Sargasso

W. Mahlon Purdin

THE SCREENMASTERS
(Volume Two)

FRONT AND BACK COVER PHOTO:

"CLOSE MOON" BY DIVERSE PIXEL

ISBN-13: 978-0692595497 (Legend, Inc.)
ISBN-10: 069259549X

www.legendinc.com
www.wmahlonpurdin.com
www.emerald.earth

1.4

AUTHOR'S ANALOGOUS NOTE

Imagine waking up, riding a horse, a thoroughbred mare, approximately fifteen hands high and over nine hundred pounds heavy. The horse is at a full gallop, nearing thirty miles an hour. She never tires. The terrain is an open field covered in high grass, so there's no telling what's underfoot. You have a saddle and stirrups, and the reins are in your hands. What do you do? You have no idea where you are, or where you are going. The only thing you know is that you are riding this horse at full speed. At first you tense and resist. The ride becomes stressful and jolting, but then you notice a rhythm in the horse's movements. You lean forward, not standing in the stirrups, but using your body and now your mind to move with the horse. The horse notices this unison and lengthens her strides in confidence, or so it feels to you. Now the two of you are riding as one. You notice the beauty of the field and the fresh air. You find the enjoyment of seeing new things from a new point of view. The horse bounds through a stream, its hooves splashing water all over you both. You laugh and lean in. You're looking ahead with awareness and presence. You're wondering what's next. You're hoping for what's next, riding on the wind.

Dedicated to

My wife, Joy,
who showed me
the new world
of true love
and real happiness.

DEDICATORY POEM

QUIESCENCE AND CONSEQUENCE
by Farson Uiost

Each morning I go outside and
  peer
Into the dark soil of my
  gardens.
Watching for those tulips to
  emerge.
Each morning I think of you,
Each morning I think of life,
Each morning I think of things
Rebuilding and teeming
For a new season of growth
And surprising beauty that
  emerges,
Not just with the bud and
  flower,
But with time and things
  being.
Not just becoming.

It isn't just the flower of spring,
And the flagrance of beauty on
  which
We feast; it is also the time
That passes, the things that
  change,
The season of abscission and
  recharge,
The long winter of quiescence
And consequence when so
  many things
Are determined with little
  outward change;
And then there I am, back
  staring
Down into the dark soil,

My eyes searching for the little
  hopeful
Sprouts scratching up for the
  warmth
And root-filling nutrient
Of a new season, another year
Of being.

Yesterday I saw one clawing its
  way
Through two inches of solid
  ice:
Its little green tip poking
  through
Just now touching its goal.
It was easy to imagine its
Relief after wondering how
  long,
How far do I have to go?
Can I do it?
I must.

In a few weeks, that little
  ice-covered
Fuse-splinter will explode
Into one of nature's
Greatest beauties, full of high
Red and green and amazing
  from
Its hardscrabble beginnings.

How little we know
Of what we truly are
Becoming.

Foreword
(from Farson's Log)

There comes a time in your life when things will clarify. You are given this great gift and are free to do with it as you please. This becomes more and more apparent as time passes.

To each of us come choices and we make them. One after the other. The accumulation of our decisions looks back at us from the mirrors-in-mirrors of time, and offers up our history.

I am writing this for you from the place beyond those mirrors. The place where what you already know means more than you think.

Life begins with a childhood that seemed to be one thing, when we were young, but turned out to be altogether another in our maturity.

At the end of that long metamorphosis you will find us waiting for you. Some of us will surprise you. Some of us will relieve you. Some of us will change you. But, here we are, waiting. We can see your struggles and sense your uncertainty. We have been where you are.

This is a translation – a map of emotions and directions – for you to use. Like explorers from the past, you may seem to be on your own – a stranger in a strange land – but you are not alone.

The winding road of life, though challenging and confusing, is the path we all must take on the way to a destination that will amaze and reward. Hidden in your every breath, concealed in your every thought, are the very secrets you seek. Fear not.

BOOK I
The Combing

"To see a world in a grain of sand
And a heaven in a wild flower
To hold infinity in the palm of your hand
And eternity in an hour."

– William Blake

Chapter One[1]

The Ice Canyons of Sargasso

1. It's Really Big

Gerald Antonoff was at his station. He was looking at the planet they were now calling "Sargasso." At least a very small part of it. *Very small.*

The planet was so large as to be almost indescribable. The largest ever known. *Solar system size.* The small piece he was looking at was an object of great interest. Throughout the portion of the vastness of Sargasso that SkyKing could see, there were multiple millions of little areas of brightness. Antonoff had no idea what they were. No one did. Nor did Farson apparently. *At least, he's been no help despite our requests.*

The lights were uneven in a somehow predictable way. Antonoff had been scanning this part of the planet for months. Through the viewer, he could always tell where he was, by using the lights. Even as the planet slowly turned,

---

[1] For readers of the first volume, The Rise of Farson Uiost: It is now approximately 2104 C.E. and 6517 E.E. For the past several years, the Moon and SkyKing, and the silent, impenetrable Emerald Earth, have all been orbiting at Sargasso recovering from all that happened, assessing things, researching, investigating each other, and generally resting, recuperating, and enjoying life.

At the conclusion of this book is a section entitled, "Front and Back Matter with Appendices," which contains a dramatis personae, a glossary, a chronology, and other information for you.

Antonoff always knew. He wasn't the only one. The entire bridge crew was aware of the intuitiveness of the lights.

Then he noticed that one was blinking.

Andrew Sortt and Farson Uiost were having a brandy. Actually, it was an Armagnac. Sortt spoke first, looking at his glass. "You know, Farson, we used to have these all over the White House."

Farson took a slow, savoring sip. "It's very nice. Many things of old Earth were very nice." Farson was looking into the glass, thinking of the aging oak casks and the flavors and colors of the brandy. This easily led him to thoughts of oak trees and camping with Karina.

It was their first night. The little converted van had all the trimmings. A queen-size bed, a bathroom, a kitchen, a shower, hot water, a refrigerator with a freezer, a generator, and even an outdoor shower. They had brought a pop-up tent to cover the picnic table, two folding chairs, and an L.L. Bean outdoor kitchen that folded up to briefcase size for stowage. Farson had spread out the doormat and hung a few strings of lights. In the twilight there were several of the little bulbs that didn't come on.

"Getting careless, Farson?" Karina was making a joke. Farson was fastidious in details.

"Not at all, Karina. I picked this one because it wouldn't be too bright." Karina looked at the lights. Then at Farson. Her eyebrows went up.

"We wouldn't want that, would we?"

2. The Blink of an Eye

Lieutenant Antonoff couldn't believe it. *Did it really just blink?* He closed his eyes and then looked again. *It is blinking.*

He grabbed a pencil and started marking in time with the blinking to record them. The pencil was making little lines with spaces at varied distances in timing with the blinks. Antonoff was hoping it would mean something. With his other hand, he tapped the device on his wrist. A holographic image of Voul's office appeared. Antonoff was still making lines and watching the light. "Commander, we've got something." Voul came into range of his screen. He was perfectly dressed in the Sker way. Crisp whites. Groomed to perfection.

"Report."

"One of the planet's lights is blinking. It was right in the middle of my screen."

"What area?"

"Just below us." Voul was thinking. He knew that area was of interest. There had been inconsistent readings, or rather consistent readings that shouldn't have been there. The Skers were concentrating on it. Their probes had been unsuccessful. There seemed to be little or no atmosphere.

A thousand miles on Sargasso was like traveling an inch or two on Earth. Or less. Maybe much less. It was impossible to know. The size assessments of Sargasso were far from complete.

"Is it continuing?" Voul could hear a scribbling sound as Antonoff's pencil grew duller.

"Yes, I am mirroring it now on paper."

"Are you getting impressions as well?" There was a slight pause, and then a heavier tapping.

"I am now," he said, pressing harder.

President Sortt was still speaking. "It's true, Farson. We both know it is. There were good things on Earth, good people on Earth, good times on Earth.

"I always wonder, though, if in all of the good, there on old Earth, was there not always something of the terrible as well."

Farson knew what he meant. The will to survive, the ambiguous philosophies, the manipulations, the wild moralities, the greed. "It's been a long time, Andrew."

"True again."

They sipped their drinks. Farson thought of Handy's incessant smoking and drinking and how it seemed to help. The situation on Emerald Earth was weighing heavily on him. So much had happened. *So many gone.* He thought that Handy would be lighting one up at this point. *And pouring himself a generous refill.*

<<Feeling a little weak, Farson?>> Handy's interruption was not unwelcome.

Farson's dad had been a smoker, and Farson sometimes smoked his pipe. It was an old, gnarled, hand-carved piece of white briar. It always felt good in Farson's hand, but he was no smoker. Karina always laughed at his amateurish attempts.

"You've gone too far with the professorial, Farson," she would say. *How many times has she said it?*

Farson knew Handy wasn't talking about smoking. He was talking about The Screen.

<<All is well, Handy. As you well know.>>
<<Just checking.>>

The Moon, SkyKing, and Emerald Earth: The three of them, so different and yet so bound together, had moved far, far away. They were now their own little solar system, orbiting a giant wall that went on forever.

It went up, down, and in all directions. It appeared to be perfectly straight. Its curvature was beyond comprehension.

The Moon had grown in population as they traveled through space over the years to get here. They had finally completed New Chicago, and built two more surface cities. Memphis had nearly a thousand people living in it. Bangor was the newest; designed for a colder climate, with snow and wind. MoonBasers were moving into Bangor with stoves and blankets. They seemed to love the rugged terrain and climate.

SkyKing had eight whorls now, and the ninth – by far the largest – was under construction.

Emerald Earth remained home to 6.8 million people. Their culture and technology were a constant source of discussion and study by SkyKing and the Moon. It was difficult to do with no contact allowed. Clearly, in the way that the planet had reappeared and had taken the Moon and SkyKing in tow, everyone knew that something significant had happened there.

When the stasis field came down, everything had changed. Emerald Earth was now a force to be reckoned with. Farson had told everyone only one thing about the people living there, "The ancients are no worry. They are us."

The three separate worlds: worlds so different. The raucous MoonBasers and their commander, Viera Nichols, living lives of complete freedom. The MoonBasers had proven to be a remarkable team. SkyKing – with its ascetic Skers and their leader, Voul Jonsn, and with commander Jim Peterson and his always-ready crew – had grown by leaps and bounds in the ensuing years of peace and predictability. Emerald Earth, with Andrew Sortt and the mysterious Emers, kept its distance, silently, completing the formation.

It had been an interesting ten years.

On Emerald Earth, it had been the longest ten years in the last 6,520.

<<*Something like that was to be expected. It's a big place.*>>

<<*Ten years. Nothing. Now, something?*>>

<<*Well, that something was always there. We just hadn't seen it yet. Or maybe it hadn't seen us.*>>

<<*The magnitudes are a little scary, don't you think?"*>>

<<*Compared to what, Uva? Even Sargasso is small in the scope of things.*>> The avian ScreenMaster adjusted her wings and brushed her hand through her soft shoulder feathers. She settled everything back into a smooth profile of dignity and power, looking at Farson.

<<*Yes, Farson. Everything is huge, and yet everything is small. When I think of Uvo, it's not the expanse of space and the great, vast Screen I think of. I think of the outer vanes of his inner feathers. I think of the soft aroma when he settled in beside me. I think of his quiet laugh and tender love. When I think of how much I miss him, I feel small, tiny, infinitesimal. Your grand scheme seems misplaced somehow — wrong to me — in his absence.*>>

<<*I feel it too, Uva. I loved him.*>>

<<*I know you think you did, Farson. My love and your love are very different, though.*>> Farson was looking at her with his mind. There was no denying the truth deep in her thoughts. <<*Imagine Karina is gone. Then you'll know.*>> Uva's mental voice had an odd twinge to it. Not threatening, but something like that. She was wishing he knew the pain she was feeling. She was wishing Farson would someday know her loneliness.

He had learned from Hattie that love has many faces: some kind and nurturing, some harsh and tough and teaching. Uva's were the latter in this moment. He knew she was screaming, with her agony, inside.

That thought remained. *Imagine Karina is gone.* Farson concentrated. Karina was currently on the Moon with Viera. Felicity and Valgary had a playdate with Prms Bensn. He had just turned three today. Farson knew everything was fine in their world. Karina was happy in Viera's company. Their friendship had grown and grown. They were more like sisters now. Farson scanned The Screen. All was well. He looked at Uva again. She was looking at him.

Farson found her unblinking stare disconcerting.

Those four words still hung in the air.

3. The Idea

Young Farson was restless. He hardly ate his breakfast, but Hattie had stood over him until he did. At school he kept looking out the window, looking at the clock. At lunch he just pushed his food around, although the ham salad sandwich did look good. He noticed Hattie had put in a Tootsie Roll. *Oh, what the heck.*

The afternoon dragged on and on like a church service. He was the first student out of the building after school. His bike seemed heavy and slow.

When he got home, he went straight up to his room. Hattie noticed. *What's he doin' up there?*

Farson was writing a note to Karina.

STAY RIGHT HERE

I wonder sometimes if I'm so isolated
That I lose out experientially.
I mean those camels, those pyramids,
That Eiffel Tower, that Lenin's Tomb.
But then I watch you falling asleep
On the couch and think of the days just past
Driving, measuring, moving furniture,
Hanging curtains, painting touch-ups,
Going out for pizza (not for me),
Talking with our daughters all day
Thinking of what my day was like,

I doubt it.
It might be nice, but in an odd Thoreauvian way
I think it might be distractive. So many new
Things to factor there than here, in fact,
Here I can concentrate on things.
Plus I do get out and about, six states,
Ten towns, shopping at the supermarket,
I average around 11,000 miles a year
Just around here. I know a lot of people,
Which makes life fun, and I still have long, long
Periods of working alone, singing alone, and
Writing alone to satisfy the soul.
So going to Fallujah or even Tikrit,
Maybe taking one of those river cruises
Down the Murat, or back to Australia sometime;
Are thoughts I have and have again.
But when one is happy where one is
It means something.
And I'm going to stay right here
Until I figure that out.

When Karina came home and saw the "note," it made her laugh. She read it again, and then she tore it up into little pieces, still laughing.

<<*You are so predictable, Farson. And yet, you think you are so clever.*>>
<<*Can you figure it out?*>>
<<*Wait a minute. Let me think. Hmm. You miss me?*>>

Farson leaned back in his chair and listened to the peepers just now starting to set the mood for long-awaited spring evenings to come.

<<*Well, of course. That's a given. You know that.*>>
<<*Really. It seemed in your 'note' that you were trying to talk yourself into something. Either that, or you were just feeling sorry for yourself. Or dreading your mundane routines. It was perfectly*

clear, however, that all the effort it took to get it to me, including going to school all day and risking an encounter with Hattie, showed a sincerity – really, a devotion, that is hard to overlook. So when you say so casually, "You know that," remember when you taught me "Everything hangs by a thread?" Without clarity of message, you must agree, anything can happen.>> No answer.

<<Farson? Knock, knock.>>

Farson was in North Conway. He had decided to go skiing at a mountain called Attitash. It was early April, maybe the last day the mountain would open for the season. He had arrived late morning, geared up, and was sitting in the middle of a high-speed quad chairlift alone, swiftly ascending to the summit for his first run. The cool air, the bright blue sky, the beauty of the mountains filled him. It was a day off. The chairlift moved swiftly over trees and trails.

On the way up the mountain, he noticed that there were bras and beads hanging from some of the trees along the lift trail: an aftereffect, he assumed, of the last big event on the mountain's yearly schedule, Mardi Gras Weekend. He watched as a particularly close tree with at least seven bras, and even more strands of brightly colored beads hanging on it, passed underneath him. He smiled. The caprice and impulses of humanity always warmed him with their whimsy. He loved the unpredictable nature of people everywhere. He knew it was one of humanity's greatest strengths: having fun. He had gone back to write the poem for Karina for that very reason. That he had chosen that day would not be lost on her. Her laughter confirmed he had made his point. It was their Door Day[2] anniversary. The day he had hesitated. The day she took control. They both knew it. It was an endless argument.

---

[2] For readers who have not read volume one, The Rise of Farson Uiost – "Door Day" is further explained there in the first one hundred pages and throughout the book. For purposes here, it was the day that Farson and Karina became equals. They were ten and eight years old, respectively.

She said he had waited too long and could have ruined everything. He said he had done it perfectly, timing it to the second. The poem was his way of saying that he had everything under control. Her laughter and, in his view, wrongful insight, made him ask for the confirmation: "Can you figure it out?" Time being no barrier to them, her request that he "wait a minute" was funny. Farson knew that he could never win the argument. He knew in his heart he had waited too long that day and that Karina had saved everything. He could rewrite history and move worlds, but the truth with Karina was always the immutable truth. They could play. They could joke. They could be in many places, in many times at once. They were true ScreenMasters of The Screen. But even with all of that power and ability, Farson knew. Karina loved him enough to risk everything. And she would do it every time without hesitation. Farson knew that that degree of certainty, of resolution, was beyond him without her. Her thought interrupted him.

    <<*It sounds like surrender to me, Farson.*>>
    <<*We've been here before, Kari. Nothing new.*>>
    <<*Where? The place where you can't do it without me?*>>
    <<*You wish.*>> They both laughed.

The ski lift arrived at the summit. Farson stood up from the chairlift and skied down the ramp. As he put his hands through the ski pole straps, he noticed Mount Washington through the bare trees. It was pure white, brilliant at the peaks, and Farson could see the tree line was just starting to green up. *It won't be long now.* The winter in New England was coming to its ever slowing conclusion. It was coming for sure, but people always wondered, "Is spring ever going to get here?" He pushed off, his skis gathering speed through the mashed potato snow. He took the easier, intermediate trail, the Upper Saco, but was thinking of the two or three expert options along the way. *It could be my last run of the year. Why not?*

On Emerald Earth he turned and looked toward the far horizon. The sky was a perfect soft orange. Those fiery red sunsets of lore were long gone now. No sun. Day and night were mechanically generated to suit human nature. This made Farson smile. *Human nature, the one truly unstoppable force.* This, to Farson, was the one truth that no one could fully dispute. The vast, past changes – great and disastrous – that it had caused, and those unknown changes still yet to come, had all been, or would be, recorded. But understood? *Never completely.* Farson faced a deep truth secretly to himself: He preferred the past, or pasts, to be more accurate. His childhood with Karina, North Conway in the winter, standing in the grocery lines, these he loved. Driving his old truck around the mountain roads and along the lakes' shores, he relished. Even the war and his experiences there, before being a ScreenMaster, were memories he revisited with frequency and emotion.

Farson looked out across the horizon of the world as it now was, so many years later, and wondered. *Does anyone remember?*

4. Farson's Log (1): The Problem with Emerald Earth

They were ahead of us: way ahead. Contact would have been destructive. The Emers had all been ScreenMasters, aware and confident, for thousands of years. They had seen so much and learned so much more. They lived on a ScreenMaster world. They had taken what was given to them and made the most of it. It wasn't easy. It never is. Over the centuries they had gained control. Not in the traditional way, but in the True ScreenMaster way: order, peace, freedom, humanity, all together.

In the beginning, the planet itself was dying. What choice did they have? I was there and that helped. There were arguments about which way to go. In the end, like fighters worn down in struggle, the two sides gave it up. There were no signed documents, no written agreements, no records. It all happened for everyone at the same moment. Unanimity. Ascension. Salvation. The TrueScreen was born. They learned to control it together, and life became heaven on Earth. The population was thinned out by design and always with care. The planet's ecology evolved perfectly in their hands. It was a world of grains and science. "The exports," I told them, "are important." One planet feeding many others. A people blessed with wealth untold who have no money.

Emerald Earth became humanity's brightest light, long shrouded in stasis, but soon shining again.

They kept asking me questions. They'd show me their amazing inventions. Some went with me when I traveled. Some went other places.

There is only one old ScreenMaster on Emerald Earth now. Handy, of course. He still lives out in the open air and shoots eagles. He was always there whenever I stopped by and still is.

I keep thinking about the little stream where Sam and I fished. Long gone now.

<<*Really, Farson? Gone?*>>
<<*Handy, don't you have anything better to do?*>>
<<*They're readying a mission. Want to go?*>>

Sam used to tell me that if you sit in a place long enough, the fish will come to you.

"Is that why you're sleeping half the time?" Sam sat up a little less slumpy. He straightened his shirt front a little. He reached into his pocket for his beat-up old pocket watch. "That thing never knows what time it is, Sam." He looked at the watch and was somehow reassured. He leaned back against the tree, checked his line, and closed his eyes again.

Voul looked at Farson, who was dressed in the usual cardigan sweater and corduroys. *There's something new about his shoes.* Farson noticed Voul's interest. "They're gyro'd. Much easier, Voul. You never feel tired at all. Nothing can penetrate the sole, and they never actually touch the ground. Traction in all situations. I can even walk on water." Voul knew Sker scripture as well as Farson did.

Voul had come a long way during all the changes. Even with the sacred scriptures being assaulted right in front of him, from events out of his control, and now by the mechanical shoes of the man standing right in front of him, he just shrugged it off now.

"Do you have an extra pair?"

"No, just this one, Voul. Want to try them on?" Farson laughed at his own joke, knowing the Skers' very strict clothing traditions. He knew only too well the things that Voul was dealing with now. Being a Sker and being in love. Dealing with MoonBasers everywhere. Joking that Voul might actually switch shoes with him was a clear sign. They were friends. Voul reacted only slightly when Farson put his arm around him and said, thinking of the coming trip to Sargasso, "Cheer up, buddy. How often does a mission like this one come around?"

People always wonder if I am really there or not. The idea of being in two places, or more, at once takes awhile to get used to. There are things you have to do first. None of them easy. It takes time to understand. That's why there are levels. It's indescribable. It is a matter of awareness. Walking and chewing gum is a good directional example. Think about it.

You have to watch where you're going, chew the gum without choking, and maximize your alertness, all the time intensely enjoying the flavors. How many places at once were you, just doing that simple human act?

Anyway, my answer to their question is, "Yes, I am here." That's enough usually. "He's one of us," they would say. Acceptance of things unknown can be a sign of great intelligence.

So when I went on the mission to the ice canyons of Sargasso, I was really there.

You wouldn't want to lose even one hair if it didn't need to happen, would you? What if you knew another one would never grow back in its place?

So, yes, I was there with them on Sargasso. It was as real for me as it was for them.

5. The Ice Canyons of Sargasso

The exploration crew had been on the shuttle for a long eight days. The preparations for departure on SkyKing had been exciting. There had been a lot of activity and even a small departure ceremony. The crew waved from the launch pad, and everything went perfectly as the shuttle, filled with hope and dreams of adventure, left for Sargasso.

Farson and Voul were together on the shuttle. There were twenty Skers and twenty MoonBasers. Viera and John Silver were on the Moon. Karina was on SkyKing with Felicity and Valgary. Captain Peterson and Brittany were on the bridge of SkyKing. Repoul Bensn was with Lieutenant Gerald Antonoff in their respective stations, as usual. The time had passed slowly. The shuttle was a large, generous vehicle with room to spare. It wasn't a luxury liner, but the food was great, everyone had their own room, and there were plenty of things to do to prepare. Everyone kept busy.

When the call came in, the idle time of waiting and preparing quickly changed into action.

"You are within range, Commander. We estimate two hours to touchdown."

Voul and Farson were talking as they got ready. Farson was telling Voul about some of the things he had learned about Emerald Earth. "They have implemented the fourth role of government activity. The basic first three were always known: fairness, operations, and planning. But then they added the fourth: humanity. It all happened at once. It was like waking up. 'The world born anew,' as the Skers like to say. President John Andrew McKinley Sortt was their leader at that time, and he still is, if we can still call it that.

"The planet is now a powerhouse beyond our wildest dreams. The population is much sparser now, but that had been a planned evolution over a long, long time.

"Now all across the vast plains and throughout the beautiful, sprawling city, there exists, universally, in all of its people, the rarest of all human qualities. The one trait that gives us hope, that allows us to build, that drives us to love. The one thing that shows that we really understand. Patience. In the quiet rustle of the vast fields, in all the work at desks and plows, there is now a beautiful sense of timelessness and patience. People work hard at their hearts' desires. Education flourishes and has created a world of highly intelligent, completely aware people who are building a wonderful new existence. Technology has evolved into a fabric that they weave into a connected community where everyone knows everything.

"In the changing planet there were decisions to be made. Habitats disappeared, and new ones were developed. Water and soil mixed. The best water anywhere. The best soil anywhere. Slowly but surely they have made the planet theirs.

Fairness. Operations. Planning. Humanity. In their hands, the garden they were given has flourished in its new reality." Voul was wishing he could have recorded the conversation. Its impact was revelational, approaching a sacrament. His attention was avid, and he found himself anticipating and relishing each word, hoping he could remember every one.

"Other than loving my sister and all that that entails," Farson said, "watching Emerald Earth being born has been my greatest pleasure. I spend as much time there as I can.

"Karina. I love her name. I say it sometimes just to hear it. Uvo was my friend. But Karina is my wife. She always has been my sister, my best friend, really. It was definitely love at first sight."

Voul was thinking of Viera in much the same way. These two men, so different in many ways, shared something deep and unspoken. They both loved forbidden women. Their growing friendship was a precious oasis where they both enjoyed relaxing together. Voul felt honored. Farson felt his aloneness soften in Voul's company. He looked at Voul and felt relief and trust. *A friend?*

Farson continued. "I wonder sometimes about Karina. Seeing her parents die. Coming to a strange home. Fitting in." *She makes me want to be in only one place all the time.* Voul was looking at Farson. Voul knew that he might never feel exactly what Farson was feeling, but he knew how powerful his own experience had been. *Viera.*

<<*Farson. Why do you say such things when you know the truth very well? You know exactly what I feel. Poor Voul struggles so with his feelings. You are almost taunting him.*>>
<<*Just making conversation, Karina.*>>

There was a silence for a few moments. Karina realized that Farson was longing for her out there. It tore at her heart. Even though she could be in many places at once now, sometimes she could not be where she wanted to be. Her own loneliness welled up. Farson noticed the silence as she departed. <<*Where are you going?*>> Faintly, he could hear the two girls laughing as their mother reentered their room on SkyKing. He smiled and turned back to the job at hand. Voul was ready to go. A voice was blaring out of the communication speakers.

"All right, drop the cocks and grab your socks, boys and girls. It's time to saddle up." Long John Silver's guttural voice over the communicator from MoonBase caused them all to start moving to the air locks. Farson was hurrying to get his suit on.

The ice canyons of Sargasso were in the deep, cold, unforgiving vacuum of space. The planet seemed to have very little gravity at all. Barely enough to stay down. The one-fiftieth G of Sargasso's outer surface was hard to explain, given its inestimable mass. The Skers "conjectured" that the nature of its mysterious interior must have something to do with its apparent defiance of physics. Repoul's theory was that the source of Sargasso's gravity was deep, deep inside. Being on the surface was like being in a plane diving through old Earth's atmosphere or a roller coaster down the steep first plunge. They would feel the stillness of the surface, Repoul had predicted, like an astronaut on a space walk from a vessel traveling thousands of miles an hour, and the near weightlessness of a steep dive all at the same time. The exploration crew on board were all mentally preparing for the long-anticipated experience of standing on Sargasso's surface as the shuttle made its final approach. They were getting into their positions and reviewing their plans to reach the blinking light at its source. "To see it with our own eyes," as Farson put it.

The ice canyons were like the valleys between huge, sharply peaked mountains. As far as the eye could see, the patterns repeated themselves, like a mirror in a mirror. The view was disorienting in its scope. The Skers had been unable to estimate the land mass of Sargasso's surface, but it was assumed that the entire surface was exactly the same. At the time when Emerald Earth had taken SkyKing and Moon in tow, they had arrived at Sargasso so quickly that the long-range monitors had only seen it briefly from afar, and even then it was still a very partial view.

The shuttle landed, the air locks were opened. The debarkation to the surface was made without delay.

Now they were standing on Sargasso. The suit technology supplied by Emerald Earth was perfect for the job. Their shoes all had little tractors and force fields that held the wearer at a constant distance from the surface. The suits were as comfortable as street clothes. Virtually unlimited in power and life support functions. Little worlds of their own. Communication was also excellent and effortless, with both "all call" and privacy features.

A general transmission came to them all.

"We have estimated that it's about a mile to the base of the mountain where the light structure is." With that information the troop of forty began to walk off in the direction indicated. Farson and Voul walked together in the rearguard. It was quiet as the group snaked around the ground features, over the ups and downs, always moving toward the objective. Voul had a question.

"Farson, when did you know?" Farson knew exactly what Voul was asking about. He knew that Skers didn't really fall in love. They procreated. They worked together. They felt attachment, but 'in love?' That was rare indeed. In their history, it had happened, but that was long ago. The Skers now were dedicated, determined, dependable, and, most of all, metaphysical about the world around them and its allurings. Voul had given up all of that denial in the instant he had met Viera. Their worlds were so different, opposites. But even in that odd and awkward moment of their first meeting, he knew. Farson was answering his question.

"*Some* might dispute my version." Farson knew Karina insisted on believing that he had at first rejected her. But he knew that the moment when he had first seen her was the "when" that Voul was asking about. For Farson and Karina it was much more complicated than that. "The truth is, Voul, there was no 'when,' really. It was more of a 'what.' It's what you know when you realize that any life without her is a life you don't want." Voul walked silently beside him. It was easy going now on flat ground. There was no dust, and no particular hurry. Silently walking along, they were both lost in their thoughts. The troops ahead of them were stopping; Voul and Farson quickly caught up.

"There it is." They were all looking at what could only be called the mountain's peak. At the distant apogee was a structure, which they could now dimly see, even with the aid of their suit's impressive optical visors.

The structure supported the distant light thousands of feet into the black of space.

SkyKing, the Moon, which seemed really close, and Emerald Earth were all floating there above them in stark and crystal-clear view, watching. The explorers turned and looked at Farson.

"Now what?"

6. The Ascent

Long John Silver, listening impatiently on the Moon, broke the silence with his usual acerbity. "The fucking suits are flyable. Walk up as far as you can and then take off."

In the beginning, the human history of Earth was a horror show of crime, hatred, prejudice, jealousy, corruption, and conspiracy. Of course, there was also love and family, kindness and generosity, hard work and ingenuity. But, the general theme was fear and greed. People were always concerned that things would collapse around them. They felt, as if suspended on thin threads, their lives were always hanging tenuously at the mercy of sudden disaster or catastrophe. Who could blame them? Thousands of years of slaughter and enslavement, of inequity and manipulation had taken its toll on the human spirit. In the final hours of laso-nuclear Armageddon, they came to their senses just before it was too late. Soldiers could no longer push the buttons of destruction and mass murder. Generals could no longer order sacrifice and senseless death by the millions. Politicians could no longer scream for revenge and righteousness. It ended not with a bang, but with a whimper of sorrow, of regret, and of exhaustion and surrender. Some have speculated that perhaps it was the sound of a baby crying alone in the smoke and flames. Some have said it was wisdom rising. Some said, "It's not over yet." But what remained in the rubble, and what emerged in the new day, has spoken a louder truth than the fear of ten thousand years ever could. Never again. This time it was for real.

Farson and Voul were walking along again. Now they were on an ever-increasing incline. The air on Sargasso's surface was thin and still, no wind at all. Their boots' efficient technology smoothed the path out but still, walking uphill, they felt the effort. Farson looked up. It looked like a hundred miles to the apogee. "This is going to take forever," Voul said. He knew Viera would hear it on her communicator. He was hoping she would be reminded of his last thought to her when they were together. *I wish this could go on forever.* She had laughed out loud and said, "You can't even keep it up for another five seconds, Voul." How true it was. Her love was explosive for him. He had not yet learned to tame it, or even to taper it. It was all out and done. She always seemed happy and satisfied for now, but he wondered, as men always have, what she really thought. He knew her mind. He knew there were no unknown places there. Years of mental discipline had taught him that his skills were thorough. Still he wondered, as men always do, what she was hiding. What did she really think? To Voul, Sker women were perfect in their simplicity and directness. One never wondered; one knew. There was no guile, no hiding with Skers. Everything was out in the open, in a Sker-only way. With Viera there were no rules, no limitations, no certainty. *No turning back.* Farson was watching Voul. Voul was wondering if Farson knew what he was thinking. Farson was smiling.

"You are right, you know." Voul looked at Farson furrowing his brow, questioning Farson's meaning. This made Farson laugh. "It is going to take forever. Let's try a shortcut." Without further discussion Farson's suit inflated very slightly, and he took off like a shot.

7. Farson's Log (2): The Incongruity

ScreenMasters do not "travel" The Screen but coexist with it in its vastness and forgiveness as men do within their own bodies. Not fully understanding it, but in full control of it nonetheless.

I can reach out and move my toes in another universe and still feel the warmth of the sun through our windows here on Emerald Earth. I can relive those moments with Karina when our hair blew in the warm breezes and our hearts beat with the unknown moment about to enthrall and enrapture; not to just watch or mentally to think them over, but to really do them again. But now, I know what I know even as I do again what I first did then. The concept was difficult to grasp in the beginning, but now it is a joy of life and a *raison d'être*. Karina laughs at me when I change something. She says I am trying to rewrite history, but the truth is a little more involved.

People say I am a complicated person working at multiple goals and aims. Really, I am very simple. I love Karina and will do anything for her happiness. When I relive those moments, I really am *reliving* them. Fully engaged, I forget it's a rerun. It's like the first time again. I don't *try* to change anything. It's just that I am so into what's happening there's no script I could follow.

In the ScreenMasters' world there is little of reality and lots of other things. People think we travel The Screen and twist time like a summer camp's gimp project in the hands of little children. The old ScreenMasters started the weave with no real knowledge of what they were doing or even why they were doing it. Sure, they have their reasons, and they have their moments. In their thinking they are too much of the temporal and unreal, rather than the eternal and immortal. That was left for us. I proved it by showing that they were really substanceless, with all their pomp and protocols. Just a little above space travelers. When I got to Level100, I woke them up. They immediately recognized the evidential incongruity of their experience at that point, even if they could not understand it. That I was not one of them was crystal clear. They thought I was alone. To them, I was the unseen discontinuity where consensus had ruled in timeless and seamless ubiquity. They stared at me as though I was so inappropriate as to be infinitely ignorable. They tried and failed in that attempt as well. The suitability of the old ScreenMasters was embedded in their laws too long taken for granted. If you were chosen, you were accepted, and you in turn accepted the ScreenMasters' way. Then I came along. Actually, they came looking for me, as if some unseen trail of custody had impelled them.

I was perfectly happy as a professor, working slowly toward a more formal relationship with my sister, and researching silly topics like creativity and tyranny, or the mathematical evolution of natural "social laws" within the paradigm of philosophical engineering. Hey, it made me happy.

When the enormous ScreenMaster barge first appeared, I had no idea it had anything whatsoever to do with me, let alone that it had come for me.

The robots had quietly preceded the ScreenMasters. ZZ<<Arkol25609 came first, ahead of them all. The barge appeared, but ZZ<<Arkol was already beside me. He was, I know now, one of the newest models and probably the smartest robot ever, but that is difficult to confirm. The IQ of these robots was estimated in the mid-four digits, in human terms, but that measurement was probably more for our own limitations in understanding than in true estimation of the robot's actual ability. CT<<Dinsil2371 came next but didn't stay very long with me. It was an inspection of sorts, I suppose. Just to see for himself. He moved slower than ZZ<< but no less deftly and certainly with more authority. Their relationship has never been settled formally, but I would say it is one of deep deference and diplomacy. When those two are together, it's obvious that some arrangement has long been made. They are friends, to be sure, but at the same time they are also competitors in some way.

It wasn't until well after my Ascension that ID>>Karo28689 appeared. She brought with her a history that, unlike other ScreenKeepers, she was willing to share. Her femaleness was impossible to overlook, and her history told a story that answered many unasked questions. Suffice it to say that "Ida," as she prefers to be called, changed my entire understanding of the old ScreenMasters. She told me their secrets, whether I wanted to hear them or not.

<<What else could I do, Farson?>>
<<You could have kept it all to yourself as the others did.>>

<<*Really? You know better than that.*>>

8. The Third Epistle: The Revelation

~ To The Skers ~

In the beginning there was our world, and our world was all. So we thought. But now, here we stand at the center of a new vast world of worlds beyond our wildest dreams. An all-in-all. It reaches out in every direction like a universe within itself. Its dark secrets are still unknown to us, but not unknown to all.

The light shineth outward like a star submerged and worlds swim within. The creatures that inhabit this new heaven and Earth are not all strangers to us, but we ourselves have become strangers in this strange place.

Your people have sailed among the stars, fulfilling the scriptures. You have altered to meet the demands of your times, but your deep inner faith has never changed. Your devotion to truth has only increased, and your love for each other has only enriched and grown. Tested you were. Still more tests remain. Hand-in-hand with the others, now there is peace.

We have our world. We have the bread and the wine. The journey of six thousand years is finally nearing an end. All is reunited and moving forward together, yet separated, too.

Dangers lurk, as always. In the power that has been given unto us we are sheltered in a vast new estate and if not safe, then at least we are safer. If not found, then at least we are not lost. If not saved, then at least we are on our way.

In the fullness of time the grace you seek will be achieved and, measure for measure, what is sown shall be reaped. This place of Sargasso was foreseen by your fathers and mothers, and if not the promised land, then certainly it is all of our destiny now. So vast are its mysteries, and so deep are its secrets that only together will we survive and thrive.

There can be no divisions now. The things that were done on old Earth are gone. The people of that planet were lost in the deep living death of evil done. Perhaps that which happened was too strident, too sweeping, but what choice was there? The inevitability of destruction was upon us. What was, was. What is, is. God's will? You must judge what's been done for yourselves. Scriptures offer no depiction or assessment of what we have done. No guideposts of piety lead to where we are now. There is no light to show us the way. Ours was a long dark tunnel of trial and devotion. We are moving beyond that now.

Now we ourselves have become the light at the end. Even you see that truth. Though your core is shaken, your faith endures. We all have gone forth, not companionless, but without history to guide us. History was our undoing. You alone were innocents. No part of the darkness. You alone were pure. The future, now, is all there is. We are alone and together. The pasts are gone.

Now come the stories of the 6.8 million ancients on Emerald Earth, the 365,000 on SkyKing, and the 15,500 pioneers on MoonBase. Together we will explore this new heaven and new Earth.

Sargasso. It is new and it is old. It is safe and it is dangerous. It is waiting and pursuing us. It is life among the stars. It is a home where we roam free.

There are also many things which have been done and undone, some written, some never to be written. I suppose that even this great world itself could not contain those stories that should have been written of changed lives unlived, of loves never loved, of hands never held.

Here are the silent testimonies of the meaningless dead, and the ordered reborn, systematic and spiritual. So many billions now gone, now apart; because of them, we shall not die; because of them, we shall not fail; because of them, we shall keep the faith to the end that never comes.

This epistle is a testament – like a newborn crying over its painful birth, its unsought emergence into the bright light of new life that it didn't want – pressing us forward.

Forever in grace and love, I am yours, always.

– Farson Uiost

<<*Very convincing, Farson. Do you think they will remember things as you want them to, so many years gone now? Do you think they will still see you as savior? Your religiosity is astounding in light of your actions.*>>

<<*Uva, the darkness you cling to is clouding your reality. Uvo's death was oblivion for me. Only you loved him more.*>>

<<*You make it seem like a small distinction, Farson. The 'darkness' you say I cling to is more than that and you know it. It is the light of a life of a thousand years. A life of wonder that took a whole race from destruction to dreams come true. Uvo was far more than just a ScreenMaster. He did for us what you did for humanity. And he did it thousands of years ago. The darkness is the light, and Uvo showed you the way. Without him where would you be?*>>

Farson had no answer for Uva's question. He was just grateful that she was still near and asking it.

9. The Light Tower

The human race had long ago come to a fork in the road, and – to paraphrase an ironically funny pseudo-philosopher from old Earth – they took it. They had no choice both in that the tragic choice was no choice at all, and that by their nature they would have wanted to go down the unknown

35

path anyway. People like to fiddle with things. Broken things first, but if nothing's broken, then they start in on things that are working well. Everything can be improved. Everyone can do more. Nothing and no one is perfect. These are universal truths for humanity, everyone knows. So, when faced with a catastrophically damaged world, cut off from everything that kept them alive, they went to work. It took over 6,500 years, but they emerged triumphant. Being a race of ScreenMasters helped, but they didn't know that secret at first. In the beginning it was just the good old human race stumbling along. The human race that had "broken" The Screen. The human race that embodied the arrogance and intolerance that caused the ScreenMasters to come racing to the Earth, intent on destroying it, before – as they saw it – it destroyed them. Little did those ScreenMasters know what a beehive they were kicking; what a whirlwind they would unleash. Far from a ScreenRent, that had damaged The Screen, humanity had actually found a new gateway to new wonders and new vistas, before completely unknown and unseen. It was inevitable. Humanity's power was growing so immense that it could not be contained any longer. Even now that truth is unknown outside the race; the secret that every human being is a ScreenMaster is safe. The old ScreenMasters think that Twill's plan worked. In a way it did. Their omniverse of order is now quiet and still, like the calm before the coming storm. They are celebrating and returning to the routines of their Screen. They are pleased like the parents who think their children are upstairs asleep; or like soldiers who believe their enemy is dead. No need to check. All is as it must be. Denial is now a river that runs deep and still through The Screen of the old ScreenMasters, exactly as Farson had planned.

Emerald Earth developed slowly but inevitably. When the realization hit that without the sun things would have to change radically, the Combing came along naturally. The calculations of how many people the planet could support were based on ancient histories back to the time when the Earth's population was under ten million, and then, with refinements, a number was devised. It was always assumed that the number could change, but, in the end, those early estimates were pretty much dead on. Getting to 6.8 million from ten billion was painful. Like a baby's painful birth, the race's new children were born by the death of their mother.

<<*That's ironic, don't you think, Farson?*>>
<<*Yes I do, Handy. Painfully so.*>>
<<*Like someone's trying to tell us something?*>>
<<*No, like an inevitability that no one needs to tell us. We just know. Life is like that. It is very sad, though. I think about it all the time. A vast uncertainty lurks around us, as if we are always on a precipice, anticipating the fall or hoping for the invisible bridge to appear. We live without safety. We live in a dubious state in which answers appear with no questions and actions are taken with no reason. It's amazing that we have survived. Even cockroaches did not make it. Just us.*>>
<<*And the eagles. They are everywhere. The only predators left. The amphibians hide from them.*>> Handy was looking around as though for his gun. <<*Even the people have changed, Farson.*>>

The residents of Emerald Earth had changed since stasis enshrouded their planet. The old ScreenMasters had hoped to destroy them, but Farson's plan tricked them. Like a thief snatching the object of his desire quickly from its weight-sensitive stand, and replacing it with something else of equal weight, and then leaving the scene with the true prize in hand, and there, in its place a worthless item.

<<*To this day, they still don't know.*>>
<<*I hope you're right, Handy. It seems hard to believe that we could have fooled them so entirely.*>>

<<*Who was it who said, 'Anyone who can handle a needle convincingly can make us see a thread which is not there?'*>>

<<*E.H. Gombrich, as you well know. Isn't that one of your favorite quotes?*>>

<<*Yes it is, Farson. I just love that image. 'A thread which is not there.' How beautiful is that?*>>

The two of them were sitting by a small stream, fishing rods leaning unused on a tree, as were they. The catch of the day was in the straw basket. "We should get going, you know. Can't just lay around here all day." Farson stood up and stretched from head to toe, like a cat. Handy was watching him. As his stretch reached its limit, he seemed to be posing like Superman in flight.

<<*Superman, Handy? What's come over you?*>>

<<*Leave me alone, Farson. I can think whatever I want.*>>

Farson was streaking up through the Sargasso night. 15,000 feet, 20,000 feet, 30,000, 40,000 feet. Inside his suit he was warm and comfortable. Drinking water and nourishment were easily within reach, and the optical visor was displaying the suit's status as well as telescoping his view of the light tower up ahead. He turned 180 degrees in flight and looked down, still climbing at the same speed. The towers were everywhere. He imagined if he went high enough, they would look like strands of hair horripilating on the skin of a vast black arm. He realized that the height at which this would be visible would have to be in the thousands of miles high, or more. *The scope of this place is mind boggling.* He turned around to look up at the tower once again. *It's still so far away. How could we have misjudged the distances so badly?* Farson began to wonder if he would ever reach it. Forty others were following him up. They were wondering the same thing. On MoonBase, watching what was happening, John Silver was screaming at his crew to recalculate the distances.

In the year 6517, the people of Emerald Earth were quite different from their antecedent population. This was part of the reason Farson had forbidden contact with them. Their appearance was startling. Everyone was at least seven feet tall, nearly hairless except for their heads, and all one skin color now: light bronze. Their bodies were all rail thin because of the perfection of the Jacobson ChainFoods, and they had never experienced illness or death themselves, or hunger or boredom, or any of the frailties that had plagued humanity through the ages. Their intelligence, in human terms, was astronomical compared to *Homo sapiens*. And as a race, they had achieved technological advances way beyond the dreams of those early humans. They were all accomplished ScreenMasters living on a ScreenMaster world. They were invincible, omnipotent, and governed by the lessons of their history and their mutual bond to The Screen. They were a new breed of human and ScreenMaster.

The religiosity and mythology of the old Screen had been cast aside like a discarded bag of old french fries. The Emers knew The Screen was what it was, not sacred, not mythical, not the word of God. They knew it was clearheaded science: an essential truth. And they had truly mastered that Screen.

Farson's example was the light that had shown them the way, but they had gone far, far beyond Farson. Even at their heights of intellect and understanding, they continued to view him as their inspirational leader. They would do anything for him.

Emers are humble, as a people, with no ambitions beyond life on Emerald Earth. It is their Garden of Eden, their Nirvana, their dream come true. For all the billions gone and for the millions now living, they have dedicated everything to life at its best. In Farson's distant youth he had come out of disaster and death into the Chamberlains' beautiful life, where he had discovered love and purpose; where he achieved fulfillment. It was his hope, and his plan, for all humans, that they would survive the ScreenMasters' harsh verdict, and live new lives. Although he never said this out loud, the Emers knew. They also knew that Farson had given up everything for them, that he had cast aside his own life and happiness for a dream that, realistically – given the facts he knew at the time and the evidence before him in those days – had no chance of coming true. But it did. That act of faith enshrined Farson Uiost in the hearts and minds of the Emers, forever and ever, without end.

On MoonBase, John Silver was furious, of course. The mission was stalled, and he wanted to know why. Everyone did. Repoul and Gerald Antonoff were monitoring the situation and running every contingency calculation they could think of. No answer could be found for what was happening. "The distances seem to be increasing at an ever slowing rate, so at first it seemed to be taking longer than we planned but now it is clear that they will never get there. Even though, to them, it may appear that they will." Antonoff knew he was over his head. Repoul took up where the lieutenant stopped.

"It's as if the planet is moving away from the team, at least their target tower is. Some kind of a weird stretching phenomenon is occurring." Silver could not take it any longer.

"Voul, what the fuck?" Voul could hear the raspy voice of Sergeant Long John Hanson Silver blasting in his ear even though he was rocketing behind Farson as they both sought the tower light structure, the reason for the mission.

"We are pursuing it now, it seems," he said calmly. "I would suggest that the others return to the shuttle and launch to follow us." Farson came on.

"Voul, you should return to the shuttle as well. I have other methods of reaching our destination." Voul was looking ahead at Farson's thin contrail when it stopped like an artist's stroke off the edge of the canvas. Voul kept looking at the emptiness where Farson had been.

"He's gone." Voul slowed his suit to a hover somewhere in the 50,000-foot range. The blinking light of the tower was receding. He slowly turned and began to descend. *He's gone.*

Farson and Karina had just returned to The Ship from the planet Beach. "It took you long enough Farson. I thought you'd never catch up." They were both a little out of breath.

"You are really fast, Kari."

"Not fast enough, apparently."

"What does that mean?"

"It means that we had better get dressed."

"All that running and that's my reward?"

<<Come on, Farson. We were down there for two days.>>
<<Time is different for me, Kari.>>

"What makes you think you deserve a reward?"

Now alone, Farson used everything he had to catch up with the tower. He used The Screen. He used his experience. He finally used another "him" up ahead. That did it. Everything seemed to be slowing down the closer he got. He had quickly realized he would never get there; the mathematics were clear. So he sent another one of him to the tower, by sight, and then joined himself there.

It was a trick that Belnad had shown him at the party. Farson had laughed and said it must be a skill from their hunter past, meaning Belnad and him. Farson knew that the Emers considered themselves to be fully human. *Noumo sapiens* was their preferred designation, but their humanity was never in question.

He came together a little too fast and fell into the cold, dark wall of Sargasso. There was a moment of confusion at impact, and then he noticed that the light itself had turned toward him, and was now shining inquisitively on him. Farson suddenly knew. *They had no idea I could do that.* Then the tower stopped. Farson had to hold on. When he looked at the light again, it seemed to have gotten a little closer. *They're looking at me.*

Then there was a light and fresh air blowing on his face. He could feel a sense of coming home.

10. The Grass Dolphins

Handy was walking through the soft golden grasses of Emerald Earth. He was happy, even though he knew he was going to be killing today. *Those damned birds.* It wasn't that he didn't like eagles; he did. He loved them in flight and the way they soared. Their regal faces with that fierce and yet not fierce beak. Those talons that could grasp a grass dolphin and lift its thirty-pound body into the sky, screaming in intelligent protest. The poor things were defenseless once the eagle saw them. Handy really loved the dolphins. More importantly, they loved him. In his years on Emerald Earth, much of the time had been spent alone, or just him and Mrs. Handy, who was not much of a casual conversationalist. "Handy, do this. Handy, do that." That was pretty much the extent of her discourse. Then the dolphins started to follow him around. He could see and feel the Emerald Earth's peatland soil slightly rolling up and down around him. Sometimes the dolphins would poke their heads up to look at him. He would always stop and talk to them. And then, they talked to him. It was a big shock when it first happened. It was like a stray thought in his head. Something like, *where is he going?* It was so clear that he thought it was audible. "Who said that?" He would say. After a while, he got it. *They are telepaths.* In the passing years, their dialogue with Handy intensified. They began to realize he could hear them. It took awhile; they are very shy creatures. In time they opened up.

Once, when Farson saw Handy, surrounded on the grass by six of them, he knew what was happening. They saw Farson watching and dove away, leaving the grass rippling as if by a light breeze. Handy was a little embarrassed at being discovered like that. He told Farson about them. Their families, their little ones, the communities they had built, their values. "They want me to stop smoking, Farson. Can you believe that?" They told him of the fear they had from the SkySpears, as they called the eagles. They told him how so many had been taken off to horrible deaths. "They like to be petted, Farson. It just gets me. They are really something. Like little children." Farson knew Handy well enough to know that this was something special to him. In a world now so changed that animals are rare indeed, these creatures were friendly, helpful, courteous, kind, and very industrious. "They are like a vast troop of Boy Scouts swimming around Emerald Earth. They are amphibious, air breathers. They're amazing. Whenever I am with them, they know the eagles don't come. Or, if they do, they know I will protect them."

"You seem to have quite a following there, Handy. There are hundreds of them around here." The ground was rolling as the dolphins circled around Handy, fins showing occasionally here and there.

"I know. It's starting to worry me. They are always around me."

"Like the Pied Piper." Handy shook his head as he scanned the sky, smiling. There were eagles in high orbit over Handy and his friends.

"Something like that, I suppose," Handy had said.

Handy walked on until the sun started to go down. He found a place to start a fire and played his guitar for a while. He was thinking about life on Emerald Earth. *It used to be that there were so many different kinds of us. Races, religions, tribes, countries, families. The Han of China. We were everywhere. Now you're lucky to ever come across another person out here. The Emers have become all one. Emerald Earth is all one. It's beautiful and its people are wonderful, the perfect human beings. They remind me of the Skers but without the gobbledygook scripture stuff. The Emers are easy to understand, open minded, pursuing lives that anyone would want. They are adventurous and brave. They are studious and wise. They love the few children they have like nothing else. They are artists, musicians, politicians, philosophers, dancers, and teachers. They are everything Earth always wanted to be. They are peaceful. They are kind. They are wonderful friends. So, why do I miss those crazy days of Earth?* He felt around in his pockets and found a cigar. Without hesitating, he struck a small laser and pulled a big drag and blew out the blue-gray smoke. The grasses rolled around in surprise.

we thought you quit handy

He laughed and found his flask. Drinking and smoking, miles out on the golden fields under a clear sky, he was happy. A song was forming in his mind. Far off on the dimming horizon, he thought he could see a harvester working its way down a row. *Tomorrow*, he thought, *tomorrow I'll quit.* He began to think about tuning his guitar. The rolling around seemed to settle down as the dolphins gathered quietly. *They like it when I sing and play.*

11. Finding Each Other

In the chronicling of the ScreenMasters some names will live forever. One of these is Catherine Jacobson, Karina's mother. That simple fact, alone, could have achieved immortality for Catherine, but her discovery and development of ChainFoods, as she named them, would have also forever placed her in the upper echelons of the pantheon of human heroes, even if she had never had a child. Together, these two realities elevated her in history, second only to Farson Uiost and his sister.

Karina was born on July 31, 2064. Her parents had been married for less than a year when the happy day arrived. Her father, Tom, was thirty-five years old when Karina was born and her mother was thirty-four. It has been said many times, that Farson and Karina had been through much before they met, and that same comment could be made of their parents. Children shape themselves after their parents, but for Farson and Karina, it was far more complicated than that.

Death and sorrow attended the birth of Farson. For Karina, her life was great, and then death and sorrow overwhelmed.

Their lives were destined for trials and challenges unprecedented, and those beginnings tested and hurt them both to a degree that was woefully undeserved by the transforming history of their ultimate achievements: they saved us all.

Farson and Karina found solace in playing together in "The Ship" and in their imaginary travels. Farson's parents died futile, senseless deaths. Karina's died needlessly on the station through corporate greed and arrogance, or as she put it, the "sad indifference" by the Earth companies to the precious lives entrusted to them.

Karina's parents had interesting and multifaceted lives prior to her birth. Both of her parents had lived their lives fully and with enthusiasm. Both of them had briefly been married before meeting each other. Their first marriages separately ended without contempt or contest. Tom's was a no-fault divorce. He and his first wife remained friends. Catherine's first marriage never really got going: She was so busy with her science that she didn't notice how "busy" her husband was in other ways. Catherine barely acknowledged the divorce papers when they came. She was helpless in the throes of the world-changing breakthroughs she was making, creating foods that would ultimately affect every human being. The end of her first marriage went almost unnoticed.

Karina's father's life also offered some insights, perhaps, to her own nature. At least historians, over the years, have found it to be so.

Tom Jacobson was awarded a hard-fought and controversial PhD degree from the Engineering Department of Indiana University. His specialty was underwater construction. His dissertation was on the transitional pressures in the synthetic bellows that determined and protected the air quality in deep diving devices. He went to the bottom of the Mariana Trench, more than 39,000 feet and over seven miles deep, to see if his theories would hold up. The training required him to qualify for deep diving, and that took almost four years for him to complete. He was twenty-eight years old when, on the bottom of the deepest spot in the deepest ocean, he saw his theory was wrong. It was a hard lesson. So many people believed that his ideas *might* be true, some that they *had* to be true. He postulated that super high pressure transitions were affected by an infinitesimally small subatomic chemistry that, in extreme pressure conditions, could be spontaneously catastrophic. His theory was in direct opposition to the currently proven science of the time. He said it was the environmental extremity itself that would cause the failure, not the science of construction that built them. His idea was that conditions so extreme that prior experimentation was impossible could by themselves create an unknown circumstance – ungoverned by engineering facts and even the pure physics – that nothing could overcome. "Extremes," he said, "by their definition, are part of the fabric that holds us all together. There are the boundaries beyond which we cannot go." If they can be ultimately overcome – or "tamed" – as he put it, then men would become omnipotent, and the fabric of space and time would be like clay in the hands of a race of eternal potters. "It would mean that there is no true science, only the will of men." It was a philosophical postulation, odd in those days of empiricism and data-driven research, and it almost got him thrown out of graduate school. If his theory had proven to be true, he could have been drowned at the bottom of the ocean by his own logic. But in his doctorate program, one professor saw it as a quest for new knowledge and understanding, and agreed to chair his committee. "After all," he said, "it is a research degree, not a degree in acceptance of things as they are."

At seven miles down in the ice-cold, ageless depths of the Western Pacific ocean, Tom saw his theory go down in the flawless performance of the bellow he just knew would fail. The scientists had been right, of course, and he was wrong. Even under the laso-electronic micrometers, there was nothing but absolute perfection in the bellow's cellular composition.

Tom remarked, sheepishly, deep in the crater of his own failure, "Hey, someone else in the engineering school wrote one on invisibility cloaks, and she got a grant from the military." Tom did achieve his engineering doctorate, but he also achieved the unwanted status of an education benchmark: "Don't do a Jacobson," was often repeated to incoming doctoral applicants.

In the aftermath of his tumultuous graduate career, degree in hand, he decided to go sailing.

Having grown up in Massachusetts, sailing was in his blood. He loved ocean racing, and after a long, stormy race off the coast of Maine, he anchored at Monhegan Island, population seventy-five. He had performed well in a 150-mile race, ending in Casco Bay, and while the other sixty-five boats went to Falmouth for dinner and drinks at the yacht club, he came about and sailed the forty miles back to the isolated island. Staying at anchor in the small harbor there, he rested for a day, and then, as the late afternoon sun was declining, accompanied by the month's second full moon rising, he went ashore in his dinghy to explore the four-and-a-half-square mile, rocky-coasted island.

Catherine was there studying seaweed.

He saw her kneeling in a tide pool, her hands in the water. Her face was haloed in the slowly setting sun behind her and reflected in the pool below her. He could see both of those faces. One bright and tanned with clear blue eyes looking down with intent. The other rippled in agitated seawater, little waves crossing her bronzed skin. Blue moons filled the sky and tide pool. Whatever she was doing, he noticed, it completely held her undivided attention.

"I got it," she said suddenly. Her forearm tensed with excitement, her hands dripping with the cool August seawater. Held in her fingers was a small, dark green crab. As she held it up closer to inspect it, she noticed Tom. "Oh," she said with an unsurprised irritation, "where did you come from?" She knew there was no one on Monhegan like him. She'd been there for two weeks. He looked more surprised than she did. Both of them had been lost in thought. She hunting her prey, he observing and imagining her. He smiled and answered.

"I was in the race." She stood up and adjusted her shirt with a wet hand.

"Why aren't you celebrating at Falmouth Yacht Club with all the boys? Isn't that what they usually do?" She was looking at him, perhaps laughing quietly inside. He didn't mind at all.

"I'm not much for parties, and I thought the island looked interesting. I thought I would explore. It's in my nature."

"Seventy-five people live here. It's not exactly an exciting place for an ocean racer." She was cradling the little crab in both hands now, looking intensely at its movements. Tom saw the crab trying to get free, but she deftly maintained control with her thumbs. It seemed like a little contest between captive and captor.

"It's pretty exciting for *him*." Tom was looking at the crab. Catherine looked down; the little thing was nearing frantic. She took the crab into one hand and picked up a jar nearby. She dipped the jar into the water and letting just a little in, along with a piece of seaweed she had snatched with the crab. Then she pushed in the crab. The ventilated top was screwed on tight. "It's a female, actually." She looked at Tom. He was wondering if she was joking. She held up the crab and the seaweed. "I have been looking for those two together for two weeks. It's sort of miraculous that I actually found them." She looked at Tom and said, "I'm Catherine, by the way." She extended her hand. He took it quickly. Her hand was slender and wet. "Sorry. It's only seawater," she said.

"I'm Tom. Nice to meet you." While she gathered up her equipment, made a few notes, took a time reading, and sealed and zipped everything safely inside, he stood by watching. Then she closed the bag and put it over her shoulder. She looked at Tom.

"What are you going to do now?" She was smiling.

"I was just going to ask you the same thing."

12. The Elevation Protocol (1)

<<*You have got to be kidding me, Farson.*>>
<<*Come on, Kari. You knew this was coming.*>>

They were standing in a hospital in a medical center in Bangor, Maine. It was 8:50 p.m.

In late July, it could be chilly at night. Some parts of the country were still deep in bathing suits and flip-flops, but in Maine they already knew winter was coming. There were just a few touches of color appearing on some of the maples. Some of the windows in the rural hospital were still open to the fresh air.

Inside, there was a clean antiseptic smell, but maybe masking something else, too. The people around them in the hospital were frozen in time, unmoving. Only Farson and Karina were moving like people.

<<*This will only take a second.*>>

<<*Very funny.*>>

They walked along the long polished corridors and through several heavy swinging doors and down a few flights of stairs. They arrived at a long room with four full beds and two more waiting. There were nurses everywhere. He reassuringly took her hand. *At least he is here.* They kept walking. Farson was definitely leading the way. She was holding back a little.

<<*How can you be so sure that your timing is just right?*>>

<<*It's what I do.*>>

<<*You are a real comedian tonight.*>>

At the bottom of the final stairway, he opened a door and led her to another; this one a double door. He turned and spoke to her. "This is it, Karina. Are you ready?"

"You've done this before, right, Farson?" She knew the answer. He was nodding.

"Many, many times. I find this part irresistible given all that has happened."

"What do you mean by that?"

"You know what I mean." He couldn't help himself. He moved closer to her. She leaned in. He could smell her hair. He took her other hand, and they looked into each other's eyes. *This is why I love him.* "We have to do this, Karina. The time has come. Trust me. It will be fine." She kissed him, not even knowing what he had just said. *This is why I love him* was her only thought, meaning his commitment to her and his willingness to always go the distance.

The room was cold. The doctors were standing around the operating table. Karina walked over and looked between the two doctors near the patient's head. She looked down closely. It was her mother. Farson was at the other end of the patient with a look that Karina had seen before. *In The Ship, when we were children.*

   <<Farson, what are you doing?>>

   <<I'm watching you, Karina. Come see.>>

This was what she had been dreading. She knew it was now unavoidable. This was not the first time Farson had tried to bring her here. It was the fourth time. She had never been able to make it through. *This time I really want to.* She couldn't explain her hesitation, but she just didn't want to see it. Farson said she had to. She knew he was right.

The time had come.

   <<I'll be right there>>

But she didn't move a muscle. Thoughts were stirring in Karina's mind: They were thoughts of life so full, and of death so abysmal; thoughts of love lost and love found; she could see the floor around them open and her parents being sucked out; she could still feel the cold, hard acrylic alloy of the compartment window as she pounded and pounded on it; she could still feel her throat aching from screaming and then crying and crying and crying; she could still hear her shoes squeaking on the tiled floor as she had walked away; she remembered worrying that the floor under her would collapse and suck her out into space; she remembered wishing it would.

Those days afterward haunted her with their emptiness. Space itself was no vacuum compared to her heart in those horrible days. The ride back to Earth was empty. The brief stay in public housing was empty. The car ride to her new home was empty. But then ...

<<*Are you coming, dear?*>>

Farson emphasized the "dear," making it humorous rather than a serious endearment. He said it as though they were heading off to a restaurant after work. She was clearly disappointed in his lack of gravity.

<<*Could you be serious just once in a while? You always avoid the truth with your stupid jokes.*>>

She had joined him at the other end now. Her mother's legs were wide spread with blue sheets draped over her knees. The doctor's blue scrubs and latexed hands were in there, too. He had probably just said something like "Puuussshhh!" Perhaps he was a little surprised at the result. The baby's head had just appeared.

"Now watch this, Kari." The scene sped up a little, there was some noise, and it was hard to tell what was being said. It was like super, super slow motion, although from no movement, it still seemed fast to Karina. The doctor was now holding the baby, she was still attached. *Fascinating.* Now something else was happening. The baby was straining to look over at Karina. The doctor's hands were attempting to prevent her. Before Karina knew it, their eyes had met.

An electric moment passed as they looked into each other's eyes. Everything stopped. It was a moment of intensity driven by extreme mutual curiosity. It was like staring into a mirror through another mirror. A tunnel of endless curving repeating images off into infinity. Karina was traveling down the tunnel; things were flashing by. She was hypnotized as images of lives merged,   thoughts combined, memories confirmed. Then the baby blinked and started to cry. The link was broken. Karina was breathless.

<<Oh my God, Farson. What WAS that?>>

<<That, my dear Karina,>> — no sign of humorous diffusion now; he really meant it — *<<was your first step toward the end of The Screen.>>*

Chapter Two
The Door Opens

13. Handy Finds He Is Happy

The harvester was nearly two miles wide and trailing three miles of large bins, processors, storage units, and, in the middle of it all, was Strapper John's home.

The rolling matrix ranged from multiple square-acre flatbeds daisy-chained together, to some elements which reached two hundred feet, high into the air, and everything was linked together by an onboard gurney system that allowed crew members to move with ease throughout the entire structure from end to end. The giant apparatus proceeded up and down the rows after rows of grains in perfect Emer harmony. Like a ship on a smooth sea, the ensemble seemed to float along with only the slightest sensation of movement. Despite the high technology of the suspension systems and anti-sway dampeners, after long periods of being on the harvesters, the farmers found themselves a little unsteady back on land. "Life's better on the harvesters," many would say. They loved to be on the move. There were hundreds of thousands of harvesters and about three million farmers, or farmhands, as they liked to be called. "Old Earth farmers were really business people trying to make a profit. We're just doing the work. We do it because we want to. We love this life." Handy had heard these exact words, or close variations, whenever farmhands were present.

Handy had spotted the harvester a few days ago and had been moved to walk out and see who was running it. He had encountered Emer farmhand families a few other times, but it had been awhile. It turned out to be a much longer walk than he had imagined. The unbroken horizon in all directions had created a distance mirage. When he stopped at the end of the first day, he realized he still had at least a couple of days to go to the point where he hoped he could wait for the harvester to come along. He also noted that the harvester appeared to be moving much faster than he had estimated. "Damn. There are no markers out here. It's like the curve of the Earth in all directions as far as the eye can see," he said to no one in sight. He stopped and dug around in his knapsack. He found a flick tent and opened it. Small as it was in his backpack, once expanded, it was a three-roomer, with a mesh skylight and front and back flaps, couches, and a cloth floor.

why do you do that

Handy knew the grass dolphins didn't like the tent. *They can't get in.* "Because everyone needs their privacy."

we do not

"Are you sure? Are you sure there aren't some places you go, just for a moment, to be alone with your thoughts?"

no such place

"Really, nowhere in your own mind where you go? To just have your own thoughts?" No answer. Handy smiled and found a cigar and his flask. He sighed as though luck had, again, treated him more kindly than he deserved. He went into the tent and sat down on one of the inflated couches. He lit his cigar and leaned back. He took a long drink from the flask, and then a long pull on the cigar. This went on for a while.

what are you doing

"Being happy." He repeated the process again, blow the smoke toward the skylight. The light outside began to dim. "Being happy," he repeated to no one.

The dolphins slowly circled the tent. More and more of them came as the night passed. "Like crows," Handy had once said. "They all come back to the roost at night." They circled far enough away to keep the tent still. The distance was much discussed among them. Some wanted to stay closer. Some felt it didn't matter. And some wanted to test their enemy overhead. They knew that eagles generally don't hunt at night. Sentries were posted just to be safe. Taking chances never paid off.

As the morning light came again, the circle of dolphins tightened.

14. Farson and the Light

It continued to stare at him on the platform. The blinking had stopped. The tower was surprisingly flexible for something so large. At the base looking up, Farson thought it was about 1,500 feet high. The whole structure was probably 150,000 feet in altitude from the surface. *It's hard to judge.* It could have been more. The tower was bent over like the end of a cane and seemed to adjust slightly with Farson's every move. He was exploring the platform, which now seemed to ring the tower. The rock was like polished black granite. Smooth to the touch. *To walk around it will take awhile.* Farson set off, the light fixture following him. He noticed a faint transmission was trying to get through his suit's communication gear. "Farson, can you read me? Over." This was repeated several times before he responded.

"Yes, I hear you. Transmission is very weak, but I can hear you, John." Silver had obviously decided to become more actively involved in the expedition.

"It's about fucking time. You've been out of contact for an hour. We are having trouble keeping a lock on your signal; you are moving so fast." Farson thought that strange. It had seemed like it had been just a few minutes, and from his perspective he was standing still.

"I'm on the tower. The light seems to be monitoring me. I'm looking around to see if there is any way into this thing." Farson thought it unlikely; he finally arrived back at his original position after circumnavigating the platform.

It was then that an opening appeared in the shining black surface. One second it was a solid black granite-like wall, and the next it was an open door to the interior. *That happened right before my eyes. They wanted me to see that.* "Wait," he said to Silver, "here it is. I'm going in." He felt no reason to share the miraculous nature of the transformation he had just witnessed. He walked in.

"Farson? That's a shitty idea. Can you read me?" Long John Silver repeated the call to Farson over and over, but there was no response. There was a short, profane burst of expletives and, after a moment or two, Gerald Antonoff's gentle voice took over.

"Farson, come in. Can you read me? Farson, come in."

There was no answer.

Even for a ScreenMaster of Farson's level of achievement, what happened next had surprised him. He was back in the attic, in The Ship, alone. He confirmed that it was in a time before Karina. It was winter, but it was warm in the attic, which it never was at that time of year. He was looking through the telescope. There was a sound behind him. "Are you comfortable?" The voice was a rich human voice, perhaps of an older man. It was reassuring.

"Yes I am. What is happening?"

"We wanted to put you at ease. Your memory of this little room was salient, and we used it." Farson was alarmed, but he was also grateful they had not gone deeper. It had been a very gentle touch.

"To what end?" There was a silence, a moment passed, as though thinking.

"We are attempting to assist you."

"Who are you?" Farson pressed the initiative. This surprised them. "We saw you blink that light. We determined there was a pattern. We thought it might be an invitation." Another pause.

"It was not an invitation."

"Then what was it?" This time the pause was much longer. Farson looked through the telescope to far-off Serendipity, a planet he had created as a boy. It had grown enormously since his first visit. The planet was now flush with technology, and it was slowly being encased with a structure that would soon cover the entire sky all around. He could sense the population digging into the planet's interior for more room. They were converting the original into something vastly different. Farson's review of Serendipity was, as usual, interrupted.

"We were warning you."

15. They Have Dinner Together

Catherine and Tom laughed briefly together as they realized they had both been thinking the same thing at the same time: "What are we going to do now?" It wasn't the last time that this would happen. It was one of those things in human relations, especially in male and female human things, that somehow makes perfect sense when there is no reason that it should. They had just met. They had been talking for less than an hour. Odds were that that would be that. But odds in human relations are hard, if not impossible, to calculate with precision. There will always be surprises.

He had been sailing alone up and down the New England coastline and sometimes entering races when the fancy struck.

Tom had a quixotic curiosity and intellect that went from thing to thing with no particular pattern or design. He had recently followed his curiosity up the coast of Maine and throughout its giant archipelago, tacking around from island to island. The Monhegan Race had been a fun two days of sailing a specific course, but now he wanted to resume wandering around doing whatever interested him: distractions of exploration. He enjoyed the natural wonders of Casco and Penobscot bays.

She had been a student who excelled in everything. She always was singularly focused and super-motivated to achieve her goals. Everything thing she did and everywhere she went was purposed and coordinated. She was a scientist in concentrated pursuit of something that could change the world. Nothing could distract her, and nothing would. Or so she thought.

It was getting late. "Where are you staying?" he asked.

"I have a small cabin here for another week. It's not much." The invitation was obvious, so they walked together to her little place. It was a sturdy structure on the side of a hill facing bravely toward the Atlantic Ocean. As they approached, it seemed to be leaning into the steady and prevailing offshore breeze. The house had a large porch and two sheds. *One of those is an outhouse,* Tom was thinking as they walked toward the porch. The land around the cabin was rough tundra, with tall grass, scrubby little bushes, coastal rocks peering through the tough soil like little islands scratching to the surface at unpredictable places throughout the view.

Because it was so isolated, the cabin had no central electricity. The island's population frowned on unnecessary modernization, favoring the natural and primitive state of nature undisturbed. Town Hall had a phone line and wind-generated electricity, but for the most part the island existed in a stream of history unchanged since John Smith discovered the Algonquin Indians using it as a fishing camp in the 1600s.

As the two of them walked in, Tom felt the cold of evening filling the rooms. "Let's start a fire," she said. Tom helped, but he could easily sense her proficiency with the wood and easily building a warm, sustainable fire. Clearly, she had done it many times. Once established, it spread warmth and light throughout the cabin. He noticed, even in the twilight, the fire's illumination easily included the cushioned chair nearby, and he assumed that was where she read and studied in the evenings.

It was still light enough, so they made some hot tea and stood on the porch looking out at the sea as the house warmed up. Tom's boat was at anchorage, easily within sight. "It's a pretty boat," she said, putting down her binoculars. "Do you always sail alone?" He noticed the sequence of compliment and question.

"Yes, mostly," he answered looking at her, "Thank you. I love the boat. I do okay in the races, against other solos, but the high-tech boats always win the trophies. I just sail to sail. To be in the wind. Races are fun to tag along in; they give me the impression I'm going somewhere."

Catherine was standing next to him, listening to the modulations of his voice, watching his body language. It was easy to surmise: *He likes me.* There had been other men who had liked her, but she never had the time to warm up a relationship, or the patience to wait and see. To her, life was a series of check boxes, steps to be taken on the way to her goal. For many years her goal was discovery, but about eighteen months ago she found one far more specific and directed. The study of seaweed and its essential nature, how it nurtures so much on the planet and gives life to so many in its astounding abundance and variety, had captured her imagination. She came to understand that all of the essential elements of life on Earth are in seaweed's chemistry. This knowledge became her touchstone in deciphering the truth of cellular growth and evolution. She found seaweed endlessly fascinating, and then it led her to study the relationships of sea animals to the wild vegetation all around them, especially the crabs. It was in that phase of her study when her first major discovery was initially made. Tom was talking again. "I really should go out to check on my boat." He said it, but his heart was not in it. *An obligation.* "It's only on one anchor." She was looking out at the boat. Forty-eight feet she calculated. Displacement probably in the 300-cubic-feet range. Two staterooms, a larger bathroom, full galley, and lounge area, with enough room for a nice navigator's station. A freezer? *Maybe.* A mast of probably over a hundred feet, with lots of sail area just for running, let alone racing. She could tell it had a wheel helm. She could see the cabin layout in her head. She was betting there was an easy ladder down. From her mental calculations she could visualize the angle and distances. *Very easy.*

"There's still an hour or so of daylight. Let's go out there together. I'd like to see it." Tom was a little surprised at that. He had worried about mentioning his boat, laying a second anchor. *It might break the spell. It could look like I am assuming.* Every captain knows that leaving a boat unattended at anchor is a risky business. He was smiling at her. *She knows I'm worried about it.*

"Sounds good." They checked the fire. The cabin had a large fireplace with a deep firebox. The fire was safely burning. Catherine put another log on it, looked up the flue and adjusted it.

"That should keep it going for an hour or so." *A time limit,* Tom was thinking. He looked at her. She was looking back, relaxed, and interested. *I can live with that.* They left the cabin and began walking down the path, back to the sea. Catherine felt light on her feet. "This is the first time I have walked anywhere without all of my gear hanging on me in all the time I've been here. I feel free." She sort of skipped ahead and turned back. "This is fun."

Tom could not know how unusual this was. How could he? But it was. Catherine never had "fun" the way other people have fun. For her it was slowly clicking micro spurs on a laso microscope while watching the inside of a microbe go past that made her happy. She enjoyed moving in that world because it was there where she knew she would make her discovery. When she was a little girl, she had lost one of her earrings. That sort of adornment wasn't anything she would worry about today, perhaps, but back then it was super important to her. She was infuriated that it could not be found. She came to the conclusion that it had to be, must be, inside the vacuum bag. Her house had a central vacuum, so she talked her dad into taking out the dust canister and letting her look through it. It took her two hours. Her protective mask was covered in dust. She was covered in dust. The garage was covered in dust. Way down at the very bottom, in the last little kitty of dust and hair and dirt in her meticulous search ... there it was. Its dangly gold sparkled through all the dust and debris, and she had snatched it in triumph so fast it had no chance to get away. She couldn't believe it. "I found it!" She yelled out and then said it at least a hundred times over the next few days. The other earring was waiting right where she put it. She wore them for weeks, with a big smile and the thought, "*That was fun.*" She repeated it over and over. "*That* was fun."

Catherine would spend weeks studying alone in her laboratory, going home only as a last resort to falling asleep at her desk again. The were no depths of calculation to which she would not go with enthusiasm in pursuit of her goal. Her conviction that the answers are always there and if you go deep enough and if you look long enough, you will always find them, was an unshakeable tenet of her life. When her friends took a night out, it was on the town, drinking and laughing. Catherine's idea of a night out was having the time to read scientific journals on obscure topics like the abilities of endophytic bacteria to promote plant growth in banana trees or articles with beta symbols in the titles and words like *Monascus ruber.* Her sort of "night out" obviously required the ability to enjoy being alone. A lot.

Tom was smiling at her. It pleased her, surprisingly. She was examining his smile. He could feel her eyes watching him. He felt a little like a lab animal being observed, which only made him smile more. She looked up and caught his eyes looking into hers.

He likes me.

16. Farson Has Landed

The idea that the blinking of the light was a warning had never occurred to anyone in the MoonKing complex: not in the five cities of the Moon; not on SkyKing; and, not even to Farson himself.

He knew that since the light had first been discovered, all options had been much discussed in every detail. But they never knew that it was a warning. Perhaps the implications were too complex; perhaps their mind-set was of unknown discovery; perhaps the mystery of Sargasso was so big and perplexing that the idea that it could, first, be aware of them, and second, be concerned with their safety, well, it just never optioned its way into the discussions. And, there had been many.

Farson was remembering the first big meeting with all parties involved. The room had been pretty full that day. The two robots, Farson himself and Andrew Sortt, and nine members of the Emer Council, as they called themselves. And Karina was there, although staying in the background.

The nine Emers in the room that day were clearly not prone, nor used, to meetings at all, which were actually never needed on their world. Communication on Emerald Earth had long since evolved beyond mere meetings. But they came to SkyKing that day. It was their first visit.

With one Emer, or nine, came all Emers in their convergent awareness and with their combined power. Farson could feel it immediately as they came in. Belnad Goethe was the Emer who most often represented the Council, but in the sense of a leader he denied any role. He said he was more like a spokesman, or an avatar, a physical presence to reassure. Belnad and Farson liked each other from the beginning. They had done much together over the "hidden" years, as the Emers referred to stasis. Belnad had never been completely happy with the abnegation of leadership, knowing there was more to his role than mere titles. *<<I am not a figurehead.>>*

<<No one would ever say that, Belnad.>>

President Andrew Sortt was speaking. "Sargasso, Farson, is a huge unknown. SkyKing was unsuccessful in explaining it, and then they have asked you for help. You have brought us all together. This has been putting us in a difficult position."

Farson knew what his old friend was talking about: The Emers knew all about Sargasso long before it was "discovered" on SkyKing. Sortt went on. "We are worried, as I said. There are still many many unknown unknowns, and with so much at stake, perhaps you should heed the warning." Farson looked over at President Sortt.

Andrew was ancient at this point, but also never changing. Nearing seven thousand years of life, Sortt was unique. "Like Lenin in his mausoleum," he would say when this topic came up. Not everyone understood his humor.

Elected several times on Earth to the highest offices, then chosen by Farson Uiost, and then again by Emerald Earth itself. He was the Emers' chosen leader in one sense, and their prisoner in another. They would not allow him to die. "You are us," the Emers had said to him. "Our child, our father, our friend, our president, as odd as it may sound. You were there at the beginning. You are a steady reminder of what we were. You are the essential link. You are irreplaceable. Your presence among us is sacred." That last part was what bothered Andrew. He remembered the avariciousness and ambition of the former planet and its frenetic and unpredictable population, all now expiated, human nature redefined. He could easily recall the guile and guilt, the manipulations of greedy plottings. It all haunted Farson like a darkening rain cloud, the deluge coming at a moment's notice.

Farson had seen the human race at its worst. He had watched the changes in the planet and then the radical transformation of its population. *Those people, so many now gone?* Was Sortt the only one left? Sortt had replied to the Emers' words, many times. "Sacred? Not one hair on my head, not one cell of my body, or any part of my being is sacred. Far from that. I am a relic."

Now he spoke with Farson with affection and trust. Sortt knew that, perhaps, Farson was his only friend now. The ScreenMaster of Earth and the last remaining, unchanged, human being on Emerald Earth had discovered something that had changed both of their lives: They really liked each other. He turned his attention to the question at hand, the one posed by the appearance of Sargasso and its impenetrable mysteries. Farson wanted to know more. He wanted to know everything. That was why he had invited the Emers to the meeting, and it was why he doubted that the Emers were telling all that they knew. In discussing the meeting with Sortt, the president had immediately understood Farson's intentions, and he also saw the potential perils.

"Of course, you have to try, Farson, but there will be risks."

"There have always been risks, Andrew."

"Not like this."

"Why not like this? We are still a small group with just one planet and alone in space. We still have to survive by our actions, not our inactions. Sargasso was 'discovered' in the process of our evasion after my Ascension. Myriad elements have led us to Sargasso. It has to be part of everything."

"Are you sure, Farson?"

"Absolutely." That first meeting lasted about an hour. It was more of an airing, in which Farson's theory that the Emers knew more than they were letting on, that they were acting on their own, outside of Farson's plan, and that the time had come to own up, was now obvious to everyone. Sortt was cautious. The Emers were stoic, but engaged. No real resolution was reached at the meeting. It was adjourned without consensus or disagreement. Farson was sure now; the Emers' response confirmed it to him. Sortt was worried. The Emers' silence was indicative, he knew, of things afoot. The Emers departed with warm goodbyes and a promise to stay in touch. Farson quickly found out that they would be in touch sooner than later.

Now standing in the attic of the Chamberlains' home, Farson appeared to be just a boy. His telescope was on its tripod, aiming through the attic's north-facing window. The old mesh screen was still there. Farson knew if he looked through the eyepiece, he would see Sirius. He knew he would not see the window's screen. It was there, perfectly invisible in the focal distancing; stretched so wide, its image dissipated. A voice spoke to him. He knew the voice, but could not place it. He found it interesting that it was audible, as if the speaker were in the room with him.

"What you are contemplating carries a great risk, Farson." The sound was not threatening, more like an intellectual concept being debated.

"How do you know what I am contemplating?"

"It is clear that you intend to enter." Now Farson recognized the voice as the one that only he could hear.

"You invited me." Another long silence. Farson went over to the telescope and looked through it. As expected, the view was crystal clear. The star shone brightly. Farson's young imagination increased the magnification, and there he was on Serendipity again. The planet was doing well. The colder climate had impelled changes; the population was doing better. They were working together. One of them noticed he was there. A crowd began to gather. Farson withdrew to the attic again. He turned from the telescope. The attic was empty.

"We warned you." Farson looked around the attic. The old desk was there with a partially disassembled computer spread out over it. There was the couch in the corner. He smiled at the memories, and then responded.

"We both know that a warning is just advance notice of something coming. You knew exactly what you were doing."

He was standing at the platform of Sargasso. He stepped through the open portal as though in a dream. His suit was still functioning perfectly. The portal closed silently behind him. He was inside.

What he was looking at was beyond belief. It was the last thing he had expected to see. Even for Farson, the first ScreenMaster to travel the layers of The Screen without limit, that first step into Sargasso had left him stunned.

Standing there, all alone, Farson could not believe what was now, so clearly, before him.

17. Tom Jacobson and Catherine Peters

Tom's dinghy was waiting, now farther from the water's edge due to Muscongus Bay's ebbing tide. "Tide's going out," he said. He looked out at his boat, still riding well. *It's stupid to leave it out there.* Catherine was being helpful in moving the dinghy. She knew he didn't need her, but it was natural for her to pitch in. Soon he was in the thwart, rowing while looking back at her; she was in the transom seat watching him. The boat was riding evenly in the slight breeze and light waves. She knew that Tom would have them out to his sailboat in no time. His arm muscles and the natural rhythm of the oars, the water dripping happily, from finish to catch, as he stroked, fascinated her. She felt like they were driving the boat forward together. Shifting her weight slightly with the stroking oars, she found the little boat responded to the extra help. It took only a few minutes to get there, but she was enjoying it immensely. She was a little sad when Tom hooked up the painter. She felt like they could have gone all the way to Falmouth.

As they climbed aboard, Catherine was assessing her previous shoreside estimates concerning the sailboat. Tom was securing the dinghy aft, and then he said, "I'm going to check the anchor." He walked to the bow and got to work. Catherine slid the hatch back and opened the doors to the cabin and went down the easy ladder without hesitation, as if she had been there many times. Once down below, she noticed how neat the boat was. Catching most men unawares in their place of habitation can usually reveal a sloppy side that Catherine found repulsive. Her philosophy was that everything has its place and everything should always be right there when you need it. She turned a full, slow 360 degrees, surveying everything. No doubt about it. *This guy is neat.*

Tom's voice came down from topside, "I'm going to put down another hook. It will only take a minute." He was now kneeling on one knee on the deck, looking down the hatch. He could see her down there. "Make yourself at home."

She could hear him walking on the deck, heading back to the bow. Then came the sounds of chains and an anchor being lowered to the seabed below.

Catherine was sitting on the edge of a padded bench behind the teak table, which was bolted to the floor in the middle of the polished cabin. She noted that there was a built-in computer, which was unusual and old-fashioned for the day, yet somehow reassuring. There was a full, modern galley. *He likes to cook.* She moved over to the refrigerator and was about to open it, when she heard Tom coming down the ladder.

"What's for dinner?" she asked. The refrigerator door was open, and she could tell the boat was well stocked.

They did have dinner together on the boat as it turned out, but with that question of "what's for dinner," Catherine knew she had opened a potential can of worms. *If he says sautéed haddock, with sushi rice and asparagus, then what?* Her favorite. She knew she was getting interested, and that could be a whole other problem. *My success percentage with men could only be made worse if I never met any. And even then it would still be zero.* She knew that her main strategy of making men think she is totally uninteresting was something she needed to find the dial for and turn it down, if not off. She knew that an opportunity to spend time with a man like Tom might never come again. It *had* come once before.

She had been a freshman in college. He was a junior from San Diego, California, and she was from Fairfield, Connecticut. He was studying marine biology. She was studying the relationship between South American kelp and semi-terrestrial crabs in the same area. *We have a mutual interest*, she had thought then. It had been a painful but interesting period for her. Never distracted, her work continued unabated, but that feeling of interest and attachment had come along. She indulged herself somewhat, but that, she knew, was not the whole truth. The whole truth was that she allowed herself to fall in love. Thinking back over all the years, she had come to the conclusion that it was a kind of *rumspringa* for her, a rite of passage. The experience had left her with a blank spot in her memory. If not blank, then smeared into out-of-focus at best. Whenever she thought of it, she mentally tried to rub it out.

Thinking of Tom, she thought, *What if he really likes me?* Catherine's intelligence, and the fact that she had three brothers, had generated in her an intense nature of constant inquiry and evaluation, a knowing curiosity, and an unquestioned sense of equality that put most men off. When she predictably inquired as to why her nature put them off, things always went from boom to bust in nothing flat. *It must have seemed rude to them, unwanted invasion perhaps.* What else was there to do? Her nature was quiet study, travel solely to conduct research, and then long periods alone writing and researching the results.

She looked down at her toes. Not particularly clean, they clearly had not been near a pedicurist's microplane or a base coat of polish for a long time. Her legs were tanned and well defined. *My legs are excellent.* She was fit, pretty, super-smart, a strawberry blonde who made men, after first being attracted to her, run in fear. All of this without the slightest effort on her part. *It's just me, my nature.* She looked at her hands. *A crabber's hands.* They were red and rough, the nails very short and out of the way. Her cuticles were red; the backs of her hands were dark from the sun and the salty tide pools.

"What are you doing?" His voice was right next to her. It startled her. Concentration was her strong suit, if timing certainly was not.

"What do you mean?" She was moving her eyes toward his face.

"I mean are you really standing there checking yourself out?"

"Of course not."

"I think you were." He moved away to reach for a loaf of bread. "I think you were standing there thinking you were not prepared for this. I think you were thinking here you are out on this guy's boat, all alone with him, and you've worn the wrong clothes."

"That's ridiculous," she said, wondering how he knew.

Tom made a terrific sandwich for them both. Bacon, lettuce, and tomato on toasted fresh oatmeal bread. He had a large bag of potato chips. Two beers, ice cold. Ice cream for dessert. When they went out on the deck after eating, it was dark. The sky was bright with stars. She looked up, relaxed. Her mind was calculating whether such a crystal-clear night sky, with such bright starlight, could make any significant additions to the nutrient concentration levels of the seaweed and ... she never finished that thought. Tom kissed her.

At first she thought he wanted to tell her something so she turned her head. Then she knew right away that he was going to kiss her. She had the option to turn a cheek. He was being a gentleman, unassumingly content with a light brush on her cheek. It could have gone either way. But she moved gently into the perfect position for a kiss on the lips. If one could have gone into their two minds at that moment, it would have looked like the sky overhead, stars flashing, lights blinking, eyes closed: a first kiss that they would both remember for a lifetime. They lingered, lips together. For the first time in a long time, Tom had taken another chance. He put himself in a situation that he knew could go either way. It was almost an involuntary movement. His desire was so strong to kiss her as she stood there, her face bathed in starlight as she looked up, he knew he could not have stopped it if he wanted to (which he definitely did not). When she kissed him back, he felt like he was going to cry. How could he have found this woman? How could this be happening?

Being so close to him, she could smell his clean wholesome nature; his hair brushed her forehead. His arms were going around her. She wanted to tell him how happy she was, how unusual a man he was. She wanted to do something. She kept kissing him, her eyes closed, the universe around them pulsing through their lips.

In the morning, she was sitting in the back of the dinghy, waiting for him to come aboard the little craft. She knew his weight would rock the boat fore and aft, and if she shifted with him, they could keep it steady. He could see that she was ready. "Catch," he said, throwing his hat to her. "You may need this." She put it on, calming her hair in the light morning breeze. He detached the painter, got in, and pushed off. As the little boat began to drift away, she noticed the name, carefully painted in gold leaf on the wonderfully rich wood grains of the transom, for the first time: *Songbird.* The name pleased her with its intended gentle image. Perhaps it was then that she fell in love with him. Perhaps it was their starlight kiss, or calm, impassioned lovemaking. Perhaps it was a combination of everything. She knew something important had happened to her. *This time it will be different.*

He shifted the oars, sweeping one gently through the water, turning the boat smoothly toward shore. "I see your fire's still going."

She looked in the direction of her cabin, and there it was. A light trail of smoke coming out of the brick chimney.

"That's odd. It should have gone out." Tom was rowing along now, in no hurry. She was subtly moving in time with his arms.

"Some fires just won't go out," he said.

She rode to shore with a smile.

<<Karina, when are you going to be ready to go?>>

<<*This isn't my first landing, you know. I've done this before.*>>

<<*You can't just hover there forever. You've got to land. The engine will run out.*>>

<<*Routier, that engine will never run out. I'd bet on it.*>>

<<*Sitwory, could you just concentrate? Please.*>>

That morning in the cabin, Farson and Karina could see them coming. She turned over and said to Farson, "We'd better get going."

<<*Sitwory, we're going to have to do this all again, you know. This has not been a proper landing.*>>

<<*Isn't it you who said, 'Even a bad landing is a good landing,' Routier?*>>

<<*Well, I wasn't talking about a landing like this.*>>

"We'd better go, Farson."
"We always go, Karina."
"Last time you cut it too close."
"I thought that was you."
"You wish."

When they opened the door, the room was warm; the fire was almost out but could be saved. Catherine was trying to calculate how the wood could have lasted so long. It didn't seem possible. But then Tom came into the cabin and stood beside her. He was carrying some more wood from the shed. Together they rebuilt the fire and settled back into its warmth.

Some fires just won't go out.

18. A Moving Sidewalk

Handy had packed up his gear, collapsed the tent, and was getting ready to go. He still had a long walk back to the city. Walking wasn't easy on Emerald Earth. Very few ever did it. Handy had developed a racketed "grass shoe," as he called it. It allowed him to stay on top of the grass, at least not penetrating too deeply, without postholing, and mostly keeping dry. He still had a heavy pack to carry, and the striding was awkward and tiring.

let us do it handy you know we can

Handy knew what the grass dolphins could do. If he dropped the pack, they would instantly get under it and carry it in front of him on their backs, happily pushing it along as though it were a game. They never tired, never complained. They loved doing it. It was fun for them. Handy felt that if he didn't carry his own pack, he was not an authentic grass walker. Still, it was a long slog and a very warm day. "We'll see." Even though he had spoken softly, the grass waved in glee. He looked around. *There must be hundreds of them.* Beneath the grass they were moving all around Handy.

Across the planet there were millions of them. The grass dolphins were on their way to becoming the most prolific life form on Emerald Earth. They were caretakers of the planet, the janitors. As the climate had stabilized, the grass dolphins had evolved into an intelligent and industrious species that was just what the planet needed. Their movements stirred the subsurface; their grazing habits enriched the environment. Like the plains buffalo of ancient history, the grass dolphin schools moved like giant smoothing hands throughout the planet, nurturing, and renewing, keeping an eye on everything. In a combination reminiscent of old Earth's hives and flocks and herds, the grass dolphins with their vast growing numbers had formed a new dynamic bio-ecology within the Emerald Earth ScreenMasters' plans. Like the ocean dolphins before them, the grass dolphins could communicate easily from pole to pole. Handy Townsend was their one point of contact with the human race. They had chosen him. At first he found them to be an annoyance, but as time passed, he came to love them. Their companionship and loyalty, their devotion and constancy reminded him of the one friendship he had cherished over all the years: *Farson.* The grass dolphins, in their companionship and omnipresence, reminded him of Farson. Farson was always with Handy. Always ready. Never beyond reach. The dolphins had become important to him. Even though he complained about them, he loved them, and they loved him.

Handy dropped his pack in exhaustion after almost two more hours of walking and carrying it. It was immediately lifted high and began to move gracefully forward as he moved. He could see the dolphins smoothly working together. Handy knew it would be safe with them.

we can carry you too handy we can get you anywhere you want to go really fast want to try it

"Oh, shut up, will you? Please? Let me just walk." He trudged off looking into the far distance. He could not see even the tip of a communications tower on the harvester on the far horizon. It was getting farther away. Handy knew it would be coming back down the next row in due course. He also knew he was in for a long, long walk. *Maybe I should let them try it.* He looked overhead, and there were ten or more eagles circling. The grass dolphins moved closer to Handy. He cocked his rifle and confirmed that there was a round in the chamber. The eagles seemed to move a little higher. Handy could feel the dolphins rhythmically swimming under his feet, and then he noticed that he was actually moving a little faster now.

It's like walking on a moving sidewalk.

19. Voul Returns to SkyKing

Returning to the shuttle without Farson was difficult for Voul. It was like coming back for no reason, a failure of sorts. Skers always completed their mission. They always stayed to the end. Now walking with the others, on the hard, cold surface of Sargasso back to the shuttle, no one spoke. As they entered the shuttle, in their gloomy preoccupation with the unsuccessful outcome of their excursion, they barely noticed the long ramp's incline as they walked in a line, the hatchways closing behind them without notice. Stowing their space suits in the equipment station, they still were silent as they settled back into the shuttle's routine for the return trip to SkyKing. It was as if a death had occurred. Farson was not aboard. Long John Hanson Silver's strident voice and harsh terminology had not changed, however, in any way.

"What the fuck is going on, Voul?" The holograph mechanism seemed to vibrate as though being pushed to the limits of its transmission specifications. Silver's face was staring at Voul. Feeling exhausted, Voul almost didn't answer, but he knew that without a response the harangue would only increase in intensity and deepen in annoyance.

"We have returned to the shuttle and are preparing to come back to SkyKing."

"Where the hell is Farson?" Voul rethought those last moments when Farson flew on ahead alone. Voul had continued to follow him despite Farson's clear instructions for him to return to the shuttle. With the aid of his visor's optical screen, he had been able to see a short flash of light on the tower structure. Voul had eventually stopped in midair and increased the magnification. It was clear to Voul that Farson had landed on the platform and somehow had gone inside. Voul remembered the feeling of being cut off, like something suddenly amputated. He finally answered Silver's question.

"That, John, is a very good question."

The shuttle ride back was a long one. Voul worked with the SkyKing crew to analyze what had happened and formulate their next steps. Silver, back on the Moon, was in and out of the conversation, always pushing profanely and asking rude, but useful questions to which no one knew the answers. Silver's frustration was growing like a volcano building up magma for eruption.

The Skers patiently persevered with their planning. MoonBasers were uneasy and restless. Jim Peterson and the crew of SkyKing were ready as always for whatever was coming.

The shuttle flew on through the dark of space, silhouetted against the vast, incomprehensible shadow of Sargasso.

Brittany was on the Moon with Viera. With the mission away for so long, they both had some time.

Viera wanted to show Brittany the Moon's exercise features. They had started in Viera's quarters with mat work and weights. Now they were heading down to the main gym. "You are going to love this," Viera said. "It's like a different world. We can adjust the gravity, the temperatures, and, even the viscosity of the water in the pool. It's amazing, and it's really fun." Brittany was walking behind Viera in the narrow hallway leading to the exercise area. She could already hear the voices of what seemed to be many people up ahead. The voices were boisterous and excited. Brittany, following Viera, was also noticing her tight uniform and how perfectly it fit her body. They were walking fast, and Brittany was working to stay up with Viera. Viera's torso was moving with muscular grace and feminine agility in the Moon's gravity. She couldn't help but think of Viera and Voul together. It made her sad. She and Voul had been so close as she grew up; their hugs and their happiness together had meant so much.

SkyKing had very few things for children to do and in those sad days after her mother's death, Voul had become a child's obsession for her. In her young fantasies, she and Voul would certainly marry someday. What does a five-year-old girl know? He was so much fun and so handsome. He was loving and gentle. In the face of tragedy, Brittany had assigned a new role to Voul. He was her "boyfriend," her love object. In her mind, it was natural and inevitable that they would marry. Even now in her twenties, with no other prospects around, she still loved him. Her resentment of Viera's marriage to Voul was not bitter, just sad. Something she endured hopelessly. Her unavoidable and yet enjoyable friendship with Viera notwithstanding, she still felt an envious jealousy, especially when confronted, as she now was, with Viera's physical beauty and natural confidence. Following along behind Viera's powerful strides, in the wake of her attractiveness, Brittany was feeling a little detached, out of place, outclassed. Truly, it was unnecessary. Brittany was one of the most popular and well-loved people on SkyKing. She was one of the first children born there. She had had a life unlike any other child in human history. She moved among the Skers and MoonBasers as though one of them. In her young womanhood she had become a beauty in her own right. As the commander's daughter she had stayed apart to some degree, but there was no one on the MoonKing complex that compared to her status. Viera knew it well. As did everyone. But in Brittany's mind she was second tier. Her mother gone; her Voul in love and married to Viera. What else was there to say?

Suddenly, Viera pushed the door open, and Brittany was confronted with a scene of bodies in motion, people everywhere: running, weight lifting, exercising, standing in groups, a vast pool with people swimming, a high tower with people climbing; the vivid scene went on as far as her eyes could see as she peered through the open door. Viera, as if on cue, turned her head back to Brittany while continuing to walk forward into the "gym" and said smiling, "Here we go."

Inside the vast room Brittany could now easily see the "pool" with people splashing near the edges, some swimming laps, some exercising in the shallows, some diving from the high towers. On the sides were weights, trampolines, and trapezes. There were rope towers, and groups of people dancing and others doing calisthenics. There were meditative groups, and people running on a track that seemed to circle the entire area. "Four miles around," Viera said. Then Brittany noticed the canopies descending from the distant roof. "Indoor skydiving," Viera said. "You've got to try that."

Brittany also noticed that in keeping with Moon traditions, nudity, and partial nudity, was everywhere, but not ubiquitous, fortunately. Then she noticed that nudity's inevitable result was also occurring freely around the stadium, as she was now thinking of it. She had stopped walking. Viera turned to see what happened. It was obvious to her that Brittany was surprised. "You've been to the Moon many times, Brittany. Don't be such a prude." It was true. She had been here many times. *Always on business.* In the dining areas and control stations, sometimes in the private quarters, but always by appointment and prearrangement. She had seen some of "the Moon being the Moon" things, as her dad referred to it. But he was usually with her, or she was with Voul. This was different. The way the MoonBasers were looking at her as she came in, dressed in Sker whites, she had realized that for the first time in her life, she was on her own. A tall, naked man walked up to her. He was blonde and fit. Maybe six feet tall. Viera moved too late to intercept, and suddenly he was standing right in front of her. Brittany could not help herself; she looked him up and down. Then down again.

"See anything you like, gorgeous?" She could sense his closeness now. Her face flushed. He noticed. "Let me show you around." He took her hand and started to lead her toward the pool.

"Hold on there," Viera said. "She's with me." He looked at Brittany. Brittany looked at Viera. Her eyebrows elevated slightly as she bit her lip. He was still holding her hand.

"Looks like she's with me now." He was gently encouraging her, and Viera was surprised as Brittany smiled and willingly went along with him, still looking back at Viera.

"Michael," Viera's command voice was mildly in play. "you treat her nicely. She's a guest. An important guest."

"Never worry, Commander. I am a gentleman." He was laughing as he said it. Viera knew MoonBase men better than most. They all acted so macho and brash, but she knew their gentle sides as well. MoonBase was a small world. There was no place for abuse or unwelcome aggressiveness. MoonBase was a wild place in some ways, but in others, it was a community of people who knew the rules. She watched them disappear into the crowd. Oddly enough, Viera was thinking that Voul would never have allowed it. She knew how much he loved Brittany and protected her. She worried what he would say. She remembered when Voul had first come to her cabin. Thinking of his reaction then, she laughed. *He would probably ask to be introduced.*

Voul was actually thinking of Viera at that very moment, alone in his sparse cabin on the shuttle, still two days out. The thought came to him to hurry, and he was disappointed in himself. Disappointed in his lack of faith, a belief of scarcity, a loss of control. *All things in their time.* The thought of the need to hurry was the issue. Where did that come from? He had felt it before: this need to rushing. To a Sker it was symptomatic of faith's decline. *I wish I were already with her.* There it was again. *Unbelievable.* The only son of Ban Jonsn – the founder of the Sker Nation – now self-caught in an act of obvious faithlessness. Even today his father's writings were still held with such sacred reverence that they were only spoken when read verbatim from the written word, never from memory. Voul's thoughts were racing. *Memory is faulty and infatuating; it's beguiling and welcoming, like an old friend coming home. Who cares what one remembers? Who cares about the feeling of a kiss just before it happens? Who cares about a mind so deep and textured that there just isn't enough time in the universe to get to know her even just a little? Who cares about standing together looking out a porthole to the moonscape, arm in arm? Who cares about that?*

"Commander?" Someone was calling him. Interrupting him. He responded impatiently, again causing him to have thoughts outside Sker normalcy.

"Yes, Lieutenant?"

"We have established communications with the Moon, sir."

"Very good." Voul, feeling the message was delivered, began to return to his thoughts, but was interrupted again by the lieutenant's continued presence. Voul was irritated at the conversation not ending. "What?"

"You have a phone call, sir." That the lieutenant was actually putting an unsolicited communication through was astonishing. But that he called it a "phone call," well that would have to be discussed later; this was after all a military operation. But before Voul could respond, the lieutenant quickly continued, "It's your wife, sir."

"Viera."

"Yes, Voul?" He was not prepared. But he was really happy.

"You called." Viera found this very funny and laughed out loud.

"Really, Voul, is that what you think? Or is it more like I just *know*. I know that alone on that shuttle, in your condition, it could be a period of deep reflection."

"It should be." His faithless fantasies needed rebuke.

"And why is that? Because of something you've done, Voul? Could that be it? Something you've done wrong?" He could see she was trying to make a point.

"It's the opposite of that. I was actually thinking of you. My mind keeps going back to the things that are us."

"Things?" Her ironic tone was obvious.

"It's you," Voul said. "I can't stop thinking about you."

"Are you surprised?" The holographic image was crystal clear. Her face was radiant to him.

"No, I am not. You've taught me all about love on your terms. I was actually remembering it, relishing it. Then I had a recurring thought that if only I could hurry things up a little I could get home to see you sooner." They were looking at each other. The attraction and affection were bridging the distance between them. They were looking into each other's eyes. He saw her thought shifting to a new topic.

"Did you know that Brittany is in the gymnasium?" That was a surprising piece of news.

"How could I know that? Brittany's whereabouts have long been firmly placed within her own domain. She is an adult Sker in so many ways, after all."

"When you called I was thinking about the evening before I left when we were standing at the portal."

"When I said, 'Let's have a baby?'"

"It was such a beautiful moment. That's what I was thinking about. And getting back to you faster."

"Why didn't you call? You should have."

"As I said, Viera, if you were a Sker, you would understand this. I was just thinking of you." Viera knew he meant "thinking" the way Skers think. They give it everything like stretching muscles and reaching higher and higher until understanding is gained, fully if necessary. It's like someone reaching into your mind and suddenly becoming you. In the sense of being one. Sker thinking is like other people's kissing. It's the beginning of a bright road with high hopes and then feeling for what comes next. It's like a time stop, meta-senses at the highest functions, fully engaged, let's go. They love it. Two of them can sit silently in a room for hours. Viera knew. She and Voul had done many times. *It's like being one.*

She was looking at him: the King of the Skers. The antipathy of all she knew. On the Moon, they had always made fun of him. His sanitary, joyless life was strange to them. Strange to her. She had spoken briefly to him only a few times before they met. They had lived in different worlds. The Moon was an open community. The Skers used to say, "hedonistic," before it was learned that MoonBasers know that carnality alone isn't all it's cracked up to be. The MoonBasers preferred "Open," meaning responsible, which they knew more closely described their society as it had evolved now.

With five surface cities, and a quickly growing population, the Moon was gaining in equality with SkyKing. The MoonKing complex was nearing three quarters of a million people. The changes on the Moon were sensible and necessary.

It's still a crazy place.

When they first met, Viera had just been playing with a certain ensign. The two of them were still on the mats laughing together and winding down from the usual after-exercise tryst, naked and flushed, when Voul was ushered in. It was a first sight to remember, for both Voul and Viera. The ensign left with appropriate discretion.

"Well, that's good to hear. I was worried you might be regressing," Viera said. He knew she was attempting to inject humor into his ongoing metaphysical dilemma. She also knew the opposing arguments in Voul's head were not equal in their powers. Voul was in love. She was in love. She knew he was changing. Voul was remembering Farson's exact words.

"We are all one." In the various meanings Farson's words could have, Voul had found one he cherished. Looking at her in the monitor, all he wanted was to take her in his arms.

"Voul, you can't go back. Your ways and mine have both changed." Viera's words were strong and warm.

He said, "All I want is to be with you. Frontward? Backward? Nothing really seems to matter anymore except seeing you."

"How's this?" She was posing with a smile in the holographic monitor.

"Much better."

"Backward, Voul?" Viera was being coy and inciting at the same time. "What does that mean?"

They stayed in touch over the next two days. When the shuttle arrived back at SkyKing, Viera transported over to greet him. Moving around on SkyKing, she realized how much the two places were helping each other. The gurney technology was wonderful on the station: easy, ubiquitous, and fast. *They learn quickly.* She thought of the transporter technology on the Moon. How much it was helping in lunar exploration and travel among the cities.

She arrived in the hangar bay just as the shuttle was landing. She could feel Voul's mind already searching for her. She let him find her, and could feel his relief. He came down the ramp to the assembled Skers and SkyKing crew. The room came to attention. He waved them off and said, "As you were." Viera watched his trim figure in perfect, crisp Sker whites moving through the crowd. It was very clear that he had only one destination in mind. When he was standing in front of her, he took her in his arms and kissed her. There was silence in the bay. Their marriage had been the biggest event in the history of the Moon and the station. It was a cultural revolution for the two peoples. As Viera and Voul embraced so intimately, the transmission was going out to the entire complex. It wasn't the first time their worlds had seen this: the Moon commander and the King of the Skers showing the world what no one ever thought could have happened. The open world of the Moon and the aesthetic, closed world of the Skers had joined in a passionate, loving, enthralling, and yes, sensual embrace for all to see at the end of their marriage ceremony. No other symbolic gesture could possibly have communicated what watching Voul and Viera kiss so intimately on that day, with such confidence and abandon, in public, had conveyed so unmistakably. Even more for the two of them.

Viera now whispered in Voul's ear as she felt his lips on her neck, "Remember, Voul, we are on SkyKing, not the Moon." He looked in her eyes; she was laughing at him.

"Not for long," he said. Taking her by the hand, they continued on through the crowd into the gurney entrance, just outside the hangar bay. Voul pushed the button, "Moon Transporter Station." The door closed with a soft hiss, and they were gone.

20. Brittany Goes Swimming

Brittany was looking at the swimming goggles Michael had handed her. "I don't have a bathing suit." This made Michael laugh. Brittany looked him over again. *A beautiful naked man. How old is he?* Michael was responding to her wandering gaze. Now she was looking at the goggles again.

"Have you looked in the pool?" Michael asked. Brittany had noticed that it was definitely bathing suit optional. "If you're nervous, let's start with a shower." At first she thought he was going to say, "Let's start somewhere else," but then when she heard him say, "the shower," she realized things may had gone from bad to worse.

Michael took her hand again and led her to the bathhouse, a massive structure along the wall of the cavernous gymnasium. As they went inside, Brittany didn't see the usual male/female designations so common on SkyKing. Inside there were numerous large cubicles, each with dressing areas, sinks, toilets, showers, saunas, steam baths, hot tubs, massage tables, warm-up rooms, and what appeared to be sleeping areas. "Make yourself at home I'll be back." She watched him leave her. *He is really good looking.* She looked into her cubicle. Apparently, as she entered she had been fully scanned. Workout clothes that seemed to be her size appeared, shoes, and all of the accoutrements she would be needing also appeared. *I could use a shower.* The lack of complete privacy bothered her, but she found that she could discreetly undress and slip into the private shower enclosure. Once in there she noticed there were no controls. With that thought, the space filled with a thick, warm mist, almost liquid. She found it wonderfully pleasing and turned her body to enjoy it. The lighting was soft. The mist changed, and she found she was covered with a soft cleansing agent. Washing, she noticed that her skin was loving the treatment. She could feel the hydration of her skin increasing and a sense of softening. Brittany exercised every day on SkyKing, so she was in great shape. Skers loved cleanliness to a fault, but this was exceptional, something else altogether. *Voul might like this.* The mist was changing again, rinsing her thoroughly from all angles. She just stood there and let the shower do its thing. *Amazing.* It would be very difficult to explain this to anyone, she knew. It was wonderful. She stretched during the drying process and found the profound and thorough movements of air in the shower chamber to be mildly arousing. The procedure ended with a very light mist of a soothing covering that smelled great and completed the cleansing process perfectly. The chamber cleared but stayed warm and now dry. The wall became a mirror. She looked at herself. Those thoughts of inadequacy appeared in her mind again, and she turned from the mirror only to find Michael standing there, smiling. He was holding a robe for her. She took it with a surprising lack of her usual self-consciousness. *I like this guy.* No one would have guessed that this was Brittany's first time ever being nude in front of a man. "Wait'll you see what's next." Brittany had no idea what was coming, but as she ponytailed her luxurious auburn hair, she realized she was enjoying herself immensely. As they entered the adjoining room, she saw a male and female standing by two draped and ready massage tables. "Take your choice," Michael said. After thinking about it for a moment, Brittany headed for the masseur. Michael, smiling, went happily to the masseuse.

The massages were performed completely and wondrously, unhurried, by an expert, and were so relaxing that Brittany almost fell asleep. The masseur gently said, "Please turn over," and without thinking, almost in a trance, Brittany moved onto her back. The massage table was warmed and softly vibrating. The masseur's hands were soft and probing her muscles. She could not remember ever feeling so relaxed and safe. She glanced over at Michael. He was still on his stomach. He and the masseuse were conversing and laughing. They must know each other. The warm hands began with her feet and worked their way over her whole body. *This is heaven.*

After the massages, Michael suggested that they lie down on the king-size lounges. There were light blankets, and Brittany found it so comfortable that she was dozing off before she knew it. She awoke refreshed. "How long have I been asleep?" Michael was still there on the lounge with her.

"About an hour."

"And you?" Michael liked that she wanted to know if he had slept.

"I just woke up too. Let's get something to eat." Brittany had just noticed that she was very hungry. She got out of bed and walked over to her clothes. She noted that her nudity was not bothering her at all now. But she dressed quickly, spent a little time in the bathroom getting ready, and walked out. Michael was waiting. He was dressed in loose clothing, light slacks, sandals, and a dark blue T-shirt. Brittany felt a little sad that he was no longer nude. She thought he would always be nude. But looking at him dressed, she liked that too. "How about vegan?" Michael offered.

"Perfect," she said. Off they went, talking on the way.

"We can swim after lunch." Somehow that idea was now not as daunting to her as it had been before.

Even though all food on the Moon and SkyKing was chainfood, it didn't matter. Vegan was a type of chainfood reminiscent of old Earth's "no-animal products" dietary preference. In those days, leaving animal products out of one's diet was an oddity, a small niche of devoted practitioners. Most people regularly ate meat, chicken, and fish. Today, for the MoonKing people, that would be monstrous, unthinkable. All life was precious and irreplaceable to them. It always had been, but old Earthers didn't bother to think about it. *That was our problem.* The ChainFoods developed by Karina's mother had long proven to be a much sought-after answer for human dietary perfection. Eating chainfood naturally adjusted your body weight and nutrition to perfection, as it was eaten. They brought health and vitality to everyone. And, they tasted great and could be made into anything one's heart could desire. The MoonBasers, of course, had synthesized a chainfood beverage, much like beer, that gently intoxicated you but never left a hangover, no matter the level of intoxication one chose. They were very proud of Moon Ale and all of its derivatives. It was one of the Moon's most famous cultural additions.

Sitting at their table, with the giant skylight overhead, it was very comfortable and cozy to Brittany. Michael was looking up. "We put that window there so we could all come down here and look up at the Earth. It was the most popular place on the Moon in its time." Brittany looked up. The window was just a black rectangle on the ceiling. No Earth. She noticed that there were over a hundred people in the cafe.

"It still seems to be pretty popular." *I can't wait to come back.*

Their food arrived, and they chatted while they ate and sipped at the ale. Michael told her about his job: civil engineering in the newest city, Bangor. He told her of its cold climate and how much MoonBasers loved it. "Did you know that we now have some SkyKing people living on the Moon?" Michael didn't know that she was Jim Peterson's daughter and that she knew everything about SkyKing and its growing population. She knew that Chicago, the oldest Moon city, was still the most popular on SkyKing. She remembered going there with her dad when she was just eleven. It was tiny then by comparison. Only twenty people. The MoonBasers were so proud of it now. They watched construction on the VT system just as people had watched the first landing on the Moon in 1969. They couldn't get enough of it. Today, with sixt thousand people living and working in Chicago (they dropped the "new" a long time ago), people had watched the much faster construction and population of Memphis and now Bangor. Brittany knew that two more new cities were in the works, Omaha and Paris, now in collaboration with the Skers. Everyone preferred living in the cities, and that had begun to include the overflow from SkyKing. Brittany knew that Voul and Viera now lived together on the Moon. Viera was determined to stay on the Moon "proper," as she called it, but she also knew that Voul was involved with the planning of Paris. *Those two lovebirds in Paris; that's just great.* Brittany had actually been to old Paris on Earth during one of the trips back and forth she had made with her father when she was just a girl. How she had loved the pastries!

"What are you thinking about, Brittany?" Michael had noticed her staring at something in the middle distance between them. She was slightly embarrassed.

"Nothing, really. I was thinking about Earth. Do you ever think about it?"

"It's difficult. We all know there have been big changes on Earth. Now what is this new Emerald Earth? Will we ever know? Will we ever be able to go there again? Yes, Brittany, I do think about it. I think about Boston. That's where I'm from." It was strange to be talking about old Earth with someone "from" there. Brittany was born on SkyKing. Michael had been on the moon since his early teens. *I think he is about twenty-eight or twenty-nine. Not thirty yet.* Their conversation lapsed as they both thought about Earth and all the changes, but even the silence between them was comfortable to Brittany. She liked the quiet. Much of her life she had been alone: an only child with a widowed dad. She remembered her dad's face when Farson told them that all humans were ScreenMasters. Many were excited to explore what that would mean. Farson told them they already knew. Her dad was the saddest she had ever seen him. It reminded her of him when her mother died. He had asked Farson about the people. Farson said, "We are all one." Her dad asked him again about all the people. He said, "Be not afraid. Life goes on." Unbelievably, he asked Farson the same question a third time, "What happened to all the people?" Farson answered him again, "They remain among us."

Her dad kept talking about "the people" over and over, as time had passed. He wondered if Farson meant that they live on in us, or if they are living among us, but we can't see them? The age-old query about death: "Where are they?" Brittany always wondered if he was really just looking for her mom. She looked up, and Michael was looking at her.

"Time for a swim?" Brittany knew what was coming. She still had no bathing suit. "Don't worry. They have suits there."

She looked at him and was wishing he hadn't said that. She had been thinking the water would feel good swimming nude. "Or not," he added. They both laughed and set off for the MoonPool.

The sidewalks whisked them to the pool area in nothing flat. She was excited by the smooth technology on the Moon, how different the Moon actually was from its reputation on SkyKing. Everything had been wonderful to her today. Standing on the sidewalk watching the Moon's interior go by, seeing the pool up ahead, she again was lost in thought. Her mother. She had died during the construction of the sixth whorl and had died saving another crew member. A lot changed in that moment. Brittany wondered what really happened to her that day. For her, life went on, but it was not the life she had known. For her dad, life sort of stopped that day.

"We're getting off here. Watch your step." Brittany oriented herself to the stepping-stone, a small piece of the sidewalk that separated and took them to the walkway at the pool entrance. The next thing she saw surprised her. The MoonPool was enormous, a lake really. There were people around but not that many. She saw that Michael was walking to the building marked "Cabana" and talking with the attendant. He came back carrying something. "Here's your suit. The spa called in your measurements ahead of time. She looked at what he had handed her: it appeared to be a ring for her finger.

"My measurements?"

"From the scanners. It's all automatic. No one knows." He was smiling. *Does he think I'm ashamed of my figure?* "But everyone does know how beautiful you are." That made her smile. "I'll meet you at the slide. Just follow the signs." Brittany walked into the changing room. Showering again was a rule, and the entire process that happened at the spa happened again. Except this time no fragrances or moisturizers. That same mildly arousing feeling also happened again. She laughed to herself. *It's just the Moon being the Moon.* When she completed her shower, the ring activated. A bathing suit appeared on her body. The suit fit well, and then it tightened up and warmed up. It warmed her whole body from head to toe. She looked in the mirror. *I might as well be naked.* It looked like it had been painted on. As she looked at herself, the suit changed color and configuration: from modest one-piece, to a racy bikini, then topless, and then completely nude, then more options she had never considered. Somehow the suit sensed when she was happy and settled on the bikini. It took her awhile to get exactly what she wanted. Playing mentally with the suit fascinated her. "Brittany, are you coming?" It was Michael outside. He had gone ahead to the pool, waiting for her, and then returned as time had elapsed to see what was holding her up.

She heard him outside and took one last look in the mirror, made a few final adjustments, and then walked through the entrance way. *It feels as though I am naked, but I'm not.* Michael was waiting, naked again. "That's quite a suit you've got, Brittany." He was looking her over.

"You're telling me? You chose the nude option. Right, Michael?"

"Always, in the gym. Except at lunch."

The pool slide was misnamed. It was more like a tower. Michael said it reached 5,000 feet at the top. "How are we going to get there?" He pointed to a seven-foot-high archway innocently standing in the middle of the soft grass. He took her hand, and they walked through it, stepping instantly out onto the top of the slide. It was cold at their new altitude, but the suit fixed that. Even her feet were warm. The "suit" seemed to surround her with warmth. She felt as if she had no weight at all. Michael, holding a backpack-like device and looking at her said, "Put this on." As she took the backpack, her suit suddenly covered her entire body, including gloves and goggles. She adjusted the colors to a bright red. Michael put his pack on, and they walked to the edge. They were very high in the air. Brittany felt a little vertigo at the edge. She steadied herself. Michael was now also dressed for skydiving. His suit was a brilliant blue. "When we jump, be sure to relax and let the rig do its job. Are you worried?"

"Yes," she said, laughing as they left the platform together. Brittany had never experienced anything like free-falling on the Moon. The inflated suit stabilized her easily and coaxed into the proper position, and then steered her in Michael's direction. They met after about five seconds and touched hands. Michael backed off to a safe distance, and his chute deployed softly, causing him to rise out of view as Brittany fell. Then Brittany's parachute deployed, and she was floating at about 2,000 feet. Michael came down to fly beside her.

"That first jump used to take months of training. Now it's only seconds, just the time to put the rig on and jump." From her altitude Brittany could see the entire gymnasium, or rather the gymnasium on the surface. There were many floors of the facility below the surface. As she descended, the air felt warmer, and she noticed that her suit was adjusting itself to become more like a bikini again. As the ground neared, the parachute enlarged and slowed her down, smoothly bringing her feet to the ground and then silently disappearing back into the pack. Michael was beside her. "Ready for the slide?" Brittany could not remember ever being so enlivened. She was excited. The skydive had been exhilarating.

"What next?" She was having a ball.

They entered the slide at a run. Michael first. His nudity was amazing to her. *He is so free and uninhibited. This is fun.* She smiled, laughing, almost wishing that she had also taken the clothing optional alternative. But her suit was still there doing its thing. *I have to get one of these.* With that thought, she flew down the chute into a waterfall. The water was warm and soft as she entered in it. She began to swim underwater. She was breathing something so clean and fresh feeling she didn't even question it. Down she went, pushed by the cascading waterfall. At first when they had reached the water's surface, she was reminded of the jump from the tower, but now the waterfall had been her parachute and the pool was the sky. She rolled over like a porpoise and looked around. Her suit was providing great visibility, and soft goggles covered her eyes. Still breathing, she realized the suit was supplying the air. It tasted fresh and cool. They went deeper and deeper underwater, the suit's buoyancy compensating as the depth increased. If there was any water pressure, she never felt it. *The suit again.* She was starting to understand that the suit was a miracle. There was a bubble up ahead, and Michael swam right through it. Brittany followed. The transition was startling. She emerged on dry flooring. It was like a garden inside the bubble. The air was warm and comfortable. She could feel that the suit had retreated. She was really nude now as the air dried her off. Michael turned to her. She began to re-form her suit. "You don't *have* to do that if you don't want to, Brittany. Relax. I want you to meet my wife. You'll like her. Don't worry. You're among friends, and you're gorgeous."

She decided to keep the suit. Although, the bikini did seem to be a little smaller.

Michael took Brittany's hand, and they walked together for a few minutes on a fast-moving sidewalk. It was hard for Brittany to guess how far they went. *Maybe three miles.* They came to a small group of houses and other buildings. She noticed three arches. One said, "Back to the MoonStation." She thought one of the others said, "SkyKing," and she couldn't make out the third one. "Where's the third one go?"

"It doesn't go anywhere. It's only for arrivals."

"Where does it come from?"

"You may see for yourself. There is a small group coming in tomorrow." With that comment, they had reached what she later learned was Michael's home. His wife met them at the door. Brittany got that feeling again. Outclassed. Brianna was one of the most beautiful women Brittany had ever seen. Tall, blonde. *Perfect body.* During the afternoon that they spent together, Brittany found that Brianna was a highly intelligent person and a key technician on the Moon. She was articulate, warm, kind, and generous. If she had one ounce of jealousy that another woman had spent the day with her nude husband, Brittany could not detect it. They had dinner, and invited her to stay the night. She said yes. Her room was large and lush. The bed was soft and big. When she lay down on it, the lights dimmed. The bed seemed to gather her up in a hug, and she was asleep before she knew it. When she awoke, Michael and Brianna were gone. Brittany realized that the quiet and comfort of their home had given her a deep, restful sleep. As she got up and moved around, she found a note. "We'll be right back." She roamed around. Their bedroom looked like no one had even been there. It was completely cleaned and made up. The kitchen and bathrooms were immaculate. Brittany took her time showering, luxuriating again in the Moon's amazing facilities. When they came back, she was sitting alone at the kitchen table having a cup of tea. Surprisingly they were dressed. Brittany, realizing she was still in the nude option, was slightly embarrassed, and started building an outfit with her suit. "You don't have to do that. We won't be leaving for a while." She relaxed again as the two of them disrobed at home. *What am I doing?* This made them happy. It was as if being nude with everybody was a way of expressing happiness on the Moon. Brittany *was* happy.

"Are the MoonPeople only happy when they are naked?" she asked.

"You could say that. But if you want to watch that group arrive from the "come only" gate, you'll have to get dressed for them."

They spent an hour together having breakfast, talking and laughing like old friends. When they dressed, Brittany found that she could coax her suit into making a really nice set of Sker whites. When Michael and Brianna saw her, dressed in the Sker way, they both made whistling noises. Even though they had all been together undressed for hours, the whites seemed to have a much-enhanced effect on them. "They let you walk around like that up there?" they asked.

They were at the arch when the travelers from Emerald Earth came through. Brittany was astounded when they told her what was going to happen. Farson had long forbidden any contact with Emerald Earth, and yet five Emers had just stepped out of the arch. They were tall and slender. Light bronze in color. Two of the men had long brown hair; one had short blond. Two were beautiful females. Brittany stood looking at them. They were profoundly human, but different, too. Their eyes were slightly larger, and their bearing was more graceful and balanced. Their clothing was uniform-like but with slight personalizations, which she did not understand: a splash of color here, a sparkle there. They moved with such poise and ease that Brittany felt clumsy and awkward around them. Brianna put her arm around Brittany. "I know what you're feeling, Brittany. I felt it too the first time. Wait until you meet them. You're going to love them. We all do."

Brittany noticed that one of the men with long hair was looking at her. He was coming over, holding out his hand. His voice was soothing and melodious. "I have not met you. I am Ian Jordan, son of Strapper John." She took his hand. It felt huge in hers. It was strong and surprisingly textured. Looking in his eyes, she found she was reeling with the knowledge of meeting the forbidden Emers like it was an everyday event. She was amazed at how they looked, like a new breed of human. *Better.* His eyes were enthralling, mesmerizing. Even though they were not all that different really – the changes were subtle, except for the height – just looking at a new type of human being was disorienting. Everything about them was fascinating, and she found herself staring. He laughed. Brittany could feel herself getting dizzy. She felt like she was falling. Ian's arms were around her; her feet were suddenly off the ground. She felt weightless in his arms. He held her for a moment, looking at her face, and gently took her to a nearby bench. "Rest a moment. You'll be all right, Brittany." She tried to speak but couldn't. *He knows my name.* Ian looked at the other Emers who were all watching. Brittany was starting to recover. "Yes, we all know you, Brittany. You are the daughter of James Peterson." Brittany found her voice again.

"You know my father?" She was starting to sit up now, Ian standing beside her. Even though Brittany was five feet, six inches tall, she still had to crane her neck to look up at him. *He's got to be seven feet tall.* She was feeling much better, composing herself. Not having ever experienced such instability before, she was at odds trying to explain to herself why such a thing had happened.

For over ten years, Emerald Earth had been within sight of SkyKing and the Moon, but no contact had ever occurred, or been allowed. Or so they had thought. Now, without ceremony or preparation all of that had been cast aside. Brittany could remember looking at the planet for years and wondering why Farson had forbidden contact. All of the mystery of the Emers had been left to the collective imagination. Farson had called them "The Elders," and he had said, "We are all one." In her imaginings of what Emerald Earth must be like, a beautiful, young, vital man like Ian Jordan had never occurred to her. She looked at him again, steadier now. *He is so handsome.* She was thinking of how she had just been in his arms. He was speaking to her.

"We well know of him, Brittany. Commander James Peterson is a hero from our distant past. He is revered on Emerald Earth." This impossible statement was made in such a matter-of-fact way, and yet to Brittany it seemed so fantastic and impossible. *These people are from the future. They know us.* Ian looked over at her as though trying to tell her something with his eyes.

"Would you like to accompany us?" Not knowing where they were going didn't cause her a moment's hesitation. She was nodding before he had even finished his sentence. She stood up, feeling much better, and walked beside him down the path, if somewhat uncertainly, although confident of her own safety. His arms holding her had given her a feeling of relief and shelter, as though encircled by calm and trust. She found herself wanting that feeling again. He was still talking. "We are here for a meeting with Farson. Have you ever met him?" Her swooning reverie was still dissipating slowly. She cleared her head.

"Yes, I have. Once." Ian looked at her, perhaps surprised. He knew that Brittany was in her mid-twenties. Thirteen years ago, she was thirteen years old when the old ScreenMasters had arrived and everything had happened; when Earth disappeared. He seemed to reach a conclusion of some kind, as though a pathway had opened.

"You were among the first born on SkyKing."

She nodded, "The first of many."

"And yet, you are not a Sker?" She had the feeling that these were questions he already knew the answers to.

"I choose their fashion style and I love their ways, but it would be stretching it to say I am a true Sker. I am my father's daughter. That's the way I look at it."

They walked on: Five Emers, two MoonBasers, and Brittany. Michael and Brianna noticed that she had clearly transferred her companionship from the two of them, to Ian. The two MoonBasers were now walking along behind the group. The hallway echoed with muted footsteps as the group proceeded.

Up ahead, Brittany could see Viera waiting for them in front of the transporter door. *We are going to SkyKing.* Brittany's and Viera's eyes met. The two of them were always friendly, and, for Brittany, somewhat competitive. Viera noticed a slight rise and fall of Brittany's eyebrows, and they looked at each other. All she could do was smile, conveying that Brittany was welcome. Viera knew why everyone always loved Brittany. So open, so beautiful, so highly intelligent. Viera admired her and her life story. *She's really kind of amazing.* She knew of Brittany's affections for Voul. *Who can blame her?* She also knew that Voul's affections for Brittany and for her, were vastly different. To a little girl of five that nuanced difference would have been ignored or unnoticed. *To me, it's all that matters.* Viera also noticed Brianna and Michael trailing along behind. Michael waved and gave her a thumbs-up, letting her know that all went well in the gym, no complications.

The transporter door opened. Michael and Brianna stopped and were clearly not going to enter. Brittany looked back at them. Ian stopped for a moment and motioned to Brittany to move to the side of the corridor with him. She thought it was his way of letting her know she was also not invited. But as they gained a slight separation from the others, once they were alone, he blocked the others' view with his body and handed her a small ring. "What's this?" she asked.

"A power source for your suit. Once we get to SkyKing, you will need it." He was smiling. She realized that he knew her Sker uniform was a projection. She looked over at Michael. He was talking to Brianna and consciously not looking in her direction. Without Ian's assistance, she realized she could have arrived on SkyKing with no clothes on

99

whatsoever. She looked back at Michael and Brianna. They were heading back down the hallway. *Are they laughing?* She looked back at Ian, who was again speaking to her. "Just put it on your thumb. That should do it." The ring fit perfectly. She didn't know what to say. "Ready?" he said. "Let's go. It's going to be quite a meeting." The two of them rejoined the others and entered the transporter. Even with her suit fully powered by Ian's amazing little ring, Brittany, grateful for Ian's thoughtfulness, still felt small and naked beside him. She saw her reflection in the polished metal of the transporter door as it closed. Her perfect Sker whites shone brightly.

Once the door was closed, Viera turned to the Emers and realized that Brittany was coming with them. She was used to Brittany's instant popularity wherever she went, but that the Emers were bringing her along was somewhat of a surprise. Viera said without commenting on Brittany's continuing presence with the little group, "Farson will join us momentarily. He wanted us to brief you on the situation first."

Brittany looked up at Ian and silently mouthed the words, "Thank you." Then she noticed Viera was watching this exchange. Brittany couldn't help thinking how beautiful Viera looked, and how happy she was to be with her again. They were now the only two non-Emers in the room. Brittany felt alive and happy. She looked around at the tall Emers, amazed at what had happened in the past few minutes. Ian was still right beside her.

Just as the transporter door closed, a hand insinuated itself through the closing mechanism's field, stopping it. As the door reopened, Voul was standing there, and he walked in. Brittany stiffened a little, realizing she had exaggerated Viera's inclusion of her alone. *Again.* It was again Voul and Viera together, with her outside looking in. Ian noticed the effect Voul's presence had on Brittany. <<*Are you going to pass out again?*>> She heard this thought like a whisper voice and turned her head to respond to Ian, but he was standing still beside her, looking straight ahead. No sign at all that he had actually spoken. *Did he really just say that or did I just think it in my head?* As she was looking at him, he turned and smiled at her. She knew. *They are telepaths.*

Voul came over happily and hugged her warmly. "Hey, Brit. Fancy seeing you here." His arms were warm. *Small compared to Ian's.*

They all transported together to SkyKing, arriving in the main conference room. A large table centered the room. There was an enormous porthole to their left. Sargasso filled its frame like a dark wall. There were refreshments available, and several crew members were in the room. They obviously recognized Brittany, but were transfixed, staring at the Emers – beings from another world, beings from the future. The room began to glow with a golden purple hue, unusually strong. All eyes turned as three robots materialized. They stood stoically strobing for a moment, perhaps getting their bearings. ZZ<<Arkol25609 and CT<<Dinsil2371 came first, followed, after a dramatic moment of waiting, by ID>>Karo28689. Their presence seemed to fill the room. Brittany suddenly realized that she had stumbled into a historic moment. *Three robots, Farson on his way: What is this?*

ZZ<<Arkol was the first to communicate to the assemblage. <<*Farson is delayed.*>> This statement was followed by a lengthy silence as the three ScreenKeepers stood as still as lifeless statues and everyone waited for more information.

Then Karina Chamberlain appeared so smoothly, like a mist of soft purple brushing the room. She seemed to shimmer as she closed her ScreenMaster robe over what appeared to be a version of Sker whites. She smiled to everyone, brushed back her hair, and said, "My brother will be here shortly."

21. Emerald Earth

Seen from space, Emerald Earth is now shades of soft amber and vivid green. The oceans are gone, the topographic diversity vastly reduced. The atmosphere surrounding the planet is now much thinner, but far richer, denser, and more consistent: a lavish and resilient shield of safety for the beings that now occupied this new home of humanity. The planet had gone through epochal changes in the hands of the Emerald ScreenMasters. They had inherited the planet from a time of troubles and decline. They had been handed an ongoing disaster, and they were confronted with terrible choices and imminent destruction. Confusion was ubiquitous in those early days of stasis and isolation.

When the old ScreenMasters had surrounded the Earth with their satellites, a sense of doom enshrouded everything. Farson told them to "Be not afraid." But the universe around them had become a blur. Many thought extinction was at hand. Farson told them to begin planning. To get to work. He told them a great secret. He explained the true nature of the situation to them, and then he watched over them for over 6,000 years.

Knowing that now, it seems like a long time, but as it turned out, there was no time to spare.

Walking around on Emerald Earth, one looks up to an empty amber sky. No clouds. No sun. The Moon is still there with its always growing and intricate space station, SkyKing, in orbit around it. To the people of Emerald Earth, the Moon and SkyKing are ancient history, like relics in a museum. What Emerald Earth and its people have achieved is far beyond the comprehension of the old Earthers orbiting nearby. The Emers harvested the geothermal resources of the Earth's core. It was all they had after the occlusion of the stasis field and their escape to open space. They reengineered their world beneath the surface and re-terraformed the planet's surface. They used, and vastly improved, the technology of the Moon's gurney system, made improvements to SkyKing's ancient transporters, and created a world like no other. The precious oceans of the world were desalinated and subsumed in an even spread throughout the new surface, creating an illimitable resource. The vegetation, so dependent on the sun, had to be altered for artificial light generated from the core and transformed by the Emer engineers. Perfect growing and habitation environments were established and, of course, the population issue had to be solved. As the secret that Farson revealed – that all human beings are natural ScreenMasters – began to sink in, getting things done became far easier. The petty aggravations and arrogances of the past were displaced by the new knowledge that Farson had given them. As the people woke up to the reality of equality and power universal, decisions were made that had to be made, and quickly, with almost no discussion and certainly no dissent.

With the process of "mending" The Screen underway, the "culling" of the population had begun immediately. In the end, birth and death became the engines that drove the future. Each new birth was a celebration, and there were very few. Death was redefined and became a sacred rededication to life and progress for the Emers. When this process began, half of the people who had ever lived on Earth were still alive. To save them was everything. The timing of population displacement and redaction was, at first, estimated as being possible within just four generations, roughly matching the life spans of those alive at the time. The Emers soon realized that that time frame would be logistically impractical and emotionally impossible, so the ultimate process spread across almost eighty generations. The longer process gave the Emerald ScreenMasters time to master the systems, and to manage and evolve the human and natural resources. It gave them time to test the ultimate transition, step by step. The new level of population naturally stabilized at around 6.8 million on Emerald Earth. Those 6.8 eight million people were all Emer ScreenMasters, all evolving at their own pace, and unified in a way that human beings had never before experienced or even imagined.

The new emergent population of Emerald Earth knew everything. They shared The Screen in ways no one had ever thought of before. It now, metaphorically, became the atmosphere they breathed. Knowing what everyone else knows was always part of human nature, but the final step of full awareness launched a new race of people with powers in aggregate that were foreshadowed in the secrets of the ScreenRent that started it all. These powers were not fully explained until Emerald Earth assumed control of the old ScreenMasters' stasis field and achieved a freedom that those who tried to enslave and kill them could not have foreseen. If the old ScreenMasters had known what they were doing when they tried to "kill" the human race, they would have done everything they could to stop themselves, but as Farson said at the time, "They know not what they are doing." The old ScreenMasters suffered for their ignorance, with ignorance. To this day, the Emers have still not detected any awareness on The Screen of what truly happened. To those old ScreenMasters, Earth and Farson are gone. That was, apparently for them, all that mattered.

How little did they know.

Far from "gone," Emerald Earth became stronger than ever, and vastly more active and dynamic than anyone could have predicted. Over the years after gaining stasis control, the Emerald ScreenMasters took more and more interest in the little colonies of old Earthers on the Moon and SkyKing. They surreptitiously sent new technologies to them – through Farson – while remaining apart and unseen as he had instructed. They knew the separation could not go on forever, but they usually followed Farson's lead in all things. Some among the Emerald ScreenMasters felt Farson was now unneeded. "Perhaps someday," the others said, "but Farson proves to us over and over that he *is* needed." The discussion went on without rancor or disagreement, more of a conversation than a debate. No hurry. No worry. It did evolve, though, that the Emers would do some things without discussion with Farson or his permission. After all, Farson was "one with all," they said. He would know.

When, in the far reaches of their time and evolution, they decided to start making incursions to the MoonKing complex, it was understood to have been inevitable. That first ultra-secret trip to see James Peterson, however, was a transformational event. In the planning of how to do it without causing a problem was much discussed. In the end, the Emers decided to act as if nothing was out of the ordinary. To do it as if it were completely routine.

When Belnad Goethe first appeared on SkyKing, it caused a shock for Commander Peterson that was an alteration of reality for him. An event that he was not prepared for.

He was alone in the navigation station, reviewing the active logs, as usual. Antonoff had mentioned unusual readings from the planet. He was going through the readouts line by line. Out of nowhere he heard someone say, "There you are. Just as we predicted." Peterson turned and saw a human being standing behind him: a person like no human being he had ever seen. Seven feet tall, bronze in skin color, handsome, clearly human, but profoundly different. Dressed in shimmering clothes that seemed to float. The atmosphere in the room had changed. Commander Peterson found he was struggling to breathe, a dizziness overcoming him.

What were the first words of this historic contact?

"Jesus, you scared the crap out of me!" He had to sit down, or he would have fallen down. Belnad Goethe stood quietly watching the SkyKing commander gather himself.

What happened next changed everything.

The archaeology of spatial time reveals to anyone who looks into it deeply enough that The Screen is there. Look at the way your hands move, even when you are not looking. You can make them do anything you want. They can reach ahead or behind in time and space. Just fractions of seconds, to be sure, but that would be enough for the informed observer. Look at how you can plan things a few seconds ahead or years ahead. You can see every detail and make them come true. You can visualize a future and live in the past, all at the same time. It's human. We all know it. These abilities are perhaps unique in the omniverse. *We are the only ones.* Our evolving children increase this uniqueness by magnitudes incalculable. The way we fall in love exponentially generates myriad alternatives beyond the wildest imagery of even our most talented artists and poets. Our structure of art and science again multiplies this singularity. When the old ScreenMasters came to Earth, they had no idea at all what we were. How could they? They thought they had seen it all over the eons. There were no surprises left in their self-declared omniscience. Do this and do that, problem solved. With humanity, they were on a blind date with a partner from another world, another existence. What we saw so clearly was invisible to them. Farson tried to tell them. He did tell them. They just did not, and could not, understand. They were like wild dogs that wandered into a world where they saw jungles and savages and trees, not the wonders and miracles in plain view. You could say they judged us by appearance. A book by its cover. A poem by its first line. They had no real tools for the job at hand. They had no experience that could guide them. They assumed superiority, but it was not true at all.

Not even close. Farson outsmarted them at every turn. Remember, they actually chose him.

He tricked them like it was a playground prank. He gave them a feigned victory. The worst insult. He escaped with his planet and his people. There was a high price to pay, it is true, but there was no contest. The alternative was an impossibility. As the years have gone by, the scope and purity of Farson's victorious ruse became clear: an artifice immaculate.

Now the Emerald ScreenMasters, the Emers, roamed free. Their world, a Garden of Eden; its people happy and fulfilled. Their skills ever-increasing, and their scope now without bounds. But something was still missing, and they knew exactly what it was.

They wanted the others back.

Commander Peterson had stayed up late that night, working alone on some of his navigation theories and to review the logs of the day. As the anchor planet now, he knew the Moon was really running the show. SkyKing was back to its routine, the crew building more whorls; the Skers were operating the station and maintaining communications, orbital stability, and all of the other life functions. The two groups still, by predilection, apart, but not as far apart as they had been. Events were drawing them closer.

After Voul had married Viera, there were more interminglings. The crew of SkyKing, the smallest of all the three human contingencies, grew lonely. The Skers had the Skers. The MoonBasers had their culture and each other. But Jim Peterson's crew felt isolated and naturally acquired an expanding interest in the Moon. It was inevitable. The Skers were taken by surprise in this, but adjusted soon enough. The population on the station had grown so much that many now commuted from homes on the Moon. Some MoonBasers were now living on SkyKing, as well. The MoonKing complex, as it was sometimes now referred to, had basically merged governments. In the way that humans almost always do, the two communities gradually but inevitably became one.

Jim Peterson liked to work at night far more than lying in bed and thinking about Joanie, Brittany's mother and his beloved, deceased wife. On this particular night, he was calculating what it would take to push a laso-com beam over to Emerald Earth and listen in. His curiosity was insatiable, despite Farson's decree.

After Belnad's shocking arrival, it took a moment for him to calm down. Slowly his breath and lucidity returned. He looked up at Goethe, a tall, bronze man with flowing brown hair; vivid, intelligent green eyes; and an inviting presence, not at all threatening in any way. He was dressed in soft amber and green colors. The cloth was strikingly beautiful. Jim wanted to touch it. There was an aura around the man that was fascinating. Jim was beginning to relax in his presence, despite the surprise. It was perfectly obvious where the visitor was from. It was as if they had always been there. Jim did have a question.

"You predicted?" *How could he know where I was going to be?*

Belnad Goethe stood looking at Commander Peterson, who was a person of lore and legend on Emerald Earth, the man who had delivered them all.

Belnad then spoke in a voice that again emphasized that these humans were very different. Jim heard the voice and felt it touch his mind.

"As we 'hoped,' I should have said." He smiled, and held out his hand to SkyKing's Commander. "I am Belnad Goethe, of the Emerald Earth Council." Jim took his hand. The grip was soft, but a weathered texture, like from the long wear of work was also felt as their hands met. Jim's own hand felt small in the grasp. There was a gentleness, however, that he found reassuring.

"James Peterson, SkyKing Commander. What are you doing here? I thought there was a 'no contact' decree."

"Things change." The look on Belnad's face and the touch of his mind communicated something to Jim Peterson.

"You *missed* us?"

"Something like that."

22. Handy Joins the Harvester

The grass dolphins had slowly but surely picked up the pace, and Handy along with them. It was like being on a very fast-moving sidewalk. He just kept marching along, but the speed of his passage was now being multiplied by the coordinated movements of hundreds of dolphins under his feet.

this is fun handy want to see how fast we can go

Handy said nothing in answer to the question. He was actually enjoying the ride. The little group was really moving now. The grasses were parting like the ocean before an old Earth vessel on the open seas. There was advance movement in the grasses several hundred feet ahead. *They have scouts out there.* Handy wondered how fast they were going. *Fifty knots, is that possible?* The harvester was coming clearly into view now. They were overtaking it.

sit down handy and we can go a little faster

Almost without thinking, as though a large hidden hand had appeared beneath him, he found himself sitting comfortably on the dolphins. They adjusted their pattern, and a bench of sorts appeared. Then armrests formed on both sides. His cowboy hat blew back in the wind of their passage, caught by the drawstring under his chin. His long hair was streaming in the breeze. He stretched out his legs, a foot stool appeared, and he leaned back in the comfortable seating, his hands behind his head. He relaxed. The warm, clean air of

Emerald Earth, the aromas of the amber waves of tall grass nearing harvest all around, the perfect weather: It all reminded him of ocean sailing in those days of old on Earth. Someone watching him go by would have to turn their head quickly. They would have felt a wake rolling by a few seconds after Handy and the dolphins had passed. They would have seen Handy moving across the great field, seated on a throne-like chair, quickly receding off into the distance. Handy leaned back and closed his eyes: *This is the only way to go.* He must have dozed off, because when he awoke, Handy found they were slowly circling the harvester complex as it made its way down the row. They had arrived.

Onboard the harvester Strapper John Jordan was watching the spectacle. His long-range sensors had early on detected someone walking in the grass. But when the walking became a much faster approach, alarms had gone off. The arrival of the dolphins and Handy had caused a sensation on the harvester. The Jordan family was one of the oldest families on Emerald Earth with a long history of farming. This was something they had never seen.

Handy was amazed at the sheer size of the structure. It took the dolphins about a leisurely half hour to circle it. *Probably six miles around.* The "harvester" was really a small city, and the "family" was its population. The Jordan family was actually over thirty family groupings and over two hundred people.

Like all things Emerald Earth, there was a lot of room on the harvester, and things were never exactly what they appeared to be. There were around 15,000 harvesters working the planet's grass fields. There was no hurry, no production schedule, no quotas. Each family had vast areas to cover, the size of old Earth countries. The structure of the families varied widely. Emerald Earth was divided into two segments: ultra-urban and techno-rural. About half of the population lived centered in Emerald City, and the rest lived on the harvesters, roaming the planet and some in stationary "supply depots," as they called them. Some of the farmhands manned the export station, working closely with the city Emers.

In due course, the grass dolphins maneuvered Handy to within easy step-off distance of the harvester. He could see Strapper John and a few others waiting for him. The harvester was moving at about forty knots. As they approached, Handy could feel his excitement of seeing them again.

When Strapper John's son, Ian, had been born, Handy had been there. He had heard Farson announce the name of the new baby. He had felt the joy of the family. A rare event. A newborn. A son. For the Jordans, it was a new future and a whole new world. Now, Handy could see John's face looking at him from the harvester. It had a look of welcoming recognition. *This could be fun.* But Handy knew there was more than fun on the agenda of this visit. As he stepped off the dolphins and took Strapper John's hand, he could tell that John Jordan could see it. "To what do we owe this honor?" he asked, smiling. "That's quite a vehicle you've got there, Handy. I thought I had seen everything on this world, but that's a new one." Handy looked out the dolphins. They were bunched up close to the harvester. He looked up at the sky and had a worried thought for a moment. The eagles were gathering.

dont worry handy we will stay under the harvester and we will be fine as soon as you want to go just let us know

The rippling grass smoothed out as the large pod of dolphins moved into position. From above, it would have looked as though the harvester had a halo around it as the grass dolphins broached and played at the edges of the wake as it traveled down the row. Handy might have realized, if he could have seen it, that the group of dolphins had vastly grown on the trip to the harvester. As Handy and Strapper John moved toward the main structure on the harvester, the eagles turned away and headed south toward the foothills and the sparse forests, the haven of their nests.

It would be a long flight for them, on empty stomachs.

23. *Songbird*

Catherine was stretching. It was morning on Monhegan. The seagulls were cawing in their uniquely melodious way on the offshore breeze that lifted them gracefully over the warm coastal rock. The waves off the island had a light, lacy spindrift like gossamer mists, sparkling in the morning sun, rising up into the early spring air.

She felt invigorated. Two days with Tom had changed things for her. She had been alone for a long time. Her only companions had been her books and research tools. Eating had been just a necessity; sleeping, an inconvenience, an unnecessary delay. Now all that was changed. She could hear him moving around inside the cabin, getting dressed, checking the fire. *Looking for me.*

She could still feel him. She quietly reveled in the memory of his intimate presence, so welcomed and so unusual. His breath on her neck had enflamed her; his passion had challenged her. His joy had given her pleasure far beyond anything in her meager past in that department. She found a deep satisfaction in being with him, as though something had clicked into place that had had no place before that moment. Sleeping with him, these past two days had been something entirely new. She was looking forward to being in bed again. It was so intimate and so fascinating with feelings and sensations she had read about, of course, but in their deep and moving reality, they were now really hers. She felt excited, alive.

The thought of her work forced its way in. Her latest discovery, just two days ago, was still fresh in her mind, but had been pushed aside, like a book at the dinner table, to make way for a wonderful meal.

She could still taste him. She could still feel him. She wanted him all over again. Her discovery could wait, but just the thought of it had caused her scientific mind to kick in. Reluctantly, she was considering the chemistry and its implications. The combinations of symbiotic and cross-species DNA were complicated and far reaching when blended with her theories and calculations. She knew she had discovered the Rosetta stone of nutrition.

She was thinking of the next steps: synthesis and permutation. She was imagining a healthier world and a much more just world, when his hands came around her sides, lightly brushing and touching her breasts, warm and soft and welcoming beneath the flannel shirt. It was a wave of pleasure, and she turned into his arms. *He is still here.* His handsome face, light beard, clear eyes. She could smell him again. His hands drew her to him. He was smiling, almost laughing, as they kissed.

Tom had awakened, somewhat disoriented. His first thought, surprisingly, was, "Where is Catherine?" Once that was answered, only then did he think of his boat. He walked quickly to the window and looked out. *Songbird* swung easily on her anchor lines. It was going to be a great sunny sailing day. The boat had done well unattended. *What was I thinking?* But then he knew exactly what he was thinking. The most beautiful, exciting woman he had ever met. That's what he was thinking. He relished in those thoughts for a moment. How he had almost passed out in passion and exhaustion. How she had gone right with him every second, never hesitating, always matching him. He had looked at her closed eyes and had watched her moving with him. Three times they had made love. He had never been so satisfied and happy in bed. She had fallen asleep before he did. In his arms. It had been unbelievable to him: this amazing woman, alone on

Monhegan Island. How they had met by accident. He was in a state of masculine disbelief. Women had always been a problem for him. He had never really met one that he could truly relax around. Catherine changed all of that. It was confusing to him. Did she feel it too? Or was it already over, as usual? He was entertaining thoughts that troubled him and amazed him. The thought of ever letting her go seemed incomprehensible. He got dressed and walked into the living room to look for her. He saw that the fire needed a log and placed two in the hearth. *Some fires just won't go out.* It was a thought he hoped was still true. As he walked out onto the porch, and saw her there, stretching in the morning air, dressed in jeans and a flannel shirt, Tom Jacobson knew he had fallen in love. He put his arms around her from behind and gently brushed her breasts. She spun in his arms and kissed him. It was a long kiss. He could hear her breathing. He could feel her eyelashes. Her lips were moving, she was devouring him, and he was going in deeper and deeper. Nothing was in their way. No impediments. Freedom of love was their only guide.

It was a kiss to remember for a lifetime. It was an embrace without end. As the years would go by, they would both remember this morning kiss on the porch, through the good times and the tough times. "Love on the porch" they would always call it. That morning, on the island, with *Songbird* waiting nearby, in each other's arms, they both knew that life had taken a new path for them. Where did it lead? Neither of them cared. As long as they were together from that moment forward. Nothing would ever be the same.

They had packed up slowly over the next two days, making leisurely trips back and forth to *Songbird* to stow their things. Catherine had cancelled her airline tickets to New York. They were going to sail there together. "It's only three hundred miles. It will be fun." Tom's casual attitude about sailing three hundred miles was reassuring to Catherine, but the scientist in her checked the weather anyway, planning for safe harbors all along the way, and checking for communication protocols from waypoint to waypoint. She investigated the shipwrecks on the route and the causes of each. She looked up the coast guard records, and she checked over every system on the boat plus the rigging, the engine, and the supplies on board. "It's not like a trans-Atlantic crossing, Cat. It's just a sail down the coast. Easy-peasy. Nice stops along the way." She laughed.

"I have to be prepared. It's my nature."

They actually weighed anchor after dinner on their third day together. *Songbird's* instrumentation was up to date, and night sailing was one of Tom's favorite things. As they sailed out of Lobster Cove on the western side of the island, Catherine looked back and could see the rays of the setting sun shining on the windows of their cabin, like a little beacon marking the place where she had found true love. She knew that image would remain with her forever. That little cabin, that fire … that fire. She was sitting beside him now. He had his hand on the helm and his other arm around her. They were sailing with just the mainsail for now.

It was easy going, and the boat was moving smoothly in a light offshore breeze. The air was warm. There were sandwiches waiting in the galley refrigerator.

No one was in a hurry to eat.

24. Uva's Stories (1)

<<*What a fine story you weave, Farson. It reminds me of watching you in your childhood 'Ship,' dreaming up worlds and wonders to astound your sister. Did you know we were all watching? You were so innocent and yet so powerful. Uvo said those two attributes were the same thing. Twill belittled Uvo as a relic of some distant past that probably never really happened.*

'The rose of the world that never was has withered away,' Twill said over and over to my husband, Farson. Twill considered you to be an idiot, an aberration.

But everything you said would happen did happen. You and your sister did change everything. When we first heard of Earth and that stupid ScreenRent, none of us could have foreseen what has happened.>>

<<What has happened, Uva?>>

<<You know what has happened, Farson. Your failure is legend now. Just as the useless death of my husband is legend. It's all lost in the flutter of brittle pages in useless history books that no one reads.>>

<<Really? I am not as dead as they think.>>

<<Are you gloating? That is not healthy, Farson. Besides, you may very well be dead. Who's to know with all of your Screen manipulations? You could be dead, Farson. Have you thought of that?>>

They were onboard a very large starship. In the vastness of space it seemed to be standing still but was actually moving at speeds many multiples of light. Farson had decided to join Uva on her voyage back to her home world. It was a long voyage through space. They could have both done it in just a few minutes on The Screen. But, she had chosen to go the long way. <<It gives me time to think.>> Farson mentioned that it was going to take over a year to get home at this pace. She had responded, <<Your years are very different from my years, Farson.>>

On their journey together she told him stories of Uvo.

Their world was a vast planet with a light, rich atmosphere. Aristealia was teeming with life. Their avian race had evolved over eons. Their keen intelligence had taken control of the planet. They became dominant. Their cities were all floating in the sky. They seldom walked on the planet. The Aristealians, as they called themselves – in their language it sounded more like a hammer strike than a philosophical statement – had their history of warring and strife and, then, their current long, long history of peace and calm. The ScreenMasters had come suddenly thousands of years ago, appearing in their skies in gigantic spaceships. It was much like Earth's experience, but for the ScreenMasters, the trip to the planet Aristealia was long-planned for recruitment and extending their hegemony. In their struggles to achieve their goals, the ScreenMasters always sought to enlarge their sphere. They wanted to spread their influence as far and wide as possible. Contact was usually peaceful and productive. Uvo was selected as ScreenMaster. In due course they also accepted Uva. They became a ScreenMaster team. It was a first in those days. The planet thrived in this new era with astonishing technology and a greatly renewed sense of discovery. The Aristealians spread their wings. Uvo was their leader, and their father. He was Uva's husband. Like the other races, they had their own ideas and notions of relationships and love and marriage. Aristealians mated for life, without ceremony or courtship, and their procreation was straightforward, without artifice or contrivance. Theirs was a world of soaring intellect and freedom. The giant avians roamed the planet. With the advent of the ScreenMasters, Uvo and Uva roamed The Screen and shared a vast and rich experience together.

In the beginning, though, Uvo was always alone, except for the robots. It was hundreds of years later that finally Uva joined him in ascension and life began anew.

She leaned back in her perch-chair, scanned the instrumentations, touched a couple of toggles, and checked the ship's vital signs. All was well. Then she began to tell Farson a story of a time when Uvo left her. Her thoughts were soft and vivid in Farson's mind.

<<*It was a hard time for me. It's not unheard of in our race for a male to leave. I just never thought it would happen to us. We were always a perfect match.*>> She stirred in her perch.

She looked like she was going to stand up, but she just adjusted her extravagant feathers, repositioned her beautiful arms and wings, and stretched out her long legs. She settled her slender head onto her chest as if it were a pillow. Farson thought she was going to sleep. He found himself moving into a more comfortable position, settling down into the curve and cushions of the comfortable chair. How he was feeling reminded him of those post-Thanksgiving meals at the Chamberlains' when everyone headed for the couches. *Tryptophan.* Instead of a drowsiness, though, Farson noticed he was in a state more like totally relaxed, with a deep receptiveness taking over. He could feel Uva's presence. *How is she doing that?* <<*Farson, you think you're the only one with a few tricks? As long as I have lived I have never met anyone so supremely sure of himself, and yet with so little knowledge and so much power. It's as though for you, those two concepts have an inverse relationship.*>> Farson had a feeling of being held down, but something else was happening that caught him by surprise. He was flying.

The air over the planet was dry like a thirsty midnight breath. There were clouds way, way below him. The wings he could see and feel were his. He tried to bank the angle of flight with no success. <<*This is my story, Farson. Settle down.*>> The flight was long; he could feel the strength of the wings, but he also could feel them getting tired. He felt hungry. The air had gotten cold. The skies were darkening. He was going down. The air warmed slightly with the lower altitude and the wings beat on. It was a beautiful experience. He was Uvo. Somehow he had become Uvo in the story being told. *She wants me to feel it.* Uvo was flying over a planet not his own. He had left his barge and was flying to a meeting or something important. He was tired. He was hungry. Farson could hear his thoughts of Uva and wishing he were with her. He soared through the sky bundled with his mixed feelings of intent to proceed and conflicting desires to turn back. *No wonder I loved him.* There was a sharp rebuke for that thought that Farson felt in his head. <<*Watch what you're thinking. I can hear you. You didn't love him, Farson. I loved him. By the end of this story you will know how true this is.*>> There was another sharp stick of pain, and he knew Uva had basically slapped him as she got back down to business.

The land came into view. It was a large planet, and yet there was very little land. What land there was, was thoroughly covered in crops and vegetation growing everywhere, as though nothing could be wasted, no space unneeded. Uvo skimmed toward a landing with tiptoe grace at great speed. He simply coasted along as the speed of the landing bled off to where he could touch the ground at a casual walk. The people watching were amazed at the large angel-like visage descending from the sky and then a slim, tall figure strolling toward them. Uvo knew his majestic appearance under flight, and the straightforward upright appearance of him on the ground were profoundly different. Aloft, he was a vision of grace and speed. On the ground, he looked like a normal individual, certainly taller than most, but with the arms and legs and the posture of a being not all that unfamiliar with swift and precise movements. On the ground, he seemed mortal. In the air, he seemed invincible. "It makes us doubly dangerous," Uvo had said to Farson. "People don't know whether to bow, run, or shake our hands."

When Aristealians and humans met for the first time, it seemed a natural alliance. Many years later, when Farson and Uvo were in orbit around old Earth, they had walked together around his giant barge, as the ScreenMasters called their starship. Farson was surprised at the agility and ease of movement as Uvo strolled beside him. He remembered thinking, "*Strange birds, indeed.*"

Uva sent another annoying sensation into Farson's head. But, this time, he struck back. There was a long silence. Then

Uva seemed to relax. <<*'That cat can still scratch,' as we say.*>>
Farson knew he had made his point.

Uvo was now approaching a crowd of dignitaries who
were waiting for him. It had been a long trip. Screen or no
Screen, the immense reach of the ScreenMasters had
discouraged and defeated many other races. It was their secret
weapon. Like the boy who could run farther than any of his
friends, the ScreenMasters knew that their vast range gave
them a huge advantage. It's hard to fight someone you cannot
find and who can be in several places at once, especially when
the one you cannot find is also extremely intelligent and
powerful. Not knowing where the ScreenMasters actually
were had proven to be a daunting challenge when attempting
to resist them.

Uvo walked up to the reception party. Speaking and
simultaneously sending the translation to their unknowing
minds, he said, "Are you ready?" Surprised that he knew their
language, they assured him that they were ready, and everyone
walked together toward a structure that looked like it was
made out of falling water.

On Emerald Earth, Farson was speaking to Andrew Sortt.
The president was over at a window, leaning on the wall in his
office. Farson was lounging on a deep maroon couch with
pillows all around. They both looked really comfortable.
Farson was continuing their discussion of the American Civil
War. He was making the point that it was never really a fair
fight right from the beginning. "Did you know there were
two million men in the Northern armies and only 850,000 in
the Southern? The North had a population of twenty-two
million; the South only had nine million including four
million slaves. They never had a chance."

Andrew was not happy with this conclusion. He had been
born in South Carolina and had grown up hearing stories of
the glory of the Confederacy. Perhaps it was all just a myth,

but to him it still seemed important to defend history as he knew it. "Still, they had their moments, don't you agree?"

Inside the liquid building, Uvo looked around. It was a continuation of the building's exterior architecture. Inside the builders had created a feeling of being behind a waterfall. It was cool. The air was pleasantly moist, like after a hard rain. It was, however, dry in the building. Uvo was enjoying himself. *It's like Aristealia*, he thought. *Things are never what they seem.*

The business at hand was crowding its way past his appreciation of the engineering ingenuity. Everyone was looking at him.

He turned to the leader, a short, stout man, with a doubtful expression, who was standing closest to him. A little too close. The man's clothing was festooned with regalia of rank and privilege, including a colorful, flamboyant sash, and his chest was adorned with several gleaming rows of flashy medals. He seemed very certain of his place and, in his mind, in full control of the situation. Uvo shook his head. *They are all the same.*

Uvo knew the circumstances very well from the knowledge he had already gained during this portion of his Ascension. Planets like this were bent toward self-destruction: rank, inequality, avarice, disregard for ecology and the future, they were rife with unjustified prejudice and arrogance. It had all happened before. The Screen was "bending" in this area, and that was always a siren call for the ever-vigilant ScreenMasters. It was their duty, their heritage, and their destiny to "fix" such things, before they got out of control. There was no choice. No matter what it took, Uvo knew his responsibility, just as ScreenMasters before him had known theirs. It was inevitable. It was inescapably predictable. The Screen must be protected.

Uvo was looking at the podium on the stage. It would take just a few seconds to climb the stairs to the stage and begin. He hesitated, and instead of proceeding onstage, he turned to face the crowd around him. "I'm going to stay down here. We are in this together. Things are going to change now. You have created a world of inequality and virtual slavery. Your rich live a life of plenty, and your poor live a life of emptiness – except for their struggling families, of course. Your poor know their children cannot improve their lives, and they know that you don't care. This is a formula for trouble. We want you to fix it. That is why I am here."

The growing crowd was restive, agitated. What the ScreenMaster said was true. It was the way things had always been: the rich and the poor. There had been eras of hope and of progress, but, in the end, these trends always recoiled back into the same old system of dominance and fear. To the ScreenMasters, it had gone on too long. They knew that this imbalance could cause trouble – had caused trouble. They could feel it on The Screen. It would be awhile before anything would actually happen to The Screen, but the ScreenMasters knew now was the time to start. Uvo's mission was to begin the process of repair. His gigantic barge was in orbit. They could all see it. They had watched him fly from space on his great wings and land here beside them. The power of the ScreenMasters was obvious to them. They had nothing to compare. The purple hue surrounding Uvo only added to his appearance of omnipotence.

Perhaps in the backs of their minds, they knew things could not continue as they were, as they had always been. But they had done nothing to really change things. With Uvo standing before them, and hearing the words he had spoken, they knew that today was the someday they had always feared would come.

"Andrew, I know you have Southern roots, but still, it was a forgone conclusion among the leaders of the North that the South would be vanquished. The historic record of the battles which the South 'won' has been drastically distorted through the years. The North had 100,000 factories in full swing and four million trained and experienced people working in them. The South was agrarian and had only a fifth of that industrial might and only 100,000 factory workers. The South was a feudal society with slaves as its most important crop. The North was a modern powerhouse of innovation, industry, and military might. The North could and did sustain 365,000 casualties, roughly 18 percent of their forces. The South, so much smaller, was debilitated by 260,000 deaths, almost 30 percent of their soldiers."

"It was David and Goliath, as you said."

"But, this time, Goliath won."

The president stood up and walked toward the decanter, casually casting a knowing question over his shoulder back to Farson. "Did he?"

Uvo took wing again and flew into the transporter point, where he was immediately transported back to his barge in midair. The people on the ground were watching as he disappeared. Onboard the barge, he watched the monitors to see what would happen. A beam of pure white reached out from the planet, but it was stopped before it could hit his barge. It was absorbed by the barge, and then it was redirected back to the planet, directly at the falling water building. The color of the beam had changed. Now it had a faint purple hue.

Uva looked up at Farson. She watched him gradually come to the conclusion that she had stopped; the story was over. She could also see his perplexity and uncertainty about what had just happened, as if he were asking, "What's your point?" She stretched her wings luxuriously and moved as though preparing to fly away.

"He ultimately destroyed the planet, Farson. It was their choice." Farson was thinking of his own experiences, and many mistakes he had made. He was also thinking of all the people on the planet in Uva's story.

"At least they had a choice."

25. Farson Goes to the Edge

It was a cold night. Farson decided to follow the doctor home. His name was Ronald Weidger, and he had lived in Ohio all of his life. But this night was testing the doctor's lifelong devotion to the place. He slammed the door behind him as he entered his home. He went directly to the phone and made a call while taking off his hat, coat, scarf, and gloves and throwing them on the chair nearby. With some extra effort, heel to toe, he kicked off both of his boots.

Speaking into the phone, the doctor was agitated. "That crazy fool is going to kill her. You guys should send someone out there or at least stand by. She's going to give birth tonight and she's probably going to die doing it. What a mess. David threw me out." The person on the other end of the call explained that with the coming storm they would make a note of the situation at the Uiost cabin, but with the reports of the bad weather coming in, it could be days before they could do anything. Then he added, "It's not your fault, Ron. You've done everything you could do. And more." The doctor hung up the phone and stared out the window. The snow outside was intensifying. Dr. Weidger noticed it was blowing horizontally outside the window. The wind was howling like a lost child.

Back in his family's cabin, Farson continued to look around. It was like it always was when he came here. He knew where everything was and where everything would be. He knew exactly how it would go. He had seen it happen many, many times.

It was the old, tarnished mirror that now always caught his attention. His own reflection in the mirror was the only thing that ever changed in the room. He could remember coming here when he was much younger. He could also remember coming here when he was much older. He had seen it all. Farson had been here so many times that the times all blended together. Everything was always exactly the same, except for his own reflection in that mirror. Seeing himself over all the years in that unchanging room, as reflected in the mirror, focused him and left him with a sense of intrusion almost like into a painting that – except for that reflection – never changed.

Looking into his own eyes in that mirror fascinated Farson. The person staring back was so real, but he could sense nothing from the reflection. It was like watching a time-lapse movie. The reflection had seen everything that Farson had seen. He wondered, if the man in the mirror had seen things that this Farson had not seen yet? *It's here where I am uncertain. Here, in that mirror, is that me? Or someone else? Almost born, never dying, always moving, always changing …which one am I now?* Farson looked around the familiar room again. It was all happening again, right before him, and it all held such far-reaching consequences. As he had so many times before, he watched and wondered: *What really happened here?*

<<*Farson, what are you doing?*>> Karina was always watching now.

<<*I am doing what you will do when you are doing what I am doing.*>>

<<*And what will I be doing?*>>

<<*Wondering, Karina. You will be wondering, too.*>> She laughed.

<<*I doubt that, Farson. I already know too much.*>> Now he knew she was laughing at her own situation, not his. It didn't make her comment grate on his mind any less, though. He knew she knew it was not true. He also knew that knowing that you can never know "too much" was part of really knowing anything. Farson knew that, in time, all intelligent people doubt and wonder and feel uncertain. The passage to the knowledge of the great unknown was always arduous and painful. Farson knew it had to be. There was no other way. Being human meant coming face-to-face with your own illusions and misbeliefs. It meant a journey of mistakes and defeats, of failure and recovery. In due course, all human beings – every incredible, and all the unpredictable variegations of the species – come to the truth of their own fallibility. It's part of being human. It's human nature, if you will. We screw things up. Then we fix them. *History in a nutshell.* He looked at Karina. She smiled brightly.

<<*I wasn't expecting contact, Karina.*>>

<<*Surprise.*>> Their hands intertwined, and they moved closer. Their reflections in the mirror were kissing. Over his shoulder Farson saw Karina looking back at him.

The mirror was always right there. It always had the same fingerprints, paint chips, and the same spreading silver tarnish behind the reflection. It was always hanging just about two degrees off-center. He always thought to straighten it, but time had taught him to change as little as possible. The old rule about changing anything changed everything was long since gone. *Unworkable.* Things are so complicated in that chain of thought that it becomes un-human in its ludicrousness. No human being can live in a world without changing it. It's just a fact. So traveling in time is just an extension of that. If you look at the stream of billions of people living throughout history, all moving through time together, and remember that they must, by their nature, change everything, have changed everything, and are still changing everything, then you know that not to change things *would* change things. So, Farson just acted naturally: Moving in time and space was as easy for him as moving around in a familiar room was for everyone else.

He looked around this particular room. His father had weakened from the emotions of his mother's long labor. In his world of quiet introspection and study, the sad reality of spending three and a half days with a woman screaming in pain, straining with life-threatening effort, dying slowly, and talking to him, in the quiet intervals, as though she desperately wanted to tell him everything about her life in every detail had taken its toll. She told him about her parents. She told him about loving him. She told him what it was like to have his baby. She told him how much she loved him. She broke his heart a hundred times in those three and a half days. She loved him. He knew that she didn't notice the flaws that so beleaguered him with self-doubt and recrimination for his lack of faith. She would wait for the baby, she had said over and over. To hold his wife in his arms, during those hours and days, was a great gift from God. When he took her hand in his, David Uiost knew he was holding the hand of an angel. Farson watched them. He listened to them. He looked at how they held hands. *Like a still life painting.* The same way Karina and he did it, fingers intertwined just so. There were so many thoughts in this room, so many memories for Farson. *So many things that changed everything. This room.* He looked back at the mirror again. Had his face changed? Was everything different again? How could he know? How many times had all of this happened?

The mirror stared back, unanswering, still off-center.

Back in his own cabin in North Conway, he put down his pen. He had been writing. It was the third or fourth draft of the poem. He couldn't recall. It was part of a series of ten poems on the same subject. In this last revision he had changed only one word. *It's too long,* he thought. He knew that poems, like water, seek their own level. *Why do I bother? I never show them to anyone.*

<<*Anyone, Farson? You know that's not true.*>>
<<*Except for you, Handy. It goes without saying.*>>
<<*But I did say it.*>>
<<*All too true. Do you like it?*>>
<<*Too early to say yet. Is it finished?*>>
<<*Yes and no.*>>

<<*What else is new?*>> It was a joke they had about indecision and always changing things. But even as Handy said it, he saw that Farson was already gone. Handy picked up the poem from Farson's desk and read it again, looking for the change Farson had just made. The mental picture of an elderly Farson sitting in a rocking chair came vividly to view in Handy's mind as he read the poem again.

I WANNA BE YOU (#4)

Your gray hair and mild eyes
Whisper of a lifetime perhaps,
Full of rich memories and battles fought,
Some lost. This has time-woven
A memory quilt that you can pull over you
As you stand there looking at me.

There are patches that clearly show
Quick repair and stitches
That could have been better.
It really looks a little too small from here.
Perhaps it's still unfinished.
I'm sitting in the ambient
Reality of the room, but you?
You have that blanket. You can throw it off

And use it as a pillow when it's warm.
You can use it, as now you do, to stave
Off the cold that's coming.
It's a shield you've earned, I think.

Your gray hair and mild eyes;
Were you always so peacefully blended?
Or did your hair once blow long in
The winds of youth and recklessness?
Did your eyes once have that talon-thrusting
Intensity that drove profit charts and
Other people crazy? Did some of those
Patches come with blood, smoke, and flames?
Were some torn out of other lives with tears?
You seem to be hiding some underneath, or
Maybe protecting them?

When it's your turn to speak
You often let it pass, unspeaking.
Let others burn their bridges, do you think that?
Or do you just listen in now, like an aficionado
At a symphony who hears all the nuances and
Subtleties of vibrations and techniques and knows
Exactly what the composer intended even with
Your eyes closed and your hands folded
Softly – untensed now – those clenches gone forever?

Or are you in there, behind all of this, scared of
The coming inexorability? Worried about all that
You have done? Regretful of so many things past?
Are you in there, tremulous with pain,
Worried of being called out, starring in your own
Tragedy, now alone, driven back onto
Yourself and your undeniable memories,
Your lack of glory and lack of courage,
Assignations of doubt and no way out?
Sitting here like a self-imposed prisoner are you

Wishing to God you were somewhere else?
Somewhere young and free again?

It's like looking into one of those mirror-on-mirror
Rooms where the images telescope away repeating,
Ever smaller but never disappearing, sort of
Bending off into eternity: me looking at you
You looking at me.
Your gray hair and mild eyes, and mine
Seem to blend together into a long, tapering
Spear thrusting into our mirror
As far as our eyes can see.

I want to be you.
Do you want to be me?

Handy put the poem back down on the wooden desktop. Spring was coming in New Hampshire, he knew. He had seen it many times. People were still dressed for winter. It was still cold, but they were now thinking of spring. He looked at the last line again. He worried about Farson's obsession with his birth and the death of his parents. Handy knew Farson had been back there too many times. His friend's self-torture and preoccupation with things he cannot change worried Handy. The pain of the poem worried him. His eyes were welling up. The things he had seen sometimes overwhelmed. He had always been there with Farson. They had done it all together. Handy's sadness was driven by his friendship and his love for Farson. By the knowledge that no matter what he did, no matter what anyone did, Farson was alone as always. *Except for Karina.* "Except for Karina." He said it out loud as the purple hue enclosed him, and he disappeared. The disruption of the air in the cabin was slight, but it was enough to gently move the poem to the edge of the table. Handy looked back and noticed it teetering, on the verge of falling to the floor. As the air smoothed out, he saw that the poem had stayed there on the table, balanced on the edge.

26. Sargasso Opens

Farson could not believe what he was looking at. Sargasso had suddenly and surprisingly opened its door. The size proportions were unscalable by the human eye, and Farson doubted there was any way that a human being could stand where he was and understandingly survey it.

Through the opening, Farson could see the vastness of the interior. It was a universe inside a planet. There were planets in the planet. They floated like clouds in the sky or islands on a vast sea. There seemed to be stars. *How can that be?* He felt like a boy in a planetarium staring at the ceiling and seeing the entire night sky with such clarity and comprehension. Just as the boy might understand his own insignificance in that moment, Farson needed no reminder. It was clear enough. So many felt that he knew it all, and so many relied on him for guidance and safety. In his plan, it had all seemed so easy. Now the crush of those decisions was weighing him down, and he felt as if his life had become hard labor. *Stooped labor.* He felt bent over by events. He felt weak and frail. He worried endlessly. *How will they all feel when they know what I know?* But before him now was a world, a universe, he had not envisioned. It was thrilling to him. He knew he could not have imagined it. He knew this was an outcome he had not foreseen.

Farson looked down. He was still standing on the platform. He looked up, and the world of Sargasso stared back at him. He was afraid to move, thinking the door would close and access would be lost. *Will it stay like that?* Would he be able to come back and look again? With that thought, the door closed. He was faced with the blank wall again. Farson searched in his suit and found a marker. He attached it to the platform. Reluctantly, he turned around and engaged his suit's propulsion system and rocketed off upward toward the Moon. Behind him, the platform, the structure, and the distances telescoped away. Outside, Sargasso assumed the shape and substance of the "planet" they had been looking at for the past ten years. Farson looked back. *How big is it?* He knew that to the people on SkyKing and the Moon, Sargasso had not changed at all. Farson also knew that after actually having visited Sargasso, he now knew far less about Sargasso than they did. *They are looking at the unknown. I have seen into the unthinkable.*

Chapter Three

Emergence

27. Farson and the President (1)

The questioning of whether the South lost the Civil War or not surprised Farson. Surely the president was not a Confederacy holdover? Throughout the long period of time since the Civil War, there were always people in the old South waving the stars and bars. There were always people with that underpinning of longing for the land of cotton and insuring that the old times there were never forgotten. Andrew was, after all, from South Carolina.

"Come on, Andrew. How could Virginia have been part of the Confederacy? The home of Thomas Jefferson? Six of the Founding Fathers were from Virginia, including Madison, Jefferson, and Washington. How could *that* have happened?"

Andrew Sortt knew full well what Farson was thinking. His beloved South Carolina was a willing part of the Confederacy. Andrew Johnson, the facilitator of Reconstruction, may have been its most famous son, though. He did have an answer for Farson, about Virginia. He believed that the Civil War was really the second, and inevitable, part of the American Revolution.

"Richmond was the capital of the Confederacy, Farson. Virginia was a slave state. Lincoln was from Illinois. Where, in all of this was your vaunted Northeast industrial behemoth? The war was actually driven by those intellectual southerners in Virginia and countered by free-thinking midwesterners. The Northeast was just the capitalist matrix for the profiteering tools of war. It was not the first time that economics overtook the philosophic underpinnings of our country."

The president took a sip of his Armagnac. He enjoyed the sensation of it in his mouth, and he swallowed slowly, reluctantly, like the last drops of a summer rain running down into a sun-warmed rain barrel. President Sortt could hear those ancient voices singing even now.

"Oh, I wish I was in the land of cotton,
Cinnamon seed and sandy bottom,
Look away, look away, look away Dixieland."

Any discussion with Farson was always fun, but this one was especially enjoyable. Sortt had lived a long time. He was a slow motion Farson. He had gone the levels and layers, but he had done it in real time, for him: four thousand and fourteen years. He had seen it all. As the true ScreenMasters grew in numbers on Emerald Earth, they learned everything themselves. Like America itself, Sortt and the Emers were self-taught.

Farson was great, the Emers all knew it; and they also knew themselves and their own increasing powers. It was decided early on that they would use every tool, and exploit every situation, to the maximum in the pursuit of their goal. Survival was everything. Sortt understood this as few others could. He did not join them as they wished. He accompanied them. Over the millennia they had come to see that President John Andrew McKinley Sortt was irreplaceable. His requests to retire were all denied. His attempts to leave were constrained. In a way, he became a prisoner of his success. Because he chose to remain unchanged in their changing world, he became a revered symbol of the human race: a touchstone, a living echo, a voice unstilled, a reminder of who they really were.

The challenge of the Emers mixing with SkyKing and the Moon was on the president's mind. He knew that the Emers were acting on their own again, without regard to all of his cautions and persuasions. No matter what Sortt said regarding what Farson wanted, or what Handy said, the Emers always did things their way. They were making decisions with far-reaching effects. He was not exactly sure what was happening for the first time in … how long? More than four thousand years. *That's a long time to think you know what you're doing and then find out you don't know very much at all.*

He turned back to answering Farson's question. "With all your professorial statistics, I am somewhat surprised that you have misconstrued why Virginia was in the Confederacy. They were in it to win it, Farson. Your guys dodged a serious bullet. It could have gone the other way in the very beginning, but when the people in the North had decided 'no slavery' – even though they themselves were slaves in another way, as time would tell – it created a do-or-die scenario. It's ironic that so many who actually believed in the underlying principles of the rebellion were persuaded to fight against it. We Southerners understood it, though. To believe in freedom and culture, one is forced to think of others. It was the kindness and human principles of Southern life that actually caused the push for abolition. We undid ourselves. Just when our argument was at its strongest, abolitionist fervor became the engine of the North's war machine. Lincoln channeled it to brutally win battles. The Union wasn't saved. It was reborn in the Civil War."

This soliloquy made Farson nervous. He was moving. No, it was more like prowling, around the room. He noticed his glass was empty, and he was thinking of having another. *Am I becoming Handy?* He put down the glass a little too quickly. He couldn't believe what he was hearing.

"You *are* a holdover, Andy. I can't believe it."

"No, I am not. I could never have supported the Confederacy, and you know it."

"A sympathizer then. I know you are not a rebel. I do think you still cherish some of their values." Sortt cocked his head at Farson.

"I hope you mean strong families, love of the land, and being free, Farson. Otherwise we could have a problem. I feel your incredulity. You should probably take a deep breath. Your sophomoric view of the Civil War as a war between North and South, good and bad, is blinding you to the real truth. It was a war over the most basic of principles: Who's the boss of who." Farson burst out laughing. The president chuckled along.

"That's a good one, Andy. Really."

"You want one more?" Farson couldn't wait.

"Yes. Definitely yes."

"The South won."

28. Sublimity

Farson was back on the butte, sitting right where so many decisions had been made. It was one of the places he liked to go to think, or play, or to be alone with Karina. It was a favorite place. On the "Butte of Decision," as history now called it, he still came here when there were really big decisions to be made. The isolation was sublime. It could be seen from miles and miles all around, and anyone approaching would be noticed long before their presence could cause a concern. Farson liked advance warnings.

He was thinking about all he had learned of Sargasso, its inestimable mass and size, of its purpose and power. He stood at the entrance of Sargasso on the precipice of revelatory discovery. Staring into Sargasso, the first shock was a distance beyond imagination, its size was immense. And then, the second shock came to Farson. There was no Screen in Sargasso, at least as he had come to know it. He knew he had been invited in by the architects of Sargasso.

There was no doubt that everything had changed from that moment on.

When the door opened for him, he had sensed something; something complex; something known and yet still unknown. When he had turned to leave Sargasso and the same door had closed behind him, he had felt a deep sense of loss, a sadness, a longing to return. He felt as though some great and good power had been cut off from him as the door had hissed closed and the impenetrable wall returned. He had turned and looked at where the opening had been, but it was as gone as gone could be. There was no sign it had ever been there, just his memory of an experience that, by everything Farson had learned up to that point, could not have happened.

The wonderful feeling of deep sublimity that overwhelmed him as he stared into the truth of Sargasso's mysteries had been intuitively reassuring and confirming of all of his hopes for humanity. When the door closed, he had felt cut off from things of great importance, of great urgency. The insight on that moment, when he saw what he saw, was still enriching him, still entrancing him. In the severing of that connection, feelings he had long sought had hugged him closely in a deep relief like love returned or a lost treasure found. But then they were cauterized with the closing of the door and the frigid return of the aloneness of being in space. The incomprehensibility of the dark wall of Sargasso's mysterious reality returned. He stared at its perspective off into infinity. He remembered just floating there, floating there, wondering what had just happened, memory erased.

He was now sitting on the butte still trying to remember, trying to indulge those feelings of respite and relief again, to regain and nurture them again. He had traveled back on The Screen, over and over, to the moment when the door started to open, but at the first sign of its opening, everything just went blank again and again. History had changed, he knew; but the new world he had seen, and that had so infused him, was gone as if it had never been, leaving him to search for his memories, so vivid and transforming, and yet just out of reach, for now.

He and Karina could relive anything, even more now as their powers had grown. Now they could see things through each other's eyes. But Farson's always infinite and omniscient Screen powers were stopped at that platform door. The power behind Sargasso had wanted him to see it. But that was all; he had seen the truth, he knew, but it had been taken away. *Why?*

What were they trying to tell him?

He now knew that the arrival of Emerald Earth, SkyKing, and the Moon at Sargasso was not a journey's end. It was the beginning. *But of what?*

Farson wanted to talk to Repoul Bensn.

The midshipman was at his station. He was watching a monitor. The recorded sequence he was watching was of flying through the "sky" over Sargasso's surface and, specifically, it was Farson's sudden flight toward the tower that was being displayed. It was the sixth time Repoul had watched this exact footage. Each time, he saw the same thing. Farson arrives on the platform, takes a few steps, and disappears. The recording continues for the next four hours with no change, just the empty platform and the black wall. Then Farson reappears, stands on the platform momentarily, turns, looks back at the wall, and then rockets away after tagging the location.

In the reappearance sequence, Repoul was sure there must be a clue. He had been studying those two seconds of digital data for several days. Using every telemetry tool of SkyKing and the Moon, the only possible anomaly he had noticed was a slight but intense increase in the data rate just before Farson reappeared. On the front end, the data stream was consistent. Deep in the underpinning equations, there was a much increased detailing. An elaboration of algorithmic results. The increase in data was just an increase in data with no expansion of knowledge or useful information. Repoul was confused by its uselessness. *As though time simply slowed way down in those seconds.* After Farson's reappearance and departure, the data stream resumed the standard levels as before. It was just those two seconds.

Repoul was resetting his instrumentation for another run through the data when Farson himself appeared on the bridge.

29. Farson and the President (2)

"Won? Oh come on, Andy, you think the South won?"

"Of course. By any measure, except geography. The South lost fewer soldiers, in every category, and fewer wounded, as well, even though they raised a million troops to the North's 1.5 million. Both sides experienced noncombat deaths at a rate nearing three times the deaths in battle, but even in that category the South did a little better. Disease was the biggest killer, especially for the Northerners. The Southern soldiers were captured at twice the rate of," he paused here for a moment as though searching for a phrase, and then said, "the Union troops." Farson noticed.

"You were going to say 'Yankees,' weren't you?" Sortt smiled at Farson's dependable perspicacity.

"The thought crossed my mind." They both turned to their Armagnacs, seeking solace for their separate forms of disappointment: Farson, that his friend still harbored such pejorative thoughts, and Sortt, for failing to speak his true mind. There was a forced muteness in the silence as they sipped their drinks. President Sortt was thinking about how he would proceed in the discussion. It remained his turn, mostly because Farson had not responded. So he continued, strengthened somewhat by a rich savoring drink of the strong spirits, "Since the term first referred to the Dutch settlers – the English were making fun of the common first and last Dutch names, Jan and Kees – and since it originally referred to anyone from the United States, and its preceding colonies, north *and* south, it might even have been more appropriate if I *had* used the term. But, knowing you, Farson, I stuck with the expected term these days. I thought you would be happier, Farson. Your implicit criticism is unwarranted, of course."

The president, noticing that Farson now had the middle distance stare of a bored student, realized that his ScreenMaster friend and companion might no longer be devoting his undivided attention to their discussion at the moment. He inquired as much, "Farson?" But as Sortt had thought, Farson was now far, far away.

He was kissing Karina. They were "under canopy" again. Her lips were passionate with excitement, and she was on top of him. They were in the middle of the landing area at the drop zone after just landing together in perfect synchronicity. They had hugged, and their canopies drifted down over them in the light summer breeze. As though the soft silk were as heavy as lead, they comically fell immediately to the ground with the parachutes. Covered and momentarily out of sight of other jumpers, they had a few seconds of quasi-privacy. They were making good use of it.

"Farson?" the president repeated his intentionally interruptive question. It had no effect that he could detect.

When Farson had asked Karina to marry him, she laughed out loud. They had returned to Monhegan Island and spent the night in the cabin there; "their" cabin as they thought of it. The cabin was empty because Tom and Catherine, Karina's to-be-parents, had gone back out to Tom's boat. They had decided to stay the night out there, so Farson and Karina took the cabin, as usual. This night was one of their favorite ScreenMaster "trips." They were sitting in front of the fire Tom had built. The fire's level of warmth and flame was perfect. The heat was warming in more ways than one. In the midst of a deep embrace of love and intimate contact, Farson had popped the question, softly in her ear. There had never been any doubt that they would marry. She knew it was what they both wanted, but when? That was the question. Having lives that intermingled with time's infinite facets and moving through it all the way others moved from room to room, they could take their pick of time and place. She had asked Farson to marry her many times, but he had always held that that was the one decision that was still up to him. "Tradition," he had said, awarded him, and him alone, the privilege to choose. They had been so many places, so many times together that she had almost stopped wondering about it. Perhaps it didn't really matter. "There are times we go to when we are already married, Karina. What's to worry about?" he had said. She knew this was true. She knew all about their lives – future and past – but this moment of proposal was the one she had never found in all their travels. She suspected that Farson was saving it, hiding it, and that he knew very well when and where it was and would be. He denied it, saying it hadn't happened yet and that there were still some mysteries on The Screen. She just shook her head in playful disbelief, and sometimes even laughed with his silliness.

"You of all people should not be talking about tradition," she had said over and over. Neither of them believed her implication.

She was in his arms. Their bodies intertwined, their lives so long bonded together. He was wondering where she ended and he began. He whispered in her ear. "Will you marry me?" He could see her soft hair move gently with his breath, as he said the words. He spoke so softly it was almost inaudible. He could smell her. Her close warmth was flushing over him. Their nearness was supremely natural and relaxing. Nothing in all the universe could match what they had always had. Farson had never had anyone but Karina. Karina maintained that she had never had anyone but Farson despite his pleadings for full disclosure about her time away at Indiana University. She just dismissed his curiosity as perverted. "How can you think such a thing, Farson?" At this moment, though, those thoughts were the farthest thing from their minds. The words hung in the air for just a few seconds as though she was savoring them. <<*At last.*>>

She said, "Yes." And then she burst out laughing.

Farson looked at President Sortt. He had said something, and he was waiting for an answer. Farson replayed the last few moments in his mind, and then answered as if he had actually been listening. "The Union took a beating, it's true, Andy. But the South was pulverized. Sherman's so-called "March," the total unconditional surrender, the brutal Reconstruction; it was the nightmare of their defeat's disaster come true for all of the Confederate states." Sortt was not at all surprised at Farson's acuity. He knew very well who and how Farson was, his one true friend. Sortt's answers flowed naturally in the discussion.

"And yet, they resurged and took over the United States by championing their definitions of freedom and individuality, and the traditional values of that old land of cotton. Lincoln's historic restatement of 'all men are created equal' was pushed to the side and redefined by wealth and privilege and class. Some men and women, as it turned out, were much more equal than others. The later years of the United States looked more like the old oligarchy of the South than the egalitarian dreams of the Roosevelts. The corporate fascism, the plantation mentality of government joined with huge business interests that Lincoln, and others after him, warned against so eloquently, ultimately took control of everything. Despite all the good, so 'nobly advanced,' in the name of progressive liberalism and collective action – and to be fair, it did save the country twice at least – there was still an irresistible, irrepressible urge to return to the domination of ascendant individuality and ill-gotten privilege: The endless battle between the safety of security vs. the freedom of equality. It's the old dichotomy of life. It's the curse of Adam and Eve. In the end, that the South won, there can be no doubt."

Farson was listening and feeling the effects of the brandy. He knew Andrew Sortt well. *Thousands of years.* He had seen Sortt in many situations and knew and trusted his old friend. Farson had no doubt about his friend's motives and intentions. He had seen Sortt always avoid negative responses and punitive sanctions. He had always, always chosen the high road in every challenge and circumstance. Farson knew that this "philosophical" discussion was just entertainment for the president.

"Andy," Farson was still playing along, "you can't mean that fear won over love. You can't mean that." Sortt looked down at his drink. It was almost gone.

"No. You're right, Farson. Love won. But that's my point exactly. At the core of the Confederacy, as at the core of the Union, love was enthroned once fear was cast aside. In many ways, slavery aside, the two sides were far more similar than different. The perception of apostasy was enraging for both sides. The bloodiest war in American history was fought over a misconception. The truth is that the peace and tranquility of the lives of Southern whites, their devotion to their land and their families, and the happiness of those days remains the dream of all human beings, as you and I have seen. Slavery was an enabling evil whose time was running out. The Civil War extended slavery, in new ways, in the world for hundreds of years more, legitimizing inhumanity in the name of whatever ideology came along. That was not the Southern cause in any way. Order. Peace. Abundance. What the South, at its core, really wanted was exactly what the North, at its core, wanted. The industrialists of the North won the war of the armies, but the South won the argument. Look at Emerald Earth. Finally, rural and urban peace achieved, universal prosperity, and abundance unprecedented. And now the final element finally comes as true humanity has taken its rightful place. It's an inclusive triumph of enormous proportions."

President John Andrew McKinley Sortt was going to add that, had the South actually won the military struggle, this triumph would have come much sooner, but he hesitated in this postulation. Six thousand years of knowing history's greatest person, as a friend and mentor, had taught him to think things over before he spoke. *He still teaches me things I thought I already knew.*

He was thinking about the Emers and all that they had done. Six thousand years in captivity had changed them. The security of stasis had given birth to a deep longing for, and love of, freedom. Their time alone had created a thoughtful and hopeful society with powers beyond the merely individual, a happiness beyond the merely personal. Those old individual and personal elements remained, though in other ways. Now Emerald Earth – peaceful, productive, inventive, and free – was the ultimate experiment: no limits, no restraints, no enemies, and no problem insurmountable. What would and could they achieve? He knew that no altering of American history would have changed anything concerning Emerald Earth. He knew it was all petty squabbling of an irrelevant past, swept aside by a startling and irrevocable future. The past was merely, as they used to say, "rearranging the deck chairs on the *Titanic*." When the ScreenMasters came to Earth, they were the tip of an iceberg that changed everything. He added as an ending, "Love won. There is no doubt, Farson. But love has proven to be the most potent weapon of all, as everyone always knew it was."

Farson was pleased with the outcome of this conversation. As always. Andrew was a true friend who, in the beginning, had distrusted Farson and fought him. But President Sortt had long learned that fighting with Farson was like fighting with sunlight: You can hide but the light always finds a way in. His friend seemed distracted again.

<< *Are you bored, Farson?*>> Farson thought at first that it was Karina speaking to him, but then he quickly realized it was Sortt. Farson was activating Screen transport as he responded.

<<*No, Andy. I'm not bored, but my drink has needed refreshing for a while. For all your talk of love.*>> Sortt watched the room fill with Farson's unique purple light, and then he was alone.

Sortt walked over to the table where the half-full decanter was waiting. He put his drink down and lifted the bottle. The rich brown liquid sloshed around as he held it. He lifted the lug cap and sniffed the contents. He replaced it and set it down. <<*You have a point there, Farson.*>>

As he left the room, he was already missing Farson. The bouquet of the brandy was still in his mind, a lush redolence of his time with his friend. He picked up Farson's empty glass along with his own. *His glass is empty, but mine runneth over.* He headed to the kitchen, where he carefully washed and dried the two crystal glasses and put them on the shelf until the next time, the beautiful decanter beside them, the Armagnac still softly moving from the bottle's motion, settling down to a rich amber stillness, as the president left the room.

"Why are you laughing, Kari?"

"Because I said 'yes' so quickly."

"What else could you do?" She was still giggling as she responded, first physically – they were still intertwined – then, after a while, she answered verbally as well.

"Fair enough." She took his hand. "You're right. My long and impatient concubinage was *finally* over, Farson. How could I ever thank you?" She was laughing at her own joke. He moved closer. He could still intimately feel the rhythm of her mirth. He whispered in her ear.

"Being my wife is all the thanks I will ever need, Karina."

There was a long pause in the conversation. This was a time when words were unnecessary. All the years of waiting were over. Even as they made love, so gently and intensely, still holding hands the whole time, they both understood that they were and always would be surrounded by vast and sweeping changes over and over again, but that *this* world – their private world, in each other's arms – would never change.

30. Emerald Earth and the Impossible

Karina stood before the first group of pre- and post-Farson human beings ever assembled. Viera, Voul, and Karina were all actually born on Earth, and Brittany was among the first born on SkyKing, but both of her parents had been born on Earth. The Emers had never known *that* Earth. Their lives began on Emerald Earth, at first in transition and then finally stable as planned. For them, old Earth was a mythical recollection, akin to prehistoric times, in their long histories.

The Emers were obviously a different breed of human being: They were taller, light bronze in color, more highly intelligent, and, in ways that were just becoming apparent, so different that, at first, people of old Earth ancestry were confused and disoriented in their presence. "Their presence" brought with it a vertigo and a sense of mental disarray for the old Earthers. It was not unpleasant, but it could be overwhelming, as it had been for Brittany. Like a barrier to go through, that first encounter was always challenging. Farson's protection from contact for the past many years had postponed the inevitable. Even now contact was being limited, by the Emers themselves, to just this contact. But as Brittany had learned, the modulation of mutual awareness, while difficult, also held the secret of contact with the Emers: It began to change you into something new from the very first moment.

Karina's thoughts swept through the group.

<<*There is no reason to delay any longer. The sooner we make the move, the better. Our final destination awaits.*>>

"Where is Farson, Karina?" Voul's use of verbal communication caused Karina to smile. She still loved the sound of a human voice. In her years of being a ScreenMaster, she had mastered telepathy and all of its intricate nuances, far richer than mere speech. To truly communicate, she knew one needed the deep interaction of thought and all that it entailed. Thought was so intimate and inclusive, so encompassing that it had no substitute. But still, the modulations of the human voice were enthralling to her. She knew it would always be part of the communication system people used. It added a drama and emotion that nothing else could. It had earned a rich history of intonations that also were indispensable. She had noticed that with Farson, speech was often used in the most intimate of situations. It added a dimension to mental contact. She was thinking of the low, rich sounds Farson could make in their loving times. She relished her memories of kissing him and of making an almost involuntary sound like a sigh and a moan combined. Her thoughts were lingering a little too long on these matters. Voul's spoken question was still hanging in the air. She chose her answer carefully. Noting the intense interest of all those present, she included a mental tonality that vastly increased its impact.

<<*He is on his way.*>>

The meeting continued for a while longer. They discussed the logistics, the communication between SkyKing and the Moon and Emerald Earth. Channels were to be opened that had long been closed and forbidden. There were protocols and upgrades to be made. Actually, they were already underway, unknown to the crews of the two satellites. Meetings would have to be held. Preparations and systems for first contact had to be solidified and practiced. It would all take time. The integration of the "crews," as the Emers called the populations, had to be handled correctly. Not exactly like early neanderthals mixing with twenty-first century humans, the blending of the old human race with the new human race would still be shocking and would take time for acclimations and adjustments. The Emers knew it must be done, the time had come.

As the meeting broke up, Ian asked Brittany a question. It took her by surprise. His voice was very soft, very soothing. She loved the sound of it. They had just transported to the Moon. She was thinking she should have stayed on SkyKing, but instead, she went along with Ian. They had remained side by side throughout the meeting and on the return trip to the Moon. Now they were there standing before the "come only" arch, out of which the Emers had emerged just an hour earlier.

"Would you like to come back to Emerald Earth with me?" The other five Emers had stepped into the arch and were gone. Ian and Brittany were alone. His voice was assuasive and assuring. Her answer was plain to see in her eyes and in her thoughts. He reached down and took her hand and removed the power ring from her thumb. <<*You won't be needing this.*>>

Still holding her hand, they stepped into the transporter. Her last thought before the transport began was that, for the first time, Voul was not a factor in a decision she was making. In fact, as she even thought of him, he seemed far away, like a name from the past.

In an instant they were there, on the forbidden planet. It had been a completely different form of transportation. Smoother, more complete, as though farther and nearer at the same time. It brought a sensation of a vast change and no effort. They had just continued walking along. It was just one step into a new world. Brittany stopped. Ian, moving naturally along, now on his home world again, felt their hands stretched to the limit and stopped as well. He looked back at her. He was fascinated at the appearance of surprise on her face and at her conflicting thoughts trying to sort themselves out. He realized that wonder had overtaken her. She could not believe what she was seeing.

31. Onboard the Harvester

"Are you hungry?"

When Handy had first stepped aboard the harvester, the moist air and light mist that surrounded the giant machine as it traversed the endless field reminded him of his own planet for some reason that he was having trouble pinning down. It had been many years since he had even thought of Oran. But the grassy aroma stirred up by the blades and brushes and vacuums of the harvester's passage reactivated Handy's memories from his distant past. *How many years?* There was no way to know any longer, so much time had passed in so many timelines. He found his mind wandering through faceted recollections that he could no longer sort meaningfully. It was like standing still in a revolving universe of blurred and blurring images that came in and out of focus with flashes and colors and sudden memories.

He remembered standing alone on a high precipice near his home. It overlooked a canyon so large and deep that on any other planet its existence would have been entirely impossible. Oran's immensity allowed for features unknown anywhere else.

He remembered standing there in the ever-present, emerging mist, that gushed from the planet's core, lush with oxygen and the aromas of Oran, so pleasing and nutrient rich. He was feeling the light winds beneath a night sky and the lone waning star so close that it dominated the rainbow night like a giant wafer pressed there, immobile, eternal, and emitting its life-giving but slowly lessening rays with just enough remaining warmth that life was still allowed.

Handy remembered thinking, "How beautiful, how magnificent, how hopelessly sad."

He remembered the reverence he felt to be in such a place. He remembered turning and looking back at his small home, nestled in the tall, elongated grasses that reached toward the sun like arms pleading and asking for more. He remembered looking back at the vast chasm beyond and below where he was standing. He remembered the sound of a river deep in the bed of the canyon roaring like a dragon. He remembered how, on still nights, he could hear its echoes in his boyhood bedroom.

Then another thought intruded, a dark one that reminded him of why thoughts of Oran were so often repressed and avoided. The memory was of scenes of death and collapse, of hopeless abandonment, and the realization of loneliness now without end. His mind recoiled. He shuddered and shook his head to change mental directions.

The soft laboring sounds of the harvester brought him back to Strapper's innocent question about his state of hunger.

"Yes. I am. Whatcha got?" John smiled and said something about rustling up a few sandwiches as he headed for the galley.

Handy remained standing on the bridge of the harvester. He could see the forward passage through the windows. He decided to walk outside and up to the very front where the "toe" of the harvester, as they called it, was pushing through the amber crop. From there, facing forward, all he could see were the great grassy fields in front of them; the view was like a form of silent flight. The harvester was aimed along the cut line in the grass edging the previous pass it had made months ago in the opposite direction. He could see new growth repeating the process, even now, grown well past the halfway-to-harvest mark. Handy had commented on the quick regrowth. "It's a bit tall, don't you think?" Strapper John knew exactly what Handy was talking about.

"Yep. It's growing faster and faster each year. It won't be long before we can't keep up. I've spoken to the city about it, as have many others. They say, 'Don't worry. It'll be okay.' But we've heard from other families that they're now encountering some new growth that is so tall they have to slow down, which only makes matters worse. When Ian comes home, he'll know what to do." Ian was Strapper's son, one of the rare additions that the population had allowed. There were actually many others, but in the relative population growth there was never any change. Handy knew that the Emers kept the population steady. Babies were allowed but only within the same algorithms and calculations that had saved the planet and, in turn, the whole human race.

The sad event of Ian leaving the fields, after his injury, was an anomaly in itself among the farming families. That never happened. But Strapper's own son had chosen the city over farming. It had not been an easy time for the family. But stolidly maintaining his belief that the Jordans were and always would be a farming family, Strapper had taken to saying at every opportunity when Ian's decision came up, "Aye, Ian may have left the fields, but the fields have never left Ian." This always made Strapper John finish with a smile, but deep inside there was a sadness that, like the grasses that carpeted Emerald Earth, seemed to have no end.

Handy had something on his mind to discuss with Strapper and the other farming families, the reason he had, after all, come out to the harvester, but first it was time to eat. Strapper announced that lunch was ready.

The two of them turned and walked from the "bow" together back to the bridge, the control center of the harvester complex. Once closed off inside, the silence spoke of the exquisite technical competency and achievements the Emers exhibited in everything they did. Handy well knew how advanced they were; but even in his knowledge and appreciation of them, he knew that what he knew was far from the totality of what the Emers had *really* achieved. Handy had discussed this deficit of understanding with Farson, expressing his concern that things were no longer completely in their control. Farson understood all too well. He and Handy had done much together, achieved great things, and saved so many. But he also understood that, with Emerald Earth's evolution, things had taken a turn they had not foreseen. They both knew that no one, not even "the great Farson Uiost himself," as Handy liked to say — with his arms spread wide for dramatic effect — could have predicted the scope of the Emers. Handy remembered Farson's response:

"'Then, I saw a new heaven and a new Earth; for the first heaven and the first Earth was passed away.' Those words, Handy, were written in ancient Earth scripture and are now true. What does that tell you?" Handy remembered thinking this question over. He remembered how Farson so often went back to the scene of his own birth. He also vividly remembered just being back on Oran in his own thoughts. He could still feel the soft breeze and the aromas lingering, so real, in his thoughts. His response to Farson's question was tentative and exploratory. He felt that his answer, even as he gave it, was merely directional.

"It could only mean one thing, Farson."

<<*Exactly, Handy. Only one thing.*>>

As Strapper and Handy started heading down to the "galley," through the passageways of the great machine complex, Handy was again caught up in the silence of its passage and its precision of operation. The hallways were pristine and polished. Each person they encountered was friendly and fit, like all Emers. The physicality of the farmers was obvious and attractive. Their free spirits reminded Handy of the MoonBasers without all the bravado and innuendos. The operation of the harvester was obviously a well-oiled machine, everyone working together in harmony and productivity, as in all things Emerald Earth. The people of the farm and the people of the city were different, but exactly the same. Handy could sense no level of discontent or malcontent. Happiness seemed to be the routine on the "farm," as they called it. The skin color and stature of the farmers were exactly the same as the city people: tall, beautiful, and bronze. But, to Handy, these people were of the earth, and the city people were of the sky, for want of a better phrase. The city people were explorers, like the Skers. The farmhands were more like the miners. Handy thought of

Ian, who had moved from one world to the other. "How is he, John?"

"Ian is doing fine as he tells it. The city gives him access to things that fascinate him: space, time, and new friends. He tells me that the history we know of SkyKing and MoonBase is just the beginning. He has been to SkyKing several times already, and I believe they are just now coming back from another big meeting there. He told me he was planning to come out here soon. It's been years since I've seen him in person. We are obviously in contact all the time. But still it would be good to see him, just to be sure he hasn't citified too much. He grew up out here, you know. It makes a difference. But as far as his work goes, he's been very successful. He works most days, right beside Belnad Goethe himself."

They decided to eat in Strapper's apartment. The food was prepared and on the table even as they sat down. Handy was thinking about all the meals he had cooked on an open fire on Emerald Earth during the long stasis. So many meals alone. He *was* a good cook, though. *Six thousand years of cooking stuff will do that.* The food looked odd to him, too perfect, but it tasted great. They ate quickly and went into one of the other rooms. It was furnished beautifully and comfortably. One wall was a series of thirty monitors, all watching various areas and activities around the harvester complex, and there was one portion of it that remained blank. "We keep it clear for incoming transmissions," Strapper said. They sat down. Strapper looked at Handy and said, "What can I do for you? To what do I owe the honor of this visit?"

Handy smiled, thinking about his arrival on the throne of grass dolphins. He took a deep breath and said, "Farson has asked me to come here and let you know that there are some big changes coming." Strapper seemed to have prepared himself for this news. He looked at the monitor, and it had changed into one huge screen. It was the same view Handy had been enjoying at the very front of the harvester. The grass was far and wide, blowing with the wind and passing smoothly underneath the view of the screen as the harvester moved. It was beautiful to Handy, almost beyond description, knowing all that he knew. *How far we have come.*

John Jordan was thinking the same thing. He was also thinking of his life, his family, his world. Change was always inevitable, he knew. Even in this world, change could be good and bad. For the first time in many, many years, he was worried. The way Handy had said it. How many years had things been as they have been? Time was hard to gauge. Like traversing distance on fields that went on forever, time just passed and passed. There were instruments to measure everything, of course, but who was counting? Who really cared? Life was what it was and what it had always been. The thought that it could change – a thought he was now forced to entertain – had not occurred to him in too long to remember. He looked at Handy, trepidatious, but ready for the answer. Handy stirred and stood up in front of the monitor, as though looking out a window. The grassy fields stretched far away. He seemed to be straining to see farther, to see the unseeable path beyond. Handy turned to face Strapper. "We're going to be moving again."

32. Viera Is Wondering

She was just standing there, having just watched Brittany Peterson and Ian Jordan walk into the "come only" transporter, holding hands. In all of her time on the Moon, she had never seen anything quite so personally shocking and disturbing as the scene of their disappearance.

The "come only" arch had just recently been set up, exclusively for Emers only. She had been informed that there would be a short, confidential visit by some of the people from Emerald Earth. That had also been shocking. For ten years, there had been nothing: no face-to-face contact with the Emers, no communications, no information other than what they could observe through telemetry and telescopes, which was next to nothing. There had been vague, speculative descriptions of their appearance, mostly way off as it turned out. There had been rumors about them, but sadly inaccurate, both in substance and in the events they attempted to describe. Despite it all, the Emers remained essentially a great unknown. It was true and widely perceived that they had sent welcome technology to the Moon and to SkyKing which was incredible and transforming. So everyone knew they were really over there, that they were well aware of the two other groups of human beings nearby in space, and that the Emers were different in almost every way from the people of SkyKing and the Moon. But no one, not one single person, had actually ever seen the Emers … until about a month ago.

This last meeting was far and away the largest group ever. Five Emers had come to the Moon via the "come only" arch. Why they wanted to come to the Moon first and then on to SkyKing was another unknown. But each time they came, they used the same route. They never stayed on the Moon for more than a few moments, but the MoonBasers would gather around when the arch activated. It had become "an event" on the Moon. Six times it had happened now. The Emers never stopped and chatted with anyone. A little girl on the Moon who had come to watch noted that one of the Emer women smiled and waved to her once. So, obviously, they were aware of the interest they were generating with each visit. The curiosity grew more and more intense with each visit. And then there was the "Brittany visit," as everyone was calling it, when she joined the meeting, obviously in the company of Ian Jordan.

Watching Brittany, who Viera loved as if she were her own daughter, leaving the Moon, hand in hand with Ian, well, that was really something. With no goodbye, and no acknowledgement at all, Brittany had just walked into the arch beside Ian and disappeared. Viera's thoughts were mirrored throughout SkyKing and the Moon: Where were they going? Why did she go? Why with Ian Jordan? There were no answers.

Viera felt like she had an obligation to tell Jim what had happened. She touched her wrist and keyed in a number on the holographic display hovering perfectly in front of her. She stopped keying and just thought, *Jim Peterson*. Another Emer improvement in their communication system, was the new intuitive recognition system. He was on the line in less than two seconds.

"Yes Viera."

"Jim, Brittany has gone back to Emerald Earth with Ian Jordan."

"You're kidding." His shock caused his words to have the hollow sound of deadness, like something heavy falling hard onto dry dusty ground.

"No, I'm not. They were holding hands." Jim was thinking that must have been an odd-looking couple. Brittany is lucky if she's five feet, five inches tall. Emers are all over seven feet. Then, he realized that for the first time, his daughter was somewhere he could not follow. She was gone without their usual discussion. Gone, of all unlikely places, to forbidden Emerald Earth.

"I thought that was not allowed."

"It's Farson's rule, but not Ian's, apparently." Jim was concerned but not overly. Everything he knew and had learned about the Emers was good. He knew she must be safe, but still, she left without even saying goodbye.

"Do we have any way to reach them?"

"Not that I know of."

Jim Peterson ended the conversation with a sullen, "Thanks for letting me know," and Viera turned to go to her office on the bridge. As she walked along, she was wondering what Emerald Earth must be like. The planet itself was a beautiful amber and green in the black of space. It could be rotated at the will of the Emers, so it sometimes shifted its position as seen from the Moon, nothing like steady old Earth. Emerald Earth could be moved whenever the Emers wanted to, and it generally stayed well out of the 100-mile range of the transporters. The Moon's telescopes were continuously searching the planet, but the Emers' ability to block any unwanted snooping was uncanny in its perfection. The Moon had tried everything in their surveillance tool bag. They could see Emerald Earth clearly with the human eye, but any magnification device or telemetry system was blocked. Details were not available. The Moon and SkyKing also knew that Emerald Earth was watching *their* every move. "Observation" was how the Emers thought of it. To them, watching the Moon and SkyKing was a given. It was a favorite pastime on Emerald Earth. How widely prevalent this predilection was among the Emers was unknown on the two satellites. They assumed the Emers were watching, but the extent of the coverage and analysis was far greater than they could have imagined. To the Emers, this pastime was academic in nature: history in action. It was fascinating and illustrative and entertaining in the same way that people watched home movies or reality television on old Earth. Emers, in the distant future, were looking back, with their own eyes, into the lives of their ancient ancestors. Almost every Emer home had a screen for viewing the people of the Moon and SkyKing. It was their window into their past.

Viera reached her office, and the door opened with a sound like a suction device releasing. It closed behind her with the same sound, in reverse, suction taking hold. The entire Moon complex was lightly pressurized to maintain air quality and dust integrity. This and many other life support systems had created clean, healthy, and enjoyable living standards on the Moon. Her office was equipped with some of the latest Emer tech including walls and furniture that could be changed in size, shape, color, and arrangement to match mood or moment. Today the office was red and white, with a sofa, large desk, and exercise area. The "windows" were large monitors that cycled through the Moon station facilities and included the public areas on SkyKing as well. The term MoonKing was used intermittently now to emphasize the unity of the two, but individually, each group stuck with their traditional designations. That is not to say that two groups were not slowly merging.

Since the shock wave event many years ago, a mutual appreciation had developed along with the ease of moving between the two locations, and, as a result, the two cultures were getting together lines were blurring, but in the minds of everyone, and due to the facts of the living arrangements, it was getting harder and harder to always know who was who. The Sker's standard white uniforms were very popular on the Moon, and the MoonBasers' attitudes about sex and relationships were slowly creeping into the lives of Skers and the crew of SkyKing. It wasn't happening all at once, but it was happening. This blending was a great topic of research on Emerald Earth, where formulas and calculations were predicting a continuing wider and wider spread of the "culture" mixings. Even Belnad Goethe had mentioned it in council after he had witnessed two Skers kissing in public. This caused a round of hilarity and comment throughout the the Emers, who considered themselves primarily descendants of the Skers and had adopted and adapted the essences of Sker teachings and traditions through the thousands of years of their development. Watching two Skers kissing was remarkable, both in the act of their touching lips, which was wild enough, but also that they were doing it in public. <<*There is no privacy,*>> Belnad had said. <<*We all know that. But still what are things coming to? People are watching way too much of the MoonKing show!*>> This caused greater hilarity and discussion that only made everyone more and more curious. The cultural changes were – to use the term so common on the Moon – "eclipsing." Belnad, known as an avid adventurer among the Emers, was rumored to have wondered out loud. <<*Will these things ever evolve among Emers?*>> This was a popular topic and an unanswered question, but no evidence of such things had yet appeared, despite the fascination from afar.

Viera had cycled her main monitor to look at Emerald Earth. She knew the planet well enough to know that she was looking down at the area of the great city. It showed as a brightness on the planet. She wondered what it was like down there. Her desk chair warmed to her body temperature and shaped itself closer to her curves and posture. She felt the embrace to be mildly arousing. *If they can make a chair do this, what wonders can they do down there?* Then she thought of Brittany. She quickly turned off the monitor and changed the directions of her thoughts. Her wrist communicator was calling. It was Long John Hanson Silver. "Yes, John?"

"We think something is happening on Emerald Earth."

"What?" There was a long pause. She repeated her question. "*What*, John?"

"It seems to be moving away." It took her a second to realize Silver was not talking about the usual movements of the planet. She snapped the monitor back on, and the visual confirmed Silver's statement.

"Where is it going?"

33. Voul Is Invited

Farson's reappearance did startle Repoul Bensn even though he had been expecting him. It had occurred to Repoul that Farson would be coming back to see the recordings again himself. Bensn had been studying continuously and carefully, over and over, during the past many days.

As the very bright purple of Farson's ScreenTransit dissipated, along with Repoul's surprise, he turned to address the ScreenMaster of Earth without salutation, as if they were already engaged in an ongoing discussion. "There is very little in the data to accurately assess the portal's re-accessibility if that is what you are interested in." Farson's seamless response reinforced the feeling that this conversation had not just started, but was a continuing dialogue between the two of them.

"Let me see the data stream again." The two of them reviewed the data together for almost an hour. Farson kept asking for slower and slower frame timing, stretching the capacities of the system way beyond its nominal specifications. Then they called Gerald Antonoff on the Moon for assistance, utilizing the lunar Emer-enhanced systems, but, again, to no avail. No further elucidation of the known facts was achieved: It was always the same. Farson arrived and disappeared for about four hours, and then reappeared. It did happen, but it also did not happen. The only record of the door opening and closing was Farson's recollection. Farson was there, then gone, then back again. Hours passed with just the blank, black wall of the tower's platform on the monitors. Their investigation of the disappearance and reappearance sequences revealed nothing, despite their high resolution values, including microscopic inspections down to the molecular level. With all of his tools exhausted, Bensn turned to the last instrument of insight: his raw and unsatisfied curiosity.

"So, what happened in there, Farson?" Bensn was nothing if not inquisitive in his nature. His hard work, continuing studies, and formulations had saved the station. His reputation for excellence and high-value, exemplary performance was second to none, with the one absolute exception – and Repoul himself would always remind anyone who needed reminding of this ranking correction – of Sergeant Long John Hanson Silver, who had selflessly thrown his life away to save a fellow crew member.

Bensn's question was waiting for an answer.

Farson knew there was no way to explain it. Looking into Sargasso, he had witnessed a future unforeseen, a new reality, an alteration of destiny. What could he say to Repoul Bensn that would not result in more unanswerable questions? He changed the topic. "Where is Voul?" Bensn reluctantly looked up from his work, the focus of his attention slowly catching up as he spoke.

"I believe Commander Jonsn is on the Moon with Viera Nichols." When Repoul looked around, the room was empty. There was a soft purple glow slowly thinning. Farson was gone; Repoul's question unanswered in his sudden solitude.

When Voul and Viera arrived on the Moon, they were intent on getting to her quarters without delay. As they marched together through the corridors, Viera thought she had better tell Voul the news. "Emerald Earth seems to be moving away. We are not sure if it's significant or just another *j'adoube*." Voul was pleased with her correct use of the chess term for adjusting the pieces. She never ceased to amaze him with her mental versatility and playfulness, and he was not thinking about chess with that thought. He increased his pace slightly and she noticed. "Whoa, boy. Let's not start running. It could cause some talk."

"Talk, Viera? That is the last thing on my mind."

Farson was already waiting in Viera's quarters. He knew Viera and Voul were coming, but he was using the time to look around. Her quarters had changed since he was last there. It wasn't just the changeling tech from the Emers. That *was* new, but that was not the difference he had noted. It was clearly a family apartment now. Skers are neat beyond description, so Voul's presence was almost invisibly sifted into the rooms' appearance. At first it looked exactly the same, but then some extra clothing (neatly folded), a different sort of comb, soap not just the right shape, and more towels. Not to mention the four-year-old's toys. *So much has changed.*

The door opened, and Voul Jonsn and Viera Nichols walked in, excited, holding hands, Viera turning into Voul's arms, expecting the apartment to be empty. Their daughter, Byn, was at the Moon's children's center, and as he looked over Viera's shoulder, through her hair and growing passion, Voul was surprised to see Farson Uiost in their room. The room where they had planned to be alone. Voul's travels and Viera's work made times like this, when they could actually be alone, rare indeed. Disappointment filled Voul's mind, but then duty called him to a more sober response. Viera was surprised when Voul seemed to be speaking to someone else.

"Farson, where have you been? We have been looking for you." Farson was wearing the usual cardigan sweater, white shirt, and corduroy pants. He was also wearing what appeared to be highly technical athletic shoes instead of the usual loafers. It seemed to be getting warmer in the apartment, and Farson knew they had sent a message ahead for the room to get itself ready.

<<*I don't want to interrupt anything, Voul. But I have a trip in mind and I want you to come.*>>

Viera was aware of a communication occurring, of course. She let Voul's hand go, turned around. She slowly walked into the room, past Farson, as though nothing unusual had happened.

"Should I make some sandwiches or is this an immediate emergency?" Farson laughed. He knew there was no time to waste, but he also knew that these two people were special and there was always time enough. He smiled at his two friends.

"Sounds good, Viera. Let's eat." One of the things people knew about Farson's communications now was that the message was always accompanied by an "attachment." In addition to the plainly spoken message he had just delivered, there was a more complete story sent along in the mental background. Viera and Voul were now concentrating on the second part of Farson's message. Viera looked at Farson.

"You are serious, aren't you."

<<*Yes, I am, Viera. He could be gone for a while.*>> As she looked at the images and nuances that came with Farson's thought, she noticed Voul was moving to a chair by the table. There was an emptiness settling in. She could feel the room starting to cool as she moved into the kitchen.

"I'll make some sandwiches."

34. Uva's Stories (2)

Uvo was on a ScreenMaster barge as it headed to Earth. The trip was exceptionally long for the ScreenMasters aboard. The starship was huge, and there was plenty of room. For the Aristealian, the vast hangars were his favorite. He could fly there. On Aristealia, flight was life. Their cities were in the sky. Everything was built and engineered to emphasize flying as the only way to go. Aristealians could walk easily, and they enjoyed their ground lives, but flying, that was where their hearts had always been. Being where flight was impossible was imprisonment to them. Spreading their elegant and expansive wings and soaring through the sky was freedom. Aristealians loved that. Even as Uvo had learned to be in more than one place at a time, to fly was still very important to him wherever he was.

Now he was soaring in the hangar farthest from the bridge. It was his favorite. While the hangar served as an access and egress to and from the ship, it was also an environment of its own. This one was jungle-like, built to suit another species of ScreenMaster, but Uvo loved the air and the moisture. He loved the currents that circulated the air. Soaring from one end to the other took about half an hour. He could coast in one direction, and work his wings for exercise, upwind, as he called it, in the other. He would often do this for days, alone. Farson was feeling the exhilaration and relief that Uvo was enjoying. He could sense the joy of movement and pleasure in flight. Farson had found that these long periods of flying in the hangar allowed Uvo to relax and achieve a meditative-like state.

Farson found it a little boring. He wanted to steer Uvo into a barrel roll, or a sharp dive, or anything to break the monotony. He could clearly sense that Uvo could go on like this forever. Back and forth. Hour after hour. Day after day.

As they flew together, Farson was finding that Uvo's mind in this relaxed state, traveled back to Aristealia and, inevitably, back to Uva. Farson was surprised at the vividity of Uvo's recollections.

"Uvo, you should eat more. You're getting too skinny."

She had been waiting for, and then watching, Uvo's approach and landing. He had soared straight in without slowing. He was actually accelerating as he swooped into their nest with whooshing noises and flapping sounds. The nest was large enough for easy, safe takeoffs and landings. As things quieted down, Uva saw her husband standing there, out of breath, obviously tired from the long exertion, and smiling broadly in her direction. She walking directly into his arms. The feathers surrounded them. Their rustling soothed her. Her own wings opened, and she hugged him to her. With four fifteen-foot wings raised high to form a "tent of marriage" – the oldest position of embracing for their race – they kissed each other in total privacy. Her mind was consumed with happiness and fulfillment. His was filled with passion and love. The two of them were identical in many ways. She was as strong as he. He was as intelligent and crafty as she. They came from similar families and loved many of the same things. They had lived together for 110 years, in harmony and caring. They counted on each other for everything and helped each other in every way. Their long lives meant there were still many, many years ahead of them. They had raised one daughter together. She was on her own with her own nest and mate. Uva and Uvo had talked of more children, but nothing had been decided. For now, they were happy. In each other's arms they relaxed. She could hear him. She had just tasted him. She still had her arms around him. His breast and throat were pressed against her. She loved the moment. "Well, Uva, you feel great to me. I have missed you so much." After a few more moments of recharge and rebirth, the two of them separated and walked to the inside of the nest. Anywhere else, their "nest" would be a mansion or a king's castle, but here on Aristealia it was just another spacious and well-appointed nest among millions. For the two of them, it was home sweet home.

Farson could feel the hard strokes as they rippled through Uvo's body. He was turning into the wind again at the aft end of the enormous hangar. The next thirty minutes would be harder on Uvo, but he seemed undeterred by fatigue or of any desire to stop that Farson could see.

On and on they went.

Uva had prepared a meal, one of his favorites. They ate together, standing, as is the Aristealian custom. It was a quiet time. Uvo's mission had been more or less successful. *There is hope.* But he knew that the planet now had a dark and dismal period to deal with. He remembered all the symbols of rank and wealth, all shining in the sunlight, then hidden in the darkness that Uvo had wrought. Standing there with Uva, he glanced through the transparencies of their home. The nest floated in the air, about 5,000 feet from the surface. It was constructed of materials that, from within, seemed not to exist. The nest hung in the sky as if it were in the open air. Inside, Aristealia's sunlight was bright and the skies were showing a deep shade of golden orange with scintillating hues of light green and soft blues, almost rainbow-like. The sky shimmered with mists of moisture and pulsed with the strong winds that moved around the planet like a river in the sky. The view from the nest showed a planet that seemed to be a serene, littoral paradise of vast oceans as far as the eye could seen. Uvo knew its history, though. Through his eyes he saw not only the details of his beloved world, but also he saw its long and virulent history of war and destruction, now overcome.

Having just come from a planet beginning the journey from savagery to the ScreenMasters' way – now long ago completed on Aristealia – Uvo's eyes were tearing with sorrow for what lay ahead. Uva was watching him. "Uvo?"

"Yes, Uva."

"You are concerned for them?"

"They are brutish and yet sophisticated. They are unaware and yet educated. They are powerful and yet misdirected. Dealing with realities they cannot change, but must change, is not their strength. It is problematical that they will accept our way and proceed to a new history." He was still looking out into the clear skies around their nest. He remembered the very same view as a child when he had taken flight for the first time, so many years ago. As he awkwardly took to the skies as a fledgling, his parents had steered him away from the single large island of Aristealia, Rilievon, back toward the seas. He remembered the harsh smell in the wind and from the clouds of darkness over the island. His parents warned him that it was war and trouble, as they steered him back to their nest.

Uvo turned to his wife. "But as we have, so can they, overcome."

The two of them stood there eating their meal and enjoying being together again. In the evening, they flew off into the clouds together. Farson was enjoying the ride with the two great avians, and was surprised, as Uva flew, inverted, under Uvo and then, when the two moved even closer and intimately linked, still seamlessly flying as smoothly as one as they had as two. Farson could sense the passionate merging of their minds and bodies. He was immersed in their pleasure, losing himself even more deeply now with their aerial bonding. The rising tides of their joining seemed to go on forever. He could sense everything – the touching was exquisite, the closeness, the deep, passionate liaison, and the surging joy of sensual abandon, all achieved thousands of feet in the clear, nutrient air of Aristealia. It was consuming him and overpowering him. He had never experienced anything like it. Then, they let go and fell through the sky as though dead.

Tumbling with Uvo, Farson was feeling abandonment, surrender, exhaustion, joy, longing. Uvo seemed immobile and helpless, lost in free fall. As they fell, Farson could feel Uva reaching for Uvo, holding on to the last vestige of her mental contact. Farson saw into her thoughts; they were rich with emotions that he had not seen before. *This is love like I have known with Karina.*

Farson found himself reaching out for Uvo, but there was nothing. Access was not granted to him even though, in a way, he was Uvo, experiencing everything as if he were. But interacting with Uvo was beyond his reach. All he could do was witness.

Farson felt Uvo waking up. Uva's mental embrace increased and suddenly they were both flying side-by-side again. Farson could feel Uvo's strokes as though they were his own. Uvo was excited again, energized. He barrel-rolled and danced through the sky. She was right beside him in perfect formation with every twist and turn. Like two ice dancers, they soared together seemingly in an immense mirror. And then Uva again passed gently under Uvo. They joined. And it all began again with even more feeling and within a much slower cadence. They flew together as one, slowly rotating over and over. It was impossible for Farson to sense any difference between them. *They are joined as one. We are.* He was amazed again. Uvo and Uva were one. Farson could feel the whole, the new.

Uva's voice slowly came to him. It flowed through a profound sense of rightness, or perfectness, of a beautiful peace that washed over Farson, who felt adream with emotion.

<<*Time to wake up, Farson.*>> He could not speak. She seemed to understand his lack of full awareness of what was happening. <<*The story's over.*>>

Farson was trying to sit up.

35. Handy and Strapper John on the Harvester

Time alone. Handy found that the harvester was so big that there was plenty of room to find a place to himself. All those years alone on Emerald Earth had taken their toll. He enjoyed the grass dolphins, and he loved Farson, and Karina too, but there were still times when he wanted to be alone. He took a long pull on his cigar, and a long draft of the drink Strapper had given him. He also had given him the bottle, which was now placed on the railing beside him. His guitar had been in his bag, but now he had it out. As he was warming up on the guitar, a poem he wrote (with some help) way back on old Earth was in his thoughts and soon in song.

Let America be America again.
Let it be the dream it used to be.
Let it be the pioneer on the plain:
A home where we roam free.

(America never was America to me.)

Let America be the dream the dreamers dream.
Let it be that great strong land of love,
Where no kings connive nor tyrants scheme:
Where no man is crushed from above.

(America never was America to me.)

Strapper John had come in as Handy began to play, and he
was there as Handy sang the entire song, some parts over and
over. Strapper was surprised. That this strange man, who came
racing up, now half drunk, on a moving throne of grass
dolphins doing at least fifty knots through the field, could
actually play a wonderful guitar and had a singing voice any
old Earth cowboy would envy, was amazing to him. A mix of
jazz and rock and cattle country, all in accompaniment to a
perfectly tuned and expertly played guitar. To him, the song
had been a masterful performance.

Strapper John could not have been happier at this
discovery. He could not stop himself from applauding. Handy
was instantly surprised and upset at this unknown presence,
and quickly put the guitar down and the poem away and out
of sight. "I didn't know you were there." Strapper noticed
Handy's peevishness at the unwelcome audience. To John it
could have been like walking in on his parents making love
and wondering what to do. To stay would be wrong, but to be
caught sneaking out could be worse. Strapper had just stood
still and watched and listened. "No one ever hears me do that
except Farson."

"And now me." Strapper looked at Handy. Handy was shaking his head no, as if to deny anything had happened.

"No, only Farson."

"I really enjoyed it, Handy. A very pleasant surprise."

"What's that supposed to mean?"

"Oh, come on. With that entrance of yours, out of nowhere, half drunk, dressed like a lost cowboy, you can't hold it against me that in my wildest dreams, I never imagine that you could sing like a rock star and play a beautiful song like that." Handy noticed the compliment within Strapper John's defense of witnessing Handy being himself. *It could have been worse.* As though hearing the thought, John laughed out loud. Handy looked at Strapper John. A tall farm Emer. They were so different from the city people. *They want to be.* He was tall in the Emer way, but probably carried a few more pounds of muscle than most. His world was enthralling. Handy loved it. He loved the movement and the endless destination. He was even starting to like Strapper John. *He likes my singing, that's something.* John laughed again. Handy suddenly realized what John was doing.

<<*Did you really just stand there and watch your parents?*>>

<<*What else could I do?*>> Now they were both laughing.

"Let's go back to the cabin so we can both have a glass."

36. The Elevation Protocol (2)

Farson was at his desk in North Conway. He was waiting for Karina. Today was the day, long arranged. All that was needed now was Karina. She had been very busy since Emerald Earth had returned. She was far more active within the MoonKing complex. Her friendship with Viera was just the beginning. With Farson's far-reaching travels and duties, he was still always available, but people always suspected that, "He's not really here." Karina, however, had the ability to "be" there. People loved her. In many ways she had taken over Farson's day-to-day duties as the true ScreenMaster of Earth, SkyKing, and the Moon. Farson told her it was purely titular. She said, "Fine," knowing nomenclature didn't really matter. To her Earth, SkyKing, and the Moon were what mattered. For some reason that she did not fully understand and could not yet articulate, MoonKing and Emerald Earth were everything as far as she was concerned. Farson could travel The Screen and deal with all of that. She only wanted to be with her family and her extended "family." Felicity and Valgary were paramount over all. Farson had quickly come to see and understand that fact. The four of them "lived" on SkyKing, and on Emerald Earth, but in truth, they mostly lived together back on old Earth. Real food, real weather, real life, as Farson called it. The girls vastly preferred the Moon, and Karina preferred Emerald Earth. But Farson loved North Conway.

It was an odd arrangement for the four of them. As new ScreenMasters, the girls were learning fast. So fast that Farson had tried to rein them in and learned what a mistake that was. "You can't make them do what you want them to do, Farson. You can only guide them and help them." It was frustrating, but he knew Karina was correct. Felicity was more like Karina. Valgary took after her father. Felicity was bossy and opinionated. Valgary was thoughtful and agreeable. Felicity liked to stay in one place or at least in just two or three. Valgary was only happy on the move, never too long in one place, and her travels were becoming more and more complex. Farson had found that if he took them both with him, or went alone with Felicity, it was too much to handle. He needed Karina. If he and Valgary went together, it was easy. She was a perfect companion.

<<*Farson, you really do think you have it all figured out. Are you completely nuts? How could you know so little about our girls, oh, great ScreenMaster of Earth?*>> Farson's thoughts were

interrupted by Karina, as they often were. Her strength had grown and grown. She had streaked through the levels and layers of The Screen. If the truth were known, she did it even faster than Farson. *She did have my help.*

Farson remembered the beginnings of Karina's Ascension. He was thinking about her first step as a ScreenMaster. They had been on Serenity.

It was dark, and they were in the top floor of a tall skyscraper overlooking the city. The room was empty except for a new sofa. <<*Farson, who are you kidding?*>>

<<*We needed a place to sit, Karina.*>>

<<*Sit? Really? That's why we're here?*>>

"Sitwory, could you please relax? I want to show you something."

"I wonder what that could be, Routier, you rascal."

"Serenity is a special place. Here, we can be alone."

"We are always alone. That's how we are."

It had been a tough time for Karina after her parents' death. She had moved to Earth and into the Chamberlains' home. The horrible little boy who taunted her slowly, changed into a friend, then into a friend like no other she had ever known, and then, slowly, into someone she loved with all her heart. Someone who became her future, her past, her present; someone who became everything. For Farson, it had been a major upheaval of a life he had considered to be perfect: just him, Hattie, Sam, and the distant scientists who provided everything and asked for nothing. Then they adopted Karina. It was horrible. She stayed in her room. Everyone fussed over her. He was alone. The one thing he feared most. He wandered around the big house: Up and down the secret staircase to The Ship, outside in the large rambling yard, down to the shed in the back where he found Sam, and where, just at the right time, their friendship began.

<<*It was the one good thing that came from those times.*>>
<<*You've got to be kidding, Farson.*>>

"Routier, you live in a dreamworld. A world all its own. I'm surprised you let me come along."

"I 'let' you?"

It seemed like a year before Karina came out of that room, but it was only a few days. Hattie had been taking food into her, and had invited Farson to come with her, but, despite his intense desire to go in, he dismissed the invitation as ridiculous. He had taken the posture that "she" did not exist. How could she? Farson's perfect universe, in which he was the only star, did not have room for anyone else. But, inevitably, they met. She thought he was an ignorant, foolish boy who had never been anywhere. He thought she was beautiful. She thought her life had been reduced to nothing. He knew his life had been changed forever.

<<*Finally, you've got it right, Farson. I'm proud of you.*>>

Farson had no response. He knew she was right. He had learned a terrible lesson that day standing outside her door after their one and only fight. He had watched and watched with all his might to see the door move, but it never did. He willed it to move, for her to open it and say everything was all right. But it never moved, until, finally, he took hold of the handle, turned the knob, and pushed it open. He will never forget what he saw as the door slowly creaked open.

<<*It was a lesson I will never have to relearn, Karina. You taught me well.*>>

Sitwory took his hand and looked into his eyes. For all of Routier's bravado and infantile drama, he was just a boy in love. She led him to the couch.

When Farson opened the door Karina knew she had won. But she also knew that she had risked much that day, and, with all the years that had passed, this knowledge of what had been at stake grew in its impact on her. *If I had known what I know now, would I have done it differently?* Stubbornness, fear, frantically trying to gain some semblance of control of her life had caused her to stay put that day, away from the door, waiting. Though they were just kids at the time, the game was very grown up in its implications. When that door slowly opened, her heart did too. She was there holding her doll, crying and smiling at the same time. Victorious and surrendering, sad that all that had happened had happened, but excited and happy that all that was to come was now coming. When their eyes met, in that moment of moments – when the door was wide open and it was all there for them both to see, no more hiding – it was the moment that changed everything.

"Routier, do you have any idea what is happening?"
"Yes, you know I do."
"I think sometimes you go too far." She closed her eyes.

In the years that ensued, through all that had happened, their love had never wavered. Farson had been born in 2063. Karina in 2064. Emerald Earth was born in 2091. He was twenty-eight, and she was twenty-six when the ScreenMasters came. From that moment on, gauging their ages became impossible. Sixty-five hundred years of Emerald Earth, moving back and forth in multiple times, sometimes for years, and then there were the pasts where Farson now spent most of

175

his time. Through it all, so many venues across time and space, there was one constant. Them.

Routier kissed her with deep emotions, his heart pounding, his head spinning. He was barely conscious in any true sense of the word. Her arms were around him, her body pressing to his, their lips still exploring sensation and rising fervor. They inched away to catch their breath, but Sitwory drew him back and kissed him again. He felt as if she had entered him and was now inside moving and stirring.

<<*What amazed me was how vivid it all was, Farson. We were millions of light-years away from that attic in Indiana, on that day when you showed me The Screen for the first time. As we traveled, we were there. It was so real. It was real. Even though you had told me what to expect, that day, I learned something about you that meant so much. Seeing it again now, it is all still there. Only you and I know what we know. Being there and all the other things that were happening gave me the strength, the courage I needed. It still does.*>>

"Sitwory." It was all Farson could manage to say.

She strolled into the cabin in North Conway as if nothing had happened. "Hi, honey. I'm home."

"Very funny," he said as she shook the snow off her boots, and started to take her coat, gloves, and hat off. "Don't get too comfortable. We'll be leaving soon." She looked at him. She knew what today was. It was the final step for her. The one thing she had put off and put off. Farson had waited patiently until it came to her: When she knew that her duties as a ScreenMaster required it. She had achieved the first of the two final steps: witnessing her own birth. It had taken years to understand that event and to come to peace with what happened. Somehow she knew that *those* eyes would be waiting for her again now. Those same eyes. The same knowing eyes. She could feel it. She didn't like it. It was a step that would take away as much as it gave. Farson had told her all about it. She had been with him many times to his beginning. They had wandered around the room, looked in the mirror, and shared his birth and his parents' death. And, though he had witnessed his own death many times, she had never been there with him. He had said, "This we do alone."

She walked into the cabin's living room. It was warm from the wood stove, and obviously Farson had rehabbed the cabin. The robots stood along the wall near the back door. They were silent and still. She sat on the sofa with a slight bounce, her hands in her lap. She sighed. All of the procrastination was over. The years of avoiding this moment seemed to evaporate. She looked into Farson's eyes. The words formed in her mind, and she spoke them out loud wondering if she was really saying them or just thinking them.

<<*Okay, Farson, let's do it.*>> Farson was looking at her with sad eyes. Karina was looking at him with questioning eyes.

<<*This time,*>> he paused and almost looked away, but held their eye contact steady, <<*you are on your own.*>>

37. Brittany on Emerald Earth (1)

She was standing just on the other side of the transporter platform, still holding Ian's hand. He was about to step off the platform into the new world, but had stopped and turned back toward her.

What she was looking at stunned her. Not only was the perspective way off, the venue before her was like nothing she had ever seen. *What has happened to me?* She looked at her companion. Something was strange. She was looking into his eyes on a level plane, not upwardly as she had since they had met. She looked at their hands still holding. She froze. The two intertwined hands were both Emer hands. She dropped Ian's and held her hand in front of her face. It was a perfect female Emer hand. She turned it over, palm toward her. It was a startlingly beautiful and light bronze in color, somewhat larger than before. The fingers were longer and more slender. The nails were perfectly sculpted. She flexed her fingers, and it was effortless. Her hand felt stronger and more flexible than ever. She looked at Ian and spoke her thoughts out loud. "What has happened to me?" He moved a little closer. He knew that there was no way he could have warned her. He knew there had been no way to explain it ahead of time. He knew that this was exactly why Farson had forbidden physical contact with Emerald Earth. This and all the other reasons. Ian knew that this transformation was only the beginning. He also had always known that a beginning would have to sometime and someday be made. *Today's the day.*

When he had met Brittany in person, he had known she was the one to begin the beginning with for many, many years. He had long prepared to say the words that Emers had dreamed of saying for thousands of years. The words that had underpinned every day of their six-thousand-year journey.

When he spoke them to Brittany Peterson, he said them with a certain reverence for her and for her ancestry and for all of the people who had gone before, the billions passed, and the billions still present. He spoke them for his own family, and most of all for himself, with the full knowledge of his role in Emer history, of his determination to bring the Combing to a final conclusion, and to bring his world into its rightful and well-earned place in human history. Interestingly, he said them very softly, looking deeply into her eyes as though searching for something, as though speaking to a lover. His voice echoed endearingly in her mind as though through the endless caverns of time.

"Welcome to Emerald Earth." His eyes were shining with anticipation.

38. Voul and Farson on the Way Back to Sargasso

Viera was not happy. The thought of Voul leaving her again after just being gone for almost a month was painful. Byn was growing and changing. Even with the excellent care of the children's center on the Moon, the dual stresses on her as a mother and as commander of MoonBase were not getting any easier. She already missed Voul even if he had just left. *We had some catching up to do.* But, she had hugged Voul goodbye and watched him walk with Farson out the door of their apartment. She remembered the excitement over having time together that she had felt as they approached the apartment only an hour ago.

She looked around the apartment as though its colors had muted and the ambience grown colder. *It's not the same without him.*

The living spaces of the Moon were large and accommodating; the commander's apartment complex was even more so. Many rooms, every possible amenity, and the new technologies acquired from Emerald Earth only made it better. She still had two hours before Byn gurneyed home from the center, using the Moon's ever and always efficient transport system, and with Voul gone and her sudden free time, she found she was struggling with what to do. She decided that she wanted to get out of their apartment, so she headed to the gym. *A hard workout will do me good.* The thought of Ensign Chambois crossed her mind, but she quickly shook her head to erase it. *That is not going to happen.*

"The problem," Farson said to Voul, "is difficult to explain."

179

They were heading for the shuttle bay. Farson had arranged for one of the smaller shuttles to be refitted for just two. There were faster ways to get where he wanted to go, but he also wanted to have the transit time to discuss things with Voul, and Farson also wanted to relax. They would need it.

As they were boarding, Farson continued his explanation to Voul about his previous visit to Sargasso, who had been admiring the sleek shape of the shuttle's new hull. "Imagine that you went somewhere but have no memories that could help you find your way back. You know you were there, but how you got there and back, that's beyond your powers of recall. As hard as you try, it's almost as though something is blocking you. What would you do?"

Voul was putting his gear down in the shuttle's main passenger area. On this main level there were staterooms, a central galley, and the cockpit area. The two of them had just entered. Voul was still looking around. There were four "couches" and two short rows of flight chairs. The pilots' stations were well forward, Voul could see the large forward windows and the flight control panels from where he was. He noted that the shuttle had at least two levels.

"I would want to go back and see what happens."

"Exactly." Now Voul was smiling as he continued.

"And I would want to bring someone with me this time." They both remembered when Farson took off on his own, chasing the tower, telling Voul to return to the mission shuttle. They both remembered Voul's reluctance and Farson's certainty. Farson knew that Voul had not been happy then or now about that decision.

"For what's it's worth, Voul, that situation was completely new to me. Chasing that tower; it never occurred to me that what happened would happen. It was like a form of sensory overload. The things I was seeing could not be, even in all of my ScreenMaster experiences, but they *were* happening. Those four hours passed like seconds to me. Now it's like it didn't really happen. Then I was standing on the platform in the exact place I was when the 'door,' or whatever it was, opened. To me, my feet had never moved; no time had passed."

On the smaller, much faster shuttle, compared to the troop carrier used for the first voyage, they estimated that the trip back to Sargasso would take about six and a half days. Voul and Farson were moving around the cabin settling in and getting things ready. They went to the staterooms on the lower level. Voul was in his compartment when Viera called him, as she was walking to the gym. "If you guys are going to hang around all day, maybe I should come over for a while." Voul knew what she meant. Their reunion had been sadly and disappointingly interrupted by Farson's urgency to get going. The shuttle was still in the bay. "I thought you were in a hurry."

Voul said, "I just saw Farson heading for the bridge." He could now feel the shuttle's systems starting to come online. "I don't think we'll be here long enough for what you have in mind." While he was smiling to Viera with the thoughts behind his last comment, he shifted his eyes from Viera in the monitor, over to a photo of his daughter he had just laid on the table of his cabin. Byn's little face starred up at him. She was holding two toys, a small grass dolphin and a cowboy with long hair. Voul had seen the cowboy ride on the power of Byn's imagination and on the toy dolphin, around the apartment many times. Handy's long hair trailing in the breeze of the girl's movements. They were his daughter's favorites. He lifted up the photo, and now he could see the faces of his wife and daughter together. He looked into their eyes. They were both looking at him, mother and daughter. Their faces seemed to be touching. Voul knew what it was like to be with them on the other side of that picture. The three of them. Voul was thinking about the many happy times they had together.

Voul could imagine hearing his daughter's predictable, inevitable question, "When will you be back, Daddy?" Voul wished he knew the answer. Instead he offered an uncertain smile to Viera. She asked the question he had imagined his daughter asking.

"That is a good question. I wish I knew." They looked at each other through the holographic monitors, his on the little ship now leaving for Sargasso, and hers on the wrist projection as she walked into the gym. He looked out of the forward windows into the immensity of Sargasso's darkness blocking out the stars. She opened the door to the Moon's gym and felt the positive air flow brush her as she looked in. There were people everywhere enjoying the day together. She took a deep breath, almost a sigh, and headed for the pool. He put down the photo but continued to look at it as the engines began to push the little spaceship farther and farther away.

A few minutes earlier, when its propulsion system had come on, the shuttle had lifted from the deck of the hangar and adroitly changed directions, heading for the hangar bay doors at a rapidly increasing speed. The acceleration had surprised Farson as he watched the monitors. They flashed through the doors, as they slowly opened, with barely any room to spare. Farson turned the shuttle on its side to perfectly time their exit. He watched the frames of the door's edges flash by as the dark night of space engulfed them. He shifted the aft monitor to view the station. It was already just a dot of light among the billions blinking back at him. Viera knew the shuttle had departed. She had waved as though he could see her.

Voul walked onto the bridge. "Was that dramatic departure really necessary, Farson?" Voul had noticed the inner edges of the hangar doors were extremely close as the shuttle exited.

"I thought we'd better get out of there before you changed your mind."

The six-day voyage took on the aspect of a long meeting between Farson and Voul. They discussed Sargasso. They discussed the Emers. They discussed the significance of Brittany's arrival on Emerald Earth. They discussed Uva and her stories. They talked about Handy being on the Jordan harvester. They talked about the old ScreenMasters and what they were doing. They discussed the mission at hand *ad infinitum* to be sure they covered every contingency possible. Voul asked why Farson had not used The Screen, "You would already be there." Farson said sometimes using The Screen is not the best way to get things done. Voul thought this over, thinking of all that Farson had done, and wondered how that could be.

Farson was pushing the shuttle's systems for everything they were worth. Voul noticed the speed was much higher than the specifications stated that the shuttle was capable of achieving. Farson said that he had installed a few improvements. He smiled at Voul. "With the help of you-know-who." The Emers.

"Sargasso is not a planet," Farson said, knowing that Voul already knew this. "It is a giant ovoid-like sphere in space and when you see what's in it, Voul, I will be very interested to hear what you think."

"What's in it? Tell me."

"I would, but I am not sure that what I think I saw is real or something else altogether. If what I saw is real, then reality has changed in a way I could not foresee. I want you to see for yourself. Maybe what you will see and what I saw will not be the same."

"Will we actually be able to get in again? You can't remember how you did it." Farson knew that was all too true.

"Yes," he said with confident, unshakable certainty. But he knew his conviction that the "door" would open again was based on faith, not on any facts at hand.

The trip was very comfortable for the two of them. Farson said that Karina might be stopping by at some point. He explained how busy she was. "In many ways she has taken over as ScreenMaster of Earth. Her travels, her constant monitoring of the issues of safety and security from the old ScreenMasters, her support and her devotion to Felicity and Valgary, her management of the robots – if that is the correct word – and her overall understanding of how things are is invaluable."

"It sounds like a business relationship." Voul was kidding, but there was truth in his jest. Farson knew. Between their daughters and "the business" as he often called it, their relationship had changed. Their responsibilities were prodigious, and the scope of their activities was still astonishing to them both. It really wasn't that long ago that the two of them were just kids playing in the attic. At least it seemed that way to Farson.

"Look at that, Kari." Farson gently pushed her head toward the finderscope above the eyepiece. She resisted. Farson looked at her. "You can't see anything until you look through it."

"You don't have to push me, Farson. I don't want to get a black eye." She slowly moved toward the scope and gently positioned her eye perfectly. She blinked. Farson had her staring into the neighbor's house about a half mile away.

"What do you see?" Karina looked up at him and then moved back down to the eyepiece. She minutely adjusted the focus knob, and the scene came into crystal clarity. She jumped back from the telescope.

"Farson! *What* are you doing?"

"Well, Voul, you could say that, I suppose. We are partners in a family business in a way. Saving the human race. She is unbelievable in her conviction that the old ScreenMasters are coming back. It's like an obsession. Everything she does has an element of assessing and improving the security of MoonKing and Emerald Earth. She knows the Emers as well as I do, but she feels that they still need our help. 'They are like babies,' she says. I tell her they have been active ScreenMasters for over six thousand years, and that we have been ScreenMasters for far less than that. She says it doesn't matter and that they are like children pushed by their parents to excel in school and college and suddenly find themselves out in the real world actually knowing nothing about the facts of life. I tell her that they have been moving on The Screen, and through time, essentially forever in human terms. I tell her that to know what they have been doing would be the work of the ages. She knows all of that, but she doesn't care. She says, 'Felicity and Valgary are the product of millions of years as well, with all of the memories and instincts of the billions of human beings who preceded them, but they are still just two little girls in a great big world that can be extremely dangerous and, at times, very malicious. They are babes in the woods, innocents in the jungle.' I think she meant both the Emers and our daughters when she said that.

"I find her arguments are difficult to dismiss. My time on Emerald Earth – *all those years* – gave me an innate familiarity with the Emers. I know how smart they are. I know how powerful they are. Belnad Goethe is beyond doubt the most amazing person I have ever known. And yet, they look to me for guidance, most of the time. They say it's because I was the first and that things happened in that genesis that have never been repeated. They say that my elevation of Karina proves it. They were all born as ScreenMasters, so the elevation protocol is a deep, dark mystery to them. They know their limits, but they push their abilities further and faster than I would have. There are 6.8 million of them, all coordinated, all working together in a seamless, flawless purpose of such high calling and importance that it took me a thousand years to just begin to understand it, and I have a long, long way to go. They still refer to me as 'master' despite my constant disavowal of the title."

"What do you *think* it is, Kari?" Farson knew it was obvious, but Kari's innocence always inspired him. She seemed powered by an engine that ran silently and independently despite the din of his antics and persistent practical joking. Nothing turned her away from the path to which she had assigned herself. It had taken awhile, but Karina was now, almost, impervious to Farson's interjections and surprises.

"It looks to me to be a terrible invasion of their privacy, Farson. Why would you do such a thing?" Farson laughed out loud. *Success!* She clearly did not approve. But she was still looking through the telescope.

"Do you want me to increase the magnification?"

Turning away from the pilot's console, Farson had put the shuttle back on autopilot, at top speed, aimed directly at Sargasso's "front door" as he put it. It would be several more days, and they had a lot to do.

"When Belnad first talked to me about Sargasso, he said something strange. 'When we first arrived at Sargasso, it was not what we were expecting.' He said it in the same way someone might say that they had chosen a movie to watch but when they got to the theater and were all settled in to watch it, the movie was not what they expected. After that he always spoke, as did all the Emer ScreenMasters, of Sargasso as though it was a completely known commodity. That first comment has always stayed with me. They were surprised at

Sargasso but it was not as discoverers; it was more like they had created it and it was not totally consistent with their design. That is not *what* he said, but that was *how* he said it."

"So, you think the Emers created Sargasso?"

"It's unclear, but I would say that their 'discovery' of Sargasso was mislabeled. Six thousand years to plan the survival of their new world, a world without a sun, a world entirely on its own, a world which had become the last refuge of humanity, perhaps a final, safe haven. Well, in that sort of desperation, anything is possible. It would certainly explain how creating something like Sargasso would be the priority.

"The Emer ScreenMasters have proven to be good friends who have terrific timing. Their introductions of new technology have always come just as they are needed. Even this ship has been upgraded recently," Farson's eyebrows went up a little," as though they knew we would be needing it."

Voul commented, "I did notice how comfortable it is compared to that big shuttle we used on the first trip." He was thinking of his sleeping compartment: a large bed, great bathroom, and how much he appreciated the perfect quiet in the room. *Plenty of privacy.* It had occurred to him that Viera and he could use the space to good advantage. Farson was not quite done yet.

"There is a scenario where the Emers could be planning something and not really telling us."

"Should we be worried?"

"No, I don't think so. There is no scenario where the Emers would do anything to harm us. Even through all the years of living among them, watching them change so methodically, watching them master and manipulate their world into a perfect Garden of Eden, I have always felt like an observer in a world I do not fully comprehend, but somehow, at the same time, always completely trusting them."

"You? Not 'fully comprehending?'"

"Yes, Voul. Remember, I was born on old Earth. I grew up there. I went to college there. I worked there. It seems like a million years ago, but it was only 'then,' you know. I am essentially far more like you, than like them." This made Voul smile. He had been born on SkyKing, but both of his parents were born on Earth. They had both died on Earth as well. He knew that this was a factor. The Skers were all born on SkyKing. Earth ancestry was part of humanity's collective knowledge, but it was fading out as the individual histories evolved. Certainly on Emerald Earth, all memory of life on Earth and any connections there had long since become part of ancient written records. The last remaining living memories of Earth were now only on SkyKing and the Moon. Those 6,500 years had taken their toll.

Except for Farson.

He still lived on Earth, on SkyKing, on the Moon, and on Emerald Earth. He knew them all very well. His perspective was unique. His experiential knowledge was refreshed all the time. Those fading memories of others were still vital and alive in him.

"I remember fishing with Sam. I remember kissing Karina by starlight in the attic. I remember Hattie, the most 'Earth-person' I have ever known." Suddenly, he was thinking of Hattie's fried chicken. How she made it will forever be a mystery, but how it tasted will be a relished memory forever as well. It was crisp. It was moist. It was spicy, but still fresh, delicious chicken. She made it look easy." *With dumplings and chitlins and spinach.* He could still taste it all.

He remembered Sam's sizzling fish, cooked in a frying pan on the top of a potbellied stove. He remembered the onions and peppers and how he always wanted to lick the plate. He remembered how the two of them "would eat their fill," as Sam had put it. There was always more than plenty. He remembered how they would sit there after eating and just talk. Cleaning up came later. Sam always felt like a meal and conversation took precedence over everything else. To him, relaxed dining was really living. Sam loved living. *Now he's long dead.*

Farson could feel the emotions piling up. Hattie and Sam were the parents he would always remember. The Chamberlains were ScreenKeepers set in place to provide a life for Karina and him. David and Mary were his birth parents, but he had no memories of them except what he had learned on The Screen. Hattie and Sam were real to him. However it had happened, however it had all been all arranged, they had loved Farson and Karina as if they were their own son and daughter. It was a bond beyond mere blood and above anything that could have ever been planned. It was just one of those things that happened. It was truth.

Farson looked back at Voul from the dreamy middle distance of his childhood musings. Voul was watching him. Farson smiled and returned to the discussion of the Emers and their doings. "It's as if they had Sargasso all planned out and ready and then it was something else. I remember watching Belnad as he told me the story. It should have been told with confidence and certainty, culminating in a story of accomplishment that ended with the wonders of Sargasso, but it was told in questioning tones, with a vast uncertainty, and his story ended in the wonder of the unknown, where only the known should have been. I could tell that Sargasso, in its reality, had surprised them."

"Frightened them?"

"Not really. I sensed more surprise than fear. They are an exceptionally brave and perspicacious people, as you know. Fear is not something that Emers know much about."

It was getting late as Voul headed back to his quarters and Farson went off to his. Voul's mind was full of growing revelations and now, even more questions.

Getting ready for bed, he put his whites in the processor and headed for the shower area. The system on the shuttle was the same new system now spreading across the Moon. Nudity was an option, and the technology easily would have cleaned his body and his clothes at the same time, even remaining fully dressed. It was an adaptation of the latest sophistications of the transporter system; a sanitizing, moisturizing, exfoliation, styling of his hair, nails, plus an overall health scan and repair, including all bodily functions. As he was leaving the bathroom, feeling refreshed and clean, Farson's thoughts reached him. <<*I think we should have a get-together. I have contacted the robots.*>> Voul knew the robots were around, but not currently aboard the shuttle. Even when they were not visible, Voul always felt they were watching. He had gotten used to it.

Just as Voul was thinking about Farson's idea, there was a slight vibration.

He knew the small ship was speeding up.

39. Brittany on Emerald Earth (2)

Brittany heard Ian speak the words: "Welcome to Emerald Earth." More than anything, she heard Ian's soft and agreeable intonation. She loved that she could also easily feel his gentle and encouraging thoughts. And more. Her mind was filling with a vast cleansing sensation as though she had just walked out of a peaceful, lonely room into an endless stadium saturated with the sounds of people talking, thinking, sharing. It was beautifully euphonious, not cacophonous. It was welcoming and receptive. It was warming and gloriously inclusionary. She was filled with a new sense of rich and variegated companionship; she felt a new togetherness that she had never dreamed of as even possible. She found it lavishly captivating and thoroughly enjoyable. She had a deep sense of gratitude and confirmation.

Her life on SkyKing had been full and actively engaging every day, but there had always been a loneliness overshadowing everything, an incompleteness. Being with her father had been her mission. When her mother died, she had adapted to new roles to meet new imperatives. Brittany had pressed on, soldiered on; a dutiful daughter set apart from others her age by her father's status; not alone, but lonely; longing, waiting for something, anything. She was reminded of her trip to the Moon's gym. It had been unsettling yet wonderful. That day, she was confronted with many very personal uncertainties and challenges, but that day also provided a new inclusiveness and sense of acceptance that she had loved passionately. It had been difficult to leave the Moon's warm embrace after visiting the "gym." She had wanted to linger, and even now she still felt an emotional pull to return; she wanted to go back; she needed to go back. It had been a great day.

Standing on the transporter platform with Ian – a man she had met just a few hours ago – she felt that same pulling sensation again. This time it was much stronger, and she knew instinctively it might be impossible for her to resist or delay. *Why would I ever leave?* It was a thought that came with a flush of discovery and relief, a feeling of finally being in the right place. She looked over at Ian. He was looking at her. The gulf that exists between people, that uncertainty of motive, that lack of full knowledge and trust of each other, that hesitation to go first or that fear of saying something wrong that could change everything – those worries were all gone. She was filled with confidence and awareness. Brittany realized something fundamental had happened: she *really* knew him. And, she knew him in a profound way that she recognized would ordinarily have taken many years to achieve. She knew the story of his birth and his naming by Farson Uiost. She remembered his family harvester, and she knew what growing up in the fields had been like for him.

She knew about Ian's terrible accident as a boy, how his life had changed afterwards, how his father had sought out the city and its technology, in the end losing his son. She knew of the sadness his father felt and the deep, aching longing for his son to return to the fields. She knew about Ian's intense urban education and the changes he went through in Emerald City. She knew of the Emer council discussions, and she knew of Belnad Goethe and his impact on Ian. She also knew all of Ian's plans and dreams. She suddenly knew everything about Ian and his world. It was effortless, natural, as if all of this knowledge and this new awareness was open to anyone, to everyone. This new consciousness solved all the problems Brittany had always experienced in getting to know people. It was as if everything she had ever known was now explained. For the first time in her life, she felt truly relaxed, surrendered.

She found that her thoughts turned to her father, and suddenly a scene of him standing on the bridge came into her mind. She knew he was trying to find her. He was worried. *Don't worry, Dad. I'm fine.* She saw him, on SkyKing, suddenly look up and around like she must be in the room with him. She could feel his relief, despite not actually seeing her. *I'm here on Emerald Earth. All is well. It's beautiful.* Jim Peterson turned and spoke to the others on the bridge, communicating that he knew his daughter was safe. They all seemed surprised, but Jim had no doubt at all that it was Brittany. Her father was smiling.

Ian was speaking to her. Only seconds had passed but to Brittany it had seemed far, far longer, as though she had lived a second life and that many years had gone by. She felt older, more mature, and yet still the same. She felt better. Much better. "It may take some time to assimilate this new situation, Brittany." He was going to apologize for not warning her about what was going to happen, but she interrupted him before he could say it, knowing exactly what he was going to say.

"If you had warned me, Ian, I would not have come and look what I would have missed. You did exactly the right thing." She had just spoken his name for the first time. He loved the sound of it in her voice and in her thoughts. She realized that when she said it, much more was communicated. The thought of embarrassment at revealing her feelings was washed away with a great sense of relief. He knew everything about her, just as she did about him. A deep bonding had occurred. Ian spoke again.

"It is more than just you and I, Brittany. It's all of us. We are all one here. It's not just a theme or a slogan; it describes our reality. Open your mind even further, relax and let go." Brittany knew exactly what to do. She closed her eyes, and she did exactly what he asked.

Her mind pulsed around the planet, its history, its operations, its millions of people. She seemed to pass through time backwards and forwards and sideways until everything was revealed to her. *No secrets here.* She saw the small families of the city, the precious children growing. She felt the unshakeable conviction of the Emers and their weariness, their readiness to finally move forward. She knew there was an exhaustion of unwavering commitment throughout them all. She saw how they studied MoonKing and mankind's history. She saw their complete understanding and determination to move beyond *Homo sapiens* into a new existence level, a higher one, a happier one, a safer one. She felt the "crowd," as she was thinking of the 6.8 million Emers in her mind, her awareness, all enjoying her emergence into their midst. To her now, this was normality, she felt contented, and nourishingly challenged. *A better way to be human.* She felt she was inside now, not outside looking in. She felt like she fit in perfectly, her place accepted naturally and without any hesitation. The crowd noticed her smooth transition and was pleased and relieved. She knew it had long been a topic of discussion. She knew that Emers had ultimately bridled at Farson's total control. She knew they had now been acting on their own for many, many years. She knew about Sargasso. Then she knew about the others and the other others. Suddenly, she was back on the platform. Her hand was still in Ian's.

Despite her efforts to relocalize her thoughts on Ian, her mind was still exploring, still learning, still reveling in her new light of knowledge and awareness, traveling all over Emerald Earth and beyond. She could feel Ian's approval. It was an experience like none other in her life. It was as if the mysteries of everything were being unhesitatingly revealed to her, and it was pleasing and reassuring and alimentary. She could feel herself growing stronger and stronger with each passing breath.

Ian's hand was warm and gentle. She could feel him urging her to physical movement. "Brittany, let's take a walk."

As she took her first steps on Emerald Earth, she noted how effortless it was. Like gliding. She enjoyed being so tall. She loved being with Ian, nothing hidden, no need to hide.

They stepped off the transporter platform together. It was like being on a fast-moving walkway. Brittany could see the destination to which they were heading, but she had no idea what it was. Even though information was pouring into her mind, she had no solid frame of reference yet to interpret it all quickly enough for this situation.

A shimmering appeared before the two of them. It was beautiful. It was astounding. It was alluring. She was drawn to it. Just as she was about to ask Ian about it, they entered it. Several steps were needed to pass through its depth. While transiting through it, she felt a sensation of transference, a changing of location, a purifying sensation, a deep sensory enrichment. She felt something wonderful building inside her, like revelation, or astonishment, or enlightenment – or all of the above – and then she stepped into a brave new world.

40. Tom Is Worried

Catherine and Tom spent another week in her cabin on Monhegan. It was a time of joy for them both. Time suspended. Joining their lives in the perfect way; no pressure, no worries, no distractions. They made love. They took walks. They went sailing. Catherine found herself savoring every moment, especially the sailing. She made him circumnavigate the island while she inspected the shoreline through his high-powered binoculars. "Can you move in a little closer?"

"Only if you want to swim for it after the boat hits the rocks and sinks."

They cooked the fish they caught. They enjoyed the wine from his boat. They were happy together. Very happy. They were enjoying themselves. Time passed as though they were in another world where time didn't really matter. A world where life was rich with affection and companionship, rich with passion and friendship, full of fascination and tenderness. It was like heaven for both of them. They shared this secret world like natives, showing each other all the nuances, the nooks and crannies of love, the hidden places of happiness. They reveled in the light of discovery. She found that, for the first time, she was sleeping well with a man in her bed. Very well.

He found that he wanted to be with her every minute. For the first time in his life he *was* truly happy, not planning a next thing, not thinking of anyone else, not wanting to be somewhere else. Contentment was not a word that he had much experience with, but when that feeling came over him during this time with Catherine, he recognized it instantly. He was surprised, relieved, and worried, all at the same time.

"I'm worried," he said that morning. She knew exactly what he meant. Something so wonderful and so seemingly perfect: It almost couldn't be real. She smiled at him and drew him close enough to whisper.

"Don't be."

The next few days convinced him. She was absolutely right.

41. ScreenBurn

Once Handy and Strapper John were back in John's office, on the harvester, the farmer quickly filled his glass with ice and poured a drink of whiskey from the bottle he had "lent" to Handy knowing full well that he would never see it again. The irony of now sharing it with Handy made him happy.

Life on the harvester gave the farmers few pleasures, but it did offer great opportunities to do things that the people in the city no longer did, and things of which the city people probably would not approve.

ChainFoods had changed everything from the first moment they were created by Catherine Peters Jacobson. Once people tasted the new foods and felt the effects on their bodies, it was no contest. With her innovative "re-assemblers," production and innovation swept through the old world's cuisine and that continued on Emerald Earth, reaching new heights even Catherine herself could not have foreseen. The re-assembler process, together with the transporter technology, actually was the key that opened the Emers' new world and, in truth, it allowed them to survive in that strange new world of stasis and isolation.

That Catherine Peters Jacobson was also Karina Chamberlain's mother only added to her historic stature. During her short life, Catherine's fame was worldwide. In her time on SkyKing, this celebrity was compounded exponentially. After her untimely death, she was elevated to the top of a pantheon list very few have ever achieved.

The ChainFoods technologies were a great gift to humanity and ultimately provided a bridge out of the syndromes of poverty and lack into a world of freedom and abundance. The ScreenMasters were part of it too, but in the final analysis, they started a process that they could not control. Farson, as ScreenMaster of Earth, was the beginning, and his creation of Emerald Earth was the dawn of a new era for the human race. In fact, it was the beginning of a new species of human being: happier, healthier in every way, and more powerful as a group than anyone could have imagined.

Looking at the whiskey in his bottle, Strapper John Jordan knew all of this. As an Emer, he was part of the wonders of Emerald Earth, but as a farmer, he was also apart from all of that by choice and by design. The "farmhands" as they liked to be called, roamed Emerald Earth in enormous harvester complexes that performed vital functions for the planet. Harvesting the basic ingredients for the ChainFoods formulas was just one of their many vital functions.

Strapper enjoyed how the whiskey coated the crystal ice cubes in the glass. He swirled them around, and the aroma of the wheat and barley and rye, among other components, wafted into the intimate air between his lips and the glass as he took a large and indulging gulp, breathing in the essence. He could feel the fluid's effect immediately as it went down.

Eyes watering a little, he turned to Handy, who was now pouring himself another. They were enjoying the moment. Handy offered John a big cigar, and they both lit up.

"This is a little decadent, Handy."

"What the hell, I'm old school." They both knew about the stigma of tobacco, but they also both knew that these cigars were vastly different from those smoked so damagingly in Earth's ancient history. John added a comment.

"But these babies really do taste great." John took a long pull and inhaled deeply, blowing smoke into the air. He knew the fabrication of the "tobacco" was a ChainFoods variation and that the "smoke" was actually a nutrient mist that was good for him. At first this healthy alternative really pissed

Handy off. "Fucking do-gooders," he had said. It was like the booze that got you good and drunk but was also beneficial in every way including feeling great the next day. "They've taken the adventure out of addiction," he had said. But in his heart he knew, like all things Emer, these new concoctions were a vast improvement. They both knew that very, very few Emers smoked anything. But as all things Emer, if you wanted to smoke, there was a provision for you. The two of them relaxed into chairs and watched the golden fields go by, as they happily puffed away.

"So you actually saw the ScreenLock?" Strapper John knew his history, but he never really imagined that he would be spending time with Handy Townsend and have the chance to discuss such things with the second most famous ScreenMaster in history. *Not counting Karina now..* But there he was, stretched out in a soft chair and hassock, smoking a cigar and pouring a new drink for himself. Strapper was wondering if they would be needing a second bottle.

"Yep." The answer to the ScreenLock question was one word, offering no invitation for further inquiry. At first it seemed that Handy had read his thought about more whiskey. Strapper was undeterred by Handy's brevity.

"Tell me more about it." Handy shifted in his seat, took a long drag, and blew the smoke slowly into the air, finishing with a series of four perfect smoke rings that flew through each other as the farthest slowed down and dissipated. He took another slug from the glass and let it slowly have its effect.

"It was a purple glow that raced around the planet, John. From where I was, it seemed like watching a welder's torch sealing us off from the outside. There was a great soundless snapping sensation. I know now that there was a brief period of time that Farson calls 'the ScreenBurn.' The best explanation I know of what he meant by that is that it was like when we kids used to look at the sun and then quickly away, but the sun's image was temporarily burned on our retinas. We used to play that game and tag each other as 'it' in the temporary blindness. It was a stupid, dangerous game, but kids are kids. Farson taught me that during the ScreenBurn, he was able to find the weakness of the ScreenMasters' plan and use it against them. The purple glow enclosing us was what we saw. The ScreenBurn was what Farson saw. He and I talked about it once. He said that was what gave him a chance; what gave us all a chance. I remember sitting there on the Butte of Decision that day, playing my guitar. When I saw it happen, there was a sense of finality. At least that's how I thought of it. As things have turned out, it was final in a way. But it was also a beginning as well. With that purple glow the die was cast, no turning back. I've always wondered what Farson was really thinking when he told Repoul Bensn to 'Push the button.'" To Strapper John, Handy seemed deeply reflective in this moment. *Probably just getting drunk.* But, as if to disprove that thought, Handy turned to him and said something that the harvester captain knew he would never forget, and that told he had overestimated Handy's apparent level of inebriation. "I bet," Handy said, "that Farson relives that moment over and over, second-guessing himself and twisting in indecision and maybe even having some regrets. You have to remember, John, what *really* happened that day."

42. Thanksgiving Dinner (1)

Karina was concerned. The invitation list was complicated. Voul and Viera, of course. Handy would come. The robots. Jim Peterson. But Brittany? That could be a problem. The menu and the venue were the easy part. Farson was very excited about the cabin in North Conway and turkey with all the trimmings. She could tell. "You do understand the problem, Farson?"

"Of course." He knew that Brittany was on Emerald Earth, and he knew what was happening to her. "'After they've seen Paree,' is that what you mean?" Karina knew that behind Farson's joking response there was real worry as well. *Brittany's metamorphosis.* Karina shrugged.

"Not really, Farson." Her concern was, would Brittany want to come under the circumstances? She was just learning the Emer ways. "It's been my experience that the thought of leaving that world and the sacrifices a return requires is not something that Brittany may want to do at this time." Karina and the girls had chosen Emerald Earth from the beginning, while Farson stuck with old Earth. For Karina, the changes of moving from one to the other were fairly easy, but the girls always balked at leaving Emerald Earth. To them, now, Emerald Earth was their home. They were just eleven, Brittany was now twenty-six. Brittany had lived all of those twenty-six years on SkyKing, with her father. The transformation for her, Karina knew, was life-changing. Brittany had always had trouble fitting in, although she was universally loved. She never really found her place of happiness since her mother died. She always had an emotional emptiness for all those years that nothing could fill. But now, Karina knew, that had changed.

"Maybe she will come. We want her to."

"Yes, we do."

It would not be easy. Ian, like all Emers, was born on Emerald Earth. Nothing would ever change that. If Brittany left Emerald Earth too soon and for too long, she would begin to revert. Having enjoyed the wonders of the planet and all of the physical, emotional, and mental marvels it bestows, both Farson and Karina knew that returning to her old self might be devastating, like an imprisonment or a shocking isolation. And if she went back to Emerald Earth, she would have to start over again. "Why do you think Ian acted so capriciously in bringing her back to Emerald Earth on the spur of the moment like that?" Karina was asking Farson a question he really didn't want to answer. In the silence, Karina saw something. "What are you not telling me?" She was not happy with the thought that he was keeping something from her.

"There was nothing 'spur of the moment' about what happened to Brittany."

Farson had spent thousands of years on Emerald Earth. He had witnessed the ascension of the planet and its people during the long stasis. He had also seen their growing power and fascination with old Earth and its history. He knew that they had concluded that they wanted it all back. Despite Farson's warnings and his teachings, the Emers had concluded that without the people of old Earth they would never achieve their goals. Partly it was the bottomless DNA pool of old Earth's population, but mostly it was the Emers' love of all things human. As they had evolved in their new world, and developed its implications, the old world and its confusing complexities and uncertainties always drew them back. In all of history, no historian had ever seen what they had seen. Emerald Earth had achieved "the dream the dreamers dream" as Handy so often sang it. But they had also witnessed the death of their heritage, the end of their history. This they could not accept. As time went by, Farson realized that the Emers were acting on their own, outside his guidance and control. They had long accepted the ban on contact between the old and new, but even Farson had told them that it would not be forever. They accepted that potential variable completely and went to work defining "forever" in their own terms. They knew that Emerald Earth was what it had to be and there was no changing that, but that knowledge only defined a new mission for them, far from dissuading them. As a group, 6.8 million Emer ScreenMasters, all working together, proved to be a power that even eclipsed Farson's. They still revered him, and his words were still gospel to them, but they assumed that his "Be not afraid" dictum, so often repeated, was actually a call to action. His also much-quoted dictum that they would ultimately achieve things "much greater than even I have done," was the inspiration for everything they did. There was no stopping them now, as Farson knew all too well. There was really no knowing all that they *were* doing. Moving Emerald Earth into proximity of SkyKing and the Moon and taking the last two outposts of humanity "in tow" was really more like taking possession of them. Moving everyone so easily to Sargasso's location was a show of power unlike anything seen before in human history, and they did it so easily that even Farson was surprised.

The isolation he had imposed on them turned out to be exactly what they wanted. Farson knew that their movements through time were now so thorough and encompassing that he found himself turning away from those thoughts, even though he knew it was important to address. *In due course,* he had said to himself. But watching the Emers build their world with such effortless expertise, seeing them make such sweeping decisions without hesitation, and viewing firsthand the happiness and unity they had built for each other, perhaps for everyone, at once made him happy and then caused him to worry. In discussions with Belnad, Farson always felt at a disadvantage. It reminded him of a professor who he had worked with at the university. The professor was a twin and had two other sets of siblings who were also twins. There was one brother who was a "singleton," as they put it. His professor said that that brother always felt like he was all alone at family gatherings. A family of seven children filled with love and the joy of being together and yet, he felt all alone. Farson understood that as he was speaking with Belnad. The Emers were all fully "joined" – as they called their fibril frame of joint awareness – to 6.8 million others. They were like one:

all fully engaged, all fully invested, all sharing in complete mutual knowledge. Like the professor's non-twinned brother, Farson had the feeling of being outside looking in.

ScreenMasters throughout the omniverse were always aware of each other, but what had developed on Emerald Earth was something altogether different. Farson had asked Belnad about it. "It's what you wanted, Farson," he had said. "You always told us, 'We are all one,' and, of course, we believed you."

Karina's question, "What are you not telling me?" still hanging in the air, seemed, to Farson, a difficult one to answer, and almost unfair of her to ask, but how could he explain it? What he was not telling her was something he didn't know. It had bothered him enormously, but, in thinking it over, he remembered a passage from Ban Jonsn's writings: "In the end, all is mystery. We cannot know the things we cannot know. That those things exist is the substance of our faith. Our faith is the evidence of things we have not seen and may never see. Not knowing is the fiber with which we weave our future. If all we do know is the full circumference of all knowledge, then it would be a prison that forever would confine us. The mysteries before us are the freedoms we cherish. Exploring uncertainties is the catalyst of our discovery." Farson had thought about that quote over and over until it was part of his deep memory. "Not knowing is the fiber with which we weave our future." The uncertainty of human life, even with ScreenMaster capabilities, persists as though it is – just as Ban had said – the central element of who and what we are. Farson's thoughts were interrupted by Karina's impatience for his response.

"Farson?"

What could he tell her of things he didn't know? Just telling her that fact would drive a conversation full of more things he didn't know. She would only grow more impatient.

"The only thing I am not telling you is that I don't know."

"Don't know what?" The inevitable response he had tried to avoid.

"I don't know why Ian did that."

At that moment Brittany was experiencing a world she could never have predicted. She was just under seven feet tall, light bronze in color, connected to 6.8 million other amazing people, and loving every second of it. Ian was talking to her. "You are going to experience a new level of existence, Brittany. Even now you can sense all of Emerald Earth watching you and experiencing everything with you. How does it feel?" This question was planned, of course. The people were waiting. Here is the daughter of James Peterson, commander of SkyKing, known only in the lore of ancient histories, and in their travels through time, standing here among them. Now Brittany Peterson was one of them. Her answer to Ian's well-planned question was one of the most fascinating events in Emer history to date; and that history was astounding in its own right. For the people of Emerald Earth, their own wonders paled before this moment of ultimate truth. What *would* she say? Brittany was having trouble speaking, but she had discovered a channel of communication with Ian that was much easier. She used it for the first time. The world of Emerald Earth was waiting.

<<*It is beautiful, Ian. I feel like I have come home.*>> The emotion she felt after saying those words swept over her with such pleasure and joy that she almost lost her balance. Ian's arm went around her to steady her. She could feel his warmth and tenderness. She looked into his eyes, and the world went away. How long had they been together? They were alone in the mountains. The dwelling around them seemed to move as they moved. She felt like there were ten of her and ten of him, all embracing in a magnification of love that she had never imagined possible. She turned toward him, and all the other Brittanys and Ians also moved. He kissed her. They all kissed

her from different angles. She could feel each one. Each one was a little different. It was a cascading embrace coming at her from every direction. She kissed him back, but now she was kissing them all in a kaleidoscope of emotion compounded beyond experience, beyond her dreams. It was enthralling. Some of them moved gently beyond a kiss. Others embraced the moment more fully, carefully. It was overwhelming her, but she was also deepening her own involvement. She was also exploring Ian deeper in some situations than in others. She found herself moving among them, searching for intensity. The sensations were a totality of inclusion, sweeping her up to levels of intimacy that surprised her and aroused her and delighted her and made her want more and more and more. Then they were alone again, just the two of them, holding hands. She was out of breath. In Ian's eyes she saw the moisture of passion rising. She asked the question. <<*Did you feel that, Ian?*>> She realized he was crying softly. Tears from years of waiting, tears from years of wondering, now culminated in an ecstasy unknown before. Even in a world of wonder, what had just happened to Ian Jordan was a shock of revelation to him and his whole world had reverberated like a new instrument in an orchestra, a new star in the skies, a new level of experience. Ian still had not answered her, so she took his face in her hands, looked him in his dark blue eyes, and kissed him again. She realized as her lips touched his that this was their first physical kiss; the others had been Emer style, no actual contact. This was old Earth, old-school style. Her style. She could feel Ian approach an oblivion of discernment as he entered new territory that he was not sure even existed. She could feel his lips searching for the right thing to do when everything was already just perfect to her. She could feel him centering on her, apart from the 6.8 million, now just her, just him. *Us.* She could feel his revelation of love. She could feel his lips parting, now knowing the way.

Karina wasn't sure what to say. She felt a little better knowing that Farson didn't know something that she also didn't know, but his doubt of events worried her. "Well, let's invite them both and see what happens." This seemed to settle her. His response was confirming.

"Sounds like a plan to me."

43. Brittany on Emerald Earth (3) / Becoming Her Own

Brittany took a deep breath, enjoying the air of Emerald Earth, and looked over at Ian: A man she had just met, and yet somehow she seemed to know everything about him.

Ian had been born sometime around 6485 E.E. With their extended life spans and travels through time, actual dates didn't really matter to them. She knew that actual ages meant nothing to the Emers. Once the population stabilization process (the Combing) began, it took 2,000 years to complete. The final population lived as long as they wanted to at physical ages they could select. Birth and death on Emerald Earth were also done in the most orderly way possible. "Caesarian transport" was how they described the birth process. The baby was meticulously transported out of the woman's body at the earliest possible moment of viability and brought to term under the perfect conditions of Emerald Earth's childcare facilities. Nothing was left to chance. All babies were "born" easily and physically perfect. They were monitored and "parented" to maturity, and then the aging process for each individual was set, monitored, and maintained throughout their lives, all under the watchful eyes of the entire Emer world. Death, like birth, was without ceremony and handled in a meticulous and predictable way. Each Emer who "passed" did so by their own choice. Living thousands of years takes its toll, and in some cases death became a welcome alternative. Death on Emerald Earth was also birth: One life ending always ushered in a new life being born. Each death and birth was experienced by all 6.8 million Emers. Each precious new life added a new living resonance in their world. These moments were cherished and experienced by everyone together.

Given these unchangeable conventions, and the 6,515 years of their history, Brittany's appearance on Emerald Earth caused quite a stir, to say the least.

Ian had been born into the farm family of Strapper John Jordan. He was Strapper John's son, and the first new child in two hundred years. Within the Jordan family, it was a great moment because the family numbers had stabilized for many years. The sanctioned birth of a new son was a family event like no other.

Ian's childhood was interesting in light of all that happened. He was raised to be a farmhand, with specialities in navigation and mechanics. Even in his early youth, he excelled in his work, and the promise of his future was bright for the family.

At the age of eleven he was involved in a fluke harvester accident that almost killed him. He was rushed to Emerald City, and after lengthy "repairs," as they called the process, and during his years of long recovery, Ian discovered that he loved the city. His family was disappointed when he said that he wanted to stay in the city. In a world of free will, there was no argument to be made about an individual's choice, but there were discussions. They had been so thrilled to have the new boy. To lose him was very hard to take. In those ongoing discussions at the time, Strapper had appealed to his son, stressing Ian's growing expertise and the future needs of their family. Ian procrastinated, saying he needed time to sort things out, but in the end there was no question in his mind. One of the reasons for Ian's determination to stay in Emerald City was Belnad Goethe, who was the head of the regeneration laboratory when Ian arrived. The blade injuries he had suffered were so severe that it took every ounce of Emer ingenuity and biological engineering finesse that the planet possessed. Ian Jordan's case became famous with everyone involved. Serious accidents were almost unheard of on Emerald Earth, and a young Emer farmhand being involved in one was a rare event.

Belnad's achievement of reconstructive perfection was heralded as transformational. During this process, the two of them became very close.

As Ian progressed, he wanted to know everything about the city and about the world beyond the farms and fields. Belnad showed him the city and the rest of their world. Together they saw the Thunder Waters of Onjagra and the Great Canyon. He saw the Hidden Ocean, and they visited the Transport Station. Together they studied SkyKing and Moon histories. He ultimately tutored at the Academy and then went on to advanced studies in the Tower, and finally Belnad showed him the Exploratorium, and they began to visit the planets.

Brittany was fascinated, watching Ian's memory play out. She felt his astonishment and his wonder as he looked around the Exploratorium. She heard Belnad explain the purposes of the facility and its incredible range of activities. She experienced Ian's revelation of Emerald Earth's true purpose, and she heard him say to Belnad, "Does Farson know about this?" She looked into Belnad's eyes with him and felt the disorientation when the older Emer said that there were some things now that even Farson did not know. After that tour, and with his new knowledge of the Emers' true mission, Ian's choice was inevitable. He was staying.

Ian reached maturity at thirty-three years. He often communicated with his family but had never returned to the farms. Strapper John had come to the city to see his son many times, but had ultimately desisted in asking him to return. In time, Strapper came to understand his son's choice and to reluctantly support it.

Ian's amazing career as Belnad's closest associate became a source of pride for the family. The pain of the family's loss never completely healed, but understanding's brush can paint a whole new picture, so those fine tinges of anguish and regret became blurred in the layers and blendings of hope and forgiving. The family realized that their son was now a pivotal figure in history. The pain of their loss was softened by the textures of humility and acceptance in the face of events beyond their control. After all, even the farmers of Emerald Earth, so independent and vital, were Emer to their core. "We are one." Farson's often-quoted words rang true.

So, Ian stayed. The family remained close through all the years, but Ian had never come back to the harvester he had so loved as a boy. Brittany now knew why. Through his mind's eye she saw his awareness of her standing beside him now. He moved closer, put his arms around her, pressing cheek to cheek. And then *he* kissed her. Brittany heard his thought as their lips met: *It works both ways, you know.* She hugged him closer and kissed him more deeply, knowing that Ian's story was now becoming her own.

44. Farson's Log (3): Thank Goodness We Were Wrong

Karina and I knew the Emers were doing something. It's like your kids are in the backyard having a great time. You wonder what they are doing but, to be honest, you almost don't want to know. Almost.

The Emer ScreenMasters, even in their own view of their history, knew that they started very slowly. From outside, the stasis enveloped the planet in a vast purple flash. But then, on the inside, nothing changed. Life went on, day by day, week by week, month by month, year by year, decade by decade, and then, century after century. Think about that. Life goes on.

The Emers did ascertain their unique situation as time went by. By the end of their first century, still small in numbers, they began to figure it out. Their analysis of the field itself, its harmonic and molecular makeup, gave them some of the keys. Eventually, their initial research led them to the mystery and then to the discovery. At first they could only determine that it was time that was being affected, but without a point of reference they could not determine *which way* time was being affected. They discovered mathematical evidence that a reversal had taken place. The details took them awhile to sort out, but they did it. Once they began to understand their situation, they were faced with a new and unbelievable reality.

Over the centuries, as the Emers began to save their planet and regain control of their destiny, old Earth, SkyKing, and the Moon faded into antiquity. Gradually, all of their energies transferred to their new world. Inexorably, its secrets slowly began to emerge.

Eventually, they confirmed that relative time, for them, had been, at first, slowed down, and then, in an unseen and unfelt reversal, drastically speeded up. They made mistakes along the way. Like the heliocentric astronomers of ancient history, they at first assumed the universe revolved around the never-changing Earth. It took more years to prove that this seemingly still Earth was actually moving faster through time while everything else had essentially stayed the same. They theorized, with no point of reference, that the rest of the universe, if not the omniverse itself, was unaffected. They finally understood that they were alone as no other race, and no other planet, had ever been.

They discovered the whole truth slowly but inescapably. It was a revelation, when it came, that seemed in its discovery cataclysmic. The sadness of losing the Moon and SkyKing and all those people preoccupied the planet. So many gone. Reality overturned. Everyone and everything was affected. It was a very special tragedy. Then, slowly, their understanding of actually being true ScreenMasters by their nature – not by selection – began to resonate. Earth Pact became the lever by which they moved their world. For some reason, this new knowledge of their stasis sped the process faster than the years racing by, and at the end of those first centuries, Emerald Earth had already begun to emerge. The essential re-terraforming of the planet continued as an existential necessity, and new capabilities that no one could have predicted emerged triumphant.

I was there, of course. It was an odd time for me. One of the things I had to come to grips with was that there were many choices of timelines for Handy and me. He called me an interloper who came and left and never joined. I saw it more as a second career. My work with MoonKing and Sargasso was one; my work on Emerald Earth was another. Handy's assignment, which he was not happy about at all, was to stay with Emerald Earth. He chose a timeline which maintained the time phasing of his birth; so, like a person stepping on a moving sidewalk and looking down, the world seemed still and unmoving to him, even as the centuries rushed by. He said, "That way I am still me." He also said, "That way no one can bother me. Except you, of course." So, I would come and go and see that things were changing in great and important ways. But Handy just rode along in a world that, to him, never changed. He would be there when we needed him at the end, but it was like a long, long prison sentence to him. "The people in the bottle" eventually took charge, and Handy was ultimately enticed to join them. It was in this second phase of his life on Emerald Earth where Handy truly regained himself and his purpose. As the Emer

ScreenMasters emerged, they saved themselves, their world, and Handy, too.

Handy had always been a great fan of Earth. His birth planet was not unlike it. Its history, however, sadly, was vastly different. I have always felt that Handy, like an orphan seeking surrogate parents, had adopted Earth as his own. Other ScreenMasters traveled beyond their homes, sometimes never to return, as in the sad case of Uvo, but Handy, once he came to Earth, never left. Through those thousands of years I watched him wobble up and down the path to which he had assigned himself. My utter dismay at his moral miswanderings sometimes made me wonder if all was well with him. He told me he was like Siddhartha on a spiritual journey, but seeing him passed out in pools of vomit and urine, his life in shambles, I was always worried. "What did you expect?" he would asked me when I inquired. Many times, I thought I had asked too much of him. In the end though, he was magnificent. Seeing him roaming with the dolphins in the immenseness of the grasses of what became the exultant Emerald Earth and watching him reach his pinnacle of success and happiness as Emerald Earth reclaimed its rightful place answered all my questions and relieved all my doubts. Handy Townsend's history ultimately *was* the history of Emerald Earth. His "humanity," if we can call it that, matured along with the changing planet. When I offered to help him achieve the upper levels of The TrueScreen, he said he had had enough change in his life and was finally content.

Without Handy, we would never have known the truth of Emerald Earth and the full range of their activities as the stasis period unfolded. Six thousand five hundred and seventeen years on Emerald Earth changed Handy, vastly for the better. The lonely drunk, the isolated and minimized ScreenMaster, he attained a stature and a personal elegance that revealed much. He was my friend from the beginning, and in the end he was a friend to humanity like no other.

Even Uvo, in his wisdom and intelligence, could not hold a candle to Handy's ultimate accomplishments.

Karina and I saw it all. He became an individual of wisdom and caring. The Emers loved him and revered him for his sacrifices and insights right up there with Karina and me. He laughed at us. "You guys are the rabbit," he would say, "and I am the tortoise who plodded and persisted and kept moving only to just finish the race, no thought of winning. But I did get there first, as usual." This always made him laugh. He was the first ScreenMaster; nothing can ever take that away. And, he was the first non-Emer to learn the secrets of Emerald Earth and Sargasso.

The Emer ScreenMasters had broken the stasis cordon in less than a thousand of their years, and from that moment on, they had worked toward new goals with a Sker-like determination and ingenuity. The Skers were always the Emers' model, and, like potters with their clay, they molded their world and their people to match their dreams. Order, discipline, imagination, faith in each other, and grand objectives to propel it all, the Emers made the most of their imprisonment, saved their planet and its remaining people, and engineered a future that no one on old Earth could have even dreamed of. A future that even I did not foresee.

They were like those children playing in the backyard. They dreamed up a fantasy world that eventually enveloped us all.

We thought we had everything under control.

Thank goodness we were wrong.

BOOK II
The Sargasso Insinuate

"The wind bloweth where it listeth,
and thou hearest the sound thereof,
but canst not tell when it cometh,
and whither it goeth."

– John 3:8
(from the Sker books of scripture)

The only thing that makes life possible
is permanent, intolerable uncertainty;
not knowing what comes next.

– Ursula K. Le Guin

Chapter Four

Here We Go

45. Indiana University (1)

When Karina arrived in Bloomington, it was at the very beginning of the intense and lengthy "Indian Summer" of 2082, which ultimately lasted into the following spring. It was the first time that winter never really came to the state. The Indiana September air was still hot as summer, and the corn fields were still radiating the intense heat. Students were dressed in light and airy clothes to fight the temperature.

As she walked toward the university's library, she felt out of place without her brother. Farson had finally gone off to New England and Harvard after a year of lingering with Karina as she finished high school. Karina had decided to go to IU and stay closer to home, near Hattie and Sam. Sam was not well. It was the first time Farson and Karina had ever been apart in almost eleven years. *Two-thirds of my life.*

They had discussed the topic of the coming separation endlessly. Every detail had been taken into account. Channels of communication had been set up and schedules established but when the day finally came, it was none the easier for all of that careful preparation. Their histories had blended into a life together. It was all they had. Hattie, Sam, Farson, and Karina: Their little family was the thread that held it all together. In each other's company, Farson and Karina had found meaning and contentment. In each other's arms, they had discovered

215

love. At the transport center in Indianapolis, their final embrace that day had been tear-soaked and prolonged, with the heat rising in Indiana and within their longing hearts. Their hands held on until the very last moment. Farson had walked into the tunnel leading to the levtrain that would drop him in Boston forty minutes later, knowing that without each other, they would again be lost in a world of uncertainty and change. He knew that Karina was worried and frightened at the prospect, which conjured up the death of her parents and the emptiness that surrounded her that terrible day on SkyKing. His last words to her – whispered through tears with lips still moist from kissing her – were still softly ringing in her ears even as she walked through the automatic iris entry into the largest building on the sprawling campus: "I love you, Karina. You are everything to me." She could still see his face wet with tears, looking at her, and his doubt about his decision to go it alone. In their earlier discussions, he had said it would be good for them, but she knew in his heart he didn't believe it. She certainly did not. Karina had smiled disbelievingly at him that day and said, "Maybe for you, *Routier*, but not for me."

They had laughed then, at her inadequate and exaggerated French accent, but, alone, she was not laughing now. Just entering her sophomore year, she realized that her vividly remembered feelings of separation that day, as they parted, had never lessened. Now those feelings had grown deeper and even more painful. Even as the library's entry device scanned her for identity proof, she knew her true identity had been stolen by circumstances she had been unable to control. Farson's willingness to leave her had shocked her system. She understood the motivations well enough, but that did not mean agreement. She walked away as though wounded: Her happiness slashed in two, her sense of confidence, stripped away, her rising sense of uncertainty swelling, her searching for Farson unsatisfied, her hoping he would return, dashed.

She was lonely and unsettled among a carefree, even frivolous, student body experimenting with freedom and independence, and all she wanted was Farson back again.

The entranceway scanner toned approval, and she walked in. She went to her study area, as if on some hidden autopilot, and sat down. As the monitor projections came up, she was still thinking of him. She was remembering "The Day of the Door," when she had stood unmoving inside her room as Farson fumed and fussed on the other side. She could see his shadow movements coursing back and forth in the small space between the door's bottom rail and the threshold. The shadows seemed agitated. They would stop suddenly, and she could imagine him reaching for the glass-faceted door knob, turning it and opening it. She could imagine him standing there, apologetic, finally agreeing that she had been correct, that he had been wrong. She was staring at the doorknob, willing it to move. Nothing. His shadow still darkened the space beneath the door. She stood still, waiting on her side: They were like two images in a mirror, unseen, unmoving, waiting for a sign that never came. Then, as now, she knew that she would have to move on. There was only so much a person could give. Only so much hope one could have. At certain points in life, things must be allowed to take their natural course. Moments of truth. Karina realized that, here at Indiana University, she had reached another one.

She turned her attention to the monitors.

Her field of study was to be microbiology, which was natural enough. Her mother had been the most famous scientist of her day, inventing and defining a whole new field of study. Even now, Catherine Peters Jacobson's star shone so brightly that had anyone known Karina was her daughter, it would have been disruptive to the quiet life she had always sought. Since witnessing her parents' shocking death in space, Karina had never spoken of it, except in quiet moments with

Farson. She realized that the Chamberlains had given her their name to protect her. Her gratitude for their care only grew when she entered school for the first time. If her name had been Karina Jacobson, she would never have had the experience of being just another student in the class. She accepted the Chamberlains' name as part of a transition to her new life. In time she embraced it as her own. When her class studied the topic of ChainFoods and the revolution that this discovery had created, she was grateful for the name change. She loved hearing the histories of her parents and how her fellow students became enthralled with their story and with the histories of her mother's discoveries. But for Karina, her own memories were so painful that she found anonymity to be the best defense. In her own way, though, she always and meticulously fostered and nurtured those memories out of a love for her parents that no amount of time or distance could ever erase. She would never allow it. She often thought of her father. The first image recalled was always the yellow repair tag she had "pinned" on the back of his pants. She could see it all too clearly in her mind, as he went down the weakened floor of the fourth whorl and out into space. Always, when she thought of her mother, the first thought was her mom pushing her to safety just before she, too, was sucked out into that merciless black void of death. After that, other memories came flowing in to heal and help her cope. There were so many good ones that even in the shadow of that overwhelming darkness, she could search and find the brighter images of happy times of being together that would help her climb out of the grief and heartache into something better, something assuasive and soothing. She had become adept at sorting through her memories to always have at hand one or two to instantly combat the sorrow.

They were at a pizza restaurant. It was her fifth birthday. All of her friends were there. Everyone had ordered. The crayons had been used, and the restaurant's coloring sheets had all been filled in. Karina and her friends were getting restless. Her dad was trying to keep everyone patient with his crazy stories of underwater wonders and anything else he could think of. Her mother was constantly looking to the restaurant's kitchen door, hoping that their four pizzas would appear. Pepperoni, double cheese, plain, and then Tom's favorite, "Everything." Her mother knew that the four delicious, hot pizzas should have been out fifteen minutes ago. But no, just as the Jacobson birthday party had arrived, an entire fraternity membership from the nearby state college had come in and ordered what seemed like a hundred pizzas. Obviously, such a ridiculously large order had slowed everything down in the kitchen. Even the fraternity brothers were getting impatient. Drinking great volumes of beer in pitchers definitely required pizza to abate the inevitable over-intoxication. The boys started to chant. "Pizza! Pizza! Pizza!" at the top of their lungs. At first the girls were surprised and slightly frightened at the commotion, but Karina saw the situation as an opportunity for fun, and she started to pound the table and shout along with the brothers. Quickly, the deep baritone of the fraternity was harmonized with the high sopranos of the young girls' voices, and the pounding on the tables took on a thunder-effect. Karina looked over and saw her father in full-throated participation, laughing, pounding, and shouting along, perhaps louder than anyone. Karina saw her mother's face suddenly show great relief as the waiters came, almost running through the kitchen doors, pizzas held high. The chanting stopped suddenly, except for Karina's dad who was in a trance-like state of involvement. His loud shouts of "Pizza! Pizza! Pizza!" were the last three to be heard in the silence of the pizzas' arrival. Sheepishly, he looked around, embarrassed to be the last to know the wait was over. Everyone laughed at him, but Karina started applauding, and everyone joined in. As though the sole champion of success,

Tom stood up and took a bow. More applause as the pizza slices were hoisted in his honor. Soon everyone was happily devouring their favorites.

When the girls joined the waiters in singing "Happy Birthday" to Karina, the entire fraternity stood up and joined in with a surprisingly harmonic addition. It was a day to remember.

Karina, sitting in her library carrel, was studying her main computer screen. It was displaying the page where she had been writing her introductory sophomore paper. The idea of an acellular vaccine to ward off aging was a popular topic in the biology school. Some students were working on the cosmetic side of the issues, others were working on the internal medicine side. Karina had centered on the genetic aspects and the well-known "generation skip" that chromosome effects often manifest. Red hair, twins, and even disorders often pass over children to grandchildren. Karina's theory was that through careful selection and gene engineering, some of the disorders infecting the genome could be eliminated altogether if the "skip transmissions" acquisition codes could be expanded and managed effectively. Her idea was centered on the reordering of individual molecules that occurred within the ingestions of ChainFoods. She saw that complex reassigning structure as a hidden tool that might be used to not only solve negative genetic inheritances, but also an instrument to drive longer life, and perhaps – this was problem she was working through now – *much* longer life. She was hoping to present her final report sometime next year. Research, for Karina, was a step-by-step, trial-and-error, failure-after-failure process guided by a determination to always finish what she started. *There are enough unfinished projects in this world already.*
And in my life.

46. Voul and Farson Return to Sargasso

"We'll be there in two more days, Voul. So let's discuss the plan again and make things as ready as possible." Voul knew Farson was determined to do things differently this time. Voul looked at the array of monitors. Port and starboard showed stars and the black of space. Aft was the same, but he could visualize Emerald Earth and MoonKing back there, which caused his mind to find a recent memory to linger for a moment on ... Viera and Byn, wishing either they were here with him or that he was there with them.

When he looked up, the forward monitors were filled with the vast flatness of Sargasso as usual.

In the preceding three days of space travel, the view had hardly changed at all. He knew they were getting closer, but from the look of things anyone would think they were heading, at apparent suicidal speeds, toward a gigantic, immovable wall. He looked at Farson for confirmation that all was as planned. "I know the perspective is unusual, Voul, but we still have a long way to go. We are on perfect track to my marker. The visuals are disorienting because of the proportions, but we are perfectly safe. Relax and enjoy the ride. Few have ever made a trip like this." Voul found that he did relax somewhat during the next day and a half. *You can get used to anything.* There were many things to do, and being alone with Farson Uiost was a pleasure to Voul. They had long-since become friends, and for Voul these past days were reassuring and, he had to admit, just plain fun. *Farson's fearless.* The ship itself was wonderfully comfortable and versatile, and he had learned much from watching and listening to Farson. Voul was thinking about how far Farson had come from those early days when the old ScreenMasters came to Earth and found him teaching political science in New Hampshire. Now Farson roamed the omniverse and drove spaceships like a pro. And, Voul noted, Farson was still the most important human being in history, married to the second most important human being in history. Then there were Farson's twin daughters, now almost five. *What a family.* His own daughter had just turned six. As he worked to prepare for the little ship's arrival on Sargasso, Voul was thinking about how many things had changed. *Is anything the same now?*

As the ship drew nearer, the monitors' reach resolved, and they could finally see the area where Farson had vanished. "Is that it?" Voul seemed a little underwhelmed. The marker Farson had placed there was flashing on the ship's proximity sensors. It was a tiny blinking light in the dark shadow of Sargasso's extravagance. "Yep, we're getting there," Farson said. To Voul, their destination hardly seemed transformational, worth all the rush and urgency. It still just looked like a great flat wall that went on forever.

"Now what?" asked Voul.

"Now we move in as close as we can, and then we wait." He was looking at the telemetry module. It was an array of holograms that changed as he studied them. Just glancing around, Farson could tell the exact position of the small ship and exactly how far they were at any time from Sargasso. Using the long-range scanners, they could now see the platform's profile at maximum magnification.

"How far out are we?" Voul asked. Farson looked up and down the array, and a distance designator appeared to indicate the answer.

"Just over six hundred thousand miles; we'll be there in a few hours." Voul was thinking that over. *The ship is really fast. Sargasso is enormous. Even now it just looks like a big flat wall in all directions. We're going be there in a few hours.*

"Is there anything I should be getting ready? We have all the gear in the armory." Farson was looking at him somewhat quizzically.

"I thought you knew."

"Knew what?"

"That we are taking the ship in with us." Farson continued working the controls and telemetry. He seemed to be trying to eke out every ounce of speed he could from the propulsion systems. Voul looked at the monitor. *We are hurtling toward the surface of probably the largest object ever found at over 320,000 miles an hour. He's trying to make us go faster.* Voul always knew that Farson was dauntless. And he was doing all of this while being in many places at once. Recalling their conversations over the past five days, Voul reviewed Farson's current activities. *He is on Uva's barge. He is traveling with Karina. He is talking to Handy about the future of everything. He is living in North Conway. He is on Emerald Earth spending time with John Andrew McKinley Sortt. And he's driving this ship as hard and fast as he can.*

Voul's plan had been to land, disembark, and then to walk to the tower as they had before. He was expecting another exciting suit-flight to the platform. He had been expecting to stand on the platform next to Farson. So, no, he hadn't been aware of Farson's new plan. *What else is new?* "No, I didn't know that, Farson. But it does sound like a good idea. At least we'll have a complete record."

"MoonBase gave us new tech for the trip. The Emers have just updated the Moon's capabilities, which were already good. This ship, among its many other features, is now a surveillance platform like nothing ever seen before. If we get inside, we'll have a record all right."

Farson was thinking of skipping rocks across the fishing stream and how he could never reach the cattails. Sam could do it easily. He laughed at Farson's always short-falling stones. He remembered Sam telling him that he was his own worst enemy. "Ya gotta let go, Farson. You're holding back. It's all out if you ever want to get there." Sam laughed and threw another one. Farson watched it sail so smoothly, not tumbling unevenly end over end like Farson's, in a long, fluid, arching trajectory into the cattails. *Way in.*

For the next two hours they flew toward Sargasso in silence. Farson was so focused on the approach that conversation seemed unneeded. Voul took the time to meditate and pray, to consider things from the Sker point of view. Things had been moving pretty fast these past days, so he was grateful for the solitude.

The two of them rode the racing ship toward their rendezvous with Sargasso: As Farson worked the ship, he was thinking, *Another hour and we will be there.* As Voul worked through his prayers, one prayer kept repeating itself. *Show us the way.*

If anyone had seen the ship pass, they could have noticed how artistically alloyed it was from stem to stern. Compared to the shuttle of the first voyage, it was small. Compared to the other ScreenMasters' enormous vessels, it was tiny, almost microscopic. But the ship was easily as large as the largest mega-yachts of the late twenty-first century of Earth. It was packed with features, highly livable, and very comfortable. "Just right," as Farson had said. When Karina had asked him about the little spaceship he had put so much work into lately, he said it was going to be his version of a "barge." When they walked through it a few days before launch, she found she loved the ship. It reminded her of their secret childhood "Ship" in the attic so many years ago, although this version was outfitted "to the nines," as she put it with a big smile. She loved the telemetry console and the ship's ability to see everything in all directions at great distances. She looked at him. <<*No neighbor will be safe now, Farson.*>> She loved Farson's quarters, and she noticed that everything was perfectly set up for two: the bedroom, the expansive living areas, the dining facilities, but the bathroom in the master suite made her pause. "Now this is very nice," she said with a heavy tone of understatement.

"Well, the Moon had some great suggestions." Karina noted the shower and other facilities were clearly new Emertech, and the dressing area was perfect, in its size and the wide variety of clothing options instantly available. Then she noticed the bathtub. It was huge, and it was unusual in its design. Farson happily demonstrated its capabilities. The water appeared instantly at exactly the right temperature, and then with another flash it was gone, and a soft couch appeared within the inset area. Then there was another shift, and a beautiful bed appeared. She looked at Farson. <<*Now that is interesting. Can we try it?*>> A few hours later, as they walked out of the hangar, refreshed and invigorated, she turned back to look at the spacecraft again. "That is really something, Farson. We could explore the universe in that thing."

"Exactly."

Then she noticed that Farson had named his ship. When she saw the name on the tapered end, she went up to him and, going deeply into his arms, she gave him a kiss to remember. They took the moment to turn, still holding each other, to look at the name and the ship together, just enjoying the moment. The beautifully presented name was like a cherished memory they were indulging together. Karina's thought at that moment was crystal clear. <<*Perfect.*>> The name filled them both with loving thoughts and memories.

Songbird.

Farson's voice sounded softly throughout the ship. "Fifteen minutes, Voul." He looked up from his books. "You should join me on the bridge as soon as you can." In a few seconds, Voul walked into the control area where Farson was closely monitoring the telemetry and position controls. Voul looked at the forward monitor, and all he could see was the dark image of Sargasso's surface. It was clear that they were now within the surface features, towers on all sides. They were moving as though through a crowded city full of skyscrapers. Farson was maneuvering the vessel, carefully navigating toward the target. Voul marveled again at how silent the ship was in its operation. It reminded him of the robots and their adroit, precise movements. As he completed that thought, there was a brief flash of faint purple, and ZZ<<Arkol25609 appeared. Clearly, Farson was expecting him, and addressed a question. *<<Are the others standing by, ZZ?>>*

<<Of course.>> The response was so matter-of-fact, so robot-like, that Farson found it reassuring. Suddenly, his concentration seemed to intensify.

"Look, Voul. There it is. Just as we planned." The ship, after traveling at top speeds for 6.2 days, and just over two million miles, was now just a few hundred yards from the platform. Hanging motionless in space, hovering in anticipation of its next move, *Songbird's* bow was pointing directing at the exact spot where Farson remembered standing just before Sargasso opened itself up and let him in. There was a long pause as Farson completed the ship's positioning. Then he said, "Now we wait."

47. What Really Happened

Strapper John regretted thinking that Handy had been getting drunk because, over the next hours in the farmer's quarters, Handy taught him more about the history of Emerald Earth than he had ever learned in school or during all of his long life on the planet. Handy told him what happened when the stasis field was activated, and how it had taken time for the field to complete itself. How people on Earth watched as the skies slowly disappeared, how the stars faded away. He told him of those days of despair and fear. He told him how Farson ultimately came to help them understand. Handy told him that those first decades were inflective, altering human life in ways never predicted, never imagined, never conceived of even in the wildest dreams of artists and poets and science fiction writers. Life on Earth was being smothered out like a soft pillow pressed over humanity's face, blocking airways and threatening beating hearts. It was a slow death, depressing and discouraging, with no way out. The ScreenMasters turned out the lights, locked the door, threw away the key, and walked away. There was no discussion, no debate, no fight. As far as they were concerned, it was problem solved. Inside, stasis had, at first, slowed everything down more and more. Predictions of a complete stop of time were rampant. Most estimated they had less than a year.

Then Farson came.

He showed them the way. He showed them his plan. In the darkness and depths of despair, his words were like light shining in a forgotten prison cell. A chance for freedom where all hope had been abandoned. He told them that he was going to change the stasis field, that there was a brief moment of time when it could be done, and he was going to do it. They didn't know that every second of their time was now taking them further and further away from the ScreenMasters. They didn't yet know how much could and would be done within Farson's new parameters. He told them that the ScreenMasters had outsmarted themselves and had given him the one thing he needed to save the Earth: time. He told them to work hard together to save their planet. He told them that there was a way to generate power and warmth from the Earth's core, but there were also horrifying and epochal decisions that would have to be made. "Everyone," he said, "must now work together or it will all end, and the ScreenMasters will be victorious despite my efforts." He showed them the way, but as he left he said, "The kingdom is within you. Look within and you will find the answers." Then Farson left them.

Handy then took a long drink from his glass and let the liquid flow down his throat with relish. Strapper John followed suit, easing the tension he had felt over the import of the story Handy was unfolding for him. They sat quietly for a few minutes, the words sinking in. John knew the story he had learned as a boy. How the world had gotten together, how the population was allowed to decline, forced to decline. He remembered the stories of the Combing ceremonies each year and the announcements of milestones and achievements. How, in the end, 6.8 million people emerged on Emerald Earth with new skills and new powers that changed everything. John knew the stories, and he knew there was much more to it. The history Handy had just explained, he also knew, was only the beginning.

"Then what happened, Handy?" Handy was taking a drag on his cigar and looking at his guitar. His fingers were moving as though up and down the frets. Handy took a deep breath and sighed.

"Then he put me in here."

"Why?"

"He wanted a witness. Someone he could trust. Someone to see it all firsthand." Handy's eyes drifted to the harvester's window. The wheat was passing by as the vast machine trekked across the endless plain. The window was open, and he could smell the world outside. It was fresh. It was alive. It was beautiful. Then he added one more comment. "It was the greatest gift of my life. Farson proved his love by taking everything away from me and imprisoning me here with all of you for 6,517 years. I complained. I bitched. I accused him of killing me. But I loved every minute. Even now, I'm free to leave, but I stay here with you and the dolphins. It's hard to explain, Strapper, but there's no doubt in my mind. Finally, after all the things I've seen and done, all the places I've been

... finally I am home." He picked up his guitar and played for a few minutes, probably warming up, and then he sang a poem. Strapper John relaxed and enjoyed it, realizing that Handy Townsend had accepted him as a friend.

THE OTHERS

They still mystify us.
They still make us happy.
They still make us wonder.
They still make us crazy.

They make us question, doubt, and hide.
They leave us filled, empty, shaken, stirred.

They burst into our lives and destroyed everything.
They burst into our lives and renewed everything.
They burst into our lives, set bombs, and ran.
They burst into our lives and took away the pain.

They were kind to us when we were young.
They scarred us as we grew.
They took our hand and said, "Don't worry."
"Things get better all the time."

They helped us up and down.
They threatened to condemn us.
They washed our hands and our feet.
How did we deserve such love?

They all are still marching beside us:
From young to old to dead.
We watch and listen and wonder
At all they did and all they said.

Strapper John listened to the fading last notes of Handy's guitar. He noted that the instrument was old, but very well kept. He also noted how, for a few minutes, the world had gone away. The rhythm of the music, the blending of Handy's rough but melodic and emotive vocal, the smell of the crops being harvested through the open window had all cast a spell. He had just relaxed and let go. It was a peacefulness that John Jordan had sorely missed since Ian's decision. Being there with Handy, and all that Handy was, relaxing and enjoying life, was a relief for him. A relief from worry and regret; a relief from uncertainty; for even though life on Emerald Earth was everything a human being could ask for, he had learned the hard way that no matter how carefully plans were laid, that no matter how hard we work to deny it, in the end life still held its surprises, good and bad; some we are ready for, some for which we will never be ready. Handy was looking at him. Not surprisingly. There were only the two of them in the room. They had been there for over an hour, together for over two. For John, it had been the best two hours he had had in longer than he cared to remember. Handy was talking to him. "Are we out of whiskey? Please say that's not true." Handy was holding an empty glass and the empty bottle. John laughed. He stood up and went to a cabinet nearby. He opened the doors and revealed at least a dozen bottles more.

"We are never out of whiskey, Handy."

48. Thanksgiving Dinner (2)

Farson wanted to have Thanksgiving dinner on *Songbird*. Karina said the cabin in North Conway would be better. Farson wanted to show off his new barge. Karina wanted people to be comfortable. They talked it over. Farson offered his best, most persuasive arguments, covering every detail, explaining it all to the skeptical Karina. The cabin it was. Farson then said that he would actually hunt for the turkey himself. The old woods were full of them, he said, and he had a hunting license, and he had a gun: a shotgun. "Who's going to pick all that buckshot out and pluck the bird? Sam's dead, Farson. You know you're not going to do it."

"I could do it."

"But you're not going to, and we both know it. I'm not going to do it, Farson. So who's going to do it?"

"Why don't you handle the food and I'll help you in any way I can?"

"Now, that sounds like a plan."

Farson ordered the robot to send out the invitations, if you could call them that.

In discussions with Karina — nothing was ever done without discussions with Karina — they had decided on the guest list. As usual, eight was the target number. Voul and Viera, Jim Peterson, Ian and Belnad, the three robots, and they decided to leave the question of whether Brittany was ready or not up to Ian, but they doubted she would attend. And, in an enlargement, they decided to invite Repoul Bensn, out of respect for all that he had done. So that came to a possible ten plus Farson and Karina. "I doubt that CT<<Dinsil2371 will attend, considering their current level of activity, but I could be wrong. That would be our biggest dinner ever, an even dozen."

Brittany's decision to come, they felt, would be too far-reaching. Leaving Emerald Earth at this point would be difficult for her. Karina felt that Repoul would decline, in the Sker way — out of his unwavering sense of duty — regardless of the tiny time loss. "So that would put us back to just eight again," she clarified.

"You never know, Karina. Sometimes a 'summons' from me carries extra weight. I'm thinking five plus three will be eight guests and us: ten." Farson looked at her, smiling. She was thinking it over. Voul, Viera, Jim, Ian, Belnad, ZZ<<Arkol25609, Brittany, and who else? Karina smiled back, knowing something was left unsaid.

"Well, if what I think you're thinking happens, wouldn't that be interesting?"

"Yes, it would."

Karina's smile had a tinge of irony. *Things are never exactly what they seem to be with Farson.* She noticed he was smiling back.

Voul and Viera accepted quickly. Having previously had the experience of a "dinner with Farson," there was no question. They didn't want to miss this one.

Jim Peterson accepted and was excited at the prospect of seeing his daughter again, but in the back of his mind, he wondered if that would happen. Karina warned him it was only a possibility.

Ian Jordan and Belnad Goethe took awhile to respond. Farson and Karina speculated that the whole of Emerald Earth was discussing all of the possibilities and potential permutations of such visits outside of Emer control. Ultimately, they agreed to come, but only after getting Farson to agree that they would handle their own transportation to and from North Conway.

ZZ<<Arko125609 agreed to attend, of course. CT<<Dinsil2371 declined after some discussion. He felt he was getting too old for such excitement, but Farson knew that his current assignment was the real reason. *<<I would like to participate in such a gathering, Farson, but as you know, my circuitry is not of the highest, most sophisticated version, and such frivolities would be completely lost on me. I would be what you might call a party pooper.>>* Farson and Karina found that comment hilarious and that CT's discussion of his circuitry and the humor he had employed was a clear sign that he was making fun of them and that while he would not attend, he would be monitoring the situation as though he were there. They heard nothing at all from ID>>Karo28689. They felt that she did not deem the invitation worth a response.

Whether or not she appreciated the inclusion was also a mystery. The silence from her was deafening. Farson and Karina discussed it at length and decided that it was a mistake to think she would like to get together with them. *Wishful thinking.* ID>>Karo28689 was the highest-ranking robot they had ever encountered. She was always courteous and without any sort of arrogance or standoffishness. When she was around, the other robots deferred to her in all things. Farson had even seen other robots seem to bow slightly in her presence. He knew she was something special and was disappointed that she had not at least responded. "Kinda rude, don't you think, Karina?"

"Can a robot be rude? It would seem outside of their protocol parameters." Farson knew she must be right, but still, it bothered him.

"So it would seem, but that's how it feels."

They both knew that inviting Handy would have been a waste of time. He was extremely happy on Emerald Earth, and they knew he wouldn't want to leave under any circumstances. *He's earned it.*

<<You got that right, Farson.>>

No response at all from Brittany, but Ian assured them that she had received the invitation.

The menu was going to be standard fare. History has it that the first Thanksgiving occurred in Plymouth, Massachusetts, around 1621. Four hundred and eighty-four years later it still survived on the Moon and SkyKing, at least for the crew, if not the Skers themselves. To say it "survived" on the Moon would be an understatement. As all things Moon, Thanksgiving was an excuse to party like there was no tomorrow.

Viera's only question about this particular Thanksgiving was aimed at the timing. The Moon was a busy place. "I can't miss *our* celebration. That's a given." Farson had assured her that the real time she would be off the Moon was less than eight seconds.

"Last time it was almost eleven seconds, Farson. People noticed."

"I'm getting better at it."

The menu turned out to be relatively simple and, of course, in Karina's hands it would be ChainFoods-based and delicious. Turkey and all the trimmings: green beans, sweet potatoes with baby marshmallows, mashed potatoes, gravy, biscuits, stuffing, of course, and several desserts. Karina had arranged through SkyKing and the Moon to actually obtain the raw ingredients for a pecan and a pumpkin pie. Ice cream was a famous specialty of ChainFoods chefs everywhere, so that was easy.

"You are actually going to make the pies?" Farson was astonished.

"Yep. Believe it or not, I have Hattie's recipes. She taught me." Farson had never seen Karina make anything and doubted the veracity of this statement.

"You mean you watched her make it. Right?"

"Yes. Over and over." They both knew what that meant.

"Maybe you should watch a few more times, Karina. Disasters at these dinners are to be avoided at all costs." He was verging on taunting her. She had never let him forget the "Paella Disaster," when he had served a burnt and inedible main course at a party they had hosted. The realization of his utter failure and embarrassment in front of their best friends still hurt whenever he thought of it.

"You should know, Farson."

49. Brittany on Emerald Earth (4)

Brittany was lost in thought. It was kissing Ian that had changed everything. She was still kissing Ian. There seemed to be no rush, no hurry. *We've got all the time in the world.* It was like a suspension of time. She had no idea how much time had or had not elapsed. It didn't matter. It was a moment that captivated and continued. She was so close to him that it was enveloping her. Like before, but now it was just the two of them. For the first time in her life, she had no thought beyond the moment she was living. She felt free like a little girl kicking up her feet in Sky Lake. Or like skydiving on the Moon toward an unknown landing. Or like running in the engine rooms of SkyKing free and unconfined by loss or pain. It was a moment of discovery and sharing; a moment of passion and patience; a moment of love like those childish indulgences in fantasy as she had grown up; it was a gift of untold proportions from a man like no other she had ever met. She kept thinking *He will break away. This can't go on forever.* But he didn't and it did. In their suspended moment of warmth and desire, he wasn't going anywhere. *Reassurance.* Brittany always expected people she loved to leave. What she was now feeling was such a deep sureness that her pain and fear dissipated, her emotions melting into a new potion of confidence never before experienced. She opened her eyes. She saw his slowly open, moist with feeling undeniable. Looking into each other's eyes, a new world appeared deep in their thoughts; a transformation had occurred. *Us.*

"What just happened?" she asked. Ian was considering how to answer.

"We just happened." He knew that in all the years of planning and simulations, what had just happened had never happened before. In all those years of observation and research, when he had chosen Brittany as the person they wanted for the first true, physical contact from the outside, nothing close to this had ever been detected or predicted. But this – what just happened – was not part of any plan or paper he had ever seen or written. Through all those years, he had found a deep happiness in the Emer ways. It was always assumed that the first Earth person would assimilate, learn their ways, and off everyone would go as before. This was beyond their planning. This was something no one could have anticipated. Brittany had changed everything for the Emers. And for Ian.

"What does this *mean*, Ian?" He was thinking over his answer, carefully calculating a response, when, without knowing why, he answered her.

"It means that everything has changed." She could hear the thoughts behind the words.

"You mean Farson was right to keep us apart?"

"No, Brittany," he was still very close to her; he could feel the gravity of his emotions as though he was falling into her, pulled into her. She could feel it, too. "It means Farson was wrong."

Ian could feel someone was trying to communicate with him. He was mystified that this was happening as he was kissing Brittany. After a few more moments, he allowed it. It was Belnad.

<<*You have an invitation from Farson, Ian.*>> Ian could feel Belnad assessing the situation he had interrupted. <<*He is making dinner.*>> They both knew what that meant. But Ian knew things were different now. He held Brittany close to him. Belnad also knew that things were changing. Their intimacy was significant to him. <<*She is also invited. If you think she's ready.*>> Ian looked at Brittany and saw the recognition in her thoughts. Affirmation. She was easily following the conversation.

<<*She's ready.*>> Ian could see a smile forming in her eyes.

50. Uva's Stories (3)

They were still in the central lounge area of Uva's vast starship.

A ScreenMaster's barge is a highly customized vessel: first, because of its constant use, second, because many ScreenMasters spend their entire lives traveling on their barge, and, third, because the truth about being a ScreenMaster is that it can be – for most but not all – very lonely. So, many choose to make their barge a home.

Farson was up and walking around now. He had found that he was free of Uva's restraints. She had released him at the end of her story. Farson had played along. Her abilities were strong and her hold had been fierce. He could have broken the mental bonds, but not without a fight, and not without upsetting Uva. He had accepted the confinement. Now walking around, he began to appreciate the vessel.

Uva had gone to some other part of the ship and left him to his own devices.

He estimated that the ship's width and length were measured in many miles. The fastest way to move around in it was obviously to fly or to use The Screen. In his relaxed state, Farson was enjoying the moving pathway also provided. He was being whisked along in silence. It was as if he was standing still and the ship was moving around him. He could see the large array of monitors and windows that lined the ship's interior, apparently from end to end. There was, evidently, no one else aboard beside Uva and him. He knew the ship was traveling at near light speeds. Looking out, he marveled again at how large The Screen was, how vast the distances were that encompassed the hegemony of the ScreenMasters. Their systems overlaid everything like a mist covering a fertile valley. He knew that the ScreenMasters' ways were the color that shaded everything; the song that no one could forget; a thread that wove through everything and that no one could see.

He had now reached what he named the Aviary: an enormous jungle of trees, vines, giant ferns, and flowers of all descriptions. There was something that looked like a rose but was as big as the tallest tree; there were roots that seemed to swarm the floor like veins in all directions; there were a thousand umbrella plants, some as large as houses, all the colors of a rainbow; and, in the misting air, there actually was something that looked like a rainbow, but to Farson it was more like a multicolored vine that grew straight down from the faraway roof all the way to the floor, thousands of shoots and canes all blending minutely together into a living arc anchored at two ends. To Farson, this Aviary was too beautiful to look away from. He was enthralled and enchanted. He realized that the slipway had slowly stopped without him noticing. It had been slowing down as he became fascinated, as though it knew he needed more time to take it all in. Suddenly, there was a loud flapping sound followed by a whooshing, like something landing at high speeds. Farson was almost knocked over by the air thrusts around him of such force and direction. Then he realized that Uva had landed beside him.

"Where do you think you're going, Farson?" Despite the tremendous effort of her abrupt landing, she appeared unruffled and calmly at ease. The vegetation around was still shaking and adjusting as Farson regained his balance and answered her.

"I was looking for you," he said.

"Well, you've found me." She made an undefinable sound that approximated a high-pitched whistle with a low, slow clicking cadence that changed with varying levels of abandon. Farson immediately recognized it from his time with Uvo as Aristealian laughter. Her beautiful and excited face confirmed it. He was learning that their odd variations of laughter could easily scale from friendly and enjoyable to intimidating and fierce, depending on the circumstance. He was trying to estimate where this latest example ranked in that hierarchy when she spoke again. "Let's go back to the lounge. Exercise is over." He noticed that the slipway had elegantly resumed its motion, only now in the reverse direction. He also noticed that it was speeding up.

When they reentered the lounge, Farson noted that it was an entirely different place now. Instead of perch-couches and a subdued decor, it now resembled the jungle of the Aviary with the beautiful umbrella plants as the main decor element. Uva invited Farson to sit with her at a table with an empty moat around it. He could sit with his feet dangling over the edge and reach the table very easily. Uva's area was different somehow, and she seemed more comfortable and at home in the arrangement. Farson was somewhat ill at ease with a feeling of awkwardness he could not explain. His area was soft and in every way fitted for him. Perhaps it was the dangling feet, a feeling of being too small, that caused it. Uva gave Farson's apparent discomfort no thought at all as food and drink appeared with a wave of her small hand. She extended her great wings, flapped them twice and resettled them, almost out of sight, on her back where they seemed to disappear. Sitting across from him was a beautiful Aristealian woman, in the prime of her life. She was probably nearing six hundred years old. He could tell she was smiling at him. His thoughts were also very clear to her.

"What did you expect, Farson? That I would be pining away, a broken widow, alone and nowhere to go?" She didn't pause long enough for Farson to even begin to form an answer. "We live, Farson. We are *alive* like no other race. We radiate life. We relish it. We make the most of it. I still fly with the wild sense of adventure that every Aristealian cherishes, and I still hope for a life worth living. I am still a

ScreenMaster, Farson. Even though you have taken much away from me, I still retain much of what was. My love for Uvo is uninterrupted and unchastened by your reckless actions. Yes, he is gone, but for me, he is alive in my sky, and his beautiful eyes are my stars. You may think whatever you wish, Farson, but you would be well advised not to overestimate your power to control everything."

Farson was suddenly at the control of another starship. He was rushing through the departure protocols. Then he saw his hands reach for the controls and realized that they were not *his* hands. He knew that Uva had begun another story.

The hands on the controls were Aristealian, and they were his too because he could feel them as if they were his own. He was Uvo again, and their ship was leaving in a hurry. He could clearly feel Uvo's thoughts. *<<Let's get out of here.>>* There was an urgency approaching panic as the ship came to life and instantly accelerated, turning at an extreme attitude as the engines kicked in at full ahead. Farson glanced at the rear monitors and briefly saw Earth growing smaller and smaller, but he also noticed that it disappeared sooner than his perspective of increasing distance would have expected. Earth simply disappeared as Uvo's ship departed. There was a flash of purple, darker and colder-looking than Farson was used to in his own experience, and then the full power of the engines formed a ScreenLink, and they were gone in a blurring transposition onto The Screen. He could feel Uvo relax physically, but Farson knew Uvo was still agitated. Whatever he was running from was a serious matter for him. Farson could tell that Uvo knew he would never really get away. He was buying time. Farson shook his head in resignation as he realized, all too clearly, what Uvo was predictably intending to do next.

With the ship settled on its course, it wasn't long before Uvo were once again flying up and down the ship's great interior. He was again lapsing into that meditative state that he seemed to love so much. Farson knew he was trapped in the monotony of Uvo's trance. So as the hours started to go by, Farson felt Uvo gradually relaxing and going into that deep, fluid, lentissimo of slow, slow motion, moving back and forth, hour after hour, with an ease of methodical movement that seem to achieve a pleasing perpetuality and peace for him. Farson found himself being hypnotized by the long flowing strokes and the inhaling, exhaling motion that accompanied the wings on their way. It wasn't long before they were both lost in the profound quietude of Uvo's slowly increasing tranquility.

It was a dark day. The sun was pressing on the sky with a lack of effect as though its ebbing power was finally reaching the end. The air was cold on his wings and heavy like tethers trying to hold him back. But he flew on. The enclosing night was empty, as though a burnt-out remnant, a shamble of nowhere, a faint shadow of other nights when things were different. Uvo knew he was responsible. He knew there was no turning back now. It was do or die, keep going into a bleak prospect of uncertainty. On and on he flew.

Uvo could still hear Twill's horrible words and feel his scaly, claw-like hands on his feathers. Uvo had known what was coming and had said quietly on The Screen, as he faced the inevitability, <<*Farson, I'm coming.*>> as though in resignation and death he knew he would find his friend. Then, Twill's fateful words: <<*You're not coming, Uvo. You're going. You're dying. All that you were, all that you stood for is dying with you now. Your plans and your dreams of a different Screen were delusions, and that has taught the rest of us who remain much indeed. That is your legacy, Uvo. Total failure.*>>

Uvo only knew that he had to keep flying. In flight he was still alive and free. As long as he could keep flying, he could still be with Uva. *I can still be with Uva.*

Farson could feel the weakening of his wings and a tiredness growing like a disease invading, like a fear growing, like a destination too far to reach. He felt Uvo's mind wandering in exhaustion, losing concentration.

In Uvo's mind, he was landing in their nest, and she was waiting. He slid and fell on landing and stayed on the floor of their home, unable to rise, exhausted. He saw her tears and helpless anguish at his collapse. He saw the distress and torture in her mind. *Uvo is dying.*

Then Uvo and Farson were flying again, up and down the ship. Uvo's tormenting and falsely reassuring images of landing and sliding home were recurring over and over, again and again. He saw Uva's face and tears a hundred times. He felt Uvo's fear of dying, of never seeing Uva again. Over and over and over. They were flying up and down the ship's interior as it rocketed on its way. Farson's depth of intimacy with Uvo's doubt, regret, and sadness infused him deeply with all the same emotions, as though it were really happening to him. Farson's tears seemed to stream behind them both as they flew into oblivion. It was unbearable and never-ending.

Farson could feel the night closing in on them as the cold, dark day of Uvo's imagination had slowly faded away. He could see the planet's stars visible now at night. It seemed better to him somehow. Night was better than the day had been. How long could Uvo keep flying? Where was he going? The Aristealian's giant wings stroked on, as though the wind was water, and he was pulling the oars of some great ship with all his might. Farson could feel the strain passing down into Uvo's legs, pressing as though pushing on the air for every advantage forward. Every ounce of Uvo's strength was pressing onward now, the effort's toll growing with each debilitating beat of his wings. The harder he tried, the more easily death approached as though the door was opening on hinges oiled with his agony. The more the pain, the further it opened.

And then, he reached the end. Tumbling dying, exhausted in every way, Uvo was falling and falling and falling. The ground was coming up. The air warmed as the altitude diminished. The ground crushed Uvo's beautiful body as the immovable met the softness of his life, his memories crushed, his hopes dashed, his heart smashed with the unstoppable impact. Farson could feel the last feeble reaching of Uvo's mind, even in the midst of disaster. <<*Uva ... Uva ... Uv....*>> Farson could feel Uvo's death as if it were his own.

Farson awoke in a panic, as from a nightmare. He was disoriented. The emotions of Uvo's last thought had migrated to his mind, and he found himself, shedding painful tears, crying out Uva's name at the top of his lungs.

Then he was alone at the table. Uva was nowhere to be seen. He could hear her name still echoing through the starship.

51. What's Happening?

Karina was studying Farson. He seemed miles away, distressed and upset. "What's up, Farson? What's happening?" He was sitting at his desk in North Conway. The snow outside had mostly melted away, but it was still cold. The winter was chronologically over, but the ground was still hard as a rock, and the skies seemed determined to constantly threaten more snow.

Spring, in New Hampshire, comes slowly along, degree by degree, weakly propelled by the anticipation, memories, hope, and faith of the people who long for those few days of shorts and sandals and even a day or two when the beaches fill with sunbathers and children with shovels and dreams of castles and dams and the sound of soft waves. Sometimes it seems like it goes from winter directly to summer, leaving people to wonder, "What happened to spring?" Farson was looking out the window at an icicle trembling from the gutter. A drop of water was teetering to release from its tip. Farson watched and waited, but it just hung there as though deciding whether to fall or freeze. He was still in the throes of Uva's agony, thinking of her stories. He was wondering if they were over. Like the tenuous drop of ice water, he could not decide. If the stories were over, it meant the end of something important. If they were not over, it meant more pain and sorrow. He was thinking about Uva's beautiful face as she landed beside him in the Aviary. Farson now loved her, just as he had loved Uvo, but this love was damaged and flawed by his own actions. Farson knew he didn't kill Uvo, but he saw her point all too vividly and was helpless to offer a counterargument. She was right. Even now, his pain was hard to bear. How could *she* bear it? How could she go on? What was it that allowed her to go forward? Was it revenge? He felt that sting. Was it love? That hurt worse than revenge. His eyes moved up to the icicle again, just as the drop fell. He turned to Karina.

"Come here," he said, patting his knee. Karina came over and joined him on the rickety old leather chair by his desk. The wheels squeaked on the hardwood floor as she settled in, their heads together. He could feel her breath on his neck. It felt wonderful. "Uva has been telling me stories, Karina. It's been tough to hear it all. The way she tells them is very moving. It's been a rough patch. She wants me to feel her pain. She blames me for Uvo's death." Karina knew all of this, of course, but having Farson say it, and think it, added to her knowledge and understanding.

"She is right, of course."

He moved a little closer; she could feel his yearning for comfort, for relief. There was only so much she *could* do. But that, she knew with all her heart, she would always, always do.

Farson wandered around Uva's barge for the remaining months of the trip. He learned how to take care of himself onboard, finding food and drink, a small place to live, and pretty much everything he could possibly need. But he was alone. Uva never reappeared out of the jungle; she never sat down with that regal way of hers and told him more stories. *Spellbinding stories.* She never rearranged anything again, not the rooms, not his point of view. They never walked again together on the slideway. There were parts of the ship that were clearly off limits. Despite his curiosity, he went along with her solitude. Uva and Farson traveled on The Screen together for almost a year, but after that first month and the three stories, she stayed away from Farson. He missed her. He wanted to tell her what he had learned. He wanted to talk about it. For her, she now had no home other than *Rachis*, the name she gave her ship. Her homenest was a bad dream, a reminder of pain, a destination she avoided. Aristealia was her home, and the only solution she could accept was to orbit the planet. She was heading there as fast as her barge would go. Farson thought to leave and get on to other things, but something held him. Something told him, there could be one more story. If there was, he wanted to hear it.

Karina and Farson slept in their bed that night. It was a deep sleep for both of them, no dreams, in each other's arms.

52. The Elevation Protocol (3)

They never really discussed Karina's experience at her birth after that day. It did come up a couple of times, but her response was always the same to his entreaties to discuss it.

"Why? You already know everything." He didn't really have an answer. She was right; he did already know everything. But he tried a different tack.

"Tell me what you were thinking." Same exact response. Sometimes he would try to ask the question in such a way that Karina would have to change her response, like "Did you see the doctor's hands release your little head, almost as if on cue?" With these sort of questions – and he had several iterations – he was always met with that look; the tilted head meant to confuse in the face of Farson's pathetic apolaustic persistence in these details. He eventually gave up.

Now they were planning the next step in her "ScreenMaster-ness," as Farson put it. "This one will complete the (he paused here looking for the right word, one that she would understand), the ... the ..." She completed his sentence for him.

"Bond?" Farson was surprised when she said it. She was exactly correct.

"How do you know that?"

<<*You told me.*>>

For the final step in her Ascension, they were back in Indiana. Karina was surprised at that. "Why did I come back here?"

"It's a *long* story." This made Farson laugh; she caught the inflection and laughed along with him. Even though she didn't know the whole story yet, just the way Farson said it told her it would be a doozy. They enjoyed the joke together. Then Karina spoke.

"I hope I'm still laughing when this is over." Farson seemed to have not heard.

The Chamberlains had lived in Ellettsville, just a few miles from the University. Their house had been preserved as a historic site, until Karina moved back in, in her mid-eighties (old Earth years). The caretakers moved to a home next door, not pleased at the change, but who would have tried to stop her? She restored every inch of the grounds and building to exactly what they had been when she and Farson were growing up. There had been some accommodations. Easy floor-to-floor access, and an extra railing on the secret staircase. But other than those few adjustments, Karina felt right at home. Except for the fact that she was alone. "Where are you, Farson?" Her voice echoed as she walked up the polished, curving stairway to the attic. The slight echo hung in the air of silence that followed. She looked at him. His eyebrows went up. He was smiling.

"I must be somewhere, Karina, don't you agree?" She knew that he meant he was not dead, which she already knew, but Farson's comings and goings were a multifaceted mystery, and always had been.

"If I am eighty-six, you must be halfway to eighty-nine." She had been born on Friday night, around 11:30 p.m., July 31, 2064. Farson had been born two and a half years earlier on Sunday morning, 3:59 a.m., February 4, 2063.

"You're pushing it." Farson did not like discussions of age.

"Still. Are you in a nursing home?"

"Let's look around the house."

They had been heading up to the attic, her in front, but this idea of looking through the old house had turned them around. Karina did not need encouragement to delay the inevitable as she went back down the stairs. <<*No hurry for that yet.*>> Farson knew he had just given her a reprieve from what she was most afraid of. Farson also knew that a stroll through their memories in the house would do them both good.

They walked through their old home. The kitchen was the first stop. The secret staircase, which went from the kitchen, all the way to the attic, began, or ended, in the kitchen depending on whatever they had been doing, and which way they were going, as children. To both of them, it seemed that the staircase was always part of everything. Farson was remembering how many times Hattie had carried him down those stairs and into the kitchen, and sat him down at the table. It could have been breakfast. It could have been lunch. It could have been dinner. It could have been all three.

"That damn boy is up in the attic again? What is he always doing up there, for the love of God?" Sam looked at Hattie. He was enjoying her pseudo-anger, knowing it was all an act; knowing she would go up and get Farson; knowing that she would pick him up and tickle him all the while carrying him back down to the table; knowing how much she desperately loved it all.

When she came back with Farson, who was laughing and trying to free himself, Hattie, tickling him and holding on tight, Hattie said to Sam, "He won't be young like this forever, ya know." Sam knew. He knew how things change, how things never stayed the same. Hattie got Farson into his chair and then put a plate of oven-hot buttered biscuits, ham and eggs in front of him. Then she put a glass of fresh-squeezed orange juice on the table. Farson was already eating.

"I can remember the smell of those biscuits, Kari, like they are right here in front of me." He had taken his old seat at the table. Karina sat down in hers. Karina remembered coming down those stairs for the first time.

Hattie said, "What's wrong, Kari? You seem so sad." Karina had taken her time coming out of her room after her arrival in the Chamberlains' home. It had only been fifteen days since her party and her parents' death. It seemed like an eternity to her. Those first days in her new bedroom, a complete stranger in a new world, a strange but happy world, had been long and lonely. She could tell from the moment she had arrived, just five days after it all happened, that the Chamberlains' home was a good one, a safe one ... except for that horrid boy who began tormenting her. He would not stop. She stayed in her room, and that didn't even stop him; he taunted her from the hallway. Finally, she came out. This was the first time she sat at a chair at the table. It was just Hattie and her. Hattie's hand was on hers. She could feel the warmth. She liked Hattie right away. Karina looked into the deep brown eyes. The care and concern were obvious and genuine. Hattie asked Karina what she would like to eat.

"Nothing."

"You sure?"

"Yes." Hattie doubted it.

"Aren't you hungry?" Karina sighed, looking around for him.

"Yes, sort of. Can I eat alone? Can I go back to my room?"

Hattie wouldn't hear of it. It had taken six days to get her out of there. *No way she's going back now.*

<<*She didn't think that, Farson. You can't fool me.*>>

<<*I know, Kari, but it is apropos, you must admit*>> No response, just a look.

"Do you know what she made that day?"

"A grilled cheese sandwich. She made those great." Farson emphasized the word "great" almost like a tiger's soft growl.

"Where were you when this was happening?"

"That's the second time today you've asked me that."

53. Thanksgiving Dinner (3)

Voul and Farson were on the bridge of *Songbird*. Everything was running very smoothly, and the ship's position had not changed. They were exactly fifteen feet from the platform, which now looked more like a very thin ledge. "You stood on that thing?"

"It was bigger then, as I recall." Farson was mentally trying to remember, but that whole period of time from when the platform "opened" to when it "closed" was very fuzzy.

"Did you land on it?"

"I must have."

"Do you remember anything after that?"

"I think I tried to move a little closer for balance. I may fallen into it with the momentum of landing there."

"You fell toward the wall? Anything else?" They looked at each other. Farson reflexively moved toward the vessel's instrumentation yoke as though to move the ship. And then he backed his hands away. There was a look of impatience in his eyes, but Voul understood. Other things needed tending to right now. Some things had to wait.

"Timing is everything," he said.

People began to arrive without ceremony at Farson's North Conway cabin. They were dressed for the late winter season. Heavy coats and boots were still required. New Hampshire's winter was still bearing down, but thoughts of warmer days, and some slight changes, were teasing their way into winter's end.

Karina was the first to arrive. They were alone. "Farson, one of these times, let's have it somewhere where I can wear heels. A little bit of fancy can make for a lot of fun."

"Fun is exactly what I have in mind." She came over to him and took his face in her hands as though she might scold him, but instead kissed him on the lips. Time stood still. They lingered. They looked in each other's eyes. A few more seconds. Then time resumed. They were still in a warming embrace, in each other's arms. He whispered softly in her ear, his breath brushing her inner feelings, "I love you."

Her joking response to his untimely intensity – people were coming – was predictable. "Routier, do you ever think of anything except sex?" Then, with a knock on the door, Voul and Viera had arrived.

"No, Sitwory, I do not. You have trained me well."

Inside, the room was warm. Some fresh air was tentatively now allowed to filter in through timidly and slightly opened windows from the infinitesimally less frigid outdoors. A few of the guests on the doorstep might have remember the smell of warming earth, and feeling of fresh breezes teasing the trees, but most had been traveling in space all of their lives. Once inside, there were twice as many stuffed chairs and sofas as would be needed, and the enormous table, now with silver settings, was big enough for a feast. The armchairs around the table were softly padded, an invitation to everyone to take their time dining. The light was soft and easy on the eyes. The entire feeling was welcoming and promising. Voul and Viera entered the room with fond greetings and then moved to the couch by the quietly slow-burning fire, its warmth filling the room.

Jim Peterson and Belnad Goethe arrived next. Jim was dressed in the working uniform of the SkyKing commander. It was rumpled and perhaps not just cleaned, but clean enough. Jim looked great. His hair was still full and extravagant, like a boy's. His face showed some age, but more, it showed his great intelligence and good humor. Jim Peterson was always a welcome addition.

Belnad seemed uneven and wary. He was dressed in normal Emer attire: shimmering garments that changed with his mood and environment. At first it looked like he was expecting arctic conditions, but he quickly adjusted once inside the room. They, too, had chosen to come in from the outside through the front door. Karina had appeared directly in the room. She spoke to Belnad, knowing this was his first trip to old Earth.

"Hey, Bel, what's up?" The seven-foot Emer shifted his attention to her. The nickname was the first he had ever heard. He was easily accommodated under the cabin's cathedral ceilings. Still, he was exceptionally tall for the group. He was looking around for a chair that suited him, perhaps to move somewhat out of the spotlight. He found what he was looking for and smoothly sat down, sinking into one of the sofas nearest to the little fireplace. He settled in and that seemed to help him relax. He realized that Karina was subtly asking if everything was okay. She had noticed.

"It's just an Emer issue that came up as I was leaving. Nothing to worry about." Ian had contacted him concerning Brittany's decision to attend. They were uncertain as to how she would hold up, leaving Emerald Earth so soon. The discussion had turned on two topics: first, the technology involved, and, second, on Brittany's strength and adaptability. Ian had said no problem, she was ready. Belnad was worried and had argued that Brittany had no idea what could happen. Brittany had restated that as far as she was concerned everything was all set. "Your dad could be shocked," Belnad said. "True," she had said, "but he, too, is very adaptable." "It could diminish your time to decide," he said. "It won't make any difference," she said. "I'm an Emer now." Belnad, despite this confident statement, knew that he was still in doubt about what would happen. Karina seemed content, if still curious, with his response.

The robot came next. ZZ<<Arkol25609 appeared in a brief, slight flash of purple in the middle of the room. He scanned around, looking for his strategic spot. He found it and turned to Farson, bowing slightly in salutation. Farson

acknowledged it. <<*ScreenMaster Uiost, what is your pleasure?*
>>

<<*Same as before, ZZ<<.*>> The robot noted Farson's
inclusion of only one of his nomenclature aspects, taking
special note that it included the first directional component of
his version identifier. *A reminder?* <<*As you wish,
ScreenMaster.*>> The robot turned to Karina, who was
watching closely and said, "Hello, Karina. Here we go again."
She laughed out loud at the robot's sense of humor and odd
intonations. ZZ<<Arkol25609 sensed her affection.

"Is that humor you are attempting, ZZ? It was really
funny. Did you intend that?"

"Well, my programs are getting older, Karina, so you are
right to question if I intended to be risible, or if some minor
malfunction had occurred. But, in this case, I *was* attempting
to be amusive. It is a social occasion after all, is it not?" This
made Karina laugh again.

"You are on a roll, Z. Keep it up."

"A 'role' as in a character in a play, or a 'roll' as in a yeast
and flour mixture that is baked and eaten?" This caused
Karina to bend over slightly with more laughter. She began to
turn away from the robot, pivoting her forearm and hand
toward him quickly until it was perpendicular to the floor,
palm out, as though acknowledging his mastery of the
moment. The robot watched the movement with interest. She
was now moving toward Viera. ZZ<<Arkol25609 was
attempting to calculate the probability alternatives that he had
offended her, or that she was pleased with his vocalizations,
when a new individual appeared in the room. No door-
knocking for this guest.

She was young, probably just twenty-two years old, with
straggly, but nice, slightly wavy, long dirty-blonde hair, some
roots unapologetically and perhaps confidently, showing. She
was dressed in black slacks and a brilliant white top under a
muted orange blazer. She was carrying a large scuffed leather

bag by its longish rolled leather handles, although it also had a shoulder strap dangling that looked well used, but not needed at the moment. Her face was clear but expressing some level of impatience, or concern, or possibly worry. It was hard to tell. Farson walked over to her. <<*This is a surprise. What should I call you?*>>

<<*Ida. It's a name I have always loved.*>> Everyone in the room had turned to the new guest, and the room was quiet. She could tell he was surprised at her appearance. <<*How did you expect me to come to your party, Farson, in eight-plus feet of bronzed alloy? There will be plenty of other robots around here to fill the void.*>> Farson turned and addressed the group as a whole.

"I would like you all to meet ID>>Karo28689. Despite the numbers, rest assured she is one of a kind." There was a silence as they assimilated the fact that the new young, beautiful, well-dressed, and smiling visitor was a ScreenKeeper. No one in the room, other than Farson and Karina, had any idea that this form was even possible for the robots. "And just before you start to wonder if there are any others like her operational now, the answer is no. The ScreenKeepers have precise rules. Masquerading as a human is definitely a rare, rare intrusion. Except in this case. She is their leader. ID>>Karo28689 is the highest-ranked individual in their species." People looked at ZZ<<Arkol25609 who had clearly bowed in her direction at the first moment of her appearance and had backed away into the corner he had earlier identified. He was now still as stone, though his visor was strobing. The room seemed unsettled by this new event.

"I won't bite," ID>>Karo28689 said in a very congenial unmistakably human tone and voice. "And call me Ida. I wouldn't miss this party for the world."

54. Brittany and Ian

Brittany and Ian were inseparable. To him, she came from prehistoric times. To her, he came from a far, distant, and compelling future. Their present was all.

Figuring each other out, if their relationship had been researched and its success estimated by Emer scientists and scholars (which it was), it could have seemed to be an equation with incompatible variables with unknown and perhaps unknowable elements embedded at every turn with undefined and unpredictable abstractions that would not resolve to any real degree of precision or to any measurable alignment toward certainty, and that would clearly result in endless insolubles repeating into an infinity of vexing failures. The relationship's success was unforeseeable at best, to say the least. The scientists found their study to be woefully impractical, opening more areas of inquiries than it resolved. Their most important conclusion was that any contact of the nature contemplated in the extensive research should be approached slowly and incrementally with extreme caution and circumspection. This did not happen.

Brittany and Ian had fearlessly approached each other, throwing caution to the wind. Their affection for each other had quickly ignited like a fuse. The scientists were waiting for an explosion or a bright flash of elucidation. Some of them worried and then recalculated; some of them tried to build modeling paradigms to influence events; some of them wisely realized that events underway were like the proverbial bell they could not unring. The volume and strength of its tolling was unstoppable. The topic of discussion now was "For whom the bell tolls," as they liked to call it. For them, it was still an experiment. For Brittany and Ian, it was a leap into the unknown that they made together with the enthusiasm of mutual attraction. Like explorers landing in a new world, having only themselves, they became inseparable.

Even in council chambers she now accompanied him. Belnad Goethe adjusted easily. To be fair, the entire planet was in full participation anyway. She had certain qualities that Belnad especially enjoyed: She was very bright, she was voraciously inquisitive, she wore the Emer embodiment extremely well, with a unique style and bearing as though she were not an interloper, but a new standard. Her presence was always welcome. She had a unique perspective, and, to him, engaged and driven as always, she was a source of enjoyment, relaxation, and pleasant surprises. He really liked her. It was mutual. Belnad and Brittany became friends.

Ian wanted to talk to her about the dinner party. He knew she knew about it, but he felt that he understood things Emer that she might not yet fully appreciate. Coming to Emerald Earth had changed her. She seemed content with that, almost ecstatic. She traveled easily within the planet's boundaries, and on the occasions when the two of them had ventured outside on The Screen, she had been a worthy companion, never missing a beat, and following the Emer ways with ease and engagement and precision, which endeared her deeply to everyone.

In fact, at this moment they were on a desert world in an unidentified system. The Emers were in the process of "forming emeralds," as they put the adjustments of various planetary compositions into something easier for the inhabitants to live with. The Emers tended to make the most of each planet's natural strengths during the transformation process. Brittany had learned that they were nearing the successful alteration of six planets, building on strengths and limiting the weaknesses within each planetary ecology. This one had accepted a growing population, still many years from its imposed limit, and which was, in fact, a vast desert tribe, nomadic by its nature, restless in its beliefs, and uncertain of its changing destiny. Ian had come to discuss the water situation. Water was the one substance that Ian and the Emers felt there could never be enough of. This planet, though mostly dry, had the needed raw materials – hydrogen and oxygen and many other vital elements – in superabundance. The question was whether to begin the process of aquanizing the planet, or to follow the ancestral desert and tribal ways, which had created lack and poverty and had empowered the chiefs as despotic rulers. Ian was sure he could persuade them to at least begin a test, in an isolated area, to show them what wonders could occur. They had resisted for a hundred years. This was his third visit to the planet, and, of course, this time, Brittany went with him.

They were meeting in what their traditions called an "ashās," based on the nomadic structures of their distant past, but for the rulers, the rudimentary subsistence of their history had now become extravagance. Their meeting area was beautifully appointed and lavish. Brittany found the interior to be amazing. *Wealth and conspicuous abundance.* She knew that even the poorest on the planet were far better off than at other times in their history, but she also knew from discussions with Ian that things had reached a point of decision. The room they were in held at least a thousand people, mostly members of one enormous ruling family. The leaders had not arrived yet, deeming it beneath their status to arrive in time to wait for their guests. Ian was used to the pomposity of this planet's "elite." They were benevolent, but often callous to the hardships their indulgence inflicted on others below them. Ruling, they said, was difficult on this planet, human beings being what they are. It took years of training and a well-developed enculturation to institutionally sustain everything. It took a lifetime of sacrifice and dedication, they said, sacrificing the simple pleasures of family life and everyday living. In so many worlds, Ian had noticed that the leaders became isolated and aloof, not by inclination, but by perceived necessity. "Rulers are few and troubles are many." This dictum from the ages was all too true, he knew. It had taken its toll. It was easy to criticize them, but Ian, as an Emer, had learned that understanding always precedes agreement. He had learned to like the rulers, and they had come to respect him and his ideas.

"Our system is much better." Ian turned to see Brittany as she plainly spoke words he had hesitated to say himself. His eyes seemed to relax in the light of her countenance. He felt as though just looking at her was nourishing. "I'm your eye candy," she had laughingly said of his lingering gazes. She seemed embarrassed whenever the topic of her beauty as an Emer came up. She could always tell what he was thinking about. But now she wanted to discuss other matters. "Everyone knows everything on Emerald Earth. The information is always right there if you want it, when you want it. Here, information is still a scarce commodity and, like the stupid money that almost ruined my world, these people are using it to boost themselves up and to keep others down, in the dark." Ian knew that the certainty in her opinions was a strength, but Emers knew that all things are relative and changing. Hard opinions, like judgements, were studiously avoided. "They need to change the atmosphere." They both knew what that would mean.

She could see the rulers arriving now. They were dressed in white robes and headdresses of great elaboration and color. These tall wardrobe accessories stood out like bright flowers blooming in the desert. Brittany giggled at their ostentatious affectation.

<<*No giggling, Brittany. It could sink our discussions.*>> He had switched to nonverbal communication because overhearing her irreverent comments, and his reaction, could infuriate their hosts, who were on the edge already with just having the two Emers on their planet. Brittany was the first female Emer they had ever seen.

<<*Okay. I'll be on good behavior.*>> Ian had heard that before.

The discussions went on for four days. While Ian was hard at work explaining, demonstrating, and negotiating, Brittany began to wander around.

Whenever Emers left Emerald Earth, a small field of amber and green surrounded them like a body halo. It was generated from a very small device embedded within them, which was also an extremely accurate scanning tool, a highly sophisticated health and vital signs monitor, a medical responder, a translator, a defense mechanism of great power, and a transporter in an emergency. The device also generated the clothing Emers chose to wear, was a protective field around them, and supplied the air they breathed.

Brittany had been looking around the village for the past two days. *I can only take so much negotiating.* She had discovered a smaller inter-family unit that she enjoyed immensely, and they had invited her back to their home again today. She was sitting in their living room, relaxing over what she decided was a dessert tea. It was invigorating and relaxing at the same time; earthy and herbal, very enjoyable. <<*Like being with you, Ian.*>> He was in the middle of an explanation of the effect the aquanizer devices would have on the planet's dune shifts that were always occurring. These shifting dunes, over time, had changed the nomadic traditions of a constantly moving population into a world with a settled people. The dunes were now cherished as essential to the culture of Simaris, as the planet called itself. Just as her thought had come to him, Ian was clarifying a fine point about how the water produced would be supremely natural. On a dry planet, water and moisture often took on aspects of divinity. The Simaris people wanted nothing but the real thing. "In the end," he was saying, "the pureness of Simaris water will be enhanced by the quality of the ingredients. Your people will ..." and then Brittany's duplicitous and arousing thought had come in. He paused in his description, a little surprised at her impetuousness, using mental communication as though a conversation was in progress, casually, almost offhandedly. His mind was filled with images of the subject she had just introduced. They had been together now for almost six months. Exploration of this topic of "being together" was a constant theme in conversations with Brittany. She loved the Emer ways, but Ian knew she wanted more. Dignitaries at the table were now looking at him, waiting awkwardly. Now, with forced extra feeling to emphasize continuity, he concluded, repeating the starting phrase, "Your people will benefit from the new abundance, and they will love you more for protecting their heritage and building their future. The aquanizers will become part of Simaris's culture, and your past will forever be its guide." There was a brief hesitation and then thunderous applause. His days of hard work had paid off. He was wondering if Brittany's interruption had somehow changed the outcome. Up to that point, Ian had been struggling to tie it all together. His untimely hesitation seemed to impart extra sincerity and conviction to his listeners. He thought, *She is from the past, but she is becoming my guide to the future.*

<<*You were so flustered, Ian. You're just lucky that you got it right.*>>

Over the next few hours, he wrapped up the successful negotiations – they were ready to try a test in the southern hemisphere, the poorest area of the planet. They decided to give the new area a name. After some discussion they all decided unanimously on "Azure." Ian could tell the demonstration was off to a good start. There were still many hours of negotiations and work left to do. Brittany spent the extra time with her new friends.

They were a small family of three hundred, living in the southern region. They were a town all their own. The patriarch was a man in his eighties, she thought, and he was handsome, strong, and highly intelligent. His family was well-enough off, but he obviously wanted more. The family had many children. She loved them and spent as much time with them as she could. The people were dark-skinned and athletic. Their scientific advances were impressive, but, in Brittany's estimation, had achieved only the levels of sophistication of a very early twentieth-century nation on old Earth. People struggled with energy, food resources, and even shelter, although life was getting better. Education had achieved a primacy, and despite the rulers' wishes to control it planet-wide. Learning, at this level of society, was virtually unrestricted and unbounded. Teachers were held in the highest esteem. The children looked at Brittany, with her amber and green aura, her stature, her clothing, and obvious power as though she were a god ... at first. Then they saw her as a teacher. When she started playing hide and seek with them, using her transporter capabilities, and then running after them out of nowhere, grabbing one of them and disappearing, only to reappear farther away, they laughed and loved her and asked her to "Do it again!" over and over. She became a friend.

Because of the translation system the Emers used, she could communicate fluently but with a humorous accent which only doubled the fun. She would spend hours with the children, teaching, playing, laughing, and helping them. The family's traditional teachers now looked forward to her visits. Brittany became closest to one special child, Riayda. She was a small child, with two older brothers. She was eleven years old. The calendar of Simaris was very close to old Earth's, so Brittany immediately connected with the girl when she heard the story of her father's death. Through tears, she heard Riayda tell of watching it happen and being hurt herself. The girl's hand had been badly damaged. It was almost useless, and she always tried to keep it out of sight.

When Ian came, late in the day, to the village and said they should begin their departure preparations, he saw the tall and beautiful Brittany on the ground, in the sand, playing a child's game of toss and grab with the children. Despite disparate appearances, he could tell that the children had accepted her as one of their own. Brittany was saddened with his news that they would soon be leaving. The children around her pleaded with her not to go.

<<*We can't stay here forever, Brittany. We have other things to attend to.*>> She wrinkled her forehead and then moved her eyebrows up and down.

<<*What are we talking about?*>> He laughed.

<<*It's time to go.*>>

<<*Just one last thing. I'll catch up with you.*>> As he transported to the departure point, she turned to Riayda and took her hands in her own, extending her amber and green field slightly. Brittany could feel her internal device scanning the girl, and as she looked into the child's eyes, she saw an astonishment as feeling returned to her hand. Brittany held on tighter. Riayda was struggling to look at her hand, but Brittany spoke to her, "Riayda, be patient for a moment with me. Relax. All is well." The child relaxed into her arms, and deeper into Brittany's aura. Brittany held her up as she was briefly overcome. In a few more moments, Brittany lowered her to the ground and released her. Soon the child looked up and saw Brittany standing over her. She sat up and immediately was looking at two perfect little girl hands. Riayda could not believe her eyes. She wiggled her fingers and held her hands together out in front of her, comparing them. *Perfect.* She stood up, shaking with joy, and looked at Brittany. A dream come true; an answered prayer. Riayda had the thought to run to her mother, and she took off, running for home, holding her hands high. Then she stopped suddenly and turned back to thank Brittany again, but there was

nothing there except the vast stretch of sand as far as her eyes could see. Her golden friend was gone.

Riayda turned back toward home and to her mother, and, padding on bare feet in the warm sand and sun, running now, toward a more hopeful future she could never have predicted.

Brittany and Ian were soon on The Screen heading home as well. The departure ceremony had been brief but confirming. They were also heading into a future that Ian knew now contained many unpredictable things. Like Riayda, he felt like running toward it.

> <<*What did you do back there?*>>
> <<*I fixed an unfairness and created a brighter future.*>>
> <<*That's exactly what I did.*>>
> <<*Great minds think alike, Ian.*>>

Belnad spoke to Ian across the eons of The Screen. <<*Is she really coming?*>>

<<*Yes, she certainly is. I will come first. She will come when she thinks the time is right. It's a big step, as you know.*>>

<<*Fair enough. See you at dinner.*>> This small jest by Belnad made Ian laugh; neither one of them had eaten in decades. He looked over at Brittany traveling beside him on The Screen. *She is changing everything.*

55. Thanksgiving Dinner (4)

The history of the pilgrims' first Thanksgiving in 1621 is such a well-known story in human history that there is no reason to repeat it. Everyone knows. As old Earth calmed down in the late decades of the twenty-first century, there was much to be grateful for, and Thanksgiving's celebration spread through all the nations as the one non-religious, non-partisan, non-nationalistic holiday that the people of the United States of Earth could celebrate together. And they did. For Farson and Karina, growing up in rural Indiana, Thanksgiving was an all-out cuisine explosion, that shook Hattie's kitchen to its core, testing her abilities to use every stove and cooking device simultaneously in the preparation of a meal that her little family would never forget, year after year. Even in Hattie's vivid imagination and dedication, she could not have known that far, far into the distant future her recipes would still be relished and followed as though roadmaps to happiness, that the memories of the tastes she had perfected would always be what Farson and Karina wanted on that special day. She might not have been able to know all of that future history, but as Hattie was preparing her famous pecan pie, she was well aware of the young girl's intense interest. "Good Lord, Kari, you're staring at me. It makes a body nervous." Karina stepped back.

"Sorry. I just want to learn how you do it."

"That's gonna take time and practice, girl, not staring."

<<*What are you doing, Karina?*>>
<<*Learning to make a pecan pie.*>>
<<*I thought so. Let me know when it's ready.*>>

She had watched Hattie many times. She had seen Hattie's beautiful hands mixing the brown sugar, white sugar, and eggs. She could see the muscles in her forearms flexing and relaxing. She had watched her fingers squeezing the filling ingredients and mixing them with handcrafted energy and expertise. Karina had watched and watched, looking for any details that would give her the secrets. The egg whites and yokes oozed into the sugar, the brown and white sweetness blending together, and then in went the chopped pecans, melted butters, milk, flour, a splash of vanilla, and the mixing and squeezing and blending of ingredients continued, again with that energy and determination, until, in Hattie's opinion it was perfect. "That's it," she would always say. Karina studied this whole process until she knew it "like the back of her hand," as Hattie's favorite gauge of knowledge acquisition expressed it.

The piecrust, the holy grail of successful pie making was, and always had been, the fateful, unavoidable final challenge to which the bakers of pies must always rise. "Forks don't lie," Hattie always said.

The ingredients were pedestrian: flour, sugar, salt, butter, shortening, and a little water. Across all the centuries, it had always been the same. But some people got compliments. "What a wonderful crust!" they would exclaim with dessert dishes almost licked clean. Others saw their dreams of success being scrapped, half eaten, down into the drain. Some pies were the topic of conversation for years. Others were simply eaten as a dessert, a fading shadow of the sought-after savor and fame. Karina had high hopes, and a wavering confidence. She always noted, however, that Hattie's expertise was on her side and her voice in her mind.

"It all comes down to two things, Kari. Get the amounts 'xactly right and never, ever use a machine when making a pie. It's all in the hands." Hattie held hers up. They were perfect, strong, female hands that could change the universe with a pie. Karina was looking at her own hands now. They seemed scrawny and weak in comparison. "Sam makes the best blueberry pie I ever tasted," Hattie stated with vicarious pride. "Never had any better, even when I make it." She was smiling. "He's got great hands." As she was walking away, Karina heard her say something else. "Use unsalted butter, keep it cold, and use ice water at the end; go slow."

"What?" Karina needed to hear that again.

"And don't over-knead it. That's a killer right there." Smiling, Hattie left the kitchen. Eleven-year-old Karina, now alone, looked around as though standing in an arena waiting for a daunting opponent to arrive. She grabbed a pencil and paper and desperately tried to write down what she had just heard Hattie say. She thought to herself, *one more time and I should have it down pat.*

There was a knock on the door. Farson walked over and opened it. Ian Jordan was standing out in the cold on the doorstep. He was alone. Farson stepped aside, welcoming the new guest into the room. "No need to knock, Ian, we were all expecting you." Ian surveilled the room like a scientist assessing an experiment. His eyes went to Belnad first, a slight nod of acknowledgement. Belnad was talking to Karina. Then he looked over at Voul, who he had known in his studies, and who he also knew had a long and special relationship with Brittany. Voul and Ian had never met, until now. Their eyes found each other: two men, six thousand years apart. One was the son of Ban Jonsn and the leader of the historic Skers. The other was a resident of Emerald Earth, and all that that entailed. They looked at each other long enough that others in the room noticed the interaction. Ian went over to Voul and extended his hand. Voul took it. Then Ian put his other hand on Voul's, and spoke to him for the first time.

"You will never know what an honor it is to meet you." Viera, who had been desperately missing Voul ever since he had left on *Songbird*, took this opportunity to move in between them and put her arms around her husband. She pressed her full body against his. Then she kissed him on both cheeks and hugged him even closer. Then she kissed him on the lips. Voul stiffened a little at this public display. Viera turned her head to Ian, smiling, still hugging Voul. "It's nice to finally meet someone who feels about Voul the way I do." She leaned toward Ian, but obviously she didn't want to break the embrace. Ian thought, *She reminds me of Brittany. No boundaries.* Suddenly, Ian could tell in her eyes that Viera had heard his thoughts. He wasn't embarrassed, but he did remember Belnad's cautionary words as he left for the cabin:

"Never underestimate them. They are us, after all." She finally stepped away, reluctantly, still holding Voul's hand, and said to Ian, "Is Brittany coming?" Before he could answer, Ian saw Jim Peterson looking over at him. His heart skipped a beat. *Brittany's father.* He couldn't keep his eyes from widening slightly. Ian's thoughts were spinning in the moment. *This is intense.* Then he realized that Commander Peterson obviously had the exact same question as Viera.

Belnad and Ian had been working on an experiment concerning the composition and the "intention" of sanidine, a mineral often found in sand, but with origins in volcanoes. Today, their research had arrived at a dark green, very common piece of felsic granite. Their instruments allowed them to trace the rock back in time. They could magnify the timeline to a degree that it would be difficult to fully explain to non-Emers, but it would be something like ten to the tenth to the one-hundredth to the one-thousandth, and that would not even come close to the full expression of the magnification details they could see. The Emers had long ago decided that looking through history, and all of its tributaries, needed a much, much closer look. Their instrumentation inventions and innovations became like temporal windows, allowing them to actually see the dark mysteries of life, and its evolutions through time, with their own eyes.

"Do you see that, Ian?" Ian was watching closely. He knew what Belnad was talking about. There was saltwater in the rock's earliest years. The saltwater trace was billions of years old. But more interesting than its age was the fact that in the saltwater there was a clear indication of vegetation.

"How could Catherine have known?" Belnad knew Ian understood the question. How *could* she have known that seaweed was the chemistry key to opening her famous ChainFoods string? How could she have known that the barrier between expectation and fact would collapse and the result would supply the exact variable to resolve her equations?

Ian asked, "Do you think she was surprised?" Belnad was nodding his head in silent appreciation. Ian's insights always made him happy.

Ian had come a long way. From the broken boy on the harvester to a full Emer scientist, keenly incisive now, learning things that no one else had ever known. From his bloody arrival and his smashed bones, to finely tuned intellect and dedicated researcher, Belnad knew that Ian was a once-in-a-lifetime companion on his journey of discovery. It was Belnad who had discovered the old ScreenMasters' weakness, and it was Belnad who defeated their imprisonment and set Emerald Earth free. It was Belnad who discovered the other others. It was Belnad who had saved Ian Jordan.

"She was a genius, Ian. A human genius. It happens. It's rare even now, but it happens. She could see things where others saw nothing. She could believe things that others couldn't even imagine. She found the evidence of things they knew did not exist. Her mathematics were flawless. Today it all seems so obvious because she triumphed over the unknown. She is still teaching us. Even now. Even you and I, Ian. She is still teaching us right now. Emerald Earth lives on because of her."

Belnad was always studying the life of Catherine Peters Jacobson, and he had all the time in the world to do it. Belnad had been studying her for hundreds of years before Ian showed up. Ian's injuries had been substantial and devastating. His father, Strapper John Jordan, was beside himself with guilt and worry over the accident and its consequences. Belnad had taken the boy into surgery. Technically, Ian was dead, but Belnad knew there was hope. He worked for many, many hours that first night. Belnad remembered the exact moment when Ian's heart began to beat again. *Born again.* He remembered when Ian's eyes opened. The Emer technology had saved Ian's life.

In their years together the two of them had explored the amazing life of Catherine Jacobson; it was not like merely meeting her and getting to know her; it was not like watching a movie of her life; they actually and intimately explored her life in ways that left nothing unknown. Her physical chemistry, her birth, her death, her marriage, her sensuality, her reproductive sequence, everything from start to finish, the birth of her only child, and her own surprising and wasteful death. They studied her until they knew everything about her that there was to know. They had explored the possibility of changing the timeline and saving her, but three thousand alternatives later, Belnad could never find one that would be acceptable or possible. He concluded that her death was a central element in human history and could not be changed. Together they had spent months and years with her as she moved through her life. They actually saw it all, many times, and then they went to work. In the tragedy of her death, her work remained incomplete in some iterational aspects. Belnad and Ian knew exactly what she was working on at the time of her death, but they could not figure out why. She had discovered how to stop the aging process. She had discovered the immunity factor. She was studying the evolving variegations of seaweed, searching for the "seaweed prime," as she noted it. She knew that the elements that seeded the oceans originated in volcanoes and in the huge sharp crater impacts that touched the core. The magma compositions were fascinating to her, occupying years of her ancillary research tracts. She had gone back to the beginning of time geologically.

Ian said, "Her work taught us how to manage the continental and oceanic crusts of the Earth. But as amazing as those revelations were, how she knew where to look, or even that there was a 'what' to look for, those are the true mysteries of her mind, and perhaps of something more." Belnad knew that Ian's observation and implied question were both deeply insightful, with an implicit significance. He hesitated, knowing the implications, but then, in the Emer way, he had disregarded caution for progress, and offered his friend another enticement to go a little further.

"In watching the raising of Karina, as a baby – you've seen it all over and over just as I have – did you notice anything in those very early years?" Ian knew he was talking about Catherine's nursing of her baby. There were many other saliences in those days: how mother and daughter communicated so easily, how Karina's early high awareness levels made everything easier, how the two of them blended into each other's lives so thoroughly; but one thing did stand out under the intensity of the Emers' research. Ian was nodding in agreement even as he asked the question.

"You think Catherine knew what was going on even then?" Belnad was very quick in responding, as though his lines in this conversation were pre-scripted.

"Yes, I do. Do you remember when Karina decided on her own to stop nursing?" Ian was nodding. "That decision, Catherine instinctively knew, was evolutionary and not just discretionary. She had felt her daughter's innate urge to keep moving despite the comfort and contentment of those treasured moments together, nurturing each other, sharing so intimately. It is now very clear to us that Catherine felt and favored, with some sadness, Karina's decision to push away, even as she sensed and savored her daughter's unquestioningly deep love; their shared emotions mixing even more deeply with her own devotion." Belnad walked over to a console. It was one of those devices they had used over and over to view the past and the history that built their future. He turned and looked back at his friend and assistant. "This seemingly small event, so detailed and discretely complex in its manifestations, was revelatory, and her research immediately took a different tack." Belnad, looking down again at the complex device in front of him, was remembering the rapture of his research, how he had been riveted to it for days and months, "rewinding" and relaying things over and over. He had seen so much in Catherine's sad and surprised eyes.

He had always felt, until Ian arrived, that he was the last of a breed of Emers who even had the capacity to see and understand such deeply human things, to notice such human subtleties. With each passing year, Emer life had become more and more encapsulating in its ultimate fulfillments; freedom had been achieved at levels beyond the aspirations of humanity's most inventive dreamers, even its poets. Catherine's history was, from the Emer point of view, finite, primitive, raw, imperfect, salacious, and fallible, and, to them, she was an exquisitely, fascinatingly imperfect human being who, for all her evolutionary faults, had given the Emers the supreme gift of infinity. In that infinity, Belnad had found the nacre that coated the grain of sand that became the perfect pearl of the beautiful world and existence that now surrounded him.

Belnad was Emerald Earth's greatest scientist and the most renowned expert on Catherine Jacobson's life. His discoveries, revealed within his exhaustive research, were the sparks that ignited the Emers' creative fire. His derivative inventions had changed everything: all because of her.

Ian had made his own decision, along the way, to study another pearl in the making, the life of Brittany Peterson. He had discovered her during research sessions with Belnad. Her life immediately fascinated him. Born on SkyKing to Earth parents, she became a Sker princess, a beloved member of the crew, a favorite of the MoonBasers, a devoted daughter, who, after the death of her mother, chose a selfless life mission assisting her father. Many had thought this was a waste of resources. But in Ian's own experience of a long recovery from disaster, he saw that Brittany's loneliness and search for meaning was a driving incentive to rebuild her life. He had seen her life, during his research, many times from start to finish, and he had explored every day and every aspect of her struggles with a microscopic intensity that brought him, in his conclusions, to a deep and empathic understanding of her. He was deeply in love with her long before they ever met that day on the Moon. In fact, he was in love long before Belnad and he figured out that, with the end of stasis, they actually *could* meet her. Ian had secretly and hopelessly, perhaps unconsciously, longed with all his heart to do just that. His studies helped his hapless infatuation, but, knowing her as intimately as he did from afar, with each day of research, he longed for more.

Ian instinctively knew that Farson was wrong about banning contact. Not completely wrong, because timing was a big factor, but wrong in the sense that Farson should have told the Emers how things really were. He should not have left them in the dark for so long, almost too long. Farson should have known better.

Ian became so deeply in love with Brittany that, once he became aware of the possibility, he knew there would inevitably come that day when he would confront Farson and tell him exactly what he thought. Belnad had tried to dissuade him, but Ian was determined. He argued to let the chips fall where they may. "The time is coming," Ian had said. Just as the little baby Karina had turned away from her loving mother, Ian argued, so, too, must the Emers act on their own. So, too, must they turn away from childhood dependencies and reach for stars of their own.

In those early days, Belnad had convinced the wounded and broken Ian to fight for his own life. Now Ian was convincing the Emers to fight for theirs.

Like Farson, Ian had lost everything and started over. Like Farson, Ian was determined to save his world, even if it meant gambling everything.

For Ian, as for Farson before him, there was now no turning back.

When Ian arrived at the door of the cabin in North Conway, Belnad Goethe was talking to Farson and Karina. They were laughing. Farson had moved to welcome him. Ian noticed that there was a young woman in the room, speaking to a tall, silent robot that had a faint aura of purple and gold surrounding it. The robot was standing in the corner, as still as the wall behind it. Ian knew it was ZZ<<Arkol25609. The woman was dressed very fashionably and was animated in her discussion with the robot. Her brown handbag in her hand moved back and forth as she spoke and gestured. Voul Jonsn and Viera Nichols were sitting by the fire. Then they were standing up and were moving in his direction.

As they approached, Ian saw Commander Peterson, Brittany's father. He was a man whom Ian knew extremely well but had never met. Ian knew of Jim Peterson's devastating sadness and sorrow, and he knew how well he masked it over the years. He knew of his fear of raising his daughter alone without his beloved Joan. He knew that Jim Peterson had bundled up his unquestioned and unconditional love for his wife after her death, had nurtured it into many times its original intensity, and had directed all of it to his daughter. Jim Peterson loved Brittany with a potency that was hard to measure, and Ian was feeling its force, now focused on him, with a disturbing vividness. Perhaps feeling the effect of the moment, Viera and Voul slowed down as they approached, watching Ian seemingly led by an involuntary urge, cross the room directly toward Brittany's dad. They watched as he neared James Peterson and extended his hand.

Looking into her father's eyes, Ian was thinking of Brittany's last bit of advice for exactly this moment. "When you meet him, don't blink. Tell him I will be there soon." Ian had looked at her in surprise. "*Will* you be there soon?" She laughed. "Who knows, Ian? But if you say that, it will make him feel better." "I can't lie to him, Brittany." She then said, "It could be true."

When she had said this to Ian, she had been smiling that sly smile of infinite possibilities that she used so well when she wanted to entice him to do so something. This conversation had taken place, a few hours ago, when she was in their home on Emerald Earth conducting research. She had created a simulation version of SkyKing's engineering room at 9.08, which meant the ninth whorl, eight levels down. She was working on a possible redesign of the bellow stabilizer technology for the refurbished connectors to the new Over-whorl, the tenth major addition to the station. He could tell she could easily be busy on this project for many hours, or even days. "But *will* it be true?" Ian hopefully had asked. Her answer was encouraging but intentionally indeterminate and equivocal. "We'll see," she said, smiling that smile again.

When Ian's hand touched her father's hand, the two men's eyes were locked together. Ian's were bright, open, friendly, and hopeful. Jim's were clouded, dark, doubting, and insisting. "Where's my daughter, Ian?"

"She'll be here soon." Ian saw the immediate relief in Jim Peterson's eyes: It was exactly what he wanted to hear.

56. Farson's Log (4)

I know that sometimes things may feel disconnected for you now. I have tried to explain the flow of The Screen whenever I had the opportunity, but it is illusive both in its extravagant scope and in its perplexing simplicity. Now, there are so many of us that The Screen is changing again. Now, another unexpected alteration is coming.

When I realized, after the initial period of adjustment and ascent, that Earth could actually be saved, it was a surprise to me, which was totally reflective of the old ScreenMasters' baseless, and yet universally accepted, assumption of their own infallibility. In a similar way, the human race had assumed itself to be in a slow decline of diminishing resources and ever-increasing disunity, almost to the point of despair. Even though we were doing better, when they came, we could feel our planet and our race straining at its limits. The ScreenMasters saved us, in a way, forcing action and unity. In another way, they were also terribly disruptive. Earth had run its course. The ScreenMasters sought erasure; I found a way to salvation.

There was some safety in distance from the ScreenMasters' plan, but there was no ultimate security. Sargasso was the magnet to the metal of our determination. It was so huge. It must mean something. We were drawn to it.

We have now been hanging around Sargasso for over fifteen years, our time. I have been inside it once, but if what I saw is true – I can barely remember anything – but if the one thing I think I do remember is true, then our adventure is just beginning. The one thing I remember – plus all of the ancillary feelings I have, intuition, if you will – tells me that we are still not safe, not yet.

Karina's conviction that the ScreenMasters are coming back is so strong that I know it must be true. *Songbird* was waiting at the gate. All was in readiness, but I wanted to have everyone together for dinner. Don't laugh. Good things happen over food. It's what I call "free time" because it affects nothing, wastes almost no time, and I can talk to them all at once, in person. That person-to-person interaction still matters, as Karina has taught me all too well. She loves it. She is making a pecan pie. Imagine. *Hope it turns out well.* Voul and Viera could not be happier in my cabin. Look at them sitting there by the fire, talking and holding hands. It's a vacation. Jim Peterson and Ian: that was interesting. Ian said the right thing. That makes me think the Brittany *is* coming, but she is traversing a huge adjustment, the first old Earth human to physically visit Emerald Earth. What will her father think? That is a vital link. Six thousand five hundred years is a long time, and there's no turning back. I will have to depend on Ian's judgment for that one. He felt it was the right thing to do, but time will always tell. Certainly there was enough preparation in his decision. (*That's a joke.*) The truth is that the Emers are a force unto themselves. I have influence, but clearly no control operationally.

I am planning a "toast," a call to the gathering to raise their glasses in honor of a coming event: To wish its outcome well; to give it their blessings; to hope for the best; to embrace the coming danger; and to prepare. It is a sort of ambush, I agree. But the dinner is fun in its own right, as well.

As I look at them, each one is pivotal in his or her own way. Think of what they have each done. Including Repoul Bensn who is not coming. Each of them has made a huge difference. They are the pantheon. The league of legends. And yet, they are just people trying to find love and meaning, like the billions who preceded them. It's amazing. I think if you asked them each what is the most important thing of all, they would say the name of another person, not the great events that swirl around us, not the disasters that they have all gone through, not the uncertain future we are working toward. No. They would all say that other person is the most important thing of all. If you asked me, I would say Karina. If you asked her? She can speak for herself. This illogical attachment of people to each other confounded the ScreenMasters. They could not see it as important when it was all that mattered. To them, the human race was an aberration, and it was an existential obstacle. Little did they know that we are the gateway; we are the hope of all survival; we are the answer to the questions they won't ask. And now, the time is coming, just as before, when actions will be taken and things will change. The ScreenMasters will be given the chance to join us, but they choose their own path. As always. How could they know? I can feel an awareness growing in them that things are not as they thought they were. It's very faint now, but that will change. We still have time, but none to waste. They *are* coming. Karina is correct.

In the meantime, we have much to be thankful for, and there is always time for expressing that.

Chapter Five

Refuge

57. Thanksgiving Dinner (5)

The table was set. The pies were cooling. The turkey was hot and ready. The trimmings were already at the table. Karina was standing nearby with a bottle of red wine. She was inviting the guests to sit down and enjoy Thanksgiving dinner together. It was 2:00 p.m. It was a bright clear day, the kind that made people think of spring and start forgetting winter's length and the need to think about staying warm. Spring was coming, everyone knew. But in New Hampshire spring comes in like a dog from the yard. You call, and he comes but never all the way. You go out to get him, and he runs away. You want to him in, but he barks and wants to play. You grow exasperated and go back inside. He barks at you to come out again. You both know that in the end all will be well, and inside, but not just yet.

There had been eight feet of snow this past year, and there were plenty of it showing. Farson could remember every storm of the past winter. He loved them all. Shoveling, snowblowing, scraping windows, and riding around in his old truck with the heater on. He was sad to see it go.

Brittany's arrival in the room was surprising in its quiet accomplishment. She was just there.

She had a question.

"Farson, why are we having Thanksgiving in April?"

"Every day is Thanksgiving Day." He had answered, not really knowing who had asked it at first. Then he saw her. He was not all that surprised. He had been expecting her after seeing Ian and Belnad. Others in the room, however, were very surprised and showed it by standing up as though a high official had appeared. Farson could tell they were at first uncertain who it was, but then they knew. Brittany Peterson was six feet, ten inches tall. *Small for an Emer.* She was very light bronze in color. She was dressed in standard Emer fashion: slacks, a tunic top. Her hair was remarkable though. It was streaked blue and pink and pixie short. Her face was bright and healthy, her posture sure and confident. She laughed at Farson's response. He was surprised at her new confidence and maturity. She spoke with a wisdom he had always known she possessed, but, now, was clearly in full bloom.

"True enough. Were that it had always been so." This comment, he knew, was from Sker scripture. Voul noticed as well. "What? You are surprised? It's still me. What did you expect?" She was looking at the other people in the room, and then at Farson, "You were wrong, Farson, to keep us apart. And you were right, too. It's not like a trip to the Moon." Viera, laughed, knowing this remark was aimed at her. She looked at Brittany, who was smiling with a warm memory of her visit to the "gym." "Do they have massages around here, Farson?" This caused some laughter and a further reduction of formality. Brittany clearly intended to have a good time.

People were starting to assimilate the new Brittany; they were adapting. Farson was about to respond to Brittany's mock question, but decided to go another way. "We do have turkey with all the trimmings. Let's eat!" With that, people took their seats and someone said, "Pass the sweet potatoes, please." Karina was pouring the wine. ZZ<<Arkol25609 was strobing in the corner. Jim Peterson was staring at his daughter as though there was no one else in the room.

The dinner became a series of conversations at the table as everyone enjoyed themselves. There was talk about Thanksgiving and how the tradition had grown. There was discussion of daughters: Felicity, Valgary, and Byn. Belnad discussed the state of children on Emerald Earth briefly. This caused the attention of everyone at the table to shift to his soft and intelligent voice. "We cherish them as nothing else, and yet only around 15,000 are growing up at any time. Our population, as you know, is set at 6.8 million. We do lose people through fatigue, accidents (although these are rare), and finally, through what we call 'resignation.' Living for thousands of years becomes a burden for some. Many of us who travel on The Screen experience so much, witness so many things, and participate in a wide range of events – it *can* wear you out. Those of us who stay on Emerald Earth seem to be more resilient and contented. We have studied the phenomenon, and our scholars have concluded that life within Emerald Earth is the optimum life for us. Just as in the old days of Earth, physical travel beyond our planet is hazardous in many ways. We have Emers now who are always away, but we are still all connected wherever we are. There are some who say it no longer matters at all where we are. We have some who orbit the planet in ships that are their permanent homes.

"The lack of children among us is an issue. Many would like to see that change. The histories of our people are very popular areas of scholarship, and I would say that most Emers are students of that long history." He stopped there, hesitating to go deeper into the actual facts of Emer research techniques. He looked over at Ian, who was already watching him, hoping he would stop right there. The issue of children was a touchy subject. Brittany had just taken her first bite of turkey.

"What is this? It's delicious," she asked.

Farson answered happily. "I was going to kill a real turkey." Everyone was listening to him now. Killing animals for food had long faded into myth. "I got the gun out and went into the woods. There were plenty of turkeys, but I couldn't do it."

"You couldn't do it, Farson?" He looked at Karina who had just interjected the question and was shaking her head at his exaggeration of reluctance. "You couldn't hit one of those birds with a choked-out shotgun if they had been as big as a barn. You scared them, that's true, shooting in all directions like that. If I hadn't stopped you, you probably would have hurt yourself, or me. The turkeys were perfectly safe." This caused laughter around the table. Farson blushed. She continued, "The gun's recoil knocked you over twice." More laughter.

"That's not true," Farson said. "Okay, I missed a few times, but in the end I decided that we could tune up the ChainFoods formula and achieve the same thing with no bloodshed. So, to answer your question, Brittany, Karina and I scanned the old birds and improved the mathematics, and we got an improved version of a ChainFoods turkey. So, I did, in fact, supply the turkey." Farson was glad that was over. The silence that filled the table was like a pausing breath. And then things resumed, leaving Farson's comment and Karina's comical looks behind, but not forgotten.

"The pies, you will be happy to know," she was still looking at Farson but speaking to everyone, "are old style. I made them by hand." Karina beamed with pride. He had seen the pies waiting in the kitchen. "They will be a treat for us at dessert." The conversations went on around the table as the feast began.

Brittany was sitting between Belnad and Ian and across the table from her father, who had still not taken his eyes off her. He was watching her move, watching her laugh, watching for anything that told him how she had changed. She was aware of his scrutiny. She found that she was constantly looking over at him but was unable to obtain eye contact. She knew her father. He was avoiding her gazes, conveniently looking at someone else when she looked at him, and then returning to his study of her as soon as she looked around or engaged in conversation with others at the table. It was a Kabuki dance of two people: so far and yet so close. Finally, he addressed her directly. "Brittany?"

"Yes, Dad." Her response was immediate, her intonation exactly the same as he had heard it countless times in the past. If he had closed his eyes, it would have been his daughter, as always, responding to his familiar conversation starter of saying her name as if it were a question. He knew she had been waiting. His next question was exactly the one she had been waiting for.

"How are you?" Three monosyllabic words, spoken throughout all of human times. Three simple words that usually invoke an offhand response like, 'great,' or 'good,' or the sometimes annoying, 'fantastic.' But this time, those three words evoked a universe of feeling, of love, of fear, of hope, of dreams, of deep resolute change, of growing up, of still being the same but wholly different, profoundly different, of sadness, of astounding joy, of a whole new world, and of a world gone away but still vividly part of her. How could she answer? She thought of a way.

Suddenly, but very gently, Jim Peterson was on a high cliff. The air was misty with warmth and light humidity. He was comfortable standing there. Brittany was beside him. Her hand was in his. They were overlooking a land of horizons and distances unlike any he had ever seen. He looked at her hand, opening it and putting it on top of his. Her hand was the hand of a woman now. It was larger than he remembered, and the light bronze color seemed to shimmer in the air of this place. She flexed her fingers as he watched. He was thinking of her little girl's hand that he had held for so many years, a hand that had sought his in sadness and uncertainty, a hand he had held in joy and recovery. He lightly adjusted her hand, linking fingers as they always did, reestablishing the bond of father and daughter. She was speaking to him.

"Dad, it's still me, but now I *am* different. When Ian invited me to Emerald Earth, I had no idea what I was doing. At first I was angry, perhaps as you are now, but then as we explored Emerald Earth and its wonders together, I came to appreciate why he had done what he did. He has studied me for so many years. He has seen my life from start to finish so many times. He knows me in a way that no one has ever known me, not even you. When I saw him on the Moon that day, I had no inkling of what was to come. But he did." Brittany moved them farther into the scene below the cliff. Jim felt it was as if by magic. Now they were standing in the grass far beneath, near a small canal. Jim could feel the grass dolphins moving under his feet. He wondered what they were. Brittany held our her hand, and they appeared all around them, their beautiful bodies and countenances showing gracefully as they moved. Jim could feel that he and Brittany were moving now, across a vast field. She had him sit down, and she sat beside him as they began to move ever faster across the amber waves of Emerald Earth. As the dolphins carried them through the fragrant grasses and beautiful and invigorating air, she began to tell him a story.

"This is a place of humanity's dreams. They have everything. Health, long life, education, science, music, travel beyond your wildest imaginations. They have peace, and prosperity for all 6.8 million Emer ScreenMasters who sweep across the galaxies and throughout all time, building, guiding, changing, and evolving everything. They have discovered the deepest secrets of life, Dad. I know what you may be thinking – and I had my doubts too – but it is true. Emers and their world are the dream of hundreds of thousands of years of suffering, anguish, prejudice, intolerance, and all the etceteras of those evils that have haunted us all for so, so long." Jim could feel her exhaustion at the thought of such useless suffering and cruelty. "I love SkyKing and the Moon and long to return to share all of this, but it will take time. I miss you every day, but they have taught me how to really watch and listen, so even though we have been apart, we have also been together. I love you more than ever, Dad, but what Emerald Earth has given me is the gift of eternity, and ..." she stopped for a moment. The silence was a richness of emotions and feelings that washed over her father like a wave of revelation. He could feel the warmth of the little girl who used to look up at him for support and compassion; he could feel the depths of their relationship enriching him even as he cherished it; he could feel her love for her mother that even now washed over him with its never-ending devotion; he could feel the innate honesty that Brittany had always, and so generously, shared with him; he could sense his daughter's earnest desire to explain everything to him. He knew she was being successful. He looked around at the beauty streaming by. He could smell the purity of the planet, and he could feel its restorative nature affecting him. He felt wonderful. She continued. " ... of love, Dad. I love Ian with an intensity and profoundness that I thought was impossible since the pain of Mom's death, but I was wrong. My love of her and you made loving Ian possible. He is so different, so compelling, and yet innocent. He is so strong and yet so incredibly vulnerable and guileless, so free and unrestrained that I have come to see that loving him is what I was born to do. We have been to worlds I almost cannot describe. I have learned things in the deep, true sense of learning. I have been changed by true knowledge and unchanged by the truth of my past. I am still me, and I am something new and distinct. When you asked me, 'How are you?' I knew the answer would not be simple." Jim Peterson was like a person watching a movie in one of those old-time Earth movie theaters who, as the movie ended suddenly, he realized that he was actually in a theater and not in the cinematographer's imagination any longer. He felt like the time to stand up and return to reality must be sadly approaching, but the grass dolphins only sped up more, and Brittany didn't move. *I guess it's not over yet.*

As they talked, time seemed to be suspended, but he still had the sensation of movement. She told him of the technology of Emerald City. She visualized the new home, and he was amazed. He could see the population moving over the planet. He could sense Brittany's certainty of her place. The city was beyond his ability to fully imagine it or comprehend what he was seeing, and as the scenes changed and the places came and went, he knew that there would never be any competition for her, or urge to return. As if she heard him, he felt her hand pressure increase slightly, and her beautiful Emer face was looking directly at him. Her next words were spoken softly, and there was no doubt in his mind that they were true as true can be. "I am home."

Then they were back at the Thanksgiving table. The pies were coming out. He could smell the rich crusts and ingredients with new subtlety. It brought back memories of his own childhood with intensity and richness he had not felt in years. He looked at Brittany. She said, in answer to his question, as if nothing had happened, "Fantastic, Dad. How are you?" He shook his head in wonder at this woman at the table beside him: his daughter, but now even more. His smile told Brittany all she needed to know. All was well. Then he said, as Karina cut the first piece for Farson, "Fantastic, as well, honey. Absolutely fantastic." She knew he meant it.

Farson took a bite. He tasted and tasted and quickly took another, smiling at his sister. "Fantastic," he said, continuing the theme, and everyone laughed. The word of the day. The pies were an enormous success; everyone wanted the recipe.

"The recipe is ... do it all by hand. Practice until you get it perfect. And, one more thing, make pies all the time. The currency of your skills in pie-making determines everything.

The more you do it, the better you get." Obviously, she must have practiced what she was preaching.

Everyone helped clean up; it was easy working together. Even ZZ<<Arkol25609 pitched in clearing the table. Ida was especially helpful in the hand-washing of the dishes – fast, efficient and very dexterous, never fumbling or dropping anything. They were done before anyone knew it. Voul and Viera put things away, Brittany and her dad spread a fresh tablecloth on the table, and, believe it or not, Ian and Belnad collaborated on making the coffee. Karina and Farson went out for more wood. Brittany heard her name a few times as everyone worked. She did a little of everything, helping everyone.

Soon enough, everyone was back at the table. Farson had placed a bottle of Armagnac on the table with ten glasses. As the bottle was passed around, he stood up. "I would like to propose a toast." Everyone touched their glasses in anticipation of raising them. But soon enough they realized it was not going to be a short toast, and they settled back to listen.

"There are times in our lives when we rest and heal. There are times when we rush to change. There are times when we plan and predict. And there are times when we must act.

"We are now completing a time of resting and planning and beginning a time of action. As you know, time is no longer our enemy, but it is also not our friend. We have time, but there is no time to waste. Karina knows, as I do, that soon enough the old ScreenMasters will be coming, looking for us. They are very close to discovering the changes we made in their plans for humanity. They *will* discover the truth. When they do, they will be upon us if we linger in doubt and debate. So, Voul and I will take the first step. It will appear to be a foolish thing to do, but, as in all things human, foolishness is often the mother of invention and frequently spawns ideas that change everything.

"We may be gone for a while. In the meantime, SkyKing and the Moon must prepare. Repoul has his instructions. Follow his lead. Emerald Earth is already prepared, as you would expect. We are now heading toward a new level of experience; we are going to see places and things unimagined; and we are going to learn more about each other than ever known before. Like a family reunited in crisis, we will grow into something new and, at first, strange, but, in time, all will be well.

"So here's to each other," he raised his glass, "and to the future we are building together." They all stood and raised their glasses and drank deeply of the moment. ZZ<<Arkol25609 stood alone in the corner. His strobing told everyone that he was preparing to begin their transits. Oddly, Ida did not raise her glass until the second half of Farson's toast and then seemed to sip her drink only enough to move the ice cubes not to drain the glass in the slightest. She was looking at Farson, who was now turning to Brittany. "And one more toast to our friend Brittany Peterson, who has passed over the Rubicon into a new world." He turned to look at Strapper John's son. "Time will tell, Ian, if your invitation was correct, but from the looks of her," Farson looked down at his hands formed in an imaginary ball, "as the old magic eight ball used to say, 'the outlook is good.'" Everyone applauded.

With that, the dinner and the toast were complete. Farson, with a wave to all, disappeared, the room awash in that deep purple hue that only accompanied Farson Uiost.

Voul moved toward ZZ<<Arkol25609 for transit, but stopped when he saw Brittany coming in his direction.

"Whoa there, Voul, not so fast." She walked over to him and as tall as he was, she still had a good nine inches on him now. As he looked up at her, he saw the same sweet face he had known for almost his whole life. She was smiling, a soft laugh. "Now I know what I must have looked like staring up at you with those little girl doe eyes." But she took him in her arms. As they hugged, Voul experienced something he had not expected. Suddenly, they were on Emerald Earth in her apartment. As he watched the room change into the Petersons' dining room, Voul felt strangely at ease. An eleven-year-old Brittany was sitting at the table. "Come over here, Voul and sit down with me. I want to tell you something." Voul was not believing what he was seeing. He knew it wasn't true, but it sure seemed to be. He sat beside her. She looked up at him. "Is this better?"

"Yes, of course it is. Your Emerald Earth form is disconcerting and intimidating. I have never seen anything like your amazing transformation; I never imagined it was even possible."

"That's only the beginning, Voul. It's why Farson forbade contact. The changes are so amazing. I wasn't on Emerald Earth for two seconds before the profound effects occurred. Basically one breath and I was in a metamorphosis that has changed me so thoroughly, that it immediately seemed natural and welcome. It was sudden and shocking, and it is still occurring. For a moment, I hated Ian like an abductor who had assaulted me, but soon enough I saw what a fundamental, essential act of true love it was. When I went to the Moon's gym that day with Viera, it was transformational for me. But when I went to Emerald Earth, it was something else altogether. All of my life, as I wandered around the Moon and SkyKing, I felt like I was looking for someone, for something. When I woke up on Emerald Earth – reborn is a better word – I knew I had finally found everything I had always been seeking." Voul listened to the little girl speaking to him. He was mesmerized by the familiar sound of her voice and the absolute clarity of her thoughts. He was happy for Brittany, and she could tell. "But there is one more thing I wanted to tell you." She moved a little closer, as she always had as a child. "I will always love you, Voul. You filled a void in my life that nothing else could fill. You gave me hope when I had lost all hope. You were a dream I loved to dream. In due course, I realized I would never have you. Viera is so wonderful and perfect for you. It did hurt, but, in a way, it helped me too. Her friendship is something I cherish now. But I will always love you. I will always be grateful to you. When Farson invited me to his Thanksgiving dinner, I knew I would accept, despite the shock it would cause my dad. I knew I would accept because Thanksgiving is the day I will always think of you." She put her arms around him, and he hugged the little girl he had so loved. She was precious to him. *This is the greatest gift I have ever received.* Hugging little Brittany again was a dream come true, a dream he thought was gone forever. His tears were a gift to Brittany, and she held on in a moment of stolen time and a moment seared into their mutual memories forever. Then she was gone. Voul was back in the cabin, standing in the room. Viera was looking at him.

"What just happened, Voul?" She could see the moistness still around his eyes.

"I said goodbye to an old friend." Viera looked around.

"Where's Brittany?" ZZ<<Arkol25609 activated their transports. Suddenly, Viera was back on the Moon, and Voul was back on *Songbird* with Farson and Uva.

Voul and Viera were both thinking of each other, wishing that they had had time to say goodbye.

The dinner was over.

The dishes done, the cabin restored to its regular appearance (a little neater), Karina sat down at the table. The last piece of pecan pie was in front of her. It had a dollop of whipped cream on it, and there was a shiny clean fork on a linen napkin waiting beside it. She lifted the fork as though in a toast, and said: "Farson, this one's for you."

No one had noticed that ID>>Karo28689 had left the party with Farson. No one except Karina, that is.

58. Sargasso Revisited

They were back onboard *Songbird* with a lapse of 1.245 seconds according to the ship's monitors. Voul was studying the screen. He noticed that at .999 seconds there was a brief interruption in the ship's data stream. Then at 1.245 another one occurred, which was the Voul and Farson returning.

"Farson, you had better look at this." Farson came over to the monitor and followed along as Voul explained the situation concerning the unknown interruption.

Farson said, "Check the readout from my first visit here. See if anything like that happened then." Voul thought about that for a few seconds. *That information could be helpful.*

"Let me consult with Repoul." He initiated communication protocols, and while he was doing that, Farson returned to the pilot's chair. He was calculating trajectory alternatives, time to designated speed, and, once that was set, he initiated a few safety programs in case his plan did not work. Then he started the simulation.

The simulation scenario played out on the monitor as if viewed from behind the vessel. *Songbird* backed up (the virtual camera always remaining in the same relative position) to about 3,500 feet from the wall and stopped. Then eight seconds later the main engines came on in a bright blue blaze, and *Songbird* blasted off at extremely high speeds directly at the ledge. In about four seconds the distance was closed, and the vessel smashed into Sargasso, completely destroying itself in an explosion, all hands obviously lost. Voul was now looking over Farson's shoulder.

"*That* doesn't look good, Farson." Voul was thinking of Viera as he said it.

"Not to worry, the simulation doesn't know everything yet. It has to learn." He looked at Voul and smiled.

Voul asked, "Can we just send the ship, without us, and see what happens?"

"Nope. We have to go with it. There's no way to get inside unless Sargasso wants us to. If the empty ship did get in, we would be left out here in our suits. When, and if, the ship came back, we would be no better off and still know nothing more than we do right now."

"But ramming the ship, as the entrance key, seems extreme, Farson."

"By my calculations and experience, I don't think it will be a problem. I expect that we will find ourselves inside Sargasso, and this time, we will have a starship with which to explore." Voul was thinking about Farson's words, "I don't *think*" and "I *expect*." *Seems a little subjective.* But he knew Farson was always right.

"You *are* always right, Farson, true?"

"I wish it were, Voul. But, no, I have been wrong many times."

"*Many* times?" Voul was getting worried.

"Let's say 'a few times.' Mostly in matters concerning Karina." Voul felt much better with that statement. He well understood that women were always an uncertainty, especially non-Sker women.

"That makes me feel a little better. I have the same problem." Farson could see that Voul was grasping at straws to build his uncertain confidence in Farson's plan.

"Right, but I did say, 'mostly,' Voul. I have also been wrong about matters concerning the old ScreenMasters."

"Really?" *This is not good.* Voul was watching Farson rerun another simulation of *Songbird* flying into Sargasso. This one began farther away, and the speed was much faster and even more explosively catastrophic. They both watched the impact erupt in total destruction again. The simulator depicted the blast radius and pieces of the little ship flying off in all directions. The pilot's area, where they both were now, was ripped open to space and tumbled from view, viciously spinning and yawing. It was clear that no one could survive such an event.

"Yes, sadly, I was wrong about Twill. I underestimated him at one point, and it could have caused real problems but it didn't. He was so caught up in the preparations for his 'Grand Ascendancy,' he didn't give all of the information he received due consideration. His ego saved us. So I guess you could say I was ultimately right about him, but that was just too close. Karina was really upset as we watched it all unfold. She said I was just lucky. I told her 'luck comes to the well prepared.'"

"What did she say then?"

"You don't want to know. For what it's worth, I learned from my mistake. Twill had his chance back then. He won't get another."

Farson was running a new simulation. This time the ship approached much more slowly, with the same result, a little less spectacular, but in the end, the failure was still stubbornly incontrovertible. The two of them stood there on the bridge of *Songbird*, watching again as the simulation's pilot's compartment twisted and turned, in pieces, off into space and then the rest of ship exploded. He turned to Voul. "Not really very encouraging, is it?"

"No, it's not."

"Well, let's keep working on it." They continued plotting new equations and variables of speed, angle, rotation, and anything else they could think of. One disconcerting explosion followed another. This went on for several hours. Farson seemed indefatigable to Voul, who gloomily concluded that this day was not going to be the best day of his life. Then Repoul called back.

"After careful review of the entire four hours and thirty-five seconds of your first attempt to enter Sargasso ..." Farson interrupted him.

"It was not an 'attempt,' Repoul. It was successful. I know what I saw. I just can't remember how I did it. Did you find anything at all to help us?"

"As I was saying ... after carefully reviewing the entire four hours and thirty-five seconds of the record of your first 'attempt,'" Farson was fidgeting and impatient with this reuse of an incorrect term, "I did notice a similar, very brief event, to the one that Voul recorded today on *Songbird*. In looking into it from every angle, scientifically and metaphorically, I have concluded that it had no effect on anything."

"But it was there?" Farson was looking for confirmation.

"Yes."

"Where did it come from?"

"Unknown."

"What did it seem intended to do?"

"Unknown."

"Were there differences between the two events?"

"Only in the most infinitesimal way. I would have missed it entirely, except that it reminded me of something."

"What was that, Repoul?" Farson felt like he was pulling the proverbial teeth in this conversation.

"Do you remember when we assumed control of the stasis field?" Farson nodded.

"Of course."

Voul was watching and listening to this exchange between Repoul Bensn, savior of SkyKing and the Moon, and Farson Uiost, the savior of humanity, and, in his opinion, the most important person who had ever lived. They seemed to be obliquely approaching a resolution and avoiding it even as they moved closer to it. On the monitor, another simulation had just concluded with the violent destruction of *Songbird* and anyone unlucky enough to be aboard her.

"Well, it was like that. As if two independent programs had touched in some extremely small way, with a tiny little effect that I can only compare to a pilomotor reflex: a hair standing on end. It passed very quickly and certainly unnoticed except in the depths of the Moon's telemetry complexes, which you know are prodigious."

"True enough. But you found it."

"Yes, it took me over an hour." Voul knew that that would have taken at least an entire day, or longer, for anyone else. He knew from his understanding of Repoul's mathematics and his history of accuracy that Repoul meant that this 'event' was either never intended to be seen at all or to be completely dismissed as insignificant, if noticed. He asked Repoul which it was. Farson was surprised that Voul had joined the interrogation. "If I had to say, I would choose the latter." Farson perked up at that.

Repoul added, "But it could be both."

"So, since we have found a replication, a similarity, then we must be on the right path, don't you agree?"

"The path to *where*, Farson? If you mean that there was some sort of intervention, I would say that may be a stretch. If you want to believe that it was an initiation sequence, there is no evidence to support that. Repoul was watching another of Farson's simulations, ending with a particularly violent explosion, on the monitor behind him. Farson turned the monitor off and answered Repoul.

"The path where we fly right into Sargasso as though that wall is not even there," Farson answered.

"Really? You think that is what is going to happen?" Farson had to think his answer over for a few seconds.

"Yes, I do, Repoul. Despite all of the evidence at hand, that is exactly what I think."

"Well, all I can say is that there is no quantifiable evidence, or even a hint of likelihood, that your conclusion that *Songbird* will sail right through Sargasso's apparently impenetrable outer shell is logical *or* probable, or in any way a credibly believable outcome. If you ask me, I would say, 'Put on your suits and do together what you did alone the first time.' That would be the logical thing to do, Farson. The introduction of a 450-foot vessel, with over 10,000 tons of mass at approximately 200,000 miles per hour into the highly complicated chemistry and molecular structure of that wall can only add to the complications of whatever happened that you cannot remember from your first 'visit.' This dubiety has been dramatically confirmed many times now in your computer simulations. It could be suicidal, at the very least, to do such a thing. If not for your own safety, Farson, certainly for Voul's. This is a risk too high to take. I advise against this course of action."

Farson looked at Voul. "What do you say? Want to try it?" Voul closed his eyes. In his mind, he was kissing Viera, perhaps kissing her goodbye. Farson continued, "I can go it alone, Voul, but then we wouldn't have the corroboration needed for the next step. What do you say?" The image of Repoul shaking his head on the communication panel's monitor was crystal clear. Voul's head, on the other hand, was perfectly still. Neither Farson nor Repoul could decipher the direction Voul's thoughts were taking at that moment. If he said, "yes," it could lead to the greatest adventure of their lives. If he said, "no," Farson would go without him. The vision of his daughter, Byn, now appeared in his mind. She was playing with the long-haired cowboy and the grass dolphin. He could hear his daughter's voice, "Come on, Handy. Let us carry you across the field. You will love it. We can do it!" It was the children's book version of Handy's visit to the harvester on the grass dolphin throne. Every child knew the script by heart. Voul looked over at Farson. He realized that Farson had chosen *him* for this mission. Not Repoul, or Karina, or even one of the robots. Farson had chosen him. He recalled his father's famous last words, cherished in the Sker nation as a call to action: "Fear not. I go to a new world with relish and excitement, leaving the old for others; choosing for myself the unknown and uncertain. It is there where our true destiny awaits." Searching for words, Voul finally found them in his memories of the miners on the Moon. They always said it at the start of every new mining expedition. He spoke, looking directly at Farson with a tenuous smile.

"Let's roll." This made Farson laugh out loud. He cut off the connection with Repoul Bensn, the Sker's face in negative exclamation. Farson imagined he was saying something like, "Don't do it," as the transmission faded away. Farson then turned to the controls and punched the ignition button, the engines roared into action, and the little vessel leaped forward, accelerating at maximum speed toward the exact spot each of the many disturbing simulations had depicted as the exploding ship's impact point. As things about them blurred with speed and intent, Farson turned to Voul and said, "Buckle up. Here we go." They both strapped in and watched through the forward view screen as Sargasso's enormity raced madly toward them.

59. There's No Turning Back Now

In 2105, Felicity had just turned seven years old, as had her sister. It was a constant discussion, bordering on argument, about who was born first. Felicity assumed she had come first. "Look how happy I always am, and look how concerned you always are. I came out looking around. You came out, a little later, worried about me. Who could blame you? One minute there we were, happy together, no problems. And then you were all alone. For the first time. You became concerned. It was our destiny: I lead, you follow." Felicity's amazing smile washed over the room. Valgary was watching this performance; she had heard it and seen it many times. She enjoyed it.

"Or, as anyone who *knows* us will agree, I *must* have come out first." Valgary's story was also well known. Felicity could have said it word for word. She liked it better the way Valgary did it. "I am the adventurous one. I am the one who likes to explore, so obviously, I found the way out first. That left *you* in there all alone. You were so happy because *finally* you were the center of attention. You could hear everyone talking about you. 'Where is she?' 'When is she coming out?' You were in heaven in there. Everyone was waiting for you, the great Felicity. I can imagine you popping your head out and giving that big, beautiful smile of yours. Everyone must have almost passed out. Meanwhile, I was out there already enjoying the new world looking for places to go and things for us to do. It was our destiny: me first, then you." The two of them laughed, as they always did, at this predictable exchange. It couldn't have mattered less to either of them. It was just fun. They knew it would never be resolved, but they enjoyed acting it out. Together. The truth was that they loved each other, supported each other, and always, always took care of each other. They could both tell the story either way and often switched back and forth, still telling it like they meant it, still always making them both look good, both of them right, just to confuse people. In telling the story, they could absolutely convince everyone that they meant it, but then would switch sides and convince them the other way. They had come to realize that it made no difference, just as their mother had told them over and over. Only Farson and Karina knew the truth, and they were not about to clear up the ambiguity. Seven years later, they knew there was no turning back now. "That bird has flown," Farson would say. Karina's response was always, "You were born together." Felicity and Valgary were the only ones who knew how true that was.

Still, it was a family topic that came up all too often, to the amusement of all.

Today was just another day on SkyKing. In a stationary orbit over Sargasso, the space station had been in the same place for over eleven years. These had been years of growth and peace and wonderful normality. A few years ago, the station had reached a population milestone of 350,000 people. The Moon had over 12,500 now, and that was going to change soon with the completion of the new surface cities, and the connecting gurney escalator. It was already obvious that many people on SkyKing would prefer to move to the Moon's surface once was it was secured. There was more space on the Moon, and, for some, it seemed more "normal," as they put it. For others, though, SkyKing was, and always would be, their home. The Skers' population had grown to fill in any absences caused by the emigrants. They calculated that within a few more years, only Skers would remain on SkyKing. It seemed inevitable.

Farson and Karina had made SkyKing one of their three main homes. Today was a day with no school, which the girls loved, and Karina had decided to spend the day at home with them. They were making breakfast for Farson, who was coming home today, and they all wanted to surprise him. "Waffles," Valgary had said, "that's his favorite." It was also hers and Felicity's, too. They needed blueberries, and they knew exactly where to get them. "Please, Mom. Please!"

Karina was at the supermarket in North Conway, third in line to the cash register. She noted that people were wearing their full summer clothing now. Spring was an unpleasant memory with its rain and wind and clouds and cold mud, as if the seasons could not decide which way to go. Summer was a welcome, if too short, relief.

The cashier was "Becky," who Karina knew from her many visits to the store. "Good morning, Mrs. Chamberlain. How are you?" She looked at the two little baskets of blueberries. "Did you find everything you were looking for?" Karina laughed inside at this question.

"Yes. We just need some blueberries for waffles. The girls are making them for their dad." That seemed to make the cashier happy, and Karina enjoyed the closeness of the little town.

"And how is Mr. Chamberlain today?" The cashier was just being logical, but still Farson would find it ironic that somehow Karina's adopted maiden name had replaced his. He would say, "Becky is living in an alternate universe," and Karina would reply, "Who isn't?"

"He is traveling, but due home this morning. We are going to surprise him." The cashier was nodding her head knowingly.

"I love surprises."

"Here you go, girls. Don't make a mess." *Wishful thinking.* Felicity was happily going over the recipe, making gestures as if she were in school at the blackboard.

"One cup of blueberries … check." Her hand went down a few inches and then swept up almost to full reach. "Baking powder … check." Her arm mimicked her words in the air again. "Eggs … check." Same thing. "Sugar, flour, milk, butter … check. We're ready to go." Just as she looked up from the recipe book, she heard the mixer abruptly and powerfully start up. Valgary was already blending the ingredients. "Val, what are you doing?"

"While you were 'checking' everything off" – she made rapid, copycat, even more exaggerated finger quotation marks in the air, to match Felicity's grand checkoffs – "I am making the waffles."

She looked away from the mixer as she said this to Felicity. She saw her sister's mouth open in surprise as flour and milk, and sugar and butter were sprayed out of the bowl in all directions.

"The mixer is on high, Val!" Valgary looked at the machine, and it was true. It was also true that the front of her shirt and pants were now soaked with milk and covered in flour, and the mixer was spewing everything everywhere, even across the counter onto Felicity. The two of them looked at the unbelievable mess and then at each other. They started to laugh. Then Karina walked in. She surveyed the situation. Both girls were covered with the ingredients of the waffles, the counter was a mess, and the mixer was still on high, its whining engine going ever faster as the encumbering ingredients left the bowl. Karina shook her head and turned off the mixer. In the silencing of the machine the sounds of their laughter filled the room.

"Well, at least the blueberries weren't in yet," Karina said to her daughters, who found this comment only added to their mirth. Even cleaning it all up and then starting over was fun. "It was all your fault," Valgary said to Felicity. This just made them start laughing all over again.

"Boy, those were terrific waffles, girls. What a great breakfast." Farson had arrived just as the second attempt was successfully exiting the waffle maker. They had eaten in the quiet, stable joy that good families throughout all time have enjoyed and cherished together. Orange juice and bacon had rounded out their morning meal. Farson was getting up to get a little more coffee and start the dishes. Karina was relaxing at the table. Felicity and Valgary were clearing the table, fighting over their dad's dishes. Valgary won and proudly went to the sink. "I have your dishes, Dad." He was smiling and aware that the two of them thought it was some sort of victory to get his instead of their own and their mom's. Valgary interjected.

"Dad, look. I have all the rest in just one trip." Farson looked at Valgary balancing three plates and glasses on her little arms and hands. It looked a little unsteady to him. Karina was right there to assist, and to avoid more kitchen calamities, "Let me help you, Val." Together they put them in the sink. There was a sudden purple flash, and Farson disappeared. The flash had come at full intensity, no slow buildup as usual, and Farson was gone instantly, as though he had never been there. No lingering purple residue as usual. He was just gone. Felicity, Valgary, and Karina has watched all of this with alarm. The girls were looking around.

"Where's Dad?" Felicity had spoken, but all three were concerned about the same thing.

"What just happened, Mom?" Karina turned and looked around the room.

"I have no idea."

60. Farson and the President (3)

"The tranquility of the South did not win the war, Andy. Their affection for a quiet, prosperous life, while admirable, was built on a casual, institutional, and unsustainable inhumanity. The South was destined to fail. It was no contest, really. Bloody, yes. But the outcome was always a foregone conclusion. Sad to say. The genuine genteelness – refined, polite, well-heeled, affluent – is attractive, but again it was based on a cruel and brutal slave culture." Farson took a sip of his brandy. He thought about its aroma. He enjoyed smelling it. His nose lingered over the glass, enjoying the bouquet, as he savored and swallowed. John Andrew McKinley Sortt was listening with doubtful anticipation as Farson continued. He knew exactly where this was going. "And if you mean, all of that aside, that the South's culture of its privileged population: freedom, rebellion, rabid prejudice, foolishness, and unrelenting and unjustified pride still endures today, you know you're wrong. Emerald Earth is proof positive." Andrew Sortt was thinking Farson's words over. He knew the ScreenMaster was correct, in a directional way, but not in every way. It was an old argument, for which there was an adequate, if not dispositive, counter. He offered it.

"Farson, imagine that you were *born* on Emerald Earth and have studied the cultures of the North and South during the Civil War period. Say you have now achieved majority in this new world, that you, and everyone, have immense wealth in old Earth terms, meaning you have everything you will ever need: shelter, education, art and culture, total freedom, the ability to travel anywhere, and even life eternal if you want it." Farson was thinking that Andy's description *was* now Emerald Earth's reality. "Which side of that war would you feel was most like yours in its essential nature: the benevolent and enslaving plantations of the racist South or the dirty, insufferable cities and exploitative factories of the North? To which form of victimization would you be most attracted?" Farson frowned at this formulation of options.

"You have vastly oversimplified the question, Andy, and you know it. An Emer would never jump to either of those stereotypes. He or she would know to look and think deeper, and in no time they would ascertain that neither the South nor the North of the Civil War era compares in any way to life on Emerald Earth. I have read their insightful and unbiased studies of Abraham Lincoln. They do not revere him as Earth historians always did. Emers see the brutality and the 'ends and means' thinking he practiced so skillfully. They are not fooled by Lincoln's brutal success in the war, or even by his 'humanity.' They do still love the Gettysburg Address, it must be said. But, Lincoln's eloquence, which they rightly

identify as politically motivated, but perhaps heartfelt as well
– although the duplicity of old Earth politicians must inform
Emer historians that even when those old leaders did the right
thing it was often done for horribly wrong reasons – especially
in the manipulative 'emancipation' of the black slaves, whose
'freedom' even hundreds of years later, by any means and
measure, still resulted in their being treated, unfairly and
without any justification whatsoever, as inferior, second-class
citizens. It cannot be disputed that the legal, social, and
political restrictions on that promising and inspiringly
determined-to-be-free element of our ancestors' population
lingered on and on, even into the days when the
ScreenMasters came to Earth. It is only on Emerald Earth
where the words of Lincoln's famous Emancipation
Proclamation actually and finally came true, 229 years later."

Farson seemed to be searching his mind for something.
Then he continued. "Shall be forever free," he said, quoting
Lincoln's famous document. "President Lincoln promised that
his government would 'recognize and maintain' the freedom
of the emancipated slaves, and that the United States
government would never repress them again. How true was
that, Andy? So, both sides failed miserably and futilely.

"All wars are won or lost, and it all means nothing, despite
the flowery speeches and political promises, if truly
reformative · changes do not occur. The fact that black
Americans remained in a second-class status, for the
subsequent 229 years between Lincoln's vaulted and revered
'Emancipation Proclamation' and the coming of the old
ScreenMasters cannot be argued. All those Confederate and
Union young men died for nothing, in the end, especially the
Southern boys. The only good that came of it was the survival
of the United States of America. We both know that." Sortt
pounced.

"Farson, that is my point *exactly*. Thank you for stating it
so eloquently."

"What? That the South saved the Union? You can't mean that."

"That's exactly what I mean, Farson. Plus, they cemented the dream of an idyllic life with freedom from want, worry, and fear, that ultimately became the refined and perfected definition of Emerald Earth, into human consciousness forever. It became the aspiration of all the non-despotic governments and philosophers from the Civil War to the emergence of Emerald Earth." Farson was shaking his head.

"And yet, no distinct period of a universal halcyonic existence ever appeared in all those years, Andy. And the suffering and inhumanity of man continued unabated. In fact it vastly *increased*." President Sortt knew better than to become annoyed at Farson's predictable persistence. He felt one more attempt to make his point could potentially turn the tide.

"Earth Pact, Farson? Does that count for nothing?" Farson understood this point well enough. He was considering giving Sortt a small victory here, but in the end, he just could not compromise into settled acquiescence.

"The nuclei-lasers impelled that document. There was no choice." From years playing verbal chess with Farson, Sortt knew a moment of zugzwang when he saw one, and dutifully made his final, futile move.

"With human beings there is *always* a choice, Farson." Farson walked to the decanter, debating whether to refill or just put his glass down. In their long history, Farson estimated that neither of them had hardly ever actually finished a glass, let alone start another. But today, for some reason, Farson was feeling a little tense. He was beginning to form the words, "fair enough," on Sortt's assertion about human vicissitudes and volition, granting him a small victory. It was, perhaps, a gesture of friendship, perhaps he was actually conceding the point initiated by Andrew's reluctant acknowledgement that Farson was right about the "gun-to-the-head" scenario that coerced the people of the late 2080s to finally give up their senseless wars and suicidal aggressions. Then, Sortt continued to his persuasive observation that human beings can always exercise free will – despite even the most dire circumstances and convoluted motives – concluding that they will always favor the possibility of peace and tranquillity, even if that decision could mean their own defeat or death.

Farson knew that Andrew's reasoning was correct. In acknowledging this, he proved his friend's point about always preferring peace over war. He was just beginning to turn from the small table, still holding the bottle of amber Armagnac and his glass and smiling as he always did at the enjoyment of their ongoing and never-ending debates about the nature of things, when the room was filled with a flash of bright purple and searing red.

In the blink of an eye Farson disappeared, in mid-thought, from the room.

Sortt watched Farson's glass fall to the carpet as if it had been suspended in space. It bounced and rolled and stopped upside down. He could see the nearly melted ice cubes on the carpet through the stubby gold-trimmed snifter's crystal glass. The room seemed suddenly very empty. Sortt had seen Farson come and go a thousand times. But never like this. It was so abrupt that he involuntarily bolted up from his comfortable leather chair in surprise.

"Farson?" he shouted. There was no response.

61. Uva's Stories (4)

It had been a lonely time for Farson. Even though as a ScreenMaster, he was here and other places as well, here on her ship was lonely. It was a huge vessel with only the two of them to inhabit it.

He would look out the vast portals and watch space go by as the months went by too. He had been on the ship for nearly a year. The last time he saw Uva had been at least eight months ago. He thought he saw her once in the Aviary, but he could not confirm it. Farson tended to hang out there, unconsciously hoping to see her. The impact of his last encounter was still strong within him. *She certainly has made her point.*

On this day, he was back in the Aviary again. The umbrella plants were just as beautiful. The air's movement made him want to fly again. He was lying on a patch of grass he had cleared, staring up at the enormous skylights that lined the interior of Uva's ship. He was thinking of how she had flown under Uvo and him. He could still feel the power of her inverted wings and the gentleness of her feathered touch.

Then, through the large, forward port, he noticed a large planet coming smoothly into view. He realized Uva's ship had entered orbit. He recognized the planet Aristealia. *She's home.*

For the next few days the starship *Rachis* was silent, its great engines off. Farson walked around as though for exercise, striding with purpose and intent, but he was *really* looking for Uva now. He had decided to walk from one end to other. He had done this many times, but now he did it, "clearing" each section as he went. He was determined to find her. It took a few days, but he did it. She was in the bow, the forward-most compartment. The last place to look.

The stars were a panorama through the curved transparency of the bullet-shaped room. Farson could see straight ahead, a new view for him after months in the body of the starship. Uva had her ship orbiting with its nose toward the planet, so that beneath the stars, Aristealia filled the view with its great beauty and the restlessness of a planet teeming with life. Farson felt awe looking down at Uva's amazing home planet. He had once been in this area of the ship before in the dark of space flight, but today she was there, sitting alone, staring down at her planet in all its sun-spilled glory.

"I'll never go back, Farson." She spoke to him as though in an ongoing conversation, even though he had not seen her for many months. No explanation offered. "It hurts just to look at it, knowing how many of us there are. How all of them are living free, together, in the peace that is the right of every Aristealian. That will never again happen for me." Farson wasn't sure what to say. He sadly agreed with her. Uva's stories had taken him to a level of understanding that could not, and would not, be denied. No words were needed. He just looked at her. Her beautiful, angular face turned toward him for the first time. "You just think you understand, Farson. It offends me that you do think that. Your empathy is sadly incomplete; perhaps your human makeup blocks you from full understanding. Uvo told me that your race is sincere and well intentioned, and that, coupled with your innate powers, you would be great partners for us. He said that you would understand." She was now staring at Farson like an eagle descending toward a hapless prey. Farson felt his arms stiffen and an immobility overtaking him. He knew exactly what was happening. He had been waiting. He opened his mind and embraced it. She could sense his joy in returning. If he could have seen her sitting there, he would have noticed Uva very slightly shaking her head, as though watching a fledgling attempting to fly: awkwardly, haltingly, crudely, ineptly flapping wings that did lift but with comical over-effort, and uncertainly.

But, now, Farson was far, far away.

Uvo's wings were flying with strength and grace, like a long-distance runner halfway home. The sky was beautiful and big; Farson looked around, and he felt like the sky went on forever. They flew through moist clouds, and he noticed how cool the air was in them, and when it warmed, as they exited the cloud, Farson could feel the rush of happiness he had experienced on previous occasions flying with Uvo. He relaxed into Uvo and felt the full extent of his old friend's physicality, from wing tip to wing tip, and from head to tail. Farson could feel the minute adjustments in position and wing-pitching that Uvo was constantly doing. He could feel each feather as it adjusted and reached for expression. It reminded Farson of stretching his own body. It seemed as if Aristealia's sky was flying them with its soft up currents and subtle changes in the winds. Farson felt like they were miles high. There was soft brushing of feathers and awareness as something flew by. It was Uva in all her glory. There are differences in the male and female Aristealians. The men are strong and piercing in flight, like fighter jets. The women were astoundingly graceful and magnificent and somewhat larger in full flight than the male. But most of all, when they spread their wings, their plumage expanded in layers and reflected the colors of the sky and sun and sea all around them. Farson was hypnotized by her appearance, and, he realized, so was Uvo. His wing movements slowed, but were now deeper in the air. He spread his wings as far as they would go. His body arched slightly, and he began to slowly descend. It took Farson a moment before he realized that Uvo was descending into Uva. Farson could feel Uvo's excitement – sharing it, really. The sky, the warm currents, the soft winds of passage, the clouds around … it was enthralling. Farson was excited. Uvo and Uva flew together for a few moments, maybe minutes; Farson could feel them embracing. He could *really* feel them. He could feel Uvo finally enter her. He could feel her relishing acceptance; more than that really, she was guiding him, surrounding him. Farson could feel her surrender, her sublimity, her domination, her love, her lust, her hunger. He could taste her yearn. He could feel Uvo's rising passion. And then he felt a bonding, an integration, a blending and swirling in which Uvo and Uva became one.

Not in the metaphorical sense, but literally. Farson was astounded. Uva seemed to have disappeared, and now there was just one great, flying Aristealian, and Farson was filled with sensations he had never experienced, could not experience. He was overwhelmed in the pleasure, and it seemed to go on and on. He could sense Uva's completeness, her rapture of sharing, but even more, it was like a birth. It was a beginning. Farson was gasping for understanding, even as he deepened into their union. Then he realized that everything he ever knew about the Aristealians was woefully incomplete. They were a race of staggering emotional power, a race that could actually change their individualities, a race that could love like no other. Now they were flying with abandon and with complete involvement with the moments of metamorphosis. Their ecstasy was a sensory overload for Farson, immediately when they joined but even more now as the intensity grew and grew the longer they flew, into something beyond Farson's comprehension. He was immersed. Everything seemed to be building toward something, but they pulled back from the edge over and over and over. Farson was growing desperate with a passion of his own which he did not understand, a longing for a release he could not comprehend, but could not resist.

And on and on they flew. The building exaltation continued seemingly without limits, and then the final climax began. Farson was with them as they were born, when they first flew, when they first met and mated. He was there at the birth of their daughter; he felt everything both as Uvo, and as Uva now. She had given him full access. Farson watched their lives in every moment and memory. He felt them fall in love in a long textured sequence as though they were both enjoying it all again and again and again. He was with them. He *was* them, a full participant in ineffable joy and unquenchable ecstasy.

And then it ended. Farson was falling, but he was with Uva now. Uvo was gone. The emptiness was excruciating. The sadness was unfathomable for him, but the pain was real. He felt suffocation. He felt anguish and ache. He felt searching and searing emptiness. He felt death rushing up as Uva fell and fell, back to Aristealia. She was alone now, defeated; she was succumbing to despair and a welcoming death. Farson realized she was committing suicide right in front of him, as the ground came rushing, rushing toward her … then nothing.

Uva, in the bow of *Rachis*, sat up with a start. "Farson!" The windows showed a stable orbit over the planet and the twinkling stars all around. "Farson!" Again, she screamed his name in her high-pitched, throating call. Nothing. The room was silent, still as a tomb. Uva remembered the rapture, her falling, and a brief flash of bright purple. Suddenly, her ship felt empty and abandoned.

Farson was gone.

62. Handy Leaves the Harvester

He thought he would be staying on Emerald Earth for several more years, but now Handy knew that would not be true. He was leaving already. Strapper John was surprised, but he knew Handy marched to a drumbeat that only he could hear. Still, it seemed a sudden departure to Strapper. "Is everything okay?" Handy smiled at his new friend. They had had a nice time getting to know each other. John had not been exaggerating about never running out of whiskey. Even though, all things being equal, Handy preferred scotch, he clearly had acquired an appreciation of the harvester's brewing capabilities, and for the smoothness and calibre of their brand. Even now, the two of them were having one last drink together, to say goodbye.

Strapper John was looking out the window. "Do they always do that, Handy?" Handy had to laugh at them. The grass dolphins: A never-ending source of surprise.

"No. No they don't. It's the first time I've ever seen them do it. But it's a pretty clear message, don't you think?" At first, it appeared to be a pillar of burning wheat. But on closer inspection, the truth was obvious. Thousands of grass dolphins had created a living tower of spiraling, turning, churning bodies, their bright underbellies flashing like flames, now reaching over one hundred feet in the air, to attract Handy's attention. Like a tapering fire tornado against the amber sky of Emerald Earth, it was one of the most beautiful things either of them had ever seen. There were eagles flying around with the turning of the tower, but its rotation was too fast, and there were no opportunities to strike.

Handy could feel the mental pressure from the dolphins for him to get moving.

we have to get going handy things are happening

Handy took another deep drink, and the ice cubes clinked against his lips and teeth. He wiped his mouth on his shirtsleeve and set the glass down. "All good things must come to an end, John."

"Don't say that, Handy. We both know it's not true." They were both smiling. Emerald Earth's 6,520-year history was all the proof either of them would ever need that good things could go on forever.

"Well, I have to go. The grass dolphins are insisting. Something's up."

"Will we know what it is?" Strapper was curious, not worried.

"I have a feeling we will all know soon enough."

"Have you heard from Farson?" Handy was thinking this over. His connection with Farson, at times strong and at times weaker, was always present. But during the past week on

Emerald Earth he had noticed a quieting, then nothing. Now the dolphin tower signal.

handy we have to go we are coming closer

He looked over at the tower, and it was moving toward him. John noticed it too. "It's really huge. How are they doing that?"

"How do they do anything? They work together and use the planet."

"They seem to like you."

"No doubt there. I can't get rid of them." The tower slowly submerged as it neared the harvester. Both men could feel the swell as it passed underneath. A raft with a shape like a chair formed at the side of the great machine, still moving, still doing its job. Handy stepped to the rail. He turned to Strapper John. "Many thanks for your hospitality, John. I came to prepare you for changes coming. Apparently, they may be coming faster than we thought. So, this is goodbye for now." They shook hands. Strapper had something more to say.

"I don't make friends easily, Handy. But you are one now. You are always welcome here. Think of it as a vacation from things. We just keep on mowing the grass and shipping it off. Never-ending. It's a life to be cherished, like all life. But for us, it is heaven. Thanks for coming. Please come back again."

"I'll be back, John. I love this place. Many thanks." They shook hands again, embracing and solidifying their time together and their friendship. A harvester captain on the great plains of Emerald Earth and a lone ScreenMaster who came out of nowhere and was now leaving for parts unknown as well. "You didn't answer my question."

Handy stepped onto the grass dolphins. They were already moving away as he said, "Farson and I are always in touch." And then they were off.

Strapper John was surprised at how fast they moved away and out of sight into the endless green and amber fields. He turned back to the operations of the harvester. He felt like it had all happened in the blink of an eye. But, actually, Handy had been aboard for almost three weeks. He called down to the operations crew.

"I want a full systems check on everything. Tighten up the entire array, secure everything for a change of course. Something's up, and we have to be ready." *For anything.*

Handy regretted not telling John the truth. He knew that saying he and Farson were always in touch was no longer completely accurate. He had noticed, just as the dolphins began to form their tower, that Farson was absent from his mind. It was disorienting.

Handy sent a powerful thought out over The Screen: *<<Farson?>>* It just echoed back unanswered. *<<Farson?>>* He sent it out again. And again.

63. Essor, This Time Will Be Different

Twill was in his glory. He had assumed the highest rank, and everything had worked out exactly as planned. He enjoyed reliving those days, forty-three years ago on the Essor's calendar, fourteen in SkyKing years. Essor was flush with the efflorescence of his extravagance and power. It was as if all of their history had destined them to this new eminence. And Twill was finally at home. At the bottom of Lake DurR, 1,900 feet below the planet's deadly bright and richly oxygenated surface and atmosphere, the denizen population had developed, over thousands of years, into a complex warren, as they called it, that happily housed the population of Essor safely, and luxuriously for the elite, who now had crowned Twill as their undisputed leader. To others, it might have appeared dark and freezing cold, but to the Essors, this was perfect heaven. Even the name Essor meant sanctuary in their language. Twill had traveled widely as a ScreenMaster, but he had quickly tired of it. To him, the universe should come to Essor, not the other way around. He wanted nothing more, as he thought of it, than to be Grand ScreenMaster and stay right there on Essor.

That's exactly what he was doing. The opulence of the superior class was sumptuous and confirming for them and disheartening and discouraging for the rest of the population, but who cared? On Essor, things were as they always had been, and as they always will be. There's no changing Essor. It is an enormous planet and the phrase "the lake" on Essor has the same meaning as "continent" or "hemisphere" or the word "everything" has for other races. There were tens of billions of Essors working within the huge planet. Specialization had evolved to such a level that each Essor had a lifetime of employment on some infinitesimally small assignment, so detailed and nuanced that it realistically could never be finished. Progress was all that mattered on Essor. Achievement was a species term for them, like evolution. Far distant from any notion of individuality, the Essor's underclass labored faithfully on their assignments all of their lives, unmindful of their insignificance and exploitation. They just were too busy to think about such things.

She had worked for years as part of a team coordinating stasis satellites around Earth with Essor's mazy systems of subterranean "composers," which were the main data conduits for all operations within the warren, and also the sole link to outside communications.[3] The innumerable redundancies built into the system's infrastructure and instrumentalities required monitoring, constant upgrades, and modifications at levels of intricacy that would have left most species in hopeless cycles of thwart and distress, but for the Essors, were

---

[3] The readers of volume one, The Rise of Farson Uiost, will remember this individual as the Essor technician who brought an issue concerning the control of the stasis field to Master Twill's attention, at her own peril, and who was dismissed as irrelevant and meaningless to his plans for his Grand Ascension and the simultaneous destruction of Earth, Farson, and all who helped him. If Twill had heeded her warning, history could have turned out far differently.

normal to the point of everyday routine. There were so many, working on every detail, that – because of this exquisite focus on every grain of even the most remote and infinitesimal root elements – things went along like clockwork: every apparent anomaly hammered into its place in the schema of operation, which constantly changed as the stream of data required. Questions were not asked because myriad options were always available to provide new pathways of observation. Questions meant doubt, or a lack of clear options, which never happened. There was always a way. The smooth operations of Essor's hegemony were made possible by the affluence of alternatives which always presented itself in the nature of things. An endless process of ever deeper analysis always led to the verities of sequence and invention; the Essor way. Except for the one time she had felt compelled to bring a situation to the attention of ScreenMaster Twill, which resulted in rejection, impatience, and, worst of all, his excruciating annoyance at her devotion to Essor's implacable proscription against insolubility. On that occasion the impossible had occurred: In her data stream analysis she had encountered an unknowable unknown. It was very small, perhaps insignificant, but that made no difference. It was a bump in the dependably smooth and unwavering certainty of Essor's system. It couldn't be there, but it was. It was an infinitely small adumbration, as she had described it to Twill, but its implication was clear. Despite her searching of alternatives, options, redefinitions; despite her repeating of past sequences, inventing new ones, and reverifying all current directions of inquiry, she had failed at resolution: Something unplanned had occurred. Her difficulty in communicating this effectively to Master Twill was understandable given her low station. His response was dismissive and final, if conditionally stated: "Let me know when and if you ever have anything to actually report on this matter. Otherwise, don't interrupt me again." Twill's disinterest was surprising to her. How could he not care? How could she have better presented it to him? She had returned to her data stream only to realize that, with the interruption, she may never catch up again. But, through assiduous attention to detail, and diligence in pressing on, she eventually did catch up again, many years later.

For her it had been an exciting time. She had clearly known that something had happened, and she continuously tracked the anomaly during the ensuing period after Twill's disregard. It slowly faded out in a diminishing pattern that became so predictable that when it finally ended, it was as though an instrument with a faulty part that very faintly affected the overall harmonic of the orchestra, noticeable only if one knew the defect's specialized signature, was finally, and inexplicably repaired. After that point, things resumed their beautiful predictability and symmetry, all in perfect balance. She was saddened, in a way, because the fact that, whatever it was, would now probably never be known. She was happy because it was over and her assigned pathway was again unimpeded by doubt or protocol requirements that could force her to leave her post again in search of guidance. Her relief was almost a sensual excitation as she pressed on past that point. To be back on track without distraction was her dream come true.

And then it happened again. With vast regret, she reluctantly backtracked down the data stream. It took awhile, so long in fact she was doubting herself ever finding it, but she did find it. It took more time to retrieve and compare the previous event with this one, and then even more time to assess the differentials, and there were many. But one thing stood out, this time. She was informed by her previous experience. Some eccentric event had entered the stream, causing a duality that diminished quickly, like a line splicing, until it also disappeared. As she tracked back up the stream to her last progressive position, she realized that this new adumbration had changed the valuations and weightings of some obscure variables, ever so slightly, and this time she saw more clearly at least one obvious implication. This, she knew, would mean another audience with Twill. She resolved to take her time and prepare evidentially much more carefully. *This time,* she thought, *it will be different.*

64. A Visit with Silver

Since the return of the happy bride to the Moon, Long John Hanson Silver was no longer in command, technically, but no one had the courage or inclination to remind him of that. In his mind, and in his attitude and actions, his command remained in full force. He was currently in the "engine room," as the crew called the great chamber where the nuclear thrust nozzles for the Moon's movements and velocity were housed and maintained. It was an enormous structure, embedded beneath the surface with an exhaust tunnel made of the most hardened materials the Moon could create. The tunnel led to the surface and was surrounded by a huge, fortified blast shield that protected the Moon from topical destruction each time the engines were fired. There were also access shafts with transitional bellows, somewhat like on SkyKing, that protected the interior of the Moon from radiation and "blow back," as the crew enjoyed calling the resulting catastrophic exhaust bursts. The entire complex was surrounded with dampeners, that expertly redirected all recoil, explosion, and seismographic energies into maximizing the directional thrust generated by the detonations. Silver's sole focus was directed at the "armory" crew who was responsible for the stocking, readiness, and unfettered access to the supply of warheads used to initiate, alter, and maintain the speed and direction of the Moon's flight in space. The devices were all of different sizes and potencies. Having them properly organized, stockpiled, cataloged, and positioned could mean the difference between life and death for the Moon. Everyone knew it. The Moon could sail along for months virtually unattended, its mass and the vacuum of space supplying the inertia of steady velocity and heading, but SkyKing always governed the movements of the Moon, acting as the helm of the formation. The slightest change in SkyKing's passage resulted in a magnification of compliance activity on the Moon. SkyKing was agile in comparison to the Moon's bulky, awkward system of steerage. What was done so easily by Repoul Bensn on the station resulted in hundreds of MoonBasers rushing into action stations and commencing laborious operations to mirror Bensn's course, speed, attitude, or sail trim corrections. Over the years the Moon's system had been augmented and refined by practice, by new EmerTech applications, and certainly by the torturous, bombastic, and all too often profoundly profane orders that Silver shouted at the top of his lungs for maximum effect. He was demonstrating his capacity for impacting events at this very moment.

"What the fuck are you assholes doing? You've got to do the big motherfuckers first, shitheads. What do you think? We're in fucking orbit? When we need to move, we'll need to move fast like a cocksucker in a gay bar, dipshits. We're not going to need those little dicks now. We need the big, manly ones up front. Get the ones like your puny little *penises* out of there and put the big fat ones in the slots. He emphasized the words "little *penises*" by holding his thumb and forefinger with, maybe, a sixteenth of an inch space between them, to amplify how small the penises of the male crew members must really be. Some of the women in the group were laughing at the men around them. The crew started to rearrange the nukes without further delay. Instead of anger or embarrassment, the men tried to get the women to push the big warheads out, shouting to them, "Hump it, girls! You know how to do it!" The women responded with appropriate remarks about how well the men seemed to be handling the small devices by themselves. Long John Hanson Silver was satisfied with the effective legerity of their collective response and let the fact that they were enjoying themselves slide. He noticed a purple hue forming in his small, enclosed command observation station. The room could hold four or five people, but Hanson was alone in there. Farson now materialized next to him.

"Master Sergeant. How are you?" Silver noticed that several of the crew members were watching.

"Farson. How's it hanging?" Farson smiled at Silver's irreverence, in no way surprised. "Karina sends her regards." Hanson wasn't quite done yet. He was hoping to offend the ScreenMaster. "How are those little brats of yours?" Farson knew this could only be the beginning.

"Felicity is happy, and Valgary is ready for new worlds." Silver was thinking of saying something about Farson's wanting manhood, with only daughters, but he let the moment for that retort pass. His visitor seemed intent on some purpose and perhaps not really ready for the continuing sexual innuendos and insults. He acquiesced. Farson spoke very clearly to his old friend. "Sergeant, we are going to be needing you and your boys and girls. How soon can you and your crew and equipment be on the surface of Sargasso?" This was unexpected.

"With the new tech we have now, four days." Farson was starting to fade out in purple light.

"Step on it, John. Trouble's coming. Be prepared to fight a holding action. The exact surface coordinates are being sent to Repoul." He disappeared. The Master Sergeant realized again that his dreams of command and situational control were self-delusion. As he was rethinking his next actions, he noticed that the crew below had stopped working and were all looking up at him.

"What the fuck?" He shouted. "Move it! Shit's comin' our way." He turned and left the command station, thinking to himself, *Viera, here I come.* The crew below resumed adjusting the stockpile. In a few hours things were set right. But word was spreading throughout MoonBase: something was happening.

65. Twill Is Alerted

Twill was in his chambers, which he had enthusiastically and vaingloriously aggrandized to a puzzling point of excessiveness that shocked even the Essors, who were universally accustomed to a level of attention to detail that left no stone unturned, no opportunity unexplored. Still, as he stood at his virtual podium, ensconced in self-indulgence, and prepared to address his realm which now included The Screen itself as well as his precious and beloved Essor, the center of his power, the last thing on his mind was that he would be interrupted. He was just about to signal to the comlaser crews to begin the transmission, when it happened.

"Master Twill?" In the deep and dark traditions of Essor, a world of welcomed shadows and beloved coldness with a people who hated and feared the deadly warmth and light that warmed so many other species, no one would ever blame the technician for following her data stream to wherever, and whenever, it led her. It was, after all, the path to which they had assigned her. But Twill stood on ceremony the way others stood on floors. It was essential to his existence. He had fought too hard and done too much to allow any diminishment of even one moment of his supremacy, even now as it was approaching fifty Essor years since his first Ascendancy. Any breach of protocol, any variation from his grand design was usually punished, immediately and mercilessly. His ruthlessness with dissent or diversion was feared so forcefully in anticipation, that in the memory of many, it had never occurred. Twill remembered, though. *Farson.* Even the briefest mental appearance of that cursed name, so briefly and dismissively coming to his mind, caused a nasty snarl to appear behind his rigid mandible, on his moist and retracting lips, and his lower talons scratched on the floor beneath him as they clenched. The flash of anger from thinking of Farson, for the first time in many years, was almost eruptive, but he kept it under control. Barely. He turned quickly to look behind him in response to his name being spoken. There was no one there. Then he looked down. He recognized her.

"You?" The word was spoken with such disdain that the technician had already retracted into her shell, a symbol of respect on Essor, or in fear of attack. Twill assumed the latter and spoke less intensely to acknowledge her surrender. "What could you possibly want?" The comlaser crews had backed off their controls, and Twill knew that everyone, everywhere, was waiting now for him. He loved the intensified moment. The cowering technician felt it severely and was attempting to formulate her response carefully. The resolute routine of her life had brought her to this moment, but in no way had it prepared her. The logic of her data stream had systematically dictated her appearance here, but now she was on her own, no protocols, no procedures, no schematic for the next step.

"Yes, Master Twill," her voice was clear but unsteady. "You told me to come back when I had something to tell you." Oddly enough, he did remember this conversation with the insignificant technician. It had occurred in the moments before his final triumph over ... he could not say or even allow himself to think that name again. His impatience was rising like magma building up inside one of Essor's towering volcanoes.

"And...?" His interrogative was almost spit out, in a hissing whisper.

"Well," she paused, composing each word, "it has happened again."

"What!?" His impatience was getting the better of him now. He had actually barked the word. She retracted slightly again, having briefly begun to extend herself, but now pressed on, holding a middle position. She was determined to stay the course this time. Fifty years had taught her much. She had relived and rethought her previous experience with Master Twill a thousand times. In some reminiscences, she realized she had been in mortal danger; in others, she realized that her fear had hindered her effectiveness; in others, she had resolved to stand her ground if it ever happened again; and in still others, she had meekly sidestepped the confrontation, ignoring the proof clearly in front of her and disregarded the anomaly in favor of the calm and predictable existence Essors loved so dearly. But, despite all of that, here she was again in the exact same situation fifty years later. She decided to say the exact words she had said before.

"There was a bump, sir." One of Twill's short and stubby arms with its scaly, clawed hand lashed out and knocked the small technician off her feet. She reflexively recoiled into her shell, tucking in as tight as she knew how, as it slid across the floor spinning to a stop several feet away, upside down. Twill stepped down from the podium and moved toward her. She retracted even farther inside as he approached. Suddenly, her protective shell, a lifelong refuge, now seemed thin and vulnerable for the first time. He stood over her. He could see her fearful eyes shining with trepidation from inside the shadow of her shell.

"What *kind* of a bump?" Ironically, he also had repeated his exact words from the first encounter. He was now bending over the technician's shell, his face getting closer. She could see the coldness in his eyes. Her voice now had a slight echoing reverberation to it. It sounded farther away than it was. Twill moved even closer. The shell shifted slightly as she tried to back away with nowhere to go. Her voice seemed far away as she answered.

"This time I was able to track the vibration and noticed that it was interruptive rather than a progressive miscue within the data stream programming. It came from outside." This brought a fury to Twill's condescending attitude, reflected in the volume of his next question. After the hissing whisper, this loud response startled everyone, and intensely focused all attention on the technician hiding in her overturned shell on the floor. This incredible misuse of his important time, and the fact that all attention had shifted from him to her, an insignificant automaton who spent her life chasing down never-ending data streams, was infuriating. But the implications of what she had just said trumped his crazed desire to kill her on the spot. He lashed out with another assault, posed as a question, not whispering at all this time.

"What did it *do?*" The small voice in the shell responded in a distancing voice, fearful, and yet courageous at the same time.

"Nothing that I could detect."

"Nothing?" He shouted it so loudly, his larynx and esophagus bulged and vibrated painfully.

"Well, not 'nothing' since it registered in the most heavily encrypted levels of the tertiary waveform polynomials, maybe even deeper. At that level there are variables and indeterminates that can obscure full and reliable observation, so approximations must suffice, and ..." Her voice had begun to grate on Twill, his impatience falling like a guillotine's blade toward its bloody conclusion.

"Stop! What in the name of Essor are you talking about?" The moment of truth had come. In all her ruminations about their previous, nearly disastrous encounter, the technician had never envisioned being knocked across the floor, being upside down, hiding in her shell, and having a screaming Grand

ScreenMaster shouting at her in front of hundreds of people, perhaps the entire planet. It was a far cry from her safe little station, deep within the warren, surrounded by her faithful and non-combative instrumentation array. She was thinking how much she wanted to be back there right now. "Speak up!" Twill's voice rattled her shell with its vehemence. She was so tight in there that her halting response was not clearly heard by Master Twill. This only angered him more. His clawed hands, together, smashed down on her shell. It hurt. Essorian shells were sentient and even erogenous at times, so this impact was shocking and painful. She realized that things were getting out of control. Her only course had to be direct and immediate if she wanted to survive. This time she shouted back.

"Someone or something caused a brief interruption of control. It was an infinitesimally modest interference with an otherwise flawless stream. It had no effect that I could determine." Twill backed slightly, shocked that so many had heard this assault on his unquestioned supremacy and control. For the first time he spoke at a lower volume.

"This happened fifty years ago?" She instinctively continued to shout.

"Yes. And I detected an echo of it again."

"When? And you don't need to scream." He was interested.

"Several days ago," somewhat softer but still perfectly clear through the chamber, her shell acting like a muffled megaphone. She was actually hiding the fact that it was a month ago. Data stream analysis generally took lifetimes, so 'a few days ago' was merely underreporting proportionably, and at this point, every word was a life-and-death matter. Twill felt like he was being battered with bad news dripping on his vaulted rock of supremacy. His next question was couched as though to the ticks of a metronome at its slowest tempo.

"Technician, what actually happened?"

"Nothing, sir."

"Nothing?"

"Yes, sir. Nothing. Which is my point. Nothing never happens. Everything always causes something in the data stream. But this did nothing."

"So nothing happened?"

"Correct." To Twill the entire conversation had a deep deja vu to it; the frustration, the pressing events of the moment, the stupid, stupid technician with a life wasted in remote and uninteresting minutia, his embarrassing reactions of fury and roiling annoyance, the waves of doubting turbulence that had followed him for all these years. He was not going to allow it to happen all over again. He kicked the carapace, and it spun like a heavy top, wobbling unevenly. He shouted it into her shell, which seemed to recoil as the words rifled in. He raised his arms in an attack posture, talons unsheathed and tensed to rip.

"WHAT HAPPENED?!" Inside she was helpless and now terrified. One Essor kicking a helpless other was almost always followed by a death blow. History was instructive. She knew it was do or die. She had planned an ultimate response, in the month of her planning: a desperate shot in the dark, the most extreme measure someone of her station could ever attempt, and only then to avoid fatal destruction. Her nervousness and fright slurred her words.

"Idon'tknowbutImayhavecoordinates!"

66. The Sargasso Insinuate

Before every momentous event in a person's life, things seem to slow down as if stretching out, extending every second. It is a suspension of normality, a pressing of the inexorable, a squeezing out of every moment for all it's worth. Once decisions are made and dies are cast, this slowing traps us in muffled sounds; we see things moving, but with so much in the scales – unfathomed changes weighting each side of success or failure – the outcome lingers before us as though suspended in our hopes and fears. There is a realization of the freedom of letting things take their course, for better or for worse. There is nothing we can do. Reality is on its way. The truth alone will set us free.

Repoul watched *Songbird* accelerate toward Sargasso. He braced at his desk as the distance, and his eyes, closed. At the last second he reopened them and what he saw left him utterly speechless. Just as in the simulations, *Songbird* exploded in a bright flash – a spectacular ball of fire and disaster. As the fateful debris spun away with death and destruction, the remote cameras showed that Sargasso remained unchanged and defiant, not a scratch.

Twill had made a decision. The regal transmission was cancelled. He ordered all Essor warships to prepare. A fleet of a thousand ships, the most powerful ever known anywhere, began to stir in the bowels of the dark planet like indigestion or hunger for a long-awaited feast. The planet was aroused to action. Twill took command of the largest ship and led the fleet into space. The insignificant technician's coordinates had been plotted into every ship's navigation, and into the seething intent of every Essor aboard. Like the armies of old, marching out to find the hated enemy, Essor's power and ferocity were now unleashed, led by the Grand ScreenMaster himself; destination: either destiny or destruction. Essor had come out of its shell.

Farson was not surprised. They had transitioned through the surface of Sargasso as though it was not there and now *Songbird* was safely inside. The view was not what Farson expected. On that first visit, what he remembered was the vivid image of Emerald Earth floating inside Sargasso with SkyKing and the Moon in a tight orbit. It had been so beautiful to him, so astounding in its implications, so outside of anything he had imagined, that he had stood there on the platform in silence, attempting to process what he was seeing. That image was what he had wanted Voul to see. Instead, the vast interior of Sargasso stretched out before him, a solar system enclosed, with planets and a single star shining brilliantly in the center. There were also moons and other objects orbiting some of the planets. Somehow, Farson knew. There were people here, and lots of them.

Voul stirred beside him He was taking off the restraints he had strapped into for blastoff. "What was that, Farson? I detected a bright flash behind us just as we entered." There had been no impact at all for them. There was a slight slowing as they went through the deep crust of Sargasso, but it had been smooth as silk. Farson had seen the flash as well.

"I think it might have appeared to anyone watching that *Songbird* was destroyed with all hands, just like the simulations." Farson's hand was on his forehead moving slowly through his hair. He realized as he spoke the words, the others would think they had died violently, and that there was nothing he could do about it. He had the sense of aloneness he had experienced in his own Ascension, of being apart, of being away. "I have lost The Screen, Voul. I cannot communicate." Voul's experience with the power of The Screen, as all human beings had now experienced in varying degrees of volition and desire, also informed him that it was gone for him as well. Farson added, "I am so glad you came, Voul."

Voul cast his eyes around the controls and monitors as if looking for something. "Something's not right, Farson." He stood up and started to walk through the cabin. He opened doors and looked in the passageways and compartments around the bridge. "I think someone is here with us now."

Farson stood up. He could feel something happening. His mind had shifted to a new gear, as though in growth or expansion, or as if a new idea had entered and excited his thoughts. New options. New possibilities. Suddenly, he knew.

"It's a different Screen, Voul. We are in a different Screen now." He was astounded. Amazed. He could sense its richness, its wealth of experience. *A whole new milieu.* He was enjoying it. Then he saw her in his mind as clear as day. He raced past Voul, saying, "Come with me."

As they left the control area, the ship was flying straight and true, no impediments anywhere, with lots of open space in all directions.

They went down the spiral staircase into the lower, main level of the vessel. Farson was heading directly for the bow. Now at a run, through the stateroom area, the galley, through the large and beautiful recreational and dining areas, through the libraries and through all of the other compartments. He came to the door of the forward observation room. He had designed it for relaxation and privacy, thinking of Karina. He opened the door to the spacious area. Foremost in the slendering taper of the sleek starship's bow, the room was still easily fifteen feet wide. There were couches, and the room was filled with the light of Sargasso's sun and the reflections of its brilliance on the orbiting planets. On the couch at the very tip of the room, sitting as though she had been there forever was Uva. She stretched her wings elegantly and then settled back again. It was an ancient Aristealian greeting. Farson had seen it many times. He was about to say something, but she stopped him. "What did you expect, Farson? That I would stay home and let you have all the fun? After all, I am a ScreenMaster, too."

When Uva experienced Farson's abrupt departure from *Rachis,* her starship, just as it had achieved orbit around the beautiful Aristealia, she had acted immediately. In the months of their passage together, she had studied Farson carefully, including the Thanksgiving interlude. Uvo had taught her much about human beings, especially their unguarded nature of thought. In her studies she learned of a secret that Farson hid well, a secret she could not fully uncover, but there were elements that she could see. Uvo had shown her how human beings interpret the powers of a ScreenMaster and how they approach it in such a thoroughly different way than others. He had shown her their ways, but he had no explanation, other than his description of them as good, well intentioned, and uniquely powerful. She took her husband at his word and in the course of telling her stories to Farson, it had been she who had learned; it had been she who had changed. The sadness of that reality had caused her to withdraw from contact for many months. She discovered that as Farson grew in his understanding of Uvo and Uva together, she had also grown in her understanding of Uvo and Farson. She had learned how wrong she had been. In their final flight together with Uvo, Uva had realized her own love for Farson, her appreciation of his love for Uvo, and by extension, of course, his love for her. She realized that he had taken a year to spend with her: a year in which he stayed with her without distraction. She came to realize what that meant, the sacrifice he had made. The joy he had in doing it. She realized that Farson, like her, could not and would not let go of Uvo. When Farson disappeared, a sadness-like grief nearly overcame her. She didn't just follow Farson to Sargasso. She chased him in desperation. It took everything that Uvo had ever taught her, it took all her own experience, including LevelTen and beyond, but, in the end, she found him and quietly entered the bow of *Songbird*, awaiting destruction or salvation, not knowing what the outcome would be just before the "impact" occurred. She had made a leap of faith to stay with Farson; she had gambled everything. Now, looking in his eyes, seeing his relief and his love, seeing he was so happy to see her, she knew she had done the right thing.

There were now two kinds of ScreenMasters: the old and the true. The old ScreenMasters had all accepted Twill, perhaps missing Farson, but bending to the arc of their own histories, they had chosen things as they were over things as they might be. The true, the Emer ScreenMasters were all the children of Emerald Earth. Farson and Karina were both old and Emer ScreenMasters. They were the only ones. The old knew nothing of the new, and the Emers knew everything, old *and* new. The Emers had proven, over 6,500 years, that they were worthy, and, well, … true. Farson loved them and had joined them to the greatest degree he could. They revered him as an avatar who embodied the past, the present, and the future. He tried to steer them into considering him as just a friend passing through, but they knew better.

Uva's appearance on *Songbird* was a surprise to Farson, but she was also a welcome addition. He could not help smiling at her. "For so long I couldn't find you, couldn't speak with you, and now you chase me down across The Screen and appear to be content with living on my little barge."

"Well, you spent plenty of time on mine. What is it you say? 'Fair is fair?'" She was obviously pleased with his confusion. "My last story had a surprise ending."

"That it did, Uva. That it did."

"Karina may not be pleased." Farson knew exactly what she was talking about.

"Karina will understand." Farson remembered that Voul was standing there with them. He began to introduce him. "Uva, I would like you to meet…" She interrupted him.

"I am well aware of the great Voul Jonsn, King of the Skers." She stood and walked to Voul. She curtsied beautifully and then extended her small hand and thin arm toward Voul. Voul took her hand in his. He had a flash of insight. She was flying through the beautiful skies of Aristealia; there was another flying with her. He blinked and saw her beautiful angled eyes looking into his, curiously searching. It was a powerful moment. "It is very nice to see you in person. In your courage and comprehension, you more than live up to your reputation." She ended their handshake, and, leaving Voul vertiginous with her praise, she turned to Farson and said, as though nothing unusual had occurred, "Where are we now?"

It was a question often asked in human history, as though not knowing was part of the fun or the danger, whichever the case may be. "Are we there yet?" was another often asked question, sometimes interchangeable with Uva's, that could introduce an additional element of urgency or impatience embedded in its speaking; or just the enjoyment of propelling the thought that it really doesn't matter "when we get there," because it's the journey, as they say. As Farson contemplated his response to Uva's less complicated question, he also considered the implications of his answer. If he told her, he would have changed the future. If he didn't tell her, then all that he had learned and shared with her would all be for nothing. First a few questions of his own.

"How did you get here?"

"I followed you. We have grown closer than you know." This caused a brief pause in the exchange as images of their last flight filled his consciousness again. It was pleasing. It was vital and virile. It was exciting, arousing. He tried to change his train of thought, but it was not easy. There was a longing for that closeness, for that completeness; it was alluring and tempting; it was love like he had only felt for Karina. Uva was looking at him. She was seeing, in her mind, the last vestiges of Uvo's presence, the last ripples of his life; the final tendrils still reaching out from the grave. She could not let him go. It was why she was here; it was like a hunger. "I had no choice."

Farson nodded. He felt it too, and like Uva, he could not dismiss it. All of it had brought Uvo back into his life; it had refreshed those memories; it had warmed him as their friendship always had, with reassurance and constancy.

<<*I know now that you did truly love him, Farson. I regret doubting you.*>>

<<*I understand your love now, Uva. I know I was to blame. How can you ever forgive me?*>>

<<*We have flown together, Farson. That is forgiveness. That is love. We have shared Aristealia. The name itself means 'courageous surrender.' The surrender of self, the courage of love. All is well, Farson. Fear not. I have joined your little flock.*>>

<<*In our ways, love and trust always go together.*>>

<<*Agreed. I may never know all the secrets of human love, but I do know trust, and I do know loyalty. In that, you and I are one now.*"

"We are in Sargasso, Uva. We are here to explore and see for ourselves what this place really is. I was briefly here before, but it has changed." Voul had stood by patiently as the two ScreenMasters had exchanged their thoughts. He could hear their conversation, of course, but had remained silent. As he spoke, they turned to him.

"What has changed, Farson?" It took Farson a few moments to gather his thoughts to answer Voul's question. It was important that he got it right. Much was hanging in the balance.

"When I stood on the platform and looked into Sargasso for the first time, I saw Emerald Earth, with the Moon and SkyKing orbiting around it. They were inside Sargasso. I had a sense of safety and of destiny. I believe it was a message. A call to action. I believe we are here to open a door. I believe we are here to save humanity one more time."

In due course, as the conversations allowed, the three of them worked their way back to the control area. After checking instruments and verifying location markers, Farson gave Voul the pilot's chair and said, pointing to the forward monitors, "Let's go."

"Where to?" Voul asked.

"Thataway." Farson was smiling as Voul brought the engines online and *Songbird* vaulted off into the unknown.

Uva was in the third seat, relaxed, enthralled, and enjoying the incredible view of a new world unfolding in front of her.

BOOK III
The Others

"We are always the same age inside."
– *Gertrude Stein*

"Love is all there is."
– *John Lennon*

Chapter Six

Ichor

67. The Star of Sargasso

They realized pretty quickly that inside Sargasso much of what they had known about space travel was completely suspended. This included the "new" Screen that Farson had detected.

It was not a vacuum, for one thing. It was thinly but adequately atmospheric. This effect only increased as they neared any of the planets. Uva, using the instruments in front of her nav station, noted that the air around the closest planet was easily dense enough for "life," by which she meant for Aristealians but it would also easily apply to humans, who actually required less oxygen. The atmosphere of Aristealia was highly livable for human beings, richer in oxygen than Earth, a lighter gravitational pull because of the makeup of the planet, and, for those lucky few who had ever visited, Aristealia had a pleasant effect for human beings: It made them feel great. Uva was busy analyzing. "It looks as though this whole interior is livable," by which she meant, flyable. Farson and Voul were suddenly filled with thoughts of flying free in space. They could feel the light touch of her wings as they spread and stroked through Sargasso's sky, as she was calling it. They were getting used to being with her.

"How far is it to the first planet?" Voul asked excited to see more.

Farson mentally noted that the new Screen inside Sargasso was just like the old one outside in its transport capabilities. It was different, though in its finiteness, enclosed in Sargasso. Within that restriction, however, Sargasso's Screen was as robust and exciting as the original. He was traveling now, as only Farson Uiost could travel.

The closest planet he saw it was teeming with life. *Human beings.* He could feel the planet-wide population, unaware of him, going about their day-to-day business. *There must be a billion people here.* He swept over the five other planets and then he circled the sun. Sargasso's vastness was difficult to comprehend, even for him, but the truth was all too clear. Farson knew. Sargasso was a closed habitat. And it had room to grow.

<<*Are the two of you getting what I'm getting?*>>
Voul nodded, wondering if he really was seeing all that Farson and Uva could see. His skills, he knew, were nowhere close, yet, to theirs. Uva hesitated.
<<*There is something odd, though, about that star, Farson.*>>

68. Karina and Viera

When Farson disappeared from their home on SkyKing, Karina told the twins not to worry. It had all happened before.

Felicity decided to enjoy her waffles, trusting her mother's insight. Valgary was worried. Even at their young age, the girls' intuition was always a factor that, Karina had learned, must not be dismissed. *Valgary's, especially.* "What's the matter, Val? Something on your mind?"

"I didn't like the way Daddy left. It seemed bad somehow."

"He's fine, honey." They looked at each other. It was clear that her daughter doubted Karina's statement. It was also clear that there was nothing either one of them could do about it. "Why don't you finish your breakfast and help clean up. I'll be back soon."

"Where are you going, Mom?" Both girls were attentive now, waiting for the answer.

"I'm going to check in with Viera."

"Can we come?" This was an old battle. They always wanted to go wherever their mother was going. Karina could feel the pull of their insistence. At first she thought no, and then she thought yes. She looked at her daughters. *Are they doing that?* The two girls, recognizing their victory, immediately started to jump up and down and get ready, quickly putting the dishes away and clearing the table. In two minutes Karina was walking out of the family's SkyKing quarters, heading down the corridor toward the escalator, two little redheads bouncing along beside her.

Viera was staring into the monitor. She had replayed the recorded event at least twenty times. As she restarted the program once again, she put in a call to Long John Hanson Silver en route to Sargasso aboard the latest Emer-enhanced Sker shuttle, *Orison*, named for the nature of its mission. "How long before you get there, John?" The answer came back with a slight distance delay.

"About two days. We are pretty busy out here." Karina knew the preparations they were making, and how rushed their departure had been. "A holding action," Farson had said. That meant that he wanted Silver to hold the position around the entry platform. Silver knew that it was an understatement, full of missing information. Against what? Against who? When? There were no answers to those questions. Silver knew he would have to be ready for anything. One quarter of the Moon's nuclear stock was now in the hold of the most advanced shuttle that the Moon, or SkyKing, had. There were over two hundred men and women aboard preparing to deploy the stockpile and mount the "guns," as they called the propellant modules that focused the blasts for the Moon's movements. Silver's crew favored this nickname for well-pumped biceps, as you might have guessed.

Over the years, the MoonBasers had become experts at aiming the nukes, and they had developed, with the help of Emer technology, the ability to "go portable" as the need arose. That capability had now been transferred to the largest shuttle, and the crew was working out the details of deploying the entire apparatus and control systems to Sargasso's surface. It was a big job.

"You have seen the record of *Songbird's* destruction?" Viera asked.

"Of course, many times. I don't believe that shit though. We'll start looking for debris tomorrow as soon as our shuttle telemetry can reach the area. At this point we are seeing nada times nothing." Viera knew all of this, of course, but hearing it was reassuring.

"Why would anyone want to fake the destruction of Farson's new barge? It seems a little futile. The record was clearly a repeat of one of Farson's simulations, but the explosion was real enough. Do you agree?"

"Your telemetry from the Moon is far better than ours out here. Until we get a lot closer, I can't answer that. Your records are clear, though. Phony fucking simulation. Real fucking explosion. It's a ballbuster of a mystery. All we've got to go on now is Farson's advance request for a holding operation. That's enough for me. I feel like a fucking idiot though, not really knowing what the hell I'm doing out here." Karina smiled at Silver's normal style of communication.

"Let's hope this all clears up as the operation progresses. Commander out."

Karina and girls had reached the escalator. Its high glass structure and suction doors offered no resistance as they moved inside with ease. The attendants were performing the standard operating procedures. The girls were peering through the entrance plates to see the moving structure within. Like a twisting rope in space, they could see the moving undulation of the long endless strip as it rotated within its width, stretching between the space station and the Moon. To them, this was exciting. To Karina, this waiting was a delay she could barely endure. Soon enough the doors opened, and the three of them stepped in. They were alone in the capsule. As the doors sealed, there was a slight shifting of balance as the mechanism activated, and then they were off. They would be traveling at speeds that would get them to the Moon, sixty-five miles away, in less than two minutes. For Karina, it was an eternity. For Felicity and Valgary, it was a carnival ride requiring squeals of glee at the beginning and noses to the windows throughout the entire trip. The image of the Moon coming up so fast and the proportions of its looming presence caused excitement and more squeals. As the capsule slowed and docked, the doors whooshed open, and the girls ran out first. Viera was waiting. They ran right into her arms.

As Viera was looking over them and she easily see the worried concern in Karina's eyes. It was a concern she shared. Karina was hoping to find reassurance in Viera, but she saw her own trepidation mirrored there perfectly. Disappointed, she walked over to Viera, and the girls made room for their mother to join the hug. The two friends embraced and despite the gravity of events and the uncertainty of outcome, they felt better. Then, Viera took Valgary's hand, and Karina took Felicity's and they walked off, the girls holding onto each other in the middle.

With a sheaf of paper with little dots and impressions beside him, Lieutenant Gerald Antonoff was studying the computer projection hovering before him. He touched his wrist, and the image changed. He touched it again, and it changed again. This went on for several minutes, screen images going forward and backward and forward again. Then a whole new set of images came on, and the process was repeated over and over. He picked up the papers and flipped through, looking for something. He seemed to find what he was looking for and compared it to the screen in front of him. He looked back and forth between the papers and the screen. He shuffled the papers until he found the one he wanted, and again looked back and forth at the screen. Then he stopped. He was looking at the monitor. He could see the room beyond through its holographic projection. He was alone in the control room, his shift almost over. Repoul Bensn would be along in a moment to relieve him. It had become their custom to operate control of MoonKing from the Moon, especially during operations. With the systems of the station now activated for orbital shift and the Moon at full alert while their shuttle was on its mission to Sargasso, the Moon's control facilities were designated as primary.

After the launch of the mission, Antonoff found himself with some extra time and little to do, so he had returned to his long-pursued research of the on and off patterns of Sargasso's blinking light. It had ceased blinking after the first mission arrived on the surface, just before Farson's brief disappearance from the platform. Lieutenant Antonoff had continued studying his dots and impressions, searching for a pattern, hoping to find some key to its mysteries. It had become a mild obsession. Watching the four hours of the recording of Farson's "disappearance," which Farson maintained was little more than four seconds, Antonoff had tried everything. Fast motion, slow motion, stop action, magnification, and every audible detector the Moon had.

Nothing. On a whim he had just tried a telescopic view where instead of just simple laso-magnification, he had enlarged the images several thousand times and then telescoped out to the limit of the device, so he had "the big picture." It was like looking at the mountain from the plain. At maximum resolution, he noted a disturbance. On further investigation, he noted that the "disturbance" was part of a pattern. At this distance, he could see very dim pulses undulating over Sargasso's surface. It reminded him of the Sargasso lights and their unpredictable but intuitive positioning effect. He began to compare the seemingly random locations of surface lights and the pulses detectable only from such a great distance, and that led him to a revelation, which he had just checked for replication proof at least eight times. His predictive formula worked every time, and it matched the pattern of the blinking light as well. His heart racing, somehow he knew exactly what it meant. *Those damn lights.* He knew that the entirety of Sargasso was telling him the secret. At that moment, Repoul walked in. Gerald Antonoff looked up and said, "You are not going to believe what I just figured out."

Once the four of them were in Viera's apartment, the girls ran for the exercise room where they knew there were things that offered fun and excitement. Even as the compartment door hissed closed behind them, Viera and Karina could hear the gravity control adjusting and the girls screaming as they began to float up from the floor. "I hope they behave themselves," Viera said. Karina knew better.

"I think your hope may be misplaced." The two women laughed, briefly distracted from their worry by the two seven-year-olds' exuberance. Both Karina and Viera envied the girls' playful diversion. Karina asked Viera the question she had been expecting. "Any news?"

"Our crew is just two days from the surface and going as fast as that shuttle has ever gone. We are all waiting. John

Silver thinks the destruction of *Songbird* was an illusion, but the explosion was real. They are still too far away for complete assurance, but there is apparently no debris field."

"Why would that happen?"

"No way to know," Viera said, "I'm glad to hear it, but I want confirmation."

Karina nodded. "I can't reach Farson, or hear him, or sense him. It has happened before. I hated it then, and I hate it now."

"I think they're inside," Viera said. Karina nodded again in agreement, but she was thinking about Farson and all that he was trying to do. She knew his hopes for the mysterious Sargasso. He had told her that it was too big to overlook. 'Something that huge,' he had said, 'must have a purpose. I want to know what it is.' Karina knew Farson's speculations and conclusions concerning Sargasso. She had seen his conviction. She knew his single-minded focus when a challenge appeared. She knew that he had reasoned it out: Sargasso was the only way. "Otherwise," he was smiling when he had continued, "there is no escape." Viera noticed that Karina's attention had clearly been distracted for a few moments. She shook her head lightly, to refocus, and turned to Viera apologetically.

"Do you have anything to eat? The girls are going to be hungry." Viera smiled at the opportunity to do something.

"Let's go see what we can cook up." They walked into the kitchen. They could still hear the twins laughing in the other room.

Master Sergeant Long John Hanson Silver was still fourteen hours out when he got the call from Repoul Bensn and Gerald Antonoff. Antonoff had stayed on duty past the end of his shift to go over his findings with Repoul. Repoul had come over on the escalator just before Karina and the girls. He was aware that they were also on the Moon now. On the faraway shuttle, Silver was not pleased with the interruption. "What do you two monkeys want? We're kinda fucking busy out here." The immenseness of Sargasso darkened all of the *Orison's* monitors as the shuttle approached. The landing area was highlighted for all to see. The scanners were searching the area of the explosion. "We still have found nothing for all our efforts." Silver had said everything in a rush of impatience. He focused his irritation on Antonoff and Bensn, but everyone knew it had nothing to do with them. Silver's assignment, "to prepare for a holding action," had caused consternation for the master sergeant. "Holding for what?" was a repeated phrase that he had blurted out at odd moments as though someone had just asked him a question, over and over since launching almost five days ago. He had driven the crew crazy, and into a frenzy of readiness for anything: The nukes were ready; the lasers were ready; the deployment plans were ready. Hanson thought that they could hold off anything ... for about thirty minutes. He had no idea what they would be holding off. He had no idea if their preparations and plans would be enough. He did not like such uncertainty. He looked at the faces of the two men in the monitor. Repoul Bensn and Gerald Antonoff had both individually and together saved the Moon and the station at least twice. His attitude softened. A little. Bensn was the first to speak.

"Lieutenant Antonoff has continued studying the blinking patterns of the light that precipitated the first landing on Sargasso."

Silver interrupted. "That light stopped blinking, as I remember."

"True, but Lieutenant Antonoff's recordings of the light have finally borne fruit." Repoul Bensn stopped to see if the master sergeant had anything to say to that. He did not, so he went on. "He has discovered something that is perhaps significant." He stopped again. Still nothing from Silver, so he continued. "The blinking of the light, taken in conjunction with the placements of the millions of others, caused the lieutenant to macro-nize the 'picture' as it were. He backed off as far as possible, and it was in that posture of high intensity investigative observation that he noticed a slight concentration of directional energy, or pulses." Silver was listening. "He concluded that the original light was not actually blinking. It was being pulsed from the other towers with very faint surges of energy, observable only at great distance, that intensified the light's power source: resulting in a 'blinking' effect. And then he noticed one additional thing." Silver seemed almost bored at this point, but still, uncharacteristically, said nothing. "With this new information in hand, the lieutenant has speculated that the resulting pulse stream formed a projection of some sort."

"A communication?" Silver's voice had a tone far different than Bensn's smooth and methodical description of the discovery had.

"Yes, sort of. It was entirely one-way. It was more like a transporter's signature than a communication, but it definitely introduced new information into the situation." He stopped for a moment, preparing for his next statement. "It spiked during Farson's first 'trip' into Sargasso, and again during the 'explosion.' The second spike was much bigger, and it has given us a scale for further conjecture."

"What does that mean?"

"It means that we can estimate that the power behind these spikes of very complex events is unbelievable. Sargasso has an enormous power source within it. Nothing we have ever seen even comes close."

"A power source? What the fuck are you talking about?"

"We're not sure. But for what it's worth, it means that Sargasso has a vast interior with a power resource beyond all human experience. The blinking light was not a blinking light. It was the first hard evidence we have that Sargasso is not at all what we are thinking it is."

"What is it?"

"The answer is uncertain, but Antonoff thinks it must be a vessel of some kind." Silver had no comment to that. He looked in the monitors. Sargasso filled the screens. He knew that if he backed *Orison* off to ten thousand miles away, it would still fill the screens.

"Vessels have crews, genius. Is that what you are saying?"

"Well, the projection from the light would suggest intent."

"Why is that?"

"Lieutenant Antonoff calculated that the pulses were focused exactly on the point where Songbird impacted. Exactly. In calculating the two trajectories – the pulses and Farson's ship – he says that at the finest magnification and the most precise calibrations we can achieve, the two met in exactly the same place and time."

"Are you saying *Songbird* was transported somewhere?" There was a long pause as Antonoff and Bensn exchanged looks. Bensn then turned to the monitor and Silver again. His face was showing signs of doubt and uncertainty, but his voice was very clear.

"So it would seem."

Viera, with Karina's friendly assistance, made tomato soup and grilled cheese sandwiches. They called the girls to come to the table. No response. They called again. Still nothing. Then they went to the exercise compartment and opened the door. The two of them were up near the ceiling upside down, wrestling over an object. They were both laughing. They had found one of Viera's personal items and were obviously in the midst of establishing who was going to control it. Viera and Karina both recognized the object and the situation. "Girls! Get down here right now!" Felicity and Valgary noticed their mother in the room for the first time. Faces reddened to match their hair color. They dropped the object as though it had scalded them. Viera lowered the gravity dampeners. She may have decreased the gravity too quickly. The girls fell to the padded floor, unable to land standing up. Viera picked up the object, noticed that it was still vibrating, turned it off and returned it to its drawer by the side of the large elevated martial arts training mat she used for close combat training. As she closed the drawer, Viera was thinking of a certain ensign.

Karina marched the twins out of the room into the kitchen area. Viera was the last one to come back to the table. The girls were now looking at the soup and sandwiches. Karina and Viera stole a knowing glance and an eyebrow moment with each other as Valgary picked up the first half of her sandwich and Felicity took a preliminary, testing sip of the soup, and both girls looked up at Viera with pleasant, innocent smiles. The three of them stared at each other for a moment. Both girls were wondering if they had offended Viera. Viera was thinking about the twins' precocious and unpredictable curiosity. It was a sort of standoff, but Viera blinked. Then, Felicity was instantly enjoying her soup as though released. Valgary began to eat her sandwich. *Is that a smirk?* Viera looked over at Karina, who was lost in thought far away.

<<*Farson?*>>

69. The Essor Fleet

Twill was flying high. His enormous fleet – armed to the teeth, sheathed by its massive formation, the outer ships positioned to create a protective shell with the great *Noctura* leading the way – moved through the black, cold of space on a heading for the coordinates the technician had gleaned from her data stream. Even though he had kicked her and threatened her as if she were the most insignificant piece of effluent that ever pushed itself out the back end of an Essor carapace, he had decided to bet everything that she was right.

It was too good to pass up. If the humans had somehow escaped, if they had actually somehow fooled him, if they were really out there on the run, well then, he was going to find them, kill them, and put this little mishap of planning and misbelieved perfection out of its misery. He could taste it: victory. He could see it: total destruction. He was enjoying every second of it: triumph. Just being in the command ship, leading a thousand warships, with myriad capabilities and powerful weapons, was a pleasure that verged on becoming the highest moment of his life. It verged on it, but it could never overtake the joy and satisfaction of his Grand Ascendancy. No. That was and always would be in a category by itself: a supreme achievement.

Then a dark shadow cast itself in his thought: Farson. He growled the name out loud. His second-in-command heard the guttural sound and recognized the name, of course. As the lieutenant commander retreated minutely into his shell at the viciousness of his commander's utterance, Twill noticed it and glared at him, annoyed, first, that he had actually spoken *that* name out loud and, secondly, even more annoyed that this underling had heard it. "As you were," Twill almost spit the words. The second-in-command seemed to be looking for something on the station floor in front of him, perhaps under the counter, perhaps up on the shelf, anywhere but in the glare of Grand ScreenMaster Twill.

Twill, looking around the main bridge, noticed the technician cowering between the exit hatchways and the navigators' stations. She saw his eye on her and withdrew into the deepest, darkest part of her shell. Someone looking around the compartment would have thought it was empty, but Twill could see her yellow eyes faintly looking out of the darkness at him, through thin slits of color. "What are you looking at?" he shouted at her. The shell shook as if to say "Nothing, nothing at all." He snorted and turned again to the main view screen set to maximum. "Are you seeing anything yet, Lieutenant Commander?" The officer indicated nothing had yet been detected.

They had set out fourteen days ago. The crews were getting used to the routines of space flight, and perhaps a little bored. Twill was anxious. *What if she was wrong?* He looked at the technician again. The shell seemed to move farther away. He turned and went to the hatches, heading for his private apartments. "If anything changes," he turned to the bridge crew, his voice raised to command tones and volume, "And I mean *anything*, I want to know immediately." He left the bridge. The feeling of relief was clearly visible as shells relaxed and the air seemed to lighten. The technician poked her head out and looked around. Her sigh of relief was clearly audible.

70. Uva Was Excited

When Farson disappeared, Andrew Sortt had picked up Farson's glass and ice cubes from the carpet and returned them to the table where the decanter of his favorite brandy stood, still three quarters full. He picked up the crystal container and admired it: its beautifully cut stopper, the graceful shape of its tall and elegant design, the rich and endearing contents within. The tall container reminded him of Emerald Earth's highest institution of learning, the Tower of Light, a statuesque, sculpted, graceful architectural structure that was the signature silhouette in the amber skyline of Emerald City, housing its most dedicated scientists, researching the deepest questions of Emer life and technology, and offering the richest new ideas and most innovative inventions that the planet could discover and generate. The Tower was the Emer's beacon of hope and promise.

With that thought, he put down the decanter and reached out to contact Belnad Goethe. <<*How are things, Belnad? Farson seems to be right on schedule.*>> Belnad was in the Tower at that moment standing beside a shimmering holographic scene of *Songbird* approaching a distant deep blue and white planet. The scene shifted to the interior of the vessel. Voul Bensn and Farson were at the main controls. It shifted again to show the elegant and lissome Aristealian, Uva, surrounded by the navigation station's instrumentations. Her undivided attention was focused on the readings and numerous holographic monitors around her.

<<*Everything is going along as planned. Except for one thing.*>>

<<*I see her. Is she a problem?*>>

<<*It is an unknown. Neither a problem nor a nonproblem at this point. She is there. But as far as we can tell, she came alone.*>> Sortt knew that the term 'alone,' for Emers, meant 'not connected.' He understood that with all of the old ScreenMasters' powers, Uva could still be an element of subterfuge if her connection to The Screen was maintained; all that she was seeing would be available to the old ScreenMasters. That would be a problem.

Belnad continued. <<*Even her absence could be noted. However, she has been out of action for a while now, so perhaps not.*>> The old ScreenMasters were rare and relatively few in number given the facts of magnitude and complexities of the omniverse, so the disappearance of even one would cause a stir of discovery and resolution. But the death of Uva's husband had granted her some leeway. She had had no interest in Screen activities for over a year. <<*There are no signs that she has been missed. She seems to be merely another passenger on* Songbird *now, if uninvited. We have noted nothing that would disturb the current situation's acceptance by all three of them. As far as we can tell, she has joined Farson in fact and in spirit. Her ship,* Rachis, *still orbits Aristealia, but she is clearly inside Sargasso, in person, and seems to be becoming part of the crew, and, from all that we can see, a welcomed member. Things are proceeding exactly as we had hoped they would even with this unexpected event.>>*

<<*And the others?*>>

<<*Given that Sargasso is doing everything exactly as planned, our conclusion is that all is well. The robots' reports are supportive of that conclusion.*>>

<<*Ida?*>> Sortt, at this point, with his continuing questions, seemed overly persistent to Belnad.

<<*Well, she is what she is. CT*<<*Dinsil2371 and ZZ*<<*Arkol25609 are able to monitor some of her activities, but if they go too far or get too close, her rebuke is fearsome.*>>

<<*Does your previous evaluation of her activities still hold in light of the current situation?*>> This was a hard question for Sortt to ask and for Belnad to answer because it brought up issues of command and control, which the Emers did not enjoy. Their world is one: Everyone always knows everything, and that is the way it had always been. That John Andrew McKinley Sortt was asking this question caused a reverberation throughout the Emer milieu that was unwelcome, an intrusive consideration that they experienced as a long discarded and discredited apostasy. They all knew, of course, that Sortt was apart from, and yet within, their whole. His history, his nature, his very essence was a vital component, and yet, also, sometimes an unwelcome reminder of all that had happened: the good, the bad, and those instinctually innate and conflicting elements of human nature that never went completely away despite the Emers' unwavering determination to achieve exactly that. His probing question about ID>>Karo28689's role and whether or not her activities were still within the accepted scope of Emer engineering was an intuitive "stab in the dark" from the

ancient president, but for the Emers, this issue was a central and an existential one. Her power and range were extraordinary; her abilities seemed unpredictable and at times even quixotic to them; but her nature was pleasing and reassuring; her mysteries were daunting and convulsing for the calm and serene Emer ScreenMasters in their quest for freedom and survival. Farson had once referred to her as a "monkey wrench," and, at another time, as a possible panacea for all the challenges of the coming changes. At Thanksgiving dinner, after saying hello, he had ignored her as if she were not there, despite her appearance (and the fact that he invited her) as an engaging young woman, dressed very fashionably, who clearly enjoyed every minute of his party, staying to the end, the last to leave. In fact, she left with Farson. The Emers had studied Ida since her first appearance on old Earth in the 1890s. They had seen and studied her growth and transformations. The role of leadership she had assumed with the robots was her first 'mystery,' as they put it, but there had been many more. In the end, there was only one conclusion, and Belnad reaffirmed it, again, for Andrew Sortt, who, having asked the question, clearly seemed to already know the answer.

<<*Yes. We feel it still must be true. She is exactly what we had hoped.*>>

Farson and Voul were enjoying *Songbird*'s silent flight though the sky of Sargasso. In the past days of exploration, they had detected three vast and distinct atmospheric fronts, that, like great moving seas, flowed over, through, and around the planets. The three seas moved in opposite relative directions. It was as though an unseen hand were stirring the rich mix of Sargasso's interior back and forth through space.

The first of the three seas they encountered was noticeably colder and almost undetectable; the second one was hot and fast and seemed the dominant of the three. And the third one was what Farson described as "serene" in its movements: temperate and predictable. They were like three vast unseen oceans encircling and encompassing the interior of Sargasso. *Songbird's* crew, in studying them, realized that life support within Sargasso was an incredibly complex and subtle system. "A metasphere," Farson had called it: a wrapper of obvious intent that was supported by great intelligence. "There is an almost a spiritual context in which everything happens." He had added, "My intuition tells me that what we are seeing and experiencing is greatly different from anything on or in the worlds and space we have known." Uva laughed out loud.

"Oh, Farson, how much you have to learn." She stood up and stretched her wings. Both Farson's and Voul's minds were filled with soaring and climbing thoughts. They could feel the winds of Aristealia on their faces, and a sense of exhilaration and relief wash over them as she flew off into the skies of their imaginations, leaving them restless and impatient to do something. *Enough of this clunky moving around in a tiny little spaceship.*

"Uva, behave yourself. You are here uninvited. Be patient. There will be time enough for your fun." She sat down again and continued her evaluation of the first of Sargasso's 'seas,' as Farson had named the three atmospheric phenomena. She had been drawn to the fastest one, the one with the most complex currents and patterns, the one she knew would be the most fun to fly in. She became absorbed again in her investigation. She had noticed that, in the areas where this sea touched the others, very interesting events occurred. Slowly, in the back of her mind, in those Aristealian recesses that only she could know, a plan was evolving. It was more like preparing for an excursion than some secret plot or scheme. She knew it would not be long now. Her wings were restless.

She was enjoying herself for the first time in many, many years. *An adventure.* She could feel her beautiful plumage rustling for flight. Her wings, now confined, soon to be set free. Even as she continued her navigational studies, and her role as an important part of *Songbird's* crew now, she could feel them reaching, straining, longing to be used for their true purpose, unfurled, unfettered, in full flight, destination unknown, gracefully lifting her into ecstasy. With her free thoughts, her calculations were coming faster and faster, her understanding growing by the second. She had a feeling of being in the right place at the right time, with the right people. She was excited.

"Farson, are you seeing what your 'seas' are doing?"

71. The Elevation Protocol (4)

The two of them were sitting at the kitchen table. It seemed lonely in the old house. It was empty without Hattie's boisterous presence, without Sam's calmness and dependability. With just the two of them sitting there at the empty table of their childhood, the void filled them. Farson noticed that Karina was crying softly. He moved to her side of the table and put his arm around her. "It just seems so distant, Farson, so long ago. Those days were so wonderful, so full of *them* and *us* and all that happened. It seems overwhelmingly sad to me now."

"We come back all the time, Kari. We relive it whenever we want. It's always there for us."

"But today is different, isn't it, Farson? This isn't a reliving. This is the end of something. It is sad."

"Is it? Or is it the beginning of something amazing, something unbelievable? I've done it over and over, and I am still here."

"Yes you are still here and that is encouraging, but remember, you and I are different. You learned that lesson long ago." He knew she was talking about the doll in the attic situation and the door day. It had not been his proudest moment, and it had been a hard lesson, an inflection point in their relationship. *One of many.* "Now it's me sitting up there alone in the attic. Somehow, I find that terrifying, Farson. Plus, you never talk about your own death, except that you've seen it. You have never invited me to go with you on *those* little trips." Farson had no response. He knew she was right. They had been to his birth many times, but the other, that moment of transition and change, he knew that he had had to do it alone, and that she would have to do it alone. He knew that the power of The Screen was, in that moment, so personal and so consequential that, events were driven by individual revelation and volition and nothing else. As close as the two of them were and are, as much as their lives had blended into almost being one, there still was this moment when the only way was alone. He could see the worry in her eyes, the knowing that irrevocable change was coming, the indulging the last lingering vestiges of the fear of the truth, like a child not wanting to grow up, like a grown-up fearing change, like almost every human being who ever lived left empty and confused by thinking of their own death. Her silent tears fell to the table, splashing on the wood grains of their childhood and in the deep textures of their memories. He felt lost in her sea of helplessness. His beloved sister, friend, lover, soulmate now faced a moment she never wanted.

72. Steady As She Goes

Farson was about to answer Uva's question about the seas of Sargasso. Being on *Songbird* was centering for him. It had been a long time since he was so centered in just one place, especially with others physically joining him. In the world of ScreenMasters it was rare that this happened. Farson remembered how Karina insisted on it. It made him smile, and then it made him miss her. Upon entrance into Sargasso, Farson knew immediately. He was on *Songbird* and nowhere else. Uva was waiting.

"Yes, Uva, they intersect with all of the planets. The pattern reminds me of the lights on Sargasso, the same intuitive feeling. If you think of it as a ventilation system, a nutrient support system, then Gerald Antonoff's idea of Sargasso being a vessel makes even more sense. It raises many more questions as well. Like, where is Sargasso going to go? What are the planets' natures? All of these people, how did they get here? There are more questions ..." Uva interrupted.

"You think you know the answers, though, don't you?"

"I have a conjecture, but I need more corroboration. We need to visit one."

"Which one?" Her graceful and delicate hands hovered over the navigation panels, as though his next words would cause *Songbird* to set a new course. He was shaking his head.

"Steady as she goes, Uva. First stop is the star. Let's see if we can figure out what is 'strange' about it, as you said." She was disappointed. There was a planet she wanted to visit. It looked like Aristealia to her. It was big, and it was blue. Somehow she knew that the flow of the seas around that planet would generate the perfect currents and atmospheric turbulences. *A second Aristealia?* Her thoughts were exciting her. Uva added some technical details for Farson.

"By my calculations we are several days out from the star, even at our current top speed. Are you sure that is our *first* destination?" He could tell she had an alternative in mind. Voul was looking at Farson as well. He said what captains had always said when the crew was getting anxious and wanted a landfall.

"Steady as she goes. Steady as she goes."

Songbird continued on her way, following a direct course to Sargasso's lone star.

73. Essor's Fleet Detects an Object

She heard someone trying to speak with her. She had tucked herself comfortably into her shell for rest. Sleep for the technician was a slow adjustment, taking long periods of peace and concentration, things undisturbed, building confidence of safety, and, of course, the pleasing cold of Essor filling her with the tranquility of familiarity and comfort.

Panau's name was given to her by her balenest siblings, based on their experience with her. Names on Essor were not given at birth, but earned. Her name meant something like mechanic, or routine, but for Essors, it had an extremely pleasing sound. Her name was pure and genuine Essor, and combined, in sound and feeling, in a clear definition: "beautiful function." For Essors, this was an exceptional name that filled the hearer with reflections of history and allure.

In the safety of her dark, cooling shell, she felt far from those days when her family frolicked on the ice of the dark caverns beneath, and relished their tempered joy of being together. Now, ensconced with her dread and fear, in the corner of the combat bridge of a giant warship traveling at speeds nearing that of the dreaded light – toward who knows what – she was worried, and her sleep was shallow and debilitating, not resuscitating. She did appreciate the isolation and quiet. Her consciousness instinctually was turning the numbers of her data stream over and over in her agile and ever-curious mind. It was in that state of restless alertness that she heard the voice – it was soft and not threatening. In her drowsiness it reminded her of those days of youth when soft voices were all around. She opened her eyes. In the dim blue light of the bridge, through her carapace, she could see a dark face outlined by the light. "Panau? We need you." She saw the friendly eyes blinking with regret for disturbing her. Everyone knew it had been a hard time for her. She poked her head out. The crew member, having said her name, now saw her face, her eyes blinking. He was thinking how beautiful she was, and why didn't he notice it earlier?

"Yes?" Her voice was unhurried, and her diction was perfect. He remembered how she spoke so rushed and nervously to Twill. She began to stand up. He noticed that she was taller than he thought. Without Twill around, her posture was strong and straight. As her shell adjusted, her normal Essor stature was evident, as well as her rank. To Twill, no rank mattered – all were below him – but now, as Panau stood there, the crew member could see that, while still young, the technician had achieved a rank higher than his, higher, in fact than almost everyone aboard the *Noctura*, a starship like no other in the fleet.

Not only was the ship Grand ScreenMaster Twill's personal barge, it was also the most advanced starship Essor's designers and strategists had ever devised. With an operational crew of two thousand, and a fearsome weapons array, her dark tapered dripstone appearance at first resembled a graceful javelin in flight, except for its abruptly flat transom, which seemed to cut the spear in half, leaving a stalagmite-like shape, as if the entire design were somehow incomplete, or interrupted, or as if it had broken off from a cavern's ceiling. It was in this transom area of the ship where Master Twill's quarters had been accommodated, partially for the more spacious nature of the area, and partially – perhaps entirely – for Twill to be as far as possible from the light of approaching stars. *Noctura* was entirely shielded from light of any kind, but in the Essor way, there were no lengths too far, or efforts too arduous, even if entirely symbolic in nature, to which they would not go or that they would not make to remain in the pure cold dark that they loved so dearly. Essor eyes shined with a light all their own: visual detectors second-to-none. They did not need light to see, nor heat to be warm; Essors were powered by a physiology of self-sufficiency needing nothing, and no one, beyond themselves. Each Essor was an island: a lone individual with a pathway prescribed at birth; a straight line from start to finish, from nativity to the final abyss of dissolution. They were destined to service and utility, lives of endless toil and detail, of futility enshrined in grand purpose.

And yet, even in such circumstances of assimilation and benign immurement, affection still found a place. Panau had noticed the soft tones of her waker. As she blinked her eyes, she saw him standing before her. His carriage was strong and slender, his shell completely out of sight in a sign of openness. His uniform was neat and proper. Her eyes briefly surveyed his face with approval. So long in the data stream catacombs, she had accepted that, if mating were ever to be part of her experience, it would have to be arranged. Now, in the pleasingly gentle gaze of the warship's lieutenant commander, she was pleasantly surprised. He was still talking to her.

"We have a question on incoming data."

"Are we at the coordinates?"

"No. Not even close."

"And ...?"

"We have detected an object far from the actual coordinates."

"There are many objects between here and there. Always." She was not impatient. She was teasing him in a very Essor way, not actually questioning his reasoning, rather asking him to enlarge his view. The actual translation would have been, 'open your shell' or something directionally like that. His eyes blinked, as he noticed the attempt at humor.

"Fair enough, Commander. I shall try." She was again pleased with his response. "The object seems to be in front of *and behind* your coordinates." She was thinking this over as he continued. "We are at the extreme-most range of our maximum sensors, so the resolutions are still intuitive and mathematical. We are months from visual."

"Let me see the data," she said. The lieutenant commander led her to a station, which she entered. It reminded her of her own station back on Essor. For a moment, she felt a longing to be away from this ship and safe within her own data stream again. As she closed the vacuum hatch, she heard the hissing of the seal. She was immersed in the thickening atmosphere of the inner station, her breathing switched to her conversion gills, and the cold of the data stream surrounded her. As the stream coursed through its logical process, the first detection came quickly along, and then there was a long silence. During this period, she found herself thinking of Twill and the crew member with the strong carriage. The data streamed through her subconscious. Her patience was as always the keystone to her success. Time passed, and her coordinates approached, but so slowly that she began to question the calculations. She accelerated the streaming with no noticeable change in result. A quick check showed the calculations were logical and correct. She returned to the main stream and realized that something was wrong, not wrong in the sense of her scientific process, or the instrumentation accuracy. No, this was "wrong" in the sense that Twill would not like it. She checked the stream one more time, enjoying the beautiful symmetry of the program's deliberations flowing through her mind. She was especially appreciating the sheer speed of *Noctura's* advanced systems, and then, cutting them off reluctantly, she opened the hatch to exit. The lieutenant commander leaped to his feet, collapsing his shell artfully, but not before she noticed its appealing appearance. His face was bright with her return and concerned with what to do next. Time was passing, and Twill would know if there had been any delay whatsoever in notifying him. She nodded a subtle greeting to the lieutenant commander which he likewise acknowledged subtly and quickly. "Notify Twill immediately. Tell him a large impediment seems to be surrounding the target coordinates and we cannot yet determine its nature or composition." *That should do it.*

The lieutenant commander straightened his carriage even further, and looked directly into Panau's eyes. She could sense his dread at the assignment, knowing too well that uncertainty and doubt in subordinates were often met with violence and Twill's demeaning vituperation. Her returning gaze gave him no quarter. Essors never hesitated on the paths to which they were assigned. But then she relented, remembering her own spinning shell and her retracting in fear from Twill's ferocity; her eyes softened in understanding and this seemed to power him to action. He turned and moved quickly to the scutelift, a device that allowed the crew to move from one location to the other via *Noctura's* outer surfaces in the tubular pathways that lined the vessel's exterior in all directions, creating the natural appearance of a living, pulsing shell of beauty and graceful design surrounding the starship. As Shals t'Bu left the bridge, Panau returned to her corner and, again withdrew into her own world, imagining she was safe with her thoughts about what would happen next.

74. I'll Be Waiting for You

The vast pod of grass dolphins moved through the amber fields, stretching in all directions as far as the eye could see, like ocean rollers intent for an unseen shore. Riding along, Handy had taken out his knapsack and rummaged through it. They were now moving so fast that even the eagles above could not devise an attack pattern that had any promise of success. One of them had attempted a dive run, but at the last moment, the huge pod had sharply changed directions (Handy had to hang on) and the bird went down into the softly waving arms of the wheat-like plants, disappearing for a flapping moment of disarray and the dolphins' harassments and then reappearing, working its wings frantically to regain a purchase and return to the sky above. As the dolphins moved away, the luckless attacker could be seen climbing arduously to rejoin its convocation in flight. The other birds seemed to slow down to assist its return, and then, again whole, the flight banked off and flew for home.

Handy found what he was looking for at the bottom of his knapsack. It was an envelope Farson had given him during the early days of stasis. Farson and Handy had spent much time together at Area 51, as Handy called his homestead during stasis, and Handy remembered Farson staring many times into the "bottle," the area beyond, for what seemed like hours. One night, toward the end of their time together there, Farson had written something on a piece of paper, folded it up, and put the envelope next to Handy's blanket. When Handy awoke in the morning, he saw the envelope. Farson was gone. On it were written these words: "Do not open until you are called." Handy had kept the envelope, unopened, waiting for a moment that fit the description. When he had gone to the Moon to get the data device from ZZ<<Arkol25609, he thought of the envelope. But he had decided that that was an assignment rather than a "calling." There had been a few other moments, some drunken, when he had taken it out and almost opened it, but, in the end, he had left it for some other, future occasion that he hoped would make itself clear when the time was right.

The twisting pillar of dolphins, calling him to action, and this sudden, rapid transit to Emerald City was clearly the moment Farson had meant.

In the wind of Emerald Earth's warmth and morning glory, he broke the seal and took out the folded sheet of paper. Farson's handwriting was easy enough to read, but then Handy had much experience over the years with Farson's angular fast-paced script. His handwriting looked beautiful to the eye with its symmetry and evenly penned strokes, but often the individual letters, and even the words themselves, were illegible in one sense and yet intuitively clear in another. If you knew Farson, the words revealed themselves, almost as thoughts to the reader. If you just let yourself go, Farson's handwriting was easy to read. Handy was letting himself go:

> You struggle, as though wrapped
> And being squeezed, life out, no hope
> Twisting to be free, nowhere to go
> Hopeless beyond saying it, lost in utterness
> Alone, in darkness, descending, so, so low.
>
> I know. Once so deep in me, I caved.
> So cold in that dark place, I came
> Close to the tip of things, nothing
> Beneath, nothing above, just me
> And the tip of the iceberg, the tunnel
> With no light.
>
> There on that balanceless point, I teetered
> Like a bottle cap spinning, eternal-less
> Empty of reason, discarded, to be forgotten
> Useless now, less than ever even imagined,
> Even dizzy-less, still spinning, knowing
> Not even obliviousness was given to me.
> Forced to witness my own torture
> Pain never became pleasure as they say
> Agony, full-throated, was mine as long
> As I chose. No filter, no dampening,
> It was pure, delivered with intent by
> An enemy all mine. All mine.
>
> I wish I could free you, but I know too much.
> There is only one way out and it's through.
> Takes your doing, not some lover's touch.
> If you make it, I'll be waiting for you.

> – *Farson Uiost*

As he finished the poem, Handy was thinking about his own life; how he had left a broken, shattered planet; how he slowly learned what had happened to it and to him; how he came to understand The Screen, at least in part; how he had come to Earth so many, many years ago; how he had lost his way; how many mistakes he had made; how his life had become so pointless; how he also had "teetered," as Farson put it; how he had met Farson and watched his friend's painful transformation; how he had experienced the heights and the depths of it all. In his thoughts he knew that Farson was talking about the two of them, and that he was also talking about the people of Emerald Earth. Handy also saw the irony in the last stanza. That encouraging last line, preceded by the stark truth of how alone we all really are, left him wondering. <<*How will we know if we make it, Farson, if we don't even know where we are going?*>> Handy's powerful thought went racing out onto The Screen into the emptiness where Farson should have been. Nothing came back. The clear amber sky seemed to warm his weathered face as he looked up, searching for his friend.

The grass dolphins were cruising along. Emerald City was still unseen, far below the horizon. Predictably, Handy took out his guitar, tuned it by ear, and, as his fingers flew up and down the frets, he figured out a melody, with a heavy beat, and then began to sing Farson's poem over and over. It was his way of exploring the words and searching for the deeper meanings. As the miles passed and the tireless dolphins faithfully pressed on, one line began to repeat, almost as a chorus, of the new song Handy had composed:

> I wish I could free you, but I know too much.
> There is only one way out and it's through.
> Takes your doing, not some lover's touch.
> If you make it, I'll be waiting for you.

He looked up and he could see just the slightest tip of the Tower of Light now appearing over the fields ahead. He knew he would be there soon.

In the distance behind, the eagles had returned to their roost on a small hillside's rocky peak. They seemed glad to be home again as they landed and strutted around awkwardly, wings tucked in.

75. Belnad, Ian, Brittany, and Handy

They had been watching for Handy, alerted that he was on his way. Through their optical scopes they could see him coming far off. The city's telemetry had noticed his movements long before Handy could see the Tower. The image of Handy, atop a throne of dolphins, guitar in hand, obviously singing with abandon and enjoyment, was a sight, projected holographically into the main control room, that none of them would soon forget. They had carefully diagnosed his mode of transportation. The collective action of the dolphins had surprised them. In the history of Emerald Earth, the dolphins had been assumed to be highly intelligent. The Emers knew that the grass dolphins were a perfect fit for Emerald Earth, and that they had tirelessly and methodically performed their instinctual duties as custodians of the planet. They were far and away Emerald Earth's most prolific life form. The Emers enjoyed studying them in their habitat. There was a branch of their science devoted entirely to the dolphins, but seeing Handy arriving, carried along so effortlessly by them, was something completely new.

Ian and Belnad were well aware of Handy's history and what it represented. They knew, after Karina, he was Farson's closest friend. Brittany had not only heard the legend of Handy Townsend and but also, growing up, she had read the children's stories, acting them out in play. Seeing him, in person, wearing a cowboy hat, with guns holstered and belted to his waist, long hair, scruffy beard, clothes dishevelled and mismatched, carrying his knapsack and guitar, she laughed out loud. Belnad looked at her disapprovingly. "Do you know who he is?" Brittany looked at Belnad, and then at Ian, who was smiling.

"Why, of course, Belnad. That is Handy Townsend, an old ScreenMaster and Farson's great friend. Who doesn't know of him?"

Brittany had gained confidence and poise in the three months she had been on Emerald Earth. Her relationship with Ian Jordan had become relaxed, intimate, and deepening every day. They had discovered an interpersonal affinity that bridged the gulf of eons between them, and her quick learning and easy, affable personality had combined to give Ian a partner of whom he had only been able to dream, but who now stood and lived beside him. He knew that his years of studying her and her world had prepared him for the day of their first meeting. But nothing could have prepared him for the way he felt about her. And, nothing could have prepared him for her amazing, innate, and unstoppable intellect and attitude. He knew the story of her mother's death, and the years of growing up with her father. He knew of her popularity on both SkyKing and the Moon. He had met James Peterson at Farson's dinner party and despite his worry and perhaps even dread – he *had* taken the commander's daughter to Emerald Earth and into its transformational environment without permission – but was greatly relieved by her father's questions and by his open-mindedness. James Peterson, Ian learned, had only one concern: Is she happy? And that information was obvious and readily available to everyone: She loved what had happened to her.

As Brittany stood watching Handy put down his stuff, and brush the dust off his clothes, she knew that the happiness and sense of belonging that had eluded her for so long was now part of every minute on Emerald Earth. More, she knew that, with Ian, her life and love was now filled to the brim and beyond with wonders she could never have imagined. Ian knew her thoughts, as all Emers always did of each other, but in this case, the knowledge was deeper and even more encompassing. She had come to him from ancient history. He had come to her from the far distant future. What they had had no precedent. What they had, they both knew, was entirely unique. Exactly the way they wanted it. She noticed that Handy was about to say something. He had been standing there looking at her. She felt like he was waiting patiently for her to do something.

"Well," Handy cleared his voice, "now we are 'crossing the Rubicon,' as Farson puts it. Is everything ready?" Belnad responded.

"We are ready to do whatever is needed." It was a simple statement, but profound nonetheless. Emerald Earth was ready to move again and to take SkyKing and the Moon with them. The Emers were prepared and, of course, fully informed. All missions off the planet had returned. Sargasso was beneath them as the three communities of human beings, in geosynchronous orbit, flew gracefully through space. During the almost eleven years they had been in this vicinity, all of them had changed. SkyKing had grown to 365,000 people onboard, nearing their population limit with the current whorl array. The Moon, through growth within the original crew and through immigration from SkyKing, was now over 15,000 people, many living in the five surface cities. Paris, the most recently completed, was filling up quickly. Emerald Earth was steady at 6.8 million people, but had changed in other ways: A refinement of operations made them the most productive agricultural resource ever known. A deepening of their research facilities had produced new technology that was revolutionizing life on SkyKing and the

Moon, as well as life on the planet itself. Belnad assured Handy that all was more than ready for the next phase. Belnad's assurance was no surprise to Handy. He had seen Emerald Earth evolve from its beginnings. More than anyone, Handy appreciated their achievements.

He was wishing someone would offer him a drink. He knew he could also use a nice smoke and a good meal. He unholstered his Colt 45 and twirled it around his finger absentmindedly, as he often did, when he was wondering what to do next. However, he usually did it alone in Area 51. The three Emers stood there watching as the gun flew off his finger and landed hard on the floor, sliding to a stop at Belnad's feet. He picked it up and handed it back to Handy without a comment. Handy reholstered it, a little embarrassed at his mishandling of the weapon. *Lucky it's not loaded.*

"Can a guy get a meal around here?" he asked.

76. Indiana University (2)

In her loneliness, Karina had subconsciously discouraged friendship, perhaps by her demeanor, but sometimes purposefully. She always felt uncomfortable if someone made overtures of wanting to be closer to her. Her studies were consuming, and her memories were dark insulants that protected her from the heat and sounds and electricity of college social life. People could sense her distance. It seemed, to many, a bridge too far, a hill too steep, a maze too complex for them to negotiate. Most of all, she really had little room left in her heart for anyone but Farson.

When Farson and Karina had first met, she was emotionally destitute, drained, and numb. The Chamberlains home was an unwanted refuge, but it was shelter from the storm that had ruined her life and left her all alone in the world. In getting to know Farson, who, at first, was a horror but who became a joy for her that healed her pain, filled the daunting void, and then taught her what love and friendship could be again, she had found the love of her life. Their explorations together in the attic had opened worlds, imaginary and real, to her that brought the light again. In its shining warmth, they both discovered a way to see the world that gave them hope and faith and purpose. In those eleven years growing up together, the thought of separation was banished like a thief who could steal their most prized possession. They barred that door with the fury of sad memories sucked into the vacuum of space, and the emptiness of death so awful that their minds snapped shut at even a hint of it happening again. Their world was perfect together in the Chamberlains' home. They relished it. They cherished it. They protected it. And then, perhaps like all things, it ended.

Farson had gone to Harvard, but it felt like another death to him. Karina was left behind at college in Indiana, but it felt like another death to her. They entered a phase of life that they did not want, but could not avoid. She had to cope. So her studies became the one place where she could run and hide.

People who knew her thought of her as the perfect student in a world of college crazies. Indiana University was a party school where virginity was discarded and the restrictions of life with parents were cast away like unwanted childhood toys. It was a constant that every night there were parties and drinking, and every morning was a time of slow recovery, a cautious reemergence. Karina typically went to bed at eleven o'clock and was up at the crack of dawn. Her roommates learned to be considerate enough, but they could not understand her imperviousness to the temptations that overwhelmed them so easily. She dressed modestly, which ironically drew attention to her, like someone wearing clothes on a nude beach. She didn't drink. She aced her classes. She didn't date, but was friendly in her own way: not judgmental at all, and always ready to help when asked. Unlike most of the students, Karina had a car, a brand-new car, a state-of-the-art car. Still only nineteen, her 2083 Solectrair Jeep was really something. Her friends admired it. Other students envied it. Karina hardly used it.

She continued to live in a college dorm. Even as the newly minted sophomores around her, including her current roommate, moved into off-campus apartments and houses, she noticed the changes, but had no interest in participating.

A new roommate was assigned to her.

It was this event, that caused the studious and solitary Karina to look up and notice that something new was happening in her world.

This new roommate had neon green hair and had spiked it high and extravagantly. It was clear that her visual and audio implants were supplying stimuli as she moved into the room, almost dancing to music in a world that only she could hear and see. She was dressed in see-through clothing that shimmered tantalizingly, always blocking any view of the essentials. Her shoes appeared to be made of glass, suspending her six inches from the floor. Her multiple travel bags followed her into the room on their own, heading to the emptiest part of the space available. She was talking, or signing, with someone unseen. Karina was watching this entrance. The new visitor to her room was looking at her over the top of her facial visor span. She was quite tall. She was thin but not skinny. Karina saw her eyebrows shoot up looking at her. "Hey," she said, as though noticing for the first time that the room was occupied. Karina was sitting at her desk, obviously in the middle of a long, intense, study session, books and papers everywhere. Karina was dressed in dorm clothing: soft flannels, slippers, and her hair was pulled back away from her face, no makeup.

The two of them looked at each other. They could not have been more different at that moment. The flamboyant new roommate stood in the soft study light of Karina's room, her height enhanced by the tall platforms of her transparent shoes. Her spiked hair lifted her appearance even higher, well over six feet. Her strobing facial span, her stylish and fantastically shimmering clothes, all gave her an otherworldly appearance in the small space as though she had appeared out of nowhere, an alien in a new world. Karina seemed small by comparison, sitting at her desk, study materials all around. In this moment of recognition, they were still looking at each other. Karina wondered, *What is she thinking of me?* The newcomer was thinking exactly the same thing. The orienting moment lingered for a few more seconds. The room quieted from the excitement of her entrance; everything had stopped moving. Karina watched with interest as the visor span disappeared. The hair spikes softened, like an illusion dissipating, into a shoulder length of silky soft brown. Her flamboyant clothing changed into a white shirt and brushed fleecy pants with low casual sandals. Now, before her, stood a young freshman, probably just eighteen years old, smiling, clearly in relief.

She sat down on the opposite bed bouncing slightly on the soft mattress, a completely different person. Her bags moved a little farther out of the way. As Karina assimilated the transformation, her new roommate spoke again. "Thank God," she said. "you're a normal person." She was looking at Karina and smiling sweetly. "Who would have thought *this* could happen at Indiana University?"

The shift from splashy, excessive socialite to someone far more like her was so extreme and sudden that it made Karina laugh. Shaking her head, she could not control her response. Maybe it was the long hours of staring into the details of her study; maybe it was always feeling like an outsider; maybe it was just the wonderfully natural young woman now sitting in front of her, but it was all very funny to Karina. Her laughter infected her new roommate. They were laughing together, each for her own reasons. The newcomer held out her hand. "Hi, you must be Karina Chamberlain. I'm Chanel Tuperstein." They shook hands, Karina still sitting at her desk, Chanel reaching across the short distance from her bed. Karina said, "You had me worried there for a moment." They laughed again.

Chanel came from one of the richest families in Chicago. Her family had wanted her to go to Columbia or one of the other Ivy League schools, but she was tired of those rarified atmospheres and wanted something "real," as she called it. No matter how hard her parents tried to steer her in the direction they had been so successful in guiding her brother to, Chanel really wanted to go to Indiana University, a state school. "It's a great university," she told her parents, but they knew its tawdry reputation, especially for freshmen.

"There won't be many girls there like you," they said.

"Then, I'll become one of *them*." Exactly what her parents were worried about.

That first night, Karina and Chanel talked into the early morning hours. Karina realized how lonely she had been. The talkative, sweet, and very funny Chanel realized how lucky she was with her new roommate. They were friends from then on.

Karina was in her quarters on SkyKing, alone, lingering in her thoughts of the past. Farson was unreachable. The Moon's operation was in full swing; she had been monitoring the transmissions. She walked over to the window of her compartment and looked out at Emerald Earth. It seemed enormous. The unimaginable backdrop of the huge Sargasso behind everything made it all seem so unreal. In their world of changes and new levels of experience, it was Emerald Earth that stood out for her. So beautiful and so different from the

Earth she had grown up with. Now, instead of a world with deep and enormous blue seas and green and brown continents overpopulated with more than ten billion people, the world was an unbroken rich amber planet with shades of light green and only 6.8 million Emer ScreenMasters who had all Ascended together during their 6,500-year history. All of the struggles and uncertainties that had been her life had never happened to them. They did have their early history of drastic change, decline, and transformation, but it was all a shared experience. The new population of Emerald Earth had never known loneliness, illness, death, or lack of anything. They were truly history's chosen people. Karina knew that they had used their great gifts well, not just to save SkyKing and the Moon, but to save all of mankind.

Farson was still preeminent, despite his protests. Now he was missing. How long had it been? It seemed like years. She remembered the first time it had happened, during his Ascension. She had experienced it as weeks and weeks, but he said it was only a few moments. She wondered if that would happen again.

They had found no debris around *Songbird's* impact area, so everyone had concluded that Voul and Farson must be inside Sargasso. *Will I ever see him again?* As she watched Emerald Earth, she could sense its slow rotating movement against the vanishing distances of the wall of Sargasso. At times she hated the incomprehensible thing. At other times, the scientist in her wondered what it was, what it could be. But more than anything, she wanted Farson back. It was then, still looking out her window, that she realized Emerald Earth was *not* rotating as she had at first thought. It was the station.

For the first time in over ten years, SkyKing was on the move again.

Chanel asked, "Can I drive?" They were walking toward Karina's new Jeep. Actually it was nearing a year old. She thought of it as 'new' because she almost never used it. When she came to IU, she had taken the levtrain to Bloomington, a half-hour ride, but the car had been sent to her a week later by the Chamberlains. Karina was wondering what Chanel's experience level was with vehicles like hers, and if she was familiar with the car's various modes of operation.

In the late '70s, the wars were raging, and most of the industrial energies of the country were directed at the desert warfare areas. The technology of her car was a direct offshoot of the bloody conflicts, a byproduct of the needs of the troops: something light and fast that could travel through the sand and dust and navigate the waterways and seashores at the same time. From the large bulky-looking, but actually very swift and nimble troop carriers so familiar on the news broadcasts came the sleek and beautiful vehicle in the garage now just ahead of the two young women walking toward it. As they approached, Karina touched her wrist device, and the roof disappeared. She could visualize the pictures from the wars of the lasocannons on gun mounts from those savage days perched over the now plush and luxurious interior. Chanel was already at the driver's side. Karina brushed her wrist again, and the whisper quiet of the vehicle's engines started smoothly. She got in on the passenger side, sitting in the form-fitting seat that felt strangely like Farson's hands and arms embracing her. The restraint system wrapped itself around her, and the car brought all of its systems online, including holographic displays, sensor arrays, access to orbital navigational devices, and launching off four of its own sensors that positioned themselves at various distances around the Jeep, waiting for further instructions. Chanel was still standing outside, waiting for permission. "Who needs to drive, Chanel? Just jump in and watch this." Chanel got right in. "Now," Karina adjusted herself so she was facing Chanel, "tell it where we're going." Chanel happily adjusted to the "driver's" seat embrace, as it performed the same positioning and safety protocols for her, eliciting a squeal of laughter as though someone was tickling her. Then she spoke to the car, in a voice a little too loud.

"Lemon Lake." The car elevated and smoothly proceeded out of the multilevel underground garage, moving at the maximum safe speed allowed by the garage driveways, and soon it came out into the sun and blasted off, about a hundred feet in the air, traveling at around 180 miles per hour, heading directly for the lake. The displays indicated that they would be at their destination in about six minutes. The advance probes had raced off and were almost there already. Chanel's soft hair was wildly streaming in the wind spilling over the car's front shields.

"Do you want to close up? It'll be less windy." Karina's ponytail was streaming in the breeze, her blouse billowing in the shield's burble. It was a very pleasantly warm day.

"Are you kidding? This is fantastic. You've never been to Lemon Lake, have you?"

"No. It always seemed that it would take too much time."

"So you know nothing about it?"

"Not really." Chanel was laughing as she threw her head back in delight. She raised her arms over her head, joyously enthralled by the ride. She had to shout to be heard.

"It's a nude beach." This revelation caused memories to immediately flow into parts of Karina's mind that she had not accessed in a long time. "Beach" was the first mnemonic stimulation her thought encountered. She vividly remembered her trips to "Beach" with Farson. How excited he had been when she finally agreed. *In more ways than one.* How anxious he was to get going, but she dragged her feet for a few more days. How, finally, they set off on the voyage, only to discover how long the voyage to the planet was. He had fallen asleep. How she had awakened him and undressed so casually in front of him. Her heart was pounding, unknown to him. How she had insisted that he "Get with it" and prepare for the landing. She had watched him undress in front of her. How young and intoxicated with the sensuality of the moment he was. He had stopped at his underwear, shy and suddenly uncharacteristically bluster-less, facing the reality of first exposure, but she said, "Off with everything, Farson. This is Beach! You know the rules." It all made her smile again just thinking about it. Chanel was talking.

"Are you okay with that?" Chanel had seen that Karina was lost in thought. She was assuming it was uncertainty and modest inexperience. Little did she know.

"We'll see." She laughed in the wind of the warm Indiana summer's car ride. Up ahead she could see the lake was looming into view. The probes were already filling the monitors with the activity at the lake. "We'll see," she repeated, her eyebrows elevating as she viewed the scenes streaming on the car's monitors. Chanel was already taking off her shirt, revealing a shimmering see-through bathing suit top that, while transparent, would make anyone look twice. Karina could see Chanel's beautiful young body blinking in and out of view with swirling colors passing all around her body. She saw Karina looking at her.

"I was hoping there would be an occasion when this suit would come in handy."

Karina could now see that the lakeside beach was crowded with IU students. It was 11:00 a.m., and the party was already in full swing. As the car oriented itself and hovered inches from the beach, the two girls got out, relaxing as their toes sank in the warm sand and into the joy of being young.

The car departed to a programmed distance awaiting Karina's call to return. People had noticed their arrival. The gregarious Chanel, now running, free and happy to her friends, was waving gayly as she approached them. Her suit's programmed pattern of hide and seek was clearly slowing down. It wouldn't be long, Karina knew, before Chanel fully embraced the spirit of the lake.

Karina was slowly stepping out of her own clothes, but still displaying a beautiful but small white bathing suit. Her hand hovered over her wrist. She was thinking of throwing her modesty to the wind and turning off the visuals entirely. The nakedness all around her was infecting her with a carefree feeling that she enjoyed. Just before she decided what to do, a soft male voice spoke to her.

"Hi, Karina." She turned and saw a young man, a very handsome young man, very nude and partially aroused standing before her. It was a boy from her bionics class. She had done a lab experiment or two with him. He had always been nice. She was surprised that anyone at the lake knew her. And then it hit her. *I am the only one who doesn't come here.* He moved closer and gave her a hug, his penis touching her briefly. It surprised her. She couldn't keep herself from looking down. He smiled.

"Let's take a swim." He took her hand and led her to the clear, cool waters of Indiana University's historic and storied swimming hole. "You're going to love it," he said. Chanel was nowhere to be seen.

Repoul Jonsn was calling her. Karina's SkyKing communicator was vibrating. She touched it. "Yes, Repoul."

"Karina, would you come to the bridge? Something's come up." She shook her head lightly to clear it and relocate. Her memories had overtaken her. She had been in a place far away in time from the task at hand. Reluctantly, she refocused and responded to the Sker.

"On my way."

77. Ready for What?

"Just how do you expect us to anchor these babies, Sarge?" Long John Hanson Silver was getting mad. The nozzles were taking a lot longer than he thought was necessary. All they had to do was set them up in the prescribed pattern and tie them securely down to Sargasso. Easy.

"Will you stop fucking around and get the cocksuckers down?"

"Nothing works. Not laser bolts. Not grav-ties. Not even plasma glue, and we even used that vibracator application thing. Nothing works. Sargasso is tough as hell." Silver was not happy, furious in fact, but something the miner had said made him think of something.

"Get the portable transporter unit. Try a micro transport of the bottom six inches of the nozzle frame into the surface. I bet that'll do it. Fuck Sargasso."

They secured the nozzle mounts and then brought down all the equipment they needed to operate them. They had been working at it for almost a week before Sergeant Silver was satisfied, and even then he kept asking for adjustments and refinements in the positioning and programming. He kept referring to the sheet of specifications he had been given. He held a conference of all his men and women, and they went over the plans again. Only after the final check was marked off on his checklist and all his questions were answered did he finally call up to SkyKing. His words were relayed to the Moon and Emerald Earth at the same time. "We are ready." He looked up and saw the three of them moving slowly overhead. They were beautiful. They seemed so close to him. He repeated the words again when asked for confirmation. "We are ready." Then he thought, *Ready for what?*

78. Panau and Twill

Twill was in his over-generously appointed and gilt-crafted, extremely spacious compartment. The windows were huge and facing aftward, away from the ship's heading, through the chopped-off tail of *Noctura's* long, reverse tapered fuselage. Twill had forced the designer to develop this space for him. That was when nobody thought the ship would ever sail.

Essors were homebodies by nature, not adventurers. No one really cared that the ship was an odd anomaly in their ship design history. Some thought it was disappointing looking. But as it turned out, Twill's ship was the most maneuverable, livable, and – because of its crew's glowing reputation – the most admired ship in the fleet.

He was sitting at the huge desk, surrounded by holographic displays from all over and around *Noctura*. He was watching every facet of the ship's company and compartments, all the while watching the rest of the fleet following in his wake. The feeling of supreme power was unbelievably pleasurable to him. The fleet had every kind of fighting ship the Essors had ever made, and all of them were brand new, or never used and perfectly maintained. Essor was a defensive planet with a cautious people. Twill's call to action and his dispatching of the fleet were unprecedented.

But here they were, racing through space as fast as they could, every second farther and farther away from their beloved home warren and balenests. It was a moment of revelation imposed upon the Essor crews by their self-proclaimed-to-be-transcendent leader. They were following him, but the gravitational pull of their true devotion was on a compass bearing back in the opposite direction. "Off into the unknown" for some races was an irresistible call to glory, but for the Essors it was the unwelcomed voice of insanity baiting them to unnatural disaster. Wary eyes watched Twill's every move.

He was oblivious to the crew's reluctant participation in his now far-famed assault on the technician's coordinates. In fact, he would have been happy if it went on forever. He was having the time of his life.

The guarded door to his chambers chimed. "What?" The interruption was unwanted to such a degree that with the mere sound of it, Twill could feel his always lurking ire awaken, ready to answer whatever annoyance was presenting itself. His second-in-command, if that is the correct term for someone in the shadow of the great Twill's authority, had entered and began speaking his obviously rehearsed report.

"The technician said that you should come to the bridge." This was not phrased in a way that Twill could appreciate. Too matter-of-fact, lacking the sufficient supplicant intonation and the appropriate phraseology of a subordinate to a superior.

"Oh she did, did she?" The lieutenant commander knew that he had repeated her exact words. He could remember the sound of Panau's gentle voice as she had said them. It was a pleasant memory.

"Yes, Master Twill. She also said to tell you, and I quote, that 'an impediment seems to be surrounding the target coordinates, and we cannot yet determine its nature or composition.'" These words were barely spoken before Twill felt a twinge shudder through his body like a neural shock, or a body blow, his ire now flaming high.

"What?!" The crew member said it again, exactly as he had the first time, enraging Twill with his seeming insensibility to the import of the words. Twill bolted up on his thick scaled rear legs, looking to his visitor like a monster set to rampage. Twill bolted for the exit, pushing him out of the way, shouting for the door to open, and moving to the corridor faster than his guards had thought possible. Twill slammed through the half-opened door, the guards jumping aside, heading for the bridge in a blind rage. The lieutenant commander was right behind him, hoping to somehow warn Panau before Twill's anger again knocked her world upside down.

Panau was at the navigation station engrossed, along with several other crew members, by the data readings pouring out of the long-range receivers. It was interesting to her that all of the readings had first gone directly to the vast computation facilities on Essor, where they were processed, recorded, evaluated, and then forwarded back to her on *Noctura*. The little group on *Noctura's* bridge was astounded at what they were seeing. It was a rare scene on the ship: crew members actually enthralled with their function and obviously enjoying a sense of discovery. As Twill burst onto the bridge, no one looked up. The data in front of them was so mesmerizing that their concentration would not be broken. Even Twill, inside his roiling emotional storm, found the calm intelligence filling the bridge arresting. He stopped and stood there, uncertain what to do. Panau turned to him and said, "Master Twill, this is something we have never seen before." She tapped her console and said, "Come and see." Like a domestic pet, deep in the welcome cold of a home on Essor, Twill obeyed her invitation and stood beside her. The crew on the bridge could not believe it and were holding their breath, but Panau pointed out a holographic image split in half by a straight line. "Our measurements indicate – and we had to go out to undiscovered exponents to reach any conclusion at all – that what you are looking at is actually a gigantic sphere, well past solar system size. It completely encircles my coordinates, but that is conjecture. The data tells us that directionally we cannot be wrong, but it is an unimaginable situation. We are scanning the object, but it would take years to complete such a survey."

Twill was uncharacteristically listening carefully. She went on. "We have no ideas concerning access to the coordinates, and in fact, we are just interpolating them, since no readings whatsoever resolve within the assumed area of the sphere." She took a soft breath and looked Twill in the eyes. He could see her intelligence for the first time. He could sense her dedication to the task at hand. He was waiting to hear what she would say next. "Even at top speed, we are still six weeks from actually being able to see the object with our own eyes on our screens." Twill moved over to his command chair, which was empty. He sat down and felt the welcomed adjustments to his comfort. His emotional state had calmed itself somewhat. He found he was grateful for her forthrightness and precision. *We are lucky to have her.* He reminded himself that it was his idea to have her come along, using a self-serving euphemism for what was nothing less than an imprisonment and forceful transfer with no concern for her assent or safety. He shrugged his hunched shoulders, extending his taloned elbows outwardly as if to say, "Whatever," and, with that self-forgiveness, spoke to her, clearly seeking further advice.

"Are we at top speed?"

"No, sir. More like three-quarters speed."

"Should we go faster?" She moved closer to him and spoke softly so that only he could hear. Twill leaned toward her.

"My recommendation is that we go to half speed, take our time, and try to figure this out. This is a great unknown, Master Twill. We should use caution." Twill reflexively wanted to disagree, but something told him she could be right. The other people on the bridge were unconsciously leaning in to hear better. The words of Twill's and the technician's conversation were inaudible except for just the two of them, but the tone of collegiality was clear. The lieutenant commander was in awe. *Panau is in control now.* Twill stood up and raised his hand. She did not even flinch. They both knew that things had changed. Twill looked at the holograph. *How can that be a curvature?* His large and scabrous hand touched her gently. She could sense a distant apology, a vague humility, a restive, evasive sense of regret. They briefly looked at each other as Twill passed her. They both had the same thought: surprise respect at discovering that indefinable essence of being truly Essor in each other: the acceptance of truth no matter what it takes, no matter where it appears; the race's saving grace.

"Make it so, Commander." With that Twill left the bridge. It was clear to everyone present that he was speaking to Panau.

79. The Riders

Songbird was rising upwind in the Sea of Knowing, as Uva called the 20,000-mile diameter stream of nanoscopic chemicals and elements that flowed more and more forcefully over them the nearer they flew to Sargasso's mysterious sun, so rich, so nutrient, so vital, so incredibly bright within its amazing interior. It was like they were being sucked in. *Songbird's* powerful engines adeptly negotiated the changeable oscillations of the currents, especially now under the control of the more than capable hands of Uva, who had assumed the pilot's chair.

"It's only natural," she said, "I have the most experience."

Neither Farson, who had traveled through time and space for the equivalent of thousands of years, nor Voul, who was an accomplished and trusted Sker pilot, could argue with her flawless mastery of the vessel.

"*Songbird* sings to me." She smiled and briefly thought of her great ship, *Rachis*, still orbiting Aristealia. She loved *Rachis*, for many reasons: her memory of Uvo in the captain's chair, and her own traveling for so many months with Farson, to mention two. All that she had learned on that ship was now serving her well; it especially reminded her of the indisputable lesson that Farson Uiost never gives up. Even now, he was watching her every move. "I have noticed something, Farson."

"What would that be, Uva?" If the truth were known, he loved having her here. She reminded him of Uvo and all the times he had had with him. They had been true friends. Uvo's death had deeply affected and impacted Farson. There was no escaping the emptiness that Farson felt with Uvo's absence or the fact that he felt responsible for Uvo's death. Uva would disagree now. But human beings harbor demons, sometimes unaware and other times with determination. Uvo's death was one of Farson's demons.

"Well, it may be hard to quantify, but I still feel it."

"What?"

"That *Songbird* is easier to fly in the center of this sea. There seems to be a slowly increasing easement in the current. We are still a great distance from Sargasso's star, but if this continues, I believe it will become a tunnel." She looked at Farson as she said the last sentence. He was thinking it over. *A tunnel in the stream.*

"A tunnel, as into something, or, a tunnel, as in around something? She smiled. Farson knew exactly what she was talking about.

"Into something."

"You think we are being invited in?"

"Yes, I do. I could be wrong. Time will tell." She settled back into the captain's chair and fussed around with the dials and screens, adjusting this and that. Then she settled deeper into the chair and leaned back. It was obvious she was expecting to be there for quite a while.

Farson and Voul had been attempting to map Sargasso's interior. They knew now that there were six planets, all more twenty-five percent larger than the Earth-size standard. They were evenly spaced, except for two empty slots, around the star and within Sargasso. The idea of visiting the star first was an easy choice because it was located, as nearly as they could calculate, smack-dab at the exact center of Sargasso. Once there, measurements and calculations should be the easiest. Since there was apparently some time available – Uva had said it could be weeks – Farson was planning to visit one of the planets. But which one? From what they could tell, the atmospheres and angle to the sun were about the same on all the planets. There were some variations, as in the variation from Moscow's cold to San Diego's warmth on old Earth, but nothing really inhospitable. They all seemed like nice worlds. He had actually briefly visited the vicinity of one, testing the interior screen of Sargasso, just after they had "arrived." He had noted many people on the world, but other exigencies drew him back to *Songbird*. Farson also noticed that Sargasso's screen did not seem to support being in more than one place at a time. When you went, you went. "What other realities Sargasso has in store for us," Farson had said, "will have to be discovered."

Uva's simple statement summed it up. "There is no manual with this thing." Farson knew that with his abilities limited, in this unknown arena, danger could lurk, although, nothing had happened to validate his caution. To the contrary, actually, their entrance had been threatening in the planning, and then, effortless in the fact. That Sargasso had a thin atmosphere that was breathable was also reassuring. It all had the feeling of being a very peaceful place. Farson had found himself relaxing in Sargasso, both times. He noticed that Uva and Voul were also quite happy. *Now there's a tunnel to the star.* Too good to be true? But Farson remembered what Uvo said about situations like this, "When something seems too good to be true, it may be good, it may be bad, but it will be interesting. Take care and figure it out. Pessimism in this life is illogical. But on every world I have ever visited, foolishness is never rewarded."

With those thoughts in mind, Farson decided to take Voul with him to the first planet.

Working with Uva and Voul, Farson determined that they had entered Sargasso into the middle of the area between what they were calling the seventh and eighth planet slots, counting the two empty areas as one and two. Uva had determined that their trajectory upon entry was very "interesting." Their original flight path as they entered had been directly pointing them at the exact center of the star. *Songbird* had veered from those bearings under Uva's control, but as she had learned to steady up within the sea's current, she had noticed that they were back on that original course and heading again. In fact, her adjustments to the currents steadily encouraged the ship right back onto that course exactly. "*Songbird* seems to be following the path of least resistance, Farson. The tunnel is becoming more clearly defined now. It is slowly but surely resolving. In a few days we will be on autopilot. Even now, I'm not sure I could turn around even if I wanted to. Which I don't. I am watching the thermal readings as we draw nearer to the star. Within the tunnel there seems to be, as I said, an 'easement' of some sort. We are safe within it. No increasing radiation, no rising heat; we are just sailing along safely separated from the changes you would expect heading closer and closer to a star. The controls seem to need adjustments less and less. It's like a slow-motion tractor beam.

"How long before the tunnel locks us up?" Uva looked at him. He was geared up in old clothing: jeans and a rough shirt, boots but no hat. It was clear he would be leaving soon. Voul was also dressed in civilian clothes. They were new, neat, but the dark colors seemed incongruent with the Voul she had known over the past weeks. She realized there was a reason for Farson's question.

"I would say you should be back no later than twenty-four hours from now. Will we be in communication?"

"I hope so, but nothing is certain in this situation, as you know." She nodded. *We are on an adventure.*

Farson and Voul spent another hour preparing, then returned to the bridge. "We will return in twenty-three hours or sooner."

Uva waved to them as the room filled with a purple hue, surrounding them both, and then they disappeared. She thought to herself about the hue now fading away. *Well, at least that's the same.*

Farson and Voul were standing on a sandy river bank. The current was being stirred up by a storm forming out over the low rolling hills. The wind and rain was causing the two explorers to lean into its force. It was midday. The light and warmth of the obscured sun was directly overhead behind the clouds. The air was rich with oxygen and moisture. They could taste the earthy mist mixing with the sheeting rain. "Let's get to some shelter," Voul said, but Farson was already heading toward a group of buildings on the edge of the hardscrabble riverside town nearby. As they ran in the rain, a sound came up behind them like thunder. Then a man on a huge horse-like beast galloped by, heading into town. Then another and another. Farson and Voul ducked onto a porch and watched. At least twenty men rode through the rain, all slow galloping with mud flying everywhere. Farson had never seen anything like it, except at the county fair in some distant past when he lived in faraway Indiana. Somehow it felt familiar to him. *This is not an advanced planet.*

Voul was moving down the porch, in the direction of the riders. Then he realized that they had stopped, were getting off their hard-breathing rides, and, after securing them to posts positioned at the side of the street, headed into the building before them. Farson realized that Voul was following them. "Do you think that is wise, Voul? We are strangers." Voul seemed not to have heard Farson, although Farson knew he had. Even as he watched, Voul was walking through the same door as the riders. Their muddy boot prints had smeared the floor so much that Voul had to take care as he walked. Farson had started to follow him in, but hesitated in the doorway, looking around. There was no electricity visible that Farson could detect. He looked at his wrist device. It was still functional. He spoke to Uva. <<*Uva, are you there?*>>

<<*Where else would I be, Farson?*>>

<<*Do you detect a power source on this planet?*>>

<<*Yes, indeed. A very powerful source.*>>

<<*The planet has power?*>> She was annoyed at this unnecessary question and did not answer. She did offer some new information, though. <<*In my surveys I am detecting a pattern in the three major emissions of the star. One stream goes through the center of the planet you are visiting, and the other two eddy around it, almost in an orbital fashion, and then all three proceed on their way. I am assuming, at this point, that they repeat this function at the other five planets. The entire system seems to be continuous. It reminds me of a ventilation system in a large building.*>> Farson decided to proceed inside.

As he stood beside Voul, he looked around. The room was lighted with oil lamps of some kind and candles placed around. There were perhaps thirty people in the room, men and women. Farson looked from person to person. They all seemed to be normal people. He sensed no danger of any kind. Then he noticed that they were all looking at him. He saw something in their eyes that surprised him. They all knew exactly who he was.

80. Indiana University (3)

The water was cool, but very pleasant. They swam together to a float about one hundred yards offshore. Karina was a good swimmer, so it was easy and enjoyable. Sean, the young man – she had remembered his name now from their work together – was a strong swimmer as well and had reached the float quickly and climbed up the ladder. He was standing there waiting for her. He helped her up. They were alone. It was a beautiful day. She could see the other students on the crowded beach, and she could hear them laughing and talking and being themselves, young and excited with life. On the raft with Sean, she still felt the loneliness that was her constant companion, that emptiness where Farson should have been. She felt a tender guilt at her even being at the lake, but even more for enjoying herself. She looked at her naked companion and laughed. Not because he was funny, but because of the situation she had gotten herself into. *Crazy Chanel.* But then she realized that Chanel was only one element of her being here; there were others, most of all her own curiosity. Her studies of life expectancy and prolonging it were so important to her that almost a semester and a half had gone by without her developing any real relationships. Except now there was Chanel; no denying that. She had been invited to parties, to join sororities and student organizations; she had been invited to weekends in Indianapolis, and even to New York, but she had always declined. Her studies and Farson were always the reasons, although she never mentioned Farson. Chanel knew about him from their talks at night and from being with her so much, but she didn't know the full story. Chanel knew that Karina's heart was somewhere else and that nothing at Indiana University or even anything or anyone else on the planet Earth would ever change that. "You love your brother?" she had asked. Karina had told her the short version that they had been adopted by the same family and were not related in the usual way. She had mentioned her parents' fate, without detailing it. She had mentioned that Farson had also come to the Chamberlains with a tragedy of his own. Chanel understood, to a degree, that they had grown closer and closer over the years. And she wondered if she would ever love someone like that. "You've never been with anyone else?"

"Absolutely not. Never will."

"Does Farson feel the same way?"

"Yes, he does. Of course." Chanel found this hard to believe, knowing college students, and even some Harvard College students, as well as she did.

"Are you sure?"

Karina was recalling this situation as Sean approached her. He was a member of Nu Tsi Tau, a fraternity, that had many members from the University's elite swimming team. It was the king of the fraternities at the University in terms of parties and reputation. She could see that he was imbued with a confidence that would always elude her. He was in his junior year, one year ahead of her, but his experience with IU's social life made her feel that he was way ahead of her.

"I take it this is your first time here?"

"Indeed."

"It is a nude beach, you know." She was still wearing her bathing suit, although it was pretty skimpy.

"You look great, Karina. And you swim well, too." She realized that for him, her swimming skills only increased his interest.

"You, too." She could not help but notice what a beautiful young man he was. Tall, muscular, a great face, waving brown hair streaked with natural highlights, a bright smile, a clear intellect, a perfect Indiana University student on his way to success. His nudity was not offensive to her. Interesting, perhaps. Her gaze passed up and down his body. He noticed and pirouetted for her, his arms raised up over his head.

"Now you." It took her a moment to realize what he wanted. Taking a breath and nervously exhaling to calm herself, she slowly turned in a circle. She could feel his eyes feasting on her. When she completed the turn, he was laughing softly. "You are blushing."

She could think of nothing to say, and then he added, "That *is* unusual around here."

There were three small tables with umbrellas on the raft, and he led her over to one and they sat down. "You have a boyfriend, I can tell. Is he here?"

"No." This was not a conversation she wanted. He noticed her discomfort and was thinking his next question over more carefully now. Then he decided on not asking it.

"It's beautiful here. I know the lake's reputation, but even if it were not nude, I would come here. It's an oasis. A place away. Have you noticed that IU seems far away from here?" She had noticed. Her studies were back there. This was a pleasant reprieve.

"Yes." He softly laughed at her again.

"Just one-word answers?"

"I'm having trouble thinking of things to say."

"Have you ever heard of the mud here?"

"No."

"Well, Indiana, as you may know, is the spelunking capital of the world. Brown County has some of the most enjoyable, noncommercial caves anywhere. But the soil, in many locations, is high in clay, which makes for great caves, and is rich and good for many crops. But it is also a vital ingredient in a very special form of massage and sunbathing that we practice here. Did you know about that?"

"No." She smiled. He stood up and took her hand.

"Let's go. You're in for a treat." Together they dove into Lemon Lake. She was thinking, though, *What have I gotten myself into to?*

Over the next two hours, Sean showed her the lake's mud pits and how to enjoy them. He had her spread the thick mud all over his body, including his head and face. She had found the thick mud at least partially insulated her from the full force of touching him, but not completely. He now stood in front of her and smiled, his white teeth blazing bright against the dark mud. Then it was his turn to mud her. He started from her feet and worked up. She flinched when he touched her. "Look," he said holding a hand full of the mud at least three inches thick, dripping. "I can't really feel anything. Relax." He proceeded to cover her from head to foot including her head and face. She deactivated her clothing as the need arose. She had found Sean's mud application process to be enjoyable, even as she resisted it at first with distraction, and then with determination. No one had ever touched her in such a way except Farson. Sean had been a gentleman, following the rules, the same rules, she had followed in her muddy applications, but still there were moments of obvious pleasure, unavoidable, both ways. They stood looking at each other. It was clear to Karina what a nice guy he was. Patient, caring, unassuming, handsome, and smart. He moved in to give her a hug. The day, the sun, the mud ... it all conspired with her habitual loneliness. She allowed it and returned it. It was a friendly hug, not a passionate one. It was nice. He was a tall, strong, wonderful young man. She might have stayed in the hug a second or two longer, her eyes were closed, if not for the clicking sound, which she immediately recognized as a recording device being activated.

"Smile!" said Chanel as her autonomous camera automatically navigated its way around, over, and under the two of them, photographing them from every angle in a few seconds. "*This* needs to be recorded for posterity!" Karina jumped back and swatted at the device like a bug bothering her, but Chanel was too quick. Naked as the day she was born, Karina's playful roommate ran away, at first backwards facing them with that laughing, mischievous face she exhibited so often, the camera still rolling.

Taking pictures of Karina, covered in mud, nude, hugging a guy she just met was over the top. Karina started to make chase, but the movements shook some of the drying mud off significant locations, so she stopped moving. In the mud-up process, removing her suit, at strategic moments, had been impossible to avoid. Topless now, she was afraid to move. The mud's grip had been proven to be tenuous. Chanel stopped and took some more images, just as Sean walked over, experiencing the same phenomenon with his muddy body, but without Karina's self-consciousness. Chanel was laughing out loud now. Karina was uncertain what to do. Sean took her hand and led her into the waters. As she sought the modesty of depth, she felt the hot mud melting away, replaced with the cool waters of Lemon Lake. It was extraordinarily enjoyable. She looked at Sean and laughed at herself.

"It's great, isn't it? Nothing like this place. He was floating on his back. Karina did the same thing, the sun warming her.

Chanel had returned to her friends farther up the beach.

The car ride home was quiet. The sun, the fun, the experience of the day had saturated them both into silence. Chanel finally spoke. "You were so lucky to have Sean for the day. Do you know who he is?"

"Not really. He is a good swimmer."

"He's the top swimmer on the best swimming team in the country. You should have seen the other girls watching you with him. They would have all changed places with you in a second. Me, too." The wind over the front spill shield again moved their hair in the wind. It was late afternoon. The sun's heat was diminishing. Karina put a sweater on over her bathing suit. "We were taking bets on what would happen."

"Nothing happened."

"Nothing?" Karina looked over at her friend.

"*Nothing.*"

Chanel laughed and said, "Wait until you see the pictures of you two mudding up."

81. News to Them

"Welcome to Range, Farson. You, too, Voul."

There were eight of them.

"We're Riders." The leader of the group said this as if it were self-explanatory. Farson and Voul were taking it all in, but it was news to them.

Dressed as cowboys, horsel rides waiting outside, tied to the hitching post, their appearance said one thing, but their knowledge of Farson and Voul said another.

"We're here on Range for about a week, and then we're off again." He waved his hand, and an image appeared in the air between the Riders and them. It was recognizable as a three-dimensional map of Sargasso, similar to the one Farson and Uva had begun to devise on *Songbird*, but this one was perfect in scale and detail. The six planets circled the star, fully surrounded in the light-blanketing patterns of the three "seas" with the three distinct colors and currents passing over, around, and through each other and enveloping the planets. One of the seas was more clearly defined by the brightest color concentration, and this one went directly through, and ghosting around each planet forming a complete, uninterrupted ring through the system, with branches reaching directly into the star's four quadrants, like four spokes of a wheel. The leader pointed to the ring and said, "We ride this one to and from the planets. There are many of us, moving throughout the system now, from all of the planets." Farson noticed that his hand lingered on the central sea of the diaphanous map-like depiction floating between them. "But, we," he indicated the eight of them, "come from here." He pointed to Azure.

The Rider leader looked at Farson. He saw Farson's uncertainty.

"Wow. You really don't know much about us, do you?" Farson and Voul knew this was true, but it was clearly a surprise to the Riders.

82. Range

It was a planet more like the old state of Colorado than anything else Farson could think of. The Riders told him that the people who came to Range were rough-edge pioneers and settlers who wanted to carve out their own independent lives. Farson and Voul spent as much time on Range as Uva would allow, and then they left when she called. Even in the short twenty-three hours they were there, they both had learned enough to want to stay. A beautiful, free planet with vast canyons, roaring rivers, and lots of room. Deer, antelope, cattle, buffalo, and wildlife of all descriptions, to a point of plethora, only made Range more endearing to them. It was like the wild west of old Earth. "Except it's not wild at all, Farson. It's more like a huge ranch." Then he added, "A home on the range." Clearly, the Rider had spoken the origin of the planet's name.

The pristine Voul seemed at ease in the dusty world of Range. Farson had seen many changes in Voul, and he knew there would be more still to come. There was a sense of acceptance in Voul and the Skers, but he knew them too well. Exigencies were to be met and mastered, and then the Skers' dreams would return. Farson knew they were a practical and pragmatic people. He also knew that the Skers never took their eyes off the prize, in the end. Adaptability for them was informed by purpose and planning.

Back on *Songbird*, Sargasso was slowly revealing itself to them and, from what they had learned so far, it was leading them to a conclusion that was not at first obvious at all. Uva agreed with their slowly forming conclusion.

"It is definitely a highly developed closed system of some sort," Uva said. "In its aggregate, it *is* like a space vessel: self-contained, independent, and dedicated to life support. It's all becoming more and more obvious to me. The seas are a complex life support system as well as a transportation mechanism for moving throughout Sargasso with ease and safety. It definitely could easily be a vessel."

The three of them had had a discussion about the nature of the star's huge and encompassing pulsing energy fields as rings or clouds, searching for another rubric to understand them. But Uva was adamant. "They are clearly not rings when seen in three dimensions. They cover the entire interior of Sargasso, so 'clouds' would also be misleading but directionally more accurate. They produce the atmosphere. They provide all the elements of weather: heat, cold, moisture, oxygen, and everything else they need. They move in a clearly defined and highly dependable pattern, mostly caused by the enormous and obviously controlled pulsating gravity fields of the star. When you see them in their true state, they cover everything in Sargasso except the star itself. They are incredibly complex oceans of energy, rich in nutrients, and all the elements of life. In fact, I would not be surprised to find that life has evolved inside of them. When you think about it, it seems obvious what to call them. These energy fields are the giant seas of Sargasso. Farson was right. Sargasso is a solar system within itself, by definition, with one big difference: It could move anywhere it wants to. It is the largest starship ever devised."

Farson was thinking about all that they had learned from visiting just one of the planets. According to Uva, Range was sparsely populated, for its huge landmass. There were approximately a billion and a half people, give or take a hundred thousand. Almost forty square miles or twenty-six thousand acres for each person. There were generous rivers and lakes, but it was all one continuous continent. There were towns and one central city, but mostly the people lived and worked their own "homesteads," all of which were huge.

Travel on the planet itself was intentionally primitive, but sufficient. The Sea of Knowing, which Uva had determined was name of the transport, was available for travel from planet to planet and within Sargasso. Range had many transport stations around the planet, available when needed.

The Riders were the one interplanetary commonality. They adjusted their appearance and modes of transportation on each planet to reflect local customs.

Uva was studying her instruments and was now talking again.

"As of a minute ago we are under Sargasso's full control, and we are heading straight toward the center of its star."

"How long before we get there?"

"Distance-wise it could be several more days. We are just entering the star's outer perimeters. But something else is happening." Farson urged her to explain. He could feel her reluctance. "It appears that a transporter-like lock is forming around us. It started slowly, but, like everything else on Sargasso, it seems to be inescapable. I would say that the lock will be complete in less than three hours. At first it started as a very thorough scan of everything and everyone on board, including health default. There have also been interesting adjustments made to *Songbird*'s operating and propulsion systems. I have detected no effect on us, other than my increasing sense of well-being and complete freedom from anxiety or worry, despite a situation in which we now have no control and there are plenty of reasons to worry. I am assuming that Sargasso wants us to relax." Farson and Voul smiled, obviously in agreement.

"I have a feeling like going home," Voul said. "And I'm excited to get there." Farson looked over at Uva. He was thinking of flying, and she noticed.

Farson said, "I feel like I should spread my wings and go with the flow." This made Uva laugh. How well she knew of Farson's love of flight, even if imaginary for him. She knew that his deep acceptance of her "stories" and his bottomless well of love for Uvo and, by association, for her, had made their bond complete. His comment made her happy. Voul looked a little confused, but to her, it was heartwarming and humorous. She appreciated it. She filled Farson's mind with intricate thoughts of maneuvers and aerial exuberance. For a moment, they were together again in the skies of Aristealia. She saw the thoughts of joy in his mind. It stopped her for a moment, realizing how thorough had been the change that had come over to two of them. He was looking at her. "Maybe we are all going home now."

83. Farson's Log (5)

The truth about Sargasso is now becoming known.

At first it was just me and my faulty memory about seeing Emerald Earth, SkyKing, and the Moon floating inside there. Even as I looked directly at them, I knew they weren't really there. I also knew that this was just the first clue that I had noticed. There had been many clues before, and there would be many more. They had been telling me what was going to happen and what I should do. Since becoming a ScreenMaster, no one could have told me anything after LevelTen: not Uvo; or the robots; not even Handy, although he did go on and on with his advice; not even Karina; and certainly not Twill in any influential way. It was always the other way around: I was always on my own, especially when decisions had to be made. Now things are changing.

When ID>>Karo28689 showed up at my party as a twenty-two-year-old woman, that was another clue, although I missed it at the time. That she only raised her glass at the second half of my toast – when I spoke of the future – was indicative and part of a labyrinthine chain of clues she has left for me since.

When I returned to *Songbird* after the dinner, she left with me, without saying goodbye to anyone. These were all clues. The ease with which we entered Sargasso was another big one. The meaningless explosion charade was another one. I'm still waiting to learn its meaning. Perhaps they were buying time.

It was Uva's "tunnel" that provided substantiation for me, at least directionally, no pun intended. Sargasso had presented itself in stages: its size, its composition, its positioning, its timing, its interior ... all parts of a whole. When the Riders told me about the transport system, I knew. As hard as it was to appreciate at first, there could be no doubt: Sargasso was a construct beyond all knowledge and control I had ever known, beyond imagination. Emerald Earth, over the 6,500 years of its history, had spawned a whole new breed of invention. The Emers had planned nothing less than the salvation of humanity. They had done it in complete secrecy. It reminds me of the Skers and their sacred solar sails; or of me with the stasis field. I was the only one who knew those secrets, and I am the only one who knows this one. Well, almost the only one. ID>>Karo28689 knows, of course. The Emers could not have done what they have done without the help of the ScreenKeepers. With the robots' leader on their side, their plans were possible, and their secret safe.

I now know that ID>>Karo28689 came to my party to protect us. Even now she is continuing to protect us. Her appearance as the young woman, Ida, was a warning to me.

Her story itself is a warning to all of us. But appearing as the twenty-four-year-old Ida Marie Rothschild – as an Ida who could never have existed – made the warning crystal clear. Things that could not be, were. Things that were, aren't. When she left the North Conway cabin with me after dinner, I heard a soft voice on The Screen speaking to me. <<*Judge not, Farson. The last shall be first and the first shall be last.*>> It took me awhile to figure out what she meant, but I did, eventually.

Now in the full control of Sargasso – just like Uva's tunnel had taken full control of *Songbird* – where we are going and what happens is controlled by others. Some elements remain for me that need to be placed in their proper order, but, like the Riders, we are now being carried along on forces we do not fully understand, toward destinations we did not expect to see.

As I look around, I already see the unpredicted and unforeseen: Uva is happy again. Voul is trusting and content. For myself, I feel a deep and welcome peace. I feel a complete reassurance from understandings I do not really have, a growing confidence in evidence I know must exist but have not yet seen. Without a doubt, without a qualm, without regret, without hesitation, I am – we are – leaping into an unknown future, and it feels good.

<<*Farson?*>> It was Karina.
<<*Where are you?*>>
<<*I'm waiting for you. Hurry up.*>>

84. It Must Have Been for You Like It Was for Me

From the back of *Songbird's* flight deck, Farson noticed that Voul and Uva were fading out in an unresolving transparency right in front of him. Then he realized *Songbird* itself was also disappearing, front to back. For a moment he was alone in the tunnel. Uva and Voul were gone. Then it all faded out.

He could see the stars flaming all around him. It reminded him of the fire in the cabin where he and Karina liked to lie down together letting the warmth lead them into each other's arms. He remembered that warmth, that fire, her, him, together. He felt a loneliness born of that togetherness, but even alone, now, he still felt that together. *Karina.* Her name often filled his thoughts, sometimes to the exclusion of all else. He remembered the first time he had ever seen her. Sam had ushered her into the Chamberlains' home, and he, just seven and a half years old, had been waiting at the door with Hattie as she came in. Farson was not happy at the intrusion. His world had been his world, and now he knew that would change. Farson saw all change as a threat in those days. His world was a "construct," too. His parents gone, he had been abandoned to an uncertain fate from the beginning.

For the first seven years of his life, taken away from a world he had never known, Farson had built a new world all his own. The deep insecurity of his beginnings gave way to the dependability of Hattie and Sam and the distant but always generous Chamberlains. Every day, every hour, every minute of his life reassured him by its consistency; things he could count on, things he could believe in; people he could trust. It was heaven on Earth for young Farson Uiost. When he heard that the Chamberlains had adopted a six-year-old girl, it all collapsed. *A girl.* Girls were the strangest of all creatures to Farson. He had seen them in school, but paid no attention. Any overtures in his direction were ignored and avoided. At home, The Ship and his telescope, Hattie's cooking and affection, Sam's steadiness … those things were his life.

Then there she was. She was wearing a frilly pink dress and shiny black shoes. Her hair was wavy wild and very blonde. Sam called her Karina. She was sad and obviously had been crying. She was beautiful to Farson. He found his new feelings were conflicting and disorienting. He had run away at first sight. Her name and her face still filling his mind. *So many years ago and nothing has changed.*

The tunnel grew in size as Voul traveled along with it, and then it disappeared.

Someone said, "transport complete and verified." There were three of them now approaching. Voul recognized Belnad Goethe, Ian Jordan, and Brittany Peterson. They came over and stood in front of him.

"Good to see you again, Voul." Belnad was smiling. Brittany came over and hugged him. Then Voul noticed that only Uva was behind him.

"Where's Farson?" Uva was looking around for him.

"He was right behind us," she said looking back, but there was no one there.

As Brittany hugged him, Voul was remembering their last encounter and all that she had shown him. He hugged her back warmly.

Where's Farson?" Voul repeated.

"Only the two of you were transferred in." Ian said. Uva and Voul exchanged looks.

She spoke first. "He was aboard, I assure you." As she said this, she offered the traditional Aristealian greeting. Everyone was looking at her beautiful wings as she refolded them and smiled and said, "Where is he?" Looking at Belnad and thinking of the tunnel they had come through, she added, "And by the way, I always knew it was you and the Emers." Belnad spoke again before anyone else could comment.

"Uva, you're right, of course. 'It' was us in some ways, but in other ways it was and is much more than *just* us. For example, Farson is not here and as of now, we cannot account for his whereabouts. It is an unknown."

Ian walked over and spoke quietly to Belnad, who then looked back at Voul and Uva. He had new information.

"Apparently, Karina is also missing."

85. Where Are We?

Farson could hear Belnad, but his attention was focused elsewhere. Karina had appeared and was running into his arms. She buried her face in his shoulders. Then she was kissing him.

<<*Don't ever do that again.*>> Farson knew this was not a request. He scanned her mind and filled it with his love. Their separation had been painful for them both.

<<*It must have been for you like it was for me when you went to Lemon Lake.*>> She pushed him away to arm's length and looked at him, his face, his eyes, the turning corners of his mouth. She saw that smile forming. She laughed out loud. Her words were spoken softly, quietly, only for him to hear.

"You've got to be kidding, Farson. You can't be serious." He was laughing. She was still holding his shoulders. He drew her back into his arms. Their bodies intertwined like Sargasso's seas, nurturing, moving, and connecting their planets, communicating everything they needed to know. Then he kissed her; a kiss never shared with another, a kiss of love and devotion, a long kiss. Humanity's most famous brother and sister in an embrace so private, so meaningful, so wonderfully personal that time was suspended in an intimacy for the ages.

Hours later she asked, "Where are we?" He pulled her closer.

"Don't you know? You must know." Then he whispered, "We're in the one place we've always wanted to be."

Farson and Karina were together again.

86. The Veins of the Gods

They called the center of Sargasso's star "Ichor," which classic mythology defined as the ethereal fluid flowing in the veins of the gods. As Voul began to learn about the Emers' achievement, he realized how perfect the name was.

As they walked around touring Ichor, Uva was thinking of the last time she and Farson had been alone on the bridge of *Songbird*, about six days out. She and Farson were falling behind the group.

She had been waiting for a moment like this.

"Farson?"

"Yes, Uva?"

"Can I talk to you seriously for a moment?" Farson well remembered their long conversations on her amazing ship, plus he certainly remembered her "stories." He turned to face her.

"Of course," he said. As she turned toward him, Farson could hear her wings rustling, and his mind began to fill with the thrill of flying. Suddenly, he was soaring again in the skies of Aristealia. He shook his head and looked at Uva. "Don't you ever think of anything else, Uva? Good heavens. Whenever we are together it seems to be the only thing on your mind."

"Well, what do you expect, Farson? If you had to carry these two things around, what would *you* be thinking about?" Farson nodded. He understood what she meant all too well. "Do *you* ever think about it?" This was a difficult topic. It involved a lot of things: sadness, death, loss, love, loyalty, faithfulness. Uva interrupted his thought, knowing exactly where it was going, and she knew, from his thoughts that he had already answered her question. "About my stories, Farson.

I wanted you to know why." He nodded in an acknowledgement of the effectiveness of her storytelling.

"I do know, Uva." He was looking straight at her and then repeated himself. "Believe me, I do know." His feelings were deep and contradictory: cherished and regretted; enjoyed and forbidden; fulfilling and exhausting; they were like a dilemma except the choices were equally alluring and irresistible.

He was lost in thought about his time with her on *Rachis*. Uva pressed on.

"Well, I want to talk about it a little bit more. Do you remember when I said that I wanted you to miss Karina the way I miss Uvo?"

"As I recall, you didn't say it that way, Uva. You said, 'Imagine she is gone.'" Uva was listening intently. Her head was at an odd angle, and it reminded him of Uvo during some of their conversations when Farson was making a point and Uvo was going to have to decide one way or the other. As her husband had done then, now Uva was doing the same thing, and Farson knew exactly what she would say next. He tried to stop her. "There's no need, Uva. Remember I was on the *Rachis* with you. I know what you know. I felt what you felt. But even more importantly, I felt Uvo feeling what you felt, feeling what he was feeling. I was right in the middle of all of that." She seemed to still want to say something, but he went on. "It was the greatest gift I have ever been given. I wish I could think of a way to repay you, Uva, but I can't. What you shared with me made us a pair in some strange sort of way, and I have embraced it. It's as though Uvo has given me a gift through you. I don't know how to adequately explain it, but I know you know, Uva. Aristealia is a planet like no other. And your people are like no other. The beauty of your world and your memories are transcendent in every way." He was looking at her. She could feel the affection. "How can I ever thank you?"

"You know I meant to hurt you?"

"I wouldn't put it that way." She bowed her head in gratitude.

"I wanted to say I am sorry, Farson. I was wrong. I never want you to feel that."

"I know, Uva. There's no need to say it." They sat together for a while. Farson had a brief vision of them soaring through the gorgeous pastel skies of Aristealia. He looked at Uva. She was staring straight ahead, eyes closed.

The others in the tour had slowed down, patiently waiting for Uva and Farson to catch up again. Voul was watching as they approached. She was smiling. He thought he could see a deep blue sky and wings soaring around him for a split-second. Then he had a sense of free falling. She came up beside him, and they continued touring the most amazing structure either of them had ever seen.

Ichor was actually a command center in the middle of Sargasso's artificial star. It was once a free star, but the Emers had captured it, harnessed it, and now they completely controlled it. They altered it, divided it, and developed attachments for a multitude of power manipulations and redirections. The star itself had a diameter of over one hundred thousand miles, and its tempered radiance filled Sargasso from edge to edge, giving them complete control of the climatology of Sargasso. They have developed derivative capabilities of the sun's emissions through the construction of foundational pathways that lead away from the star to orbiting turret assemblies. With these devices, channeling the seas became routine. It took a long time, but the three currents were ultimately positioned perfectly, pooling around each planet's docking areas and proceeding on, in a nearly perfect circle, around and around Sargasso. In the case of the third, more focused, current, they had programmed it to pass directly through the center of each planet, with transport hub stations positioned strategically beneath the surface along its path, with two large stations on the surface where it entered and exited each of the planets. Controlling the flow rates through these "veins," as they called them, was Ichor's main function, but there were others.

The tour of Ichor continued.

It was also the control center, or "bridge" of Sargasso. During the tour, Voul had noticed that the Emers routinely used the name Sargasso in describing the larger structure. It did not surprise him.

Knowing what Farson had told him about the Emers, he knew that time, for them, was everything. It was their tool, their ally; it was their goal, and their reward. Voul realized that they must have christened Sargasso with that name long before Antonoff had started calling it that when he thought it was just a big planet, before they realized Sargasso was a structure built for a purpose. When the Emers showed them the engine room, it was very clear that Sargasso was an immensely complex and powerful tool in their hands.

Then the Emers told them that they were preparing to get Sargasso "underway."

In their shock at this revelation, Uva and Voul had the exact same thought in their minds. "Where's Farson?"

The Emers seem unconcerned with his whereabouts and were very busy with testing their systems, centering the power grid, surveying the surrounding space to great distances, being sure all components were secure and ready. The inspections teams were reporting back from all areas of Sargasso with reports on planets, moons, and the long-planned upcoming operations.

Voul and Uva were on Ichor's bridge when the report came in. "The Essor fleet has slowed down. Estimate time to sensor range is four weeks, arrival in six." Then another report came in.

"SkyKing and Moon are moving into position." Then another.

"Emerald Earth is ready and waiting." Then another.

John Silver was screaming into his communication device. "Where the fuck is everybody? What's the holdup? You rushed us out here for what ... to wait around with our cocks hanging out?"

87. Here's Hoping

He was sitting in his office. The ancient desk seemed small in the large oval room. They had tried to maintain a continuity to the distant past, but it had been impossible. His office was now in the heart of Emerald City. There was no Washington D.C., no Pennsylvania Avenue, no Potomac River, no Arlington Cemetery, no Capitol Building. Those were all just words in the history books of ancient times. Like Rome, and Sparta, and Mesopotamia, the United States of America and Earth were now footnotes in scholarly tomes stacked and stored, and mostly forgotten, in libraries and archives that few ever referenced. Emerald City was like nothing in history. It had no predictive antecedents. It had no rivals in its power. From his office, Andrew Sortt could see everything. Direct access to all 6.8 million Emers, direct access to Ichor and Sargasso, the Moon, and SkyKing; he could move easily to anywhere, including on the transport channel to all of Sargasso's planets and moons and satellites. He could see the Essor fleet approaching. He could see SkyKing and the Moon moving to their assigned coordinates. The ponderous rotation of Sargasso was underway. It was all going exactly as planned. He was surrounded by a wavering field of images radiating in all directions. He moved his hand, and a perfect image of Emerald Earth appeared, beautifully and elegantly floating near the seemingly straight wall of

Sargasso, which vanished in all directions into the mystifying perspective of its enormous size. Sortt backed off on the magnification until the entire sphere of Sargasso was visible. He plotted the Essor flight's location. *Still at least four weeks away.* He knew that the fleet had slowed down and was still decelerating. *They must suspect something.* Sortt knew of the Essors from the Tower's research documents. He knew they were a cautious people, but he also knew that Twill could be brash. Sortt felt the urge to speak with Farson. He put the call through. Farson's face appeared, along with Karina. They looked happy.

"Together again, I see." Andrew Sortt genuinely loved them. He had seen them both through all the years. Karina looked beautiful and young. Farson seemed to never change. Their faces appeared on Sortt's giant monitors. The transmission was clear and steady. Farson knew that while the Emers had complete control and that they used their power with confidence and ingenuity, his family was beyond their control. "How are the girls?" Just as he said it, Felicity and Valgary came into the picture. They waved at him.

"Hi, Uncle Andy," they said as though in one voice, and then a powerful image appeared in his mind. It was a giant dish of ice cream with blueberry syrup and two cherries on top. They saw his recognition of the image and ran laughing from view. *What power they must have to do that so easily.* He knew that penetrating Sargasso's fields and Emerald Earth's security systems with such ease was indicative of the twins' mental powers and of an innate understanding of The Screen itself. *They made a child's joke.* Karina was next to speak.

"As you can see, Andy, they are well. Eleven going on thirty. Well, not really. They are still just girls, but sometimes I wonder at the things they can do." Sortt knew that the girls had been born on Emerald Earth and all that that entailed. He also knew that, like Farson and Karina, they were immune to the changes that Brittany had gone through. The scanners had no effect, and in all of the instrumentation and verification protocols that Sortt and the Emers controlled, Farson and his family were invisible. The Emers had tried everything with no effect. *They come and go within a reality that we cannot affect.* Sortt changed the topic.

"Farson, what do you think of the Essor fleet's apparent cautiousness?" He answered without hesitation.

"Twill will be Twill. You can count on it." The communication ended after a few more exchanges. Andrew Sortt invited Farson and Karina and the girls to visit him. The promise of Armagnac and conversation was well received by Farson. The twins were assured that their hearts' desire, ice cream, would be waiting for them. Karina was thinking of seeing Brittany again. They were all excited at the prospect. An image of a giant cherry rotating on the matrix of floating monitors surrounding Sortt made him smile. Karina, however, bringing reality back to the moment, was now shaking her head.

"Andy, we are where we need to be right now. Sargasso's going to be tested. It's an all hands on deck situation, as you know." He did know. Six-thousand five-hundred-plus years in the making with many elements only now moving into place, the time for decision and commitment was at hand. He nodded.

"Well, okay then. We'll all be together soon enough anyway. Hopefully." Farson was looking at Sortt. They both knew that what was coming would take more than wishful thinking and hopeful words. It would take everything and everyone. Big events were coming, and the two old friends were, again, ready for anything.

88. The Elevation Protocol (5)

Karina wiped the tears from her eyes, stood up from the table, took one long last look into her brother's empathic eyes, and then turned toward the staircase. Farson watched as she took the first step, and then the next, until she was gone from his view. He sat back down at the table to wait.

Each step up the long stairway was a step she did not want to take. She knew the rules, Farson had told her many times. It didn't make it any easier. She remembered flying up and down these stairs, running without hesitation or doubt. The familiar stairway of adventure now seemed like a grim gallows she was ascending. She could see the last step at the top coming. She stood in the attic. There was the window where, as children, they had watched the universe. There was the desk where Farson had worked. There was the couch. There was the old rocking chair. Someone was in it. It was rocking slowly, methodically, back and forth. Approaching from behind, she could see the gray hair, then the wrinkled hands resting on the arms of the chair. She could see the fingers drumming with a steady, but somehow impatient, rhythm. She recognized her own hands, the way they moved. She could even feel them. A voice was speaking to her.

"You have finally come." The voice was frail but clear.

"The time is right." The same voice, only much younger.

"Ask your questions." Karina remained behind the chair, unable to face the older her. Not moving, barely breathing, standing still, she began. Her questions, of course, were as expected.

"How old are you?"

"Ninety-six in old Earth years."

"Will you die today?"

"You know I will."

"Are you unhappy?"

"No."

"Are you in any pain?"

"Not physically." That answer was equivocal. It needed explanation.

"Mentally then?"

"You know the answer to that."

"Where is Farson?" The person in the chair stirred to turn to look at her. Karina moved away to the other side, still avoiding that moment. *Not yet.* "Is he dead?" There was a long silence. She had returned to sitting normally in the chair, and the rocking had resumed. Karina knew what she had to do.

Moving to the front, she looked down at the woman. Her eyes were averted, no eye contact. Karina was feeling an urgency now. *Look at me.* Her will had no effect. The woman spoke, still looking down at her lap.

"Death is not something to ask about. Life is all that matters. Ask me something else."

"Do you still love him?"

"With all my heart."

"Do you miss him?"

"Not as long as we live."

"We? Do you mean Farson and you? Or do you mean you and me?" Karina was staring at her, willing her to look up. Now desperately seeking eye contact. Then, she did look up and directly into Karina's eyes. There was a bright flash, a whiteness that overwhelmed, an occlusion of life forces forcing them upward. Karina saw everything as a great circle, birth-life-death-birth-life-death-birth-life-death, over and over, until the natural order was unclear, unneeded, unwanted. She could sense it all, so richly, so wonderfully, so thoroughly. A great feeling of relief swept over her, through her. She was reliving it at super speeds, then in slow motion, then backwards and forwards, sideways. She was crying. She was laughing. She was lost in passion. She was safe inside a deep patience. She was learning. She was forgetting. She was dying. She was alive again. She was still. Like a candle slowly burning out with the world melting around her, her head slumped, her arms slipped off the rests, her feet relaxed in surrender. She slumped in acceptance. She died with their eyes locked together. And then there was a quiet that washed over the room, their attic, their Ship, their love, over everything. She blinked and the room was empty, the bright light gone now in the fading sun of a late afternoon. The room was empty. No chair, no other her, no couch, no desk, just boxes and memories stacked in attic storage. The third floor of an old house. Karina felt lost in a world of memories, and yet it all seemed so real. She put her hand on a box, lightly covered in the dust of decades. She looked at her fingers, feeling the dust and the wonder of what just happened.

Farson had come up the stairs and was now beside her. He took her hand. They walked back to the table down in the kitchen. He made some coffee, and they sat quietly for a while. Finally, she reached across the table and took his hand. It was warm in hers. Standing up, she said, "Let's go, Farson. There is so much to do."

Two coffee cups, half filled, were still cooling on the table. She thought, *Perhaps they will be there for years.* The breeze through the windows ruffled the curtains gracefully as the door to the outside clicked closed behind them. Their steps could be heard softly going down the porch stairs, down the front walk to the street.

They turned and looked back once. The house seemed the same as ever, but they knew that was no longer true.

Chapter Seven

The End of Time

89. Handy on *Songbird*

To him, it was a wonder, that little ship. He moved around inside, looking things over. How he had come to be onboard was another story.

After arriving at Emerald City with the help of the skillfully escorting grass dolphins, and after his discussions with Belnad Goethe, Ian Jordan, and Brittany Peterson – with assurances from them that all was ready – he was ushered into a dining room for a meal that he felt was long overdue. "Gets mighty hungry out on the grass," he said to no one, for other than Handy, there was no one at the table or in the room. He was alone.

He walked over to the ChainFoods diverter and was greeted by a pleasant-sounding female voice. "With what would you like to start your dinner?" Handy thought this was too good to be true. *Been a long time since I heard anything like that.* Handy's answer was easy and rolled off his tongue.

"Scotch. Glenmorangie. The oldest one you have."

"Would you like that in a glass or a bottle?" Handy laughed. *She doesn't know me.*

"Bottle with an empty glass, except for three ice cubes."

"As you wish." There was a soft tone, and a light blinked in front of the little door in the middle of the table. Handy waved his hand to key the holographic prompt and exactly what he ordered appeared. One of the ice cubes clinked in adjustment.

Handy picked up the bottle and removed the seal, noting happily that it was corked. He reached to his gun belt and removed his laser from one of the cartridge loops. He adjusted it to traction and withdrew the cork effortlessly. He poured a few fingers over the ice and took a long slow drink, emptying the glass, of course.

"Now I want the best steak you have, barbecued and served medium rare. With steak fries, and fresh corn. Some powder biscuits and butter, too."

"As you wish." Handy noticed that the voice almost sang the three words again. They sounded more like a chime than a sentence. The light blinked again, Handy waved his hand and pulled the flat serving tray over so that it was in front of him. He opened the napkin, tucked it into the top of his shirt, and then lifted the fork and steak knife. For the next half hour, Handy enjoyed his meal and drank half of the bottle of scotch. When he was done, he reached back over his head, clasped his hands and stretched, at which point he farted. Then he belched with great satisfaction.

"Do you know anything about cigars?"

"I know everything about cigars."

"If I give you some parameters, will that help?"

"Judging by what I know about you, Mr. Townsend, I would say a forty-nine ring, seven-inch Churchill to start, with a maduro wrapper, long filler, and an excellent binder. How am I doing?"

"So far, so good."

"We will model it after the Oliva company's top inventory in the late 2020s." The light blinked again. Three cigars appeared with an ashtray, a clipper, a box of cedar matches, and another glass with three fresh ice cubes, but this time filled with scotch." *She's learning.*

Handy saw his guitar in the corner.

"One more thing," he said. "Could you ask Brittany Peterson to join me for a few moments?" The three-word chime acknowledgment sounded again, but no blinking light or waving of his hand was required this time.

Handy was playing his guitar and singing Farson's poem again. He loved the chorus.

> I wish I could free you, but I know too much.
> There is only one way out and it's through.
> Takes your doing, not some lover's touch.
> If you make it, I'll be waiting for you.

Both glasses were empty now, and the scotch in the bottle was very, very low. Handy was getting tired. It must have been over an hour since his last request. He leaned the guitar against the edge of the table and was mechanically reaching for the bottle again when he heard the door behind him open.

He noticed that she spoke in a voice with vocal characteristics very similar to the diverter's, or so it seemed to him.

"Hi, Handy." Brittany stood there in all of her six-foot, ten and a half inch glory. Her high boot-like shoes made her even taller. Her light bronze skin seemed to shine on him. She was dressed in the Emer standard, but somehow she looked just a little bit prettier than the others. She was thin, auburn brunette, and obviously very healthy. *A whole new breed of human.* She was looking at him looking at her.

"You know I can tell what you are thinking, right, Handy?" He had not forgotten; it just wasn't at the top of his mind at the moment.

"I got nothin' to hide, Brit." She laughed.

"We both know that's not true." She moved over next to him, and pulled out a chair, and sat down. He could sense her. The air between them now had a scent that reminded him of the wheat when it flowers, or when the grass dolphins move around him in the night. He could not hear her breathing; there was a silence around her, a deep peacefulness, an undisturbed ambience of gentle contented awareness. Again he was reminded of the grass dolphins and how naturally they moved and how certain they were of things, how their company made him happy. He spoke to her again.

"You are happy here, I can tell."

"Yes."

"How does your father feel about it?"

"He has accepted it, I believe. He really likes Ian. But I miss Dad terribly. I feel as though I have abandoned him. Left him all alone." They let some time pass in silence. Then Handy took a deep breath and sighed.

"You know, you and I are alike in some ways, Brittany." He liked to say her name. "Anyone looking at the two of us: me, a drunken, messed-up, washed-up-make-believe cowboy reaching for an empty bottle like a loser, and you, a beautiful young Emer woman, pristine and proper, dressed perfectly and with an unmistakable and immaculate posture of grace and obvious high intelligence, would doubt the similarities. A total mismatch, you and I, they would think. *The beauty and the beast.* "But, they would be wrong, wouldn't they?" He could tell that she understood.

Handy took the last drink of scotch, after first offering it to her. She declined. "I, too, left my planet behind and everything I had ever known. I went forth companionless and with no predictable future of any worth. I was a first, as you may know, just as you are." She was looking at Handy with respect and awe. A living myth right in front of her. *But, not a myth now.* Now, he was sitting next to her. He was a real person speaking to her. Despite appearances, Brittany realized that Handy was very pleasant company. Interesting and intimate in his conversation. She liked the smell of his cigar. He was still speaking. "But you, Brittany, are different from me. You have a future. You have a life. You have someone who understands. You are very young, and everything is going your way. True?"

"True." He could tell there was the one exception in her thought, one hesitation in her complete happiness. Her dad's absence. Their separation. Time drifted by as Handy smoked his cigar and took another drink, just water and ice now. The diverter, sensing a need, chimed. He held up his hand, signaling that he had had enough.

"Why do you think I am here?" Handy stood up for a moment and took off his guns and laid them on the table. The sound of the leather holster, the brass cartridges in the belt's loading strip, and the large silver buckle landing on the dark shiny wood created the image of a soldier dropping his gear after a long day at war. Brittany was watching as he tossed his cowboy hat onto the table as well. It was dirty and stained with sweat. With its removal, Brittany noted a handsome shock of dark blonde hair had burst free. Some strands fell across his forehead. He brushed them away.

"I would assume you are here because Farson told you to come here." Handy nodded his head. *No surprises with her.*

"I think, Brittany, that he wanted me to come here to tell you and the Emers something." Brittany showed no signs of speaking. Handy went on. "I think he wanted me to tell you that some things don't come easily in these sorts of transitions." Nothing from Brittany. She was watching and listening. "He has made it through a few of his own, you know. He is worried that the Emers are struggling with the ultimate outcome. He wanted you to know that just pushing through such times can create a hidden doubt and this doubt will bring you to a difficult inflection point where decisions must be made. You will feel alone." Brittany realized suddenly that Handy was no longer speaking to just her. He was speaking *through her.* He was speaking to the entire population of Emerald Earth, using her as the conduit. She was surprised at his acumen even as she understood his intention. It was clear to her that she had underestimated Handy's true nature. His mask of insouciance and irresponsibility had distracted her from his true skill and virtuosity as a ScreenMaster, old school. She had been warned, and yet, still, she was easily outmaneuvered. She could sense that all of Emerald Earth was now in full and attentive attendance to this conversation. She could also feel Handy's true affection and caring. She knew his misdirection and manipulations were a compliment to her. Emerald Earth was applauding her participation, her adaptability. She also knew that Handy was aware of her recognition now about what was happening. He smiled. "Farson told me that you, Brittany Peterson, would be the best person to speak with about this. He felt that you would know, from your own current experiences, that even in the throes of wonder, there can still be doubt. I have seen Farson endure what he considered total defeat. I have seen his failure in his heart and mind. I have watched him climb back up on the horse, and try again and again and again. I have watched his torture, and I have felt his pain." Handy's voice shifted tone slightly. "Many of you may have studied why he and I are such friends. Just as Brittany and I may seem a mismatch, so do Farson and I, as do all of the Emers and I; unless you know the truth."

Handy began a description of events that would be long discussed in Emer research. Clearly, the whole world was listening intently.

"When I came to Earth, I was broken and destroyed. My own precious world had been crushed, and, I, its sole survivor, had fared little better. But Earth saved me with its crazy innocence and its ferocious curiosity and its absolute faith in an uncertain future. I came here at a time in your far, far distant past to hide and recover. Over all those years I have seen humanity's struggles and now your approaching triumph. Farson says I am the sole witness to the full story. I know what humanity is, and I know what it can become. It is in that context that Farson and I became such good friends. It was in that friendship where I have again seen your race's tendency to repeat history over and over until it is finally altered, redirected, and redefined. All of your doubts, your loss of self, the twists and turns of human nature that have hindered and propelled you, I have seen again and again in Farson's ascendancy and life as a ScreenMaster, and in your own long, winding, conflicted history.

"He calls the moment we are now in, a 'balanceless point,' where things can and will go one way or the other. One way is the emptiness of the past, and more repetitions. The other way is whatever destiny awaits you all in the future. He wants me to tell you that it is up to you. No one can do it for you. He says there is only one way and that you will know it and what to do."

Handy could feel the reverberations of his soliloquy coursing through the Emers. There was a profound silence. He had struck a chord that's resonance was beyond the human ear, beyond hearing of any kind. It was the call of destiny spoken by one who knew. The Emers were mentally bowing to the moment – a sacred moment for them. It was a moment that had come with no warning, but it was a moment long predicted: a moment of reassurance; a moment of truth.

Handy had one more thing to say. His voice was now as crystal clear as an Emerald Earth sunrise. "Farson told me to tell you that, if you make it, he will be waiting for you."

Handy looked over at Brittany. She had been born on SkyKing. She had followed the Sker ways. She had passionately loved Voul Bensn as a little girl growing up. She was the first to enter Emerald Earth from the outside. She was the first Emer not born on Emerald Earth. Her head was bowed with respect, but not, Handy sensed, from the import of his comments, but in humility of being his chosen channel to the world of the Emers. She knew that her place in Emer history was now secure forever. She was stunned at his confidence in her. She looked up. Tears were sparkling in her clear blue eyes. Handy could sense a shaking in her assurance. He reached out and put his arm around her. Maybe it was her father's absence. Maybe it was the weight of the moment after all. Maybe the little girl who was always loved by everyone all of her life found, in this moment, a new definition of belonging. Whatever it was that caused it, Brittany took Handy's arm and pulled him closer in a long hug and cried on his shoulder. Not racking tears, but tears of love of joy and tears of a new hope. The Emers felt it all as intimately as if they were there with Handy, leaning on his shoulder, their tears wetting her cheeks. Handy's heart was full to breaking as they all entered his consciousness, through hers, and a force of knowledge and understanding swept them all together in a moment like no other in their long history. Handy was thinking of Farson's poem, its power, its meaning, now lying wrinkled and worn in the bottom of his dusty knapsack, the last stanza again singing itself over and over in his mind.

Over the next few days, the Emers and Handy began to make their plans together, one of which was to lend *Songbird* to Handy to use for whatever he needed to use it for. Some of the other items included briefing Handy on all the details of Sargasso. Even for a ScreenMaster who had seen as much as he had: his own planet's destruction, the forming of a new universal order of ScreenMasters, all of his years on Earth and then Emerald Earth, and so much more, the truth about Sargasso was a real surprise full of mysteries wrapped in hope and in faith for a future that none could completely see or define. He listened and learned as only one who has the understanding and wisdom of true experience can. Some of it was wonderful. Some of it was sad to him. The role the Emers had taken on so selflessly, and all of its implications made

Handy look at them with new eyes. One quiet night when he was alone, he cried for them. He knew now what they were doing. It made him think of his old planet and how things might have been had his race produced people like the Emers. Was he crying for his planet and its eternal sorrow, or for the Emers and their immense sacrifice? Handy was not a person to overthink everything, but he knew that it made no difference, the cause of his emotional response. It was a culmination, a coming together of many factors. That he felt this deep bond and inexorable affection for them was all that mattered. The truth had its own power and its own resolutions. He knew that truth could be understood, but never changed. As Farson often said, "The truth is always true. There's nothing we can do." Handy always enjoyed the perfect rhyme in that statement.

Now he knew his job on Emerald Earth was done. He still had a few last items to attend to, but he could sense the moving-on urge gathering power within him. It had been a long time since he had had that restless feeling. For so long he had been carrying out Farson's plan. Now, Farson was lending him his wonderful ship and setting him free. *I bet he's glad to be rid of me.* With that thought, Farson entered his mind. <<*Whoa there, Handy. You and* Songbird *are on another assignment. It's temporary. You're not 'going away.' I think you'll enjoy the new venture. You deserve it. Go forth and explore. Stay in touch.*>> Handy was relieved to hear from his old friend, but when he tried to respond, the connection was gone. Three words hung in the air, and caused him to tear up again: "You deserve it." *I must be getting old. Emotions are pouring out.*

When he asked them how he could get Farson's ship when it was still inside of Sargasso and he was on Emerald Earth, they said no problem. Don't worry. You'll be joining the ship inside. He felt their confidence and control; it was the same high confidence he had sensed in Farson's thought, and it made him believe that everything was going along as planned, but it also made him wonder, *what are they not telling me?*

They had told him to just let them know when he was ready, and he almost was, but there was one last item on his pre-trip preparation list: saying goodbye to the grass dolphins. He knew that was not going to be an easy thing to do.

They were waiting for him.

He had returned to the docking station, where he had entered Emerald City, and simply walked back down the access stairs and then out into the grass.

His special grass shoes performed their jobs perfectly, even better with the Emers' improvements. He looked down at them. A slight tinge of purple surrounded them, and they were steadier and drier than ever. His grass shoes used to feel heavy on his feet, but now they were invigorating and light as a feather. It was as if they were floating. He felt like he could walk with them forever.

Suddenly, the dolphins were underfoot everywhere. He could feel himself being lifted slightly and then moving away from the station. He could also feel his deep affection for them and his relief at being with them again. Handy loved the dolphins.

handy we want to show you something we missed you

Living a long, long time can sometimes make one think one knows everything and has seen everything. Sometimes the old become cynical and withdrawn as though exhausted and disgusted. They may give up on life, but have not died yet. Handy had seen it happen. A sad ending.

Handy's own life had had enough sadness and disappointment to earn well that very sad disjunctive finality. It could have happened to him easily enough. He could have just stayed anonymous. In fact, when he had first met Farson, Handy already knew he was sliding down that slippery slope. Drinking, smoking, carousing, indolence, and sloppiness had seeped in; they were running on their predictable and degenerative course with power and enthusiasm, and he knew it. Farson changed all of that. *For everyone.*

Handy had quickly learned in Farson's presence that knowing there is always much more to know is the secret to learning, the secret to happiness. Farson had taught him the reversible lesson that when you think you've got it all, you lose it all; and just when you think you've lost it all, you gain it all back. That palindrome-like tautology was the best explanation of The Screen Handy had ever heard. Change infuses all of life like a mainline injection of imagination and invention. In all the things that Farson had taught him, there was one that he considered the greatest of all. That was what Farson called the greatest skill, and what Handy knew was the greatest gift of all: patience. Farson had called it *his own* greatest gift as well. Farson knew that patience takes faith, and it takes knowledge. Patience had given Handy new hope and purpose.

So, knowing all that he did know, and having seen all that he had seen, he had come to "say goodbye" to his friends, the amazing grass dolphins of Emerald Earth.

That intended conversation was about to take a turn into something so new and unexpected that Handy would soon feel the swirling vertigo of the unforeseen looming up and taking him, like a giant wave, to an overpowering moment he was not expecting. Handy was in for a surprise.

The grass dolphins formed a tube around him and dove down through the grass. Handy had the feeling of speeding up as they passed through the dense subsurface and entered the less viscous and more fluid area deeper down. Down and down they went. Handy's ears popped. He was in an air pocket within the dolphins, perfectly comfortable, breathing easily. The air was fresh and rich. *How are they doing this?* He looked around. He could not believe what he was seeing. Beyond the wall of dolphins he could see clearly for what looked like miles all around. The material was crystal clear and had a consistency of light olive oil and an aroma like seaweed in the surf. It was clear as a bell. It was like flying. He thought they were heading for a structure of some sort, and then he realized they were coming up on many structures. *A city?* Even as he thought it, the huge pod of dolphins, holding him within it, accelerated, heading straight for the nearest one.

did you think we had no home handy

"I did wonder," he said, his voice echoing in the bubble.

It took him awhile to grasp that the oxygen-rich fluid was breathable, and it took longer to get used to it.

relax handy it is really nice

In due course it became second nature. He found it cleansing like an Emer scan; his body adapted, he was enjoying every minute. They gave him what they called "a uniform" and then they told him their next surprise.

we are going with you

When Handy was returned to the surface, he was still wearing their "uniform." It was exceptionally comfortable and seemed to need no care at all, drying off by itself in seconds, always looking and feeling fresh and clean.

As he walked up the access stairway, Brittany was waiting for him. She looked him over. *He's lost weight or something.* His hair was shorter and fell attractively over his forehead. He was walking with determination and purpose instead of the old wandering soul that Handy Townsend was famous for. He walked up to her, and she noticed that he was taller now. He took her hands in his and kissed her cheeks. "Great to see you, Brit. But, it's time for me to go."

"Belnad is waiting." She smiled, still holding his hand. They started off at a brisk walk. She sent a message ahead. <<*We are on our way.*>> She felt Belnad's affirming response and Ian's anticipation. She also felt Handy's awareness of the communication. Handy, as always, preferred speaking whenever possible.

"Do they know what's been happening?"

"Of course. We all do. It's pretty exciting, really." She looked over at him. He was skeptical, doubting that anyone could completely know what had happened under the amber waves of Emerald Earth. She laughed. "The Emers have been here for 6,525 years, Handy. They know it all." He still looked at her with a dubious expression. To him what the dolphins were doing was unbelievable, but he should have known. Brittany sped up her pace a little, now leading him. "The dolphins have come out of the closet, to use an old Earth saying. We knew it was just a matter of time. They are like the rest of us, Handy."

"How's that?" he asked. Not quite clear what she meant.

"They don't want to lose you either."

90. The Elevation Protocol (6)

She knew he was looking at her. She wanted to look back, but she was thinking about what had just happened when she had looked into her *own* eyes at the moment of her death. What had she seen there? A great circle had completed itself. She could remember looking into her own baby eyes and all that had happened in that moment of birth. And now those old eyes were there, too. She seemed to flash through the cycle after cycle of baby eyes, old eyes, and over and over like an electron orbiting an atom ever faster, or flash cards that won't stop. The locations she could see in the cycling were "most likely," not actuals, and the circling of her life sped up and up and then slowed down and down.

Behind those young eyes and those old eyes, everything in between was a blur of rich experience, stirring up knowing, swirling up doubts and worries, shaking confidence and building it all up again, over and over, altogether until ... gaining ground, she was struggling to look at him. As things clarified, she could see that he was still looking at her. Little Farson standing outside her door and then the great ScreenMaster, larger than life: she could, at once, see both of them now. Farson the boy and Farson the man; she knew his every thought and all of the reasons behind everything. Her lover, how she loved him: She could relive their first kiss but now through him. She could feel her own giving and taking. She was kissing him kissing her kissing him. She was loving him loving her. She felt their lives intertwining like lightning crossing the skies, or warm rain falling onto the summer grass. Her view expanded to the whole universe and beyond even that, and then it telescoped back to just his young lips waiting that day ... waiting to taste hers. Then deeper into a blending where they were not two but one. It was a sensation like being inside him and then being him inside her. She knew he was experiencing it as well. Time suspended. Reality altered. They were in their future, in their past, in their present. In a fulminant lucidity, she saw something new, something unbelievable. All that had happened in both their lives, within their combined and separate circles, had become clear, like grains of sand magnified to boulders, and a surprising new expanse of infinity now lay clearly before her. Beauty beyond beauty. Joy beyond joy. Love in its purity, a pathway to something so wonderful that she was enraptured with just the possibility of discovery, excited with mystery, fulfilled with anticipation. So was he.

<<*Farson, what is happening?*>>
<<*Something that just is.*>>

She knew there was nothing else to say. No explanation adequate. But he, too. was rapt with beginnings and endings.

For the first time, he felt a new completeness with her; it was like the rush of an addictive drug, irresistible in its overwhelming power and triumphant sensation. He was startled with their union's thrall, with the sheer pleasure of the moment for them. To be so much closer, when he had thought their closeness was perfect in all of its textures and intensities: to be so much more in love when he thought his heart was already bursting; to see her in such a new, revealing light and across seamless dimensions nearing infinity; to be her. It was an ecstasy beyond extraordinary, beyond anticipation; it was a flawless vision of beauty and of love's exquisite intercourse. They were now intertwined like spiraling vines, together reaching toward the sky, through all time, through lives only now truly just beginning. He was quivering in anticipation. She was ready for anything. They were together, rising.

91. The Fleet Approaches

Panau had been studying the data which was streaming through several of her floating monitors. She was walking back and forth from one to the other.

Twill had come into the command area twice over the past six weeks to check on things, but he had said nothing, and then returned to his quarters, which, on both occasions, had caused a silent, deafening collective sigh of relief across the bridge.

Panau was clearly in charge now. Twill was a prisoner of circumstances, like everyone else, and she was the commander in control.

As everyone knew, though, circumstances could change swiftly.

Lieutenant Commander Shals t'Bu was working at his station, and watching Panau. From spinning upside down on the bridge deck after Twill's callous backhand, to now being the de facto captain of the greatest Essor warship that had ever sailed, Shals knew that he had witnessed a legend being born. Twill's provoking and ever-angry nature was well known on Essor, and even more so on *Noctura*. Panau's perseverance and calmness in the face of uncertainty had changed everything: for the ship, now tranquil in its mission; for the mission, now being conducted with intelligence and caution; and, last but not least, for Shals, who had discovered, in his deep and abiding admiration of her, something entirely new was happening for him. He had fallen in love.

"Commander t'Bu, could I see you for a moment?" Her use of the respectful phraseology for his lower rank pleased him and accelerated his already enthusiastic response celerity. Quickly, but with appropriate dignity still maintained, he went to her.

"Yes, Commander t'ul'Dak?" She looked at him. She knew he was supportive.

"Call me Panau." He nodded to her. In his thought, he had already been thinking of her by her first name anyway. There was a happiness in his demeanor that he was having difficulty disguising. She noticed. "I have been looking this data over, and I believe we need to consult with Master Twill once again. Would you please ask him to come to the bridge?"

"May I ask what the topic is? Master Twill will want to know." Panau knew full well the reasons for needing all the details before approaching the unpredictable Grand ScreenMaster.

"Certainly. Two things, with a few added details to assist you. First, there appears to be an armed detachment waiting for us on the object, directly ahead on our current course, as if they knew we were coming and from exactly where. Their weapons may cause us trouble. Second, there is a planet and two satellites nearby; one is natural and one is artificial, and they are moving together, with the planet, into a position where they are protected by the weapons." Shals had a question.

"The planet is moving?"

"Absolutely. It also seems to be controlling the two satellites' movements.

"I am detecting harmonic residue of what could only have been a large explosion, or explosions, in the area as well. No debris, so we have to assume vaporization, which affects upwardly our estimation of the weapons' power. We will be in range of the weapons, by my estimate, in less than two days, but I could be wrong. For all we know we are already within range."

Shals nodded respectfully and turned 180 degrees on his heels and strode, with urgency, in the direction of Twill's quarters. Panau watched him leave. *He seems nice.*

Twill was sleeping. It was more like a deep dormancy in the cool space of his sleeping quarters. Essors sleep for long periods and then don't sleep for even longer periods. But when they do sleep, they go deep. Dreaming is their one pleasure, stolen in those hours and days of sopor, preferably days and days, and more days. Twill had been sleeping for almost six days. There is nothing better for an Essor than six or seven days of rest. It is like a vacation. They are away. Far away, in a dreamland none can share.

He heard someone calling. In a deep silent state of sensory deprivation, sounds can seem like spears of light thrust painfully into the cool, embracing dark. The proper way to wake an Essor is over many hours, using all of the accepted techniques: slow rocking, soft shell massage, sometimes gentle tugs on the arms and legs, sometimes warm air blown gently across the face. Inside the balenests of Essor, there were even more erogenous rituals that gained the best and most desirable and enjoyable transitions. What Twill was experiencing was more like a pounding on a door, or a rude dousing. As he emerged, his anger grew with every blink of his eyes. He pushed out his appendages and craned his neck around. There, standing beside him, fearfully and cautiously calling his name using Twill's self-chosen, supremely honorific title, was the lieutenant commander. *The same one as before.* "Grand ScreenMaster Twill …"

"Shut up!" Twill's harsh command had an instant result. The lieutenant commander moved back a few steps, standing silent and still. Twill was up, but not yet awake. He was moving, awkwardly still half asleep, to his desk. He motioned with his hands that Shals should just stand fast as he regained his composure. Essors all understood this situation. Awakenings took time. There was no other way. In due course, he began to recover. He stood up, holding up a hand to keep the lieutenant commander, who clearly wanted to talk with him, at bay. He walked to the large circular window that framed the stern of *Noctura* and stood there looking back at the obedient fleet following him into the unknown. A thousand ships, perhaps three hundred thousand Essors, all in pursuit, all in readiness, all awaiting whatever commands Twill would ultimately issue. To their deaths, if necessary. He had no doubt that they were all prepared. Twill, filled with his own importance, was free of any doubt about his situational omnipotence. No one would question him; they would not dare.

In the vast fleet behind him, many were wary and watching. Twill had his unknown detractors and doubters. His Ascension was magnificent, everyone at the time had agreed. Some thought pompous was a better word, but none doubted that he had achieved supremacy. Essor had only one ScreenMaster, and he was preeminent; the master of their fate, the captain of their race's soul. He turned gracefully, refreshed and primed, to face the lieutenant commander. "Report." The word was spoken so quickly, Shals tensed. At first it had sounded like the Essor word, "tel'lm'he," which, spoken that way, had the meaning of initiating a rapid retreat. He was thinking, for a moment, that Twill had said, "Run!" Collecting himself and correctly sorting out Twill's diction, he began his reply.

"Commander t'ul'Dak has asked me to invite you to the bridge for a consultation."

"Why did she not come herself?"

"She is immersed in the data evaluations and has discovered something which she wants to share with you. The information is on the bridge, and she is still working toward a full conclusion."

"What 'conclusion' is she working toward?" This was said with a suspicious edge, a tone of doubt, concern of guile.

"Master Twill, she has explained to me that our long-range sensors have detected a detachment on the surface of the object, and they appear to be armed with weapons of undetermined power and range. She also wanted me to tell you that there is a planet with two satellites in the area, apparently moving to position themselves under the protection of the weapons."

"The planet is moving?" This was incredulous to Twill.

"Yes, Master Twill. And it seems to be bringing the two satellites, one natural and one not, with it."

"So they know we are coming?"

"Yes, Master Twill, so it would appear. Commander t'ul'Dak is concerned about estimating the range of the weapons. She feels we are still two days out. But she asked me to convey to you that she could be wrong."

"Could we already be within the weapons' range?"

"I believe that is exactly what she wants to discuss with you on the bridge." Twill looked at him in disbelief. First, that the lieutenant commander hadn't mentioned the danger first, and second, that precious seconds were passing with his beautiful starship fortress perhaps exposed. He pushed the lieutenant commander aside and marched through the door

without another word. Shals walked over to Twill's massive
desk and waved his hand over the communications lights.
"Panau?"

"Yes, Shals."

"He is on his way toward you with rapidity."

Panau used her time well. She knew Twill was charging in
her direction, but she also knew that when it came to life-
and-death issues, especially when his own life and death were
included in the equation, Twill could listen. The calculation
technique she was using to evaluate the weapons deployed to
the surface of Sargasso was, she knew at this range, the
proverbial dim candle over the dark abyss. However, she was
able to gauge the strength of the transporter beams holding
the devices in place. The mass and force being used were such
that the conclusion of their immense power could not be
avoided. Range of fire efficacy was another issue. She could
tell that the "weapons" were really thrusters of some sort, and
a quick scan of the moon, the natural satellite in the mix,
revealed them to be a propulsion system capable of moving it.
Assuming that the thrust could also be throttled into a
weaponized discharge, she saw that the range could easily be
at least to where they had been a week ago, but certainly well
within reach of where they were now. With that concrete
conclusion in hand, she issued an order no one was expecting.
"All stop! General quarters! All hands to battle stations!" The
ship and the fleet immediately began an emergency reverse
course heading in a maneuver that would be long
remembered as the t'ul'Dak Dictate, and came to a stop in
space as ordered.

Not only had she taken command of *Noctura*, she was
now commanding the entire fleet.

As Twill negotiated the pathways from his quarters to the
bridge, the abrupt reversal of the ship's direction caused him
to miss a step and bump into the bulkhead, paining his arms,

as strong as they were. His head had come very close to smashing into the wall. Some of the Essors escorting the Grand ScreenMaster were toppled over and spinning. They required assistance to right themselves. There were crashes and bangs in Twill's ears as the ship's equipment shifted and tore from clamps and holding irons. But he never missed a beat. In fact he entered the bridge at a run, or at the pace Essors considered full speed. He was in no mood for small talk. "Report, t'ul'Dak! What is the situation?"

"I have ordered the fleet to a full stop. It is now clear that we are well within the range of the weapons on Sargasso, and we have no idea what they are or what they are capable of."

"Who cares? This fleet is impervious. We fear nothing."

"Master Twill, I estimate that the thrusters are also used to move that moon, which has a mass of approximately $7.34767309 \times 10^{22}$ kilograms. They have ten of the thrusters pointing directly at us. In simulations, we have seen that if the muzzle bore angle is even in a minute degree fluted in a positive manner – and that would certainly suit the purpose of propulsion – then, at our distance, the blast radius would easily engulf our entire fleet with unknown, but certainly violent, effect. We have no choice but to stop and assess before rushing into such a hazardous and unknown battle configuration. I was sure you would agree, so I saw no reason to delay." Twill was again faced with the technician's (as he still preferred to think of her) flawless reasoning. She was inviting him to review the data with her. He came to her side, and the two of them concentrated together on the information. As it began to sink in, Twill again put his claw-like hand on her shell and patted it. She appreciated his open acknowledgement of agreement. The crew members on the bridge were again astounded at Twill's sensible response. He turned with a snarl to the room, and they all went back to work.

Shals t'Bu relaxed but wanted Twill to remove his touch from Panau. Even as he returned to his post, still a little winded from running after Twill, he kept an untrusting and suspicious eye on Master Twill. Panau had one more piece of information to offer Twill. "There has been an explosion in the area, but no debris."

"That's odd," Twill replied.

"Not if vaporization occurred. It would make perfect sense. From our estimates, the power of the weapons is more than sufficient to make quick work of any unwanted ship in the area. It would be a mere 'pop' for those guns." Twill was considering the implications of that statement.

"Any further suggestions?"

"Keep the fleet on high alert. Move *Noctura* forward at one-third speed, along with two other ships. Keep our weapons on standby, and the fleet in reserve. Attempt to appear as non-threatening as possible. We need to investigate this situation. Our original coordinates were developed from the stasis termination sequence and involved the control protocols, as I mentioned at the time. The distances involved, together with the clear inference of the existence of what must be the planet we thought was destroyed, requires us to move forward, regardless of risk. I am sure you want to know what happened." Twill was thinking that he would rather be on one of the other ships right now, somewhere further back, away from the immediate danger. She went on. "If they fire, there is no place to hide. We are fully exposed. I could be wrong, but it appears we have entered into a trap and, as of now, there is no way out. Our only option is to approach with caution, but without the appearance of armed aggression or of being in an attack posture."

"The humans have done all of this?"

"I would say so, Master Twill. Without a doubt."

Twill pushed a crew member out of his seat in the navigation area, almost knocking him over, and sat down heavily, stressing the chair. He was clearly in frustrated resignation to a fate almost worse than death: the loss of control in every way; he was now a victim instead of a victor; now a mere participant instead of a conquering hero. His shell felt heavy, his arms as listless as wet rags, his taloned hands scraped together like the branches of Essor's luscious sky vine trees that rubbed together dryly, bark against bark, as they grew, reaching for the retched sun with no purpose. He sat in the chair fighting anger, feeling a deep, vexing annoyance. He noticed a coming dread that he had not felt since Farson's – a hated name he resented even thinking of – so-called Ascension so many years ago. His triumph then was so sweet, to be so savored, and reimagined so extravagantly, over and over. What a pleasure that had been. He vowed to himself that it would be so again. He could feel the volcano within stirring, the magma of his hate beginning to flow. In some ways it was gratifying, thinking of crushing the great Farson Uiost once more. The reality of the situation escaped Twill, perhaps through self-deception, perhaps through an approach so deeply determined in Twill's own thought that no cooling advice could penetrate or persuade him. Now he clearly saw the path to victory was in deceit, and the technician's plan was playing perfectly into his hand.

He turned to her and said, "Proceed. We will see."

Panau recognized Twill's intent was different from her own. *For now*, she thought, *he is allowing me to proceed.* She turned to Shals and saw that he was watching closely. She subtly turned her shell in the way that Essors assume an en garde posture. Shals noticed it immediately, as did others on the bridge. Twill was oblivious in his ruminations.

"Ahead one third, lieutenant commander t'Bu," she said efficiently. Ask the *Reticulator* and *Trion* to join us and to follow our readiness status and course and speed exactly. Tell them we must appear to be non-threatening. As we approach, we will broadcast the appropriate greetings. Tell them to listen for further instructions." Then she turned to Twill once more. "Master Twill, I have to warn you that I do not expect this maneuver to be successful. My best estimate is that we have less than a day before whatever those devices are designed to do, are activated and we are ..." Twill shot back at her.

"Destroyed? Is that what you think?"

"No sir. I was going to say, 'and we are ... in a position to more accurately assess our options.'" He shook his head, calming himself.

"Let's hope that your 'estimate' proves to be more than a naive euphemism." He was speaking very softly now, just to her. "We have come a long way, you and I. Don't think for a second, though, that I will ever let them get away again." He was growling his words, and his face was so close she could feel his breath on her. It was cold and dry and susurrant.

Twill's snarling disposition's obsession was echoing in his certainty and focused on one thing: reaching the final resolution of this vexing situation. *As soon as possible. This must end. Once and for all. No matter what.*

92. The End of Time

Karina was thinking it over. Her completion of Farson's elevation protocol had been the missing link. Seeing her own death had actually been a pleasure of some kind: perhaps because it was finally over, perhaps because in holding her own hand, she had felt the peace of the "circle" from birth to death, perhaps because now she knew that those terms had far less meaning than she had thought; perhaps because now life meant so much more. There were still unanswered questions: Where was Farson at her death? Why was she dying? What happened when she did die? She also realized some of the truths about time that Farson had tried to teach her, and that now she had experienced herself. Birth to death and everything in between had given her a perspective so few had ever seen, and had flushed her assumptions and pre-convictions like debris to be washed away in a receding tide. She was left with understandings about herself that were now pathways she could walk from the present to the past to glimpse the future, or that she could use to just linger in time as she wished.

She turned to Farson. "The Emers have put an end to time, haven't they? You and me, Valgary and Felicity, Brittany, Handy, and all of them, it's all the same, isn't it? Each of us went through it. Brittany in going to Emerald Earth was transitioned. Handy with the dolphins, they did it to him. The Emers all saw it together, all at once. The girls were born on Emerald Earth. And you fought your way through all those levels to find it. Now you have shown me. It's a new level of existence, of awareness, which I know now is the same thing. Part of me wants to know how you could do something like this to me, and part of me is thanking you for such a gift. In some ways I feel lost; in others I feel found; in every way I feel freer now. I feel so free it's a little confusing. She was looking at herself through Farson's eyes. They were both looking at her together. She saw herself looking back, and that connection occurred again.

She was suddenly getting out of Sam's car in front of the Chamberlains' home. She saw the curtains in the window move to the side. Then she could see the little girl walking up the front walk, holding Sam's hand.

"You were watching me the whole time from inside?"

Farson laughed. "There are no secrets now." He looked at her standing there. She was so beautiful to him, so relevant, so important, so present. She had always been that way. When you lose everything, everything becomes new. Karina had the ability to look at things so many others had seen and to intuitively understand what eluded so many. Her experiences were concepts to her, messages from past truths, harbingers of futures coming. She was the arbiter between. Farson had seen her struggle; he had seen her triumph; he had seen her sorrow; he had seen her joy. Now it was unceasing, their togetherness. It was a melding, a blending, a combining; irreversible, invincible, triumphant. Farson knew that her patience had led them home.

"In some ways, that is correct, Kari. The Emers have put an end to time, *as we knew it.* It still passes. We still bide in our share of it. If you are including a fatefulness, or an immutability, in the Emers' definition, then that would not be correct. Now, you and I have completed the circle. Valgary and Felicity were part of it from birth. The four of us are free as no others have ever been free. The Emers are certainly great, but we still are what we are."

"Are what, Farson?" She moved closer. And closer. Time slowed for them, and they took their time. *All the time in the world.* Their thoughts were one. In due course, Karina had her answer without words. She just knew.

"We are," she said aloud, "all together." Even as she said it, she could feel his confirmation.

93. The Future of Everything

Noctura moved through the dark of space without stealth now, slowly approaching as though scheduled and expected. *Orion*, a somewhat smaller starship, and *Reticulator*, somewhat larger, both trailed behind, matching course and speed exactly. On the bridge, Panau had been carefully monitoring all activity for the past five days of their approach. The size of Sargasso had astounded her, frightened her, and she had slowed the three ships even more. Now, as its wall filled their screens, she slowed again. The three ships were inching closer, more to satisfy Twill's demands, than for any real purpose. Panau already knew all she needed to know. If left to her own devices, she would have turned the fleet around and gone home to Essor, hoping there would be no pursuit. She knew that even Essor's great fleet, the best they could and would ever muster, was totally outclassed. Twill, on the other hand, saw victory within his grasp.

"Speed it up, technician. Let's go." She looked at Twill in the navigator's chair. He seemed to overflow the seat, and to be very uncomfortable in it. She wanted to make him happy. The other path caused her to cringe, but in this case she felt that, for the good of all, she needed to resist Twill's unjustified self-confidence. And, she had been studying the situation intently.

"Master Twill, we must remember that the thruster weapons, all ten of them, are aimed at us, and our research indicates their power is considerably more than is ours to resist them. There is one more thing." She saw his eyes thin to a glare. Even in his weakest moments, Twill's glare was fearsome. He was waiting. "The planet and its satellites have moved to a specific location for some reason. It may be so that they are under the protection of the guns, but it may also be for another reason. Given the size of the object, and the fact that the planet and its satellites have come here in the first place, I am wondering ..."

"Wondering? Is that what you are doing? Wondering?"

She continued, "Perhaps I should have said, I am *persuaded* that it may be to seek shelter within the object."

"Within it? Do you see an entrance anywhere?"

"No, Master Twill. I do not. That is what worries me."

Belnad stood up – he had been bending over the console in front of him – and stretched his seven-foot body, reaching almost to the ceiling of the control room. "How far away are they now?" He was asking Ian Jordan, who was across the room, hunched over another console. Beyond the two of them, at least a hundred other Emers were in the large room, all working at their stations, holographic images floating in front and around them all. One of the Emers seemed to be in the center of a giant holographic sphere coated on its entire inner surface with images of the action all around in every direction. The Essor fleet was clearly in view. The room was a beehive of activity. Ian checked with the two Emers working with him and said, "They are essentially here. Even though they keep slowing down, we are within each other's weapons range for sure at this point. The fleet itself could fire on us now, but the distance would definitely affect their accuracy. Those three ships are on our doorstep."

"What do you think is their intention?"

"I would say they are acting as a reconnaissance patrol, assessing the situation. Their caution indicates that they are aware of the peril, but I doubt they have anything like full knowledge of their situation. The nozzles from the Moon have been the main target of their sensors."

"Do you think they have any idea what's coming?"

"I doubt it. They could be thinking about what's inside Sargasso and that there may be some way in and out, but I doubt they have gotten very far beyond that. I am a little surprised at their caution. We always thought it would be an all-out assault coming in at full speed. Twill is not known for his circumspection. The extra time, ironically, has been helpful to us."

Farson and Karina, with Valgary and Felicity, were inside the home that the Emers had given them on the estate. It was an architectural wonder of angles and clear shields, warm light, perched on the very edge of the Butte of Decision, although avoiding the historic spot by half a mile. As in the days when Farson's great decisions had been made, the butte was still one of the most remote locations on Emerald Earth. No access except by The Screen itself or by an impossibly long trek on foot, although one had made it. The Emers had put all of the technology their city was so famous for into Farson's and Karina's home and into the happiness of its four inhabitants. Inside, they were all sitting at a table, playing a board game, using pocket lasers and solid holographs. They were laughing and having a good time. Valgary and Felicity were playing as a team against Farson and Karina. The girls were winning. Farson was whispering to Karina their new strategy. He hoped that in making a move that held the potential for disaster, his daughters would hesitate to destroy their parents' hopes for victory. He was hoping that they would avoid the "death blow," as he called it. He touched his laser and executed the move. The girls countered without hesitation, and the game was over.

"We win, Dad. That was stupid." Karina was laughing.

"I told you it wouldn't work," she said. The girls wanted to know what she meant.

"Oh, your father thought he could rely on your good nature and affection and that you would not crush him like a bug." Valgary and Felicity exchanged looks. Then they burst out laughing.

"Silly Daddy." At that moment they all felt the vibration. It was soft and lasted for about two minutes. Then everything fell silent again.

Taking Karina's hand, Farson said, "It has begun." Karina squeezed his hand and nodded.

"So it would seem." The girls had stopped laughing.

Shals t'Bu realized something astounding. The surface of the object was changing before his eyes. "Commander t'ul'Dak, are you watching this?" Indeed she was. He saw her nodding. Twill was on his feet and wondering why everyone was addressing the technician as though she were in charge.

"What is that?" he demanded. Panau did not move her eyes from her observation as she answered.

"I think an opening is being created. Lieutenant Commander, notify the fleet." And then she added, "All stop."

ID>>Karo28689 stood on The Screen, watching. She knew she was directly over Sargasso's star. She dropped off The Screen and entered Sargasso, then appeared in the control room, silently. She had just traveled over six light-years in seconds. Belnad had been expecting her. "What is the aperture?" she asked.

"Over 7,000 miles. We are just a few minutes away."
She disappeared in a soft pulse of pure purple.

Twill's excitement was palpable. "Energize the weapons. This is our chance." The crew turned to Panau. Twill screamed at the top of his lungs, "Do it!" They turned to their instruments and began the initialization process. *That damned technician. We should have had them armed the whole time.* Panau was watching what she thought would be her last moments alive. She noticed activity on the surface.

"Brace for impact!" She shouted as the room filled with light. She saw two streams coming at them, one from the opening and another from the weapons on the surface of the object. She looked at Twill. His face was bright with anticipation, but he was stopped in mid-thought. She saw his eyes strain in her direction, and then he was gone. The lights coming from the object extinguished, and the room returned to normal. The lasers dissipated with no effect. "Stand down! Stop our attack. Deactivate the weapons. Power everything down." Panau t'ul'Dak had given the orders. She was in command now.

The communication from ID>>Karo28689 was crystal clear. <<*We have him.*>>
Belnad gave a new order. "Proceed."

Ian added, "Aperture is complete." A vibration filled the room, and there was a loud buzzing sound. Then everything went quiet.

Brittany was standing at Ichor's monitors inside Sargasso. Emerald Earth, the Moon, and SkyKing were exactly where Ian had said they would be, in Sargasso's seventh planetary slot. "They are so beautiful," she said. Then another vibration quivered through the room around her.

"I'm a little disappointed, girls. I would have expected you to show more patience. Victory was assured. You could have played with us a little." Valgary took the lead.

"Oh, Dad. We've played this game too many times with you to fall for that. If you could have, you would have done the same thing, as you have so many times. It's usually us feeling the sting of defeat and wondering if you really love us." Then they felt the second vibration. They all knew what that meant. Farson stood up.

"Time to go." Karina and the girls watched as he disappeared.

Panau found that Shals was standing beside her. Twill had gone into the light. Now a second flash, a much longer flash was still filling the ship. The monitors and sensors indicated that they were in a huge force field of some sort. She ordered *Orion* to reverse course and was told the ship's controls were not responding, She had Shals check with the fleet and was told the same situation existed there. "So, we are captured?" Shals' question hung in the air.

Panau answered, "We are restrained, but everything is still functional." Then Farson Uiost appeared beside her. A large silver and blue robot came with him. Panau looked at the two of them. Farson was dressed in corduroys and a cardigan sweater. He wore a white shirt and soft shoes. He was haloed in purple. The robot's posture was relaxed and aware. It was the robot who spoke first, with a clearly feminine voice. "Greetings, Commander Panau t'ul'Dak. Are you aware of your situation?" Panau was thinking it over. All ships immobilized. Grand ScreenMaster Twill gone. The guns of the humans all in full operational mode. Their power was filling the room and her mind with the realization that there was no doubt of the situation at all.

"We are at your mercy." She moved a little closer to Shals. In all of Essor history only Twill had had contact with the human race. Essors all knew the stories. They were twisted to suit the ego and whims of Twill, of course. He had always made humans seem so weak and so easy to defeat. He referred to them as "go'w'ats," the Essor word for the weakest creatures ever to evolve on their planet. They were small, slimy, and squished around, absorbing droppings and the filmy scum in the dark recesses of Essor where no one ever went. Essors considered them the lowest form of life. Now, looking at Farson who was slightly taller than she, she thought he looked nothing at all like a go'w'at. In fact she found his soft skin and clear eyes interesting. She felt that the robot's voice was confident but unthreatening. Their words, though spoken in a language she had never heard, were somehow perfectly understandable. Then she felt the power of Farson's thought.

<<Panau, you are not in danger.>> At first she thought he had spoken, but she had been looking right at him and knew he had not. *What is that?* was her first thought, but then she realized what had happened. She also noted that with his thought had come a great calming down as though Farson had reached in and quieted her pounding heart. *<<We are not so different.>>* Again a pleasing sensation went through her. She looked at Shals and could easily see his calmness and that he was unafraid, not in bravado, but in fact. She knew there was now nothing to fear. *<<The entire fleet is hearing this, Panau. Every crew member is feeling what you are feeling.>>* More sincerity. It was like a tranquilizer. Composure in the

face of the strangest "attack," if that was what this was, that any Essor had ever experienced. She felt a serenity, a relief like Essors often felt on returning home. <<*We are going to release you and your fleet. You are going home unharmed. You have earned it. Your actions have indicated an intelligence and a commitment to truth that Essor is going to need. Twill will not be coming, at least for now. ID>>Karo28689 is informing The Screen of the changes.*>> Panau looked at the robot. Its faceplate was strobing a dark purple, some parts shading to red. She could sense communications underway. She noticed that her own hand was touching Shals' now. She was thinking how Farson had called it her fleet. <<*Essor will be without a ScreenMaster for a time. We want you to lead them. It will not be an easy time. But, I will be with you.*>> Panau moved closer to Farson. He could tell she wanted a closer look. He stood still. Her face neared his, her oval openings surrounded by gently rounded scales, her vertical pupils, her beautiful eyelids blinked so close to him that Farson imagined he could feel the air move between the two of them. He noticed an earthy aroma like leaves in autumn outside his North Conway cabin. Her opal-like eyes staring at him. He felt the mental power; he felt the intelligence. He felt her eyes searching his, slight movements, her slitted pupils dilating slightly in and out.

"You are Farson Uiost."

<<*Yes.*>>

"This is a ScreenKeeper?" She indicated ID>>Karo28689, who bowed her head slightly to acknowledge Panau.

<<*Yes. A very powerful ScreenKeeper. Their leader, in fact.*>> Panau again had the feeling of being engulfed in peace, in truth. She was amazed and awed, and humbled. She had heard nothing but evil about humans, and now she felt nothing but affinity and friendship from them. She had heard of the horrible miscreant Farson Uiost who had tried to destroy Essor and everything else. Now that he stood before her, she found him appealing and interesting, the furthest

thing from fearful and destructive possible. She saw how much like her he was. *No wonder Twill hated him so.* Farson heard her thought.

<<*Twill did not hate me, Panau. He feared me. Change to Twill was disaster afoot in his world. Something to be chased down and squashed. I tried to warn him. I showed him a better way. But he was blinded by rage and power, a disastrous combination.*>>

"He told us you were dead, that your world was dead. He shouted it at us again and again."

<<*The loudest voice does not always convey the deepest truths.*>> She looked around the bridge. Everyone was standing still at their stations. Shals was beside her.

"Is he dead?" Farson put his hand on the edge of her shell. He was surprised that it felt like satin, and surprised at its warmth. She liked his touch. Shals moved a little closer.

<<*Not dead, but gone.*>>

"Will we ever see him again?"

<<*Doubtful, knowing him as I do. But, if you do, he will be very different from the Twill you've known. He has wrought some pretty serious events on The Screen. The ScreenKeepers have a duty to perform. Twill has a rendezvous with a destiny of his own creation.*>> He was thinking to himself, *time will tell.*

"Time will tell?" She had heard his thoughts. He smiled.

<<*Yes, Panau. Time will tell. Time always tells.*>>

"What happens now?"

<<*Look at your monitors.*>> Panau's day had already been shocking, but one more revelation remained. They were back at Essor. Somehow the entire fleet had been transported back to Essor. After months in flight to "the object," they had returned instantly. The beautiful Essor floated in the black of space, its bright sun lighting the planet's face. She found herself longing to be home again, in her balenest, with time to explore her new affection for Shals t'Bu. Her relief was welling up.

"I am not sure what to say."

<<*Essor is fully aware of what has happened. Your courage and intelligence is being applauded everywhere on your planet. Twill's hold, now broken, is revealed as based on fear. A new leader, one respected and beloved, has taken his place.*>>

"Me?"

<<*Yes, Panau. It is a new beginning.*>> She could see the purple hue building on the bridge.

A golden accompaniment was blending in as ID>>Karo28689 said to Farson, <<*Farson, we still have much to do. We must go.*>> Panau heard them.

"Will I see you again, Farson?" He was fading out. In fact, he was gone when she again felt his thought.

<<*You can count on it, Panau. We will meet again.*>> There was a purple and golden swirl of fading light before them in the room. Panau and Shals watched it fade away like a sunset.

The fleet had been orbiting Essor for two days, a month in Earth days. The planet was in shock and relief. The balenests were alive with the implications of what had occurred. They were now a race with no ScreenMaster, where before their ScreenMaster had been supreme. They were hearing the story of Panau t'ul'Dak over and over, her legend growing with each retelling. Slowly the ships were reberthed, one by one, into the subterranean world of the Essors. Soon only Panau's ship, *Noctura*, remained in orbit. She and Shals were alone on the ship, the crew gone home. They were in Twill's quarters, looking out the huge oval-shaped window at Essor below. "Do you think we could ever return to the surface, Panau? The old stories the elders told were of a world of light and hope. Do you think it could ever happen again?" Panau thought of her station deep in Essor and her data stream. There was a part of her that wanted to go back there and get to work, leaving all of this to others. She had been happy parsing the stream of data, a stream that now would be abandoned and yet had been so important. She took a deep breath. She noticed Twill's sleeping quarters and felt her heart long for rest.

"Shals, at this point I would say anything is possible, wouldn't you?" She took his hand and led him to the sleeping area. His heart was pounding as his eyes searched hers. They went in and closed the door as Essor, far below, turned slowly in the light of its star.

In transit Farson had a question. <<*What next, ID*>>*Karo28689? It's been a busy day.*>> He noticed that she had reassumed a human form, the same young, stylish woman who had attended his dinner party.

<<*Call me Ida, Farson. You know I like it better. There is still much to do. How about you inform Uva, and I attend to the others?*>>

<<*Sounds good. But I have one other stop to make.*>>

Ida was gone. Farson was not sure she had heard him.

94. Handy in Sargasso

During a tour of *Songbird*, that the Emers ultimately arranged, Handy went to the bow and surveyed the room where Uva had stowed away. He went back through the upper staterooms and through the three decks. The lower deck held the engine room, pristine and quiet. The middle, or main, deck held the galley, dining rooms, several more staterooms, Farson's suite, the main entrance area, and other areas not yet explored. The upper deck held the operations compartment, the captain's quarters, where Handy was going to be staying, and the bridge. Interestingly, Handy noticed that the ship also had an exterior deck and a large area "outside." He felt this was for atmospheric flights, and landings on the ground. During the tour, he was also told that *Songbird* could float as well as fly, operating as a vessel at sea if desired or needed. They had told him that, whenever he was ready, he could activate the main system by keying the password phrase they had showed him how to create.

Now, alone on the starship, he was sitting in the pilot's chair. Everything was ready. The inside of Sargasso was as big as a huge solar system. There were six planets to explore, plus now, Emerald Earth. He felt like he was on vacation. In all of his time as a ScreenMaster, he had never had such a feeling of being safe and free. There had always been a job he had to do. There had always been a burden to bear. Now he was free to go anywhere, do anything he wanted. He sighed. <<*Thanks, Farson. You are a good friend.*>> He was going to add, "my only friend," but in saying goodbye to Brittany, Karina, Belnad, and Ian, he had realized that that was no longer true. *I have many friends now. I am not alone.*

Minutes passed as Handy thought it all over. *So many years, so many sad things. Now this.* He was quite happy with the turn of events. "Light her up," he said the password phrase out loud. There was a soft whisper as the systems all came on flawlessly. A soft female voice asked, "Where are we going, Handy?" He pointed out the front view screen and replied.

"That-a-way." *Songbird* leaped from the docking mechanisms and was out in the open space of Sargasso in nothing flat. The monitor chimed, "Cruising at sixty percent. Awaiting further instructions."

away we go handy this is fun

Surprised, he turned to see the dolphin ship in the side monitors. Their ship was textured like scales. The whole ship seemed to be alive. At rest, it was a large sphere, bigger than *Songbird*. It changed shape as it accelerated, becoming like a large reflection of *Songbird* as though in a carnival mirror. It was a well-crafted imitation of *Songbird*, as though drawn by a child's hand. Handy laughed. They were exactly the same out here as they had been on the planet. Always trying to impress him, never leaving his side.

The two vessels flew off into Sargasso's night.

where are we going handy we need to have some place to go

"Where do you want to go?"

with you

Handy spoke to *Songbird*'s control again. "Let's go to here. He was pointing to a planet." How long before we arrive?"

"At our current speed, we will arrive at the planet in five days."

"Whoa, slow down there little Birdie. There's no rush."

The long distance telemetry showed the planet Range as a tiny speck of light. Handy was relishing the prospect of a planet where the skies were never cloudy, where the animal life roamed free, where the rivers roared like channeled oceans, and where sitting beside a flickering campfire, he knew he would certainly be singing a chorus he had learned long ago in a simple life that helped a mauled and mangled ScreenMaster begin a process of recovery from losses unimaginable and from a loneliness so enormous that it still filled his despair with disorientation and disarray.

He looked around the beautiful ship and out at the dolphins so faithfully energetic in their devoted companionship. Soon he was humming the chorus, and then singing.

> Oh give me a home where the buffalo roam,
> Where the deer and the antelope play,
> Where seldom is heard a discouraging word,
> And the skies are not cloudy all day.

The dolphins were listening and moved their ship a little closer as *Songbird* slowed down.

wait until handy sees who we have brought with us

95. The People of Earth

When *Songbird* had eventually achieved orbit around Range, Handy went down to the planet. He set up a small camp near one of the huge rivers, along the bank, facing toward Sargasso's sun. It was warm, but pleasant. *A perfect place.* Handy had built a small fire and made some coffee. He was relaxing and enjoying the flavors and aroma. The air was calm. *Songbird's* instrumentation told him that it was approximately 1.25 times larger than Earth. The rivers coursed the planet like the stitching on a baseball, and the population was spread evenly throughout, except for the city, New Sacramento.

From his studies of the enormous Sargasso, assisted by *Songbird's* archives and data reserves, now streaming directly from Ichor's central banks, he knew that the number of cities on the six planets was very limited. Most of the planets had one, one had two, and one had none. Range had the single city of New Sacramento.

Songbird had informed him that while appearing rustic, Range had its sophistications too. Very little happened on the planet without New Sacramento knowing about it. So, he was not surprised when *Songbird*, through its communication systems, informed him that he would soon be having visitors. He sipped his coffee, peacefully waiting.

They arrived riding on Range's version of horses, known as horsels. Instantly recognizable, but on closer inspection they were taller, thinner, and, for want of a better word, furrier than he expected. The gravity on Range was about eighty percent of Earth standard, which made being on the planet easier and, from Handy's point of view, a little more fun. The horses ran with an easy agility.

we are watching handy

This made him smile. The land areas of Range were so dry, even with flowing rivers, that the dolphins had decided to stay in orbit.

we can swim you know our ship is very adaptable

Handy knew they could be right beside him if he needed them, but Range felt safe; in fact all of Sargasso felt safe. He knew if the dolphins thought he needed them, nothing would stop them.

you got that right

Handy laughed. They were making fun of him and his cowboy style of talking. But Handy knew that things had changed for him. Agreeing to wear the "uniform" they had provided had just been the beginning. His transformation in the depths of Emerald Earth had "reset" Handy to younger, healthier, much better posture, adding a few extra inches. It had also created an inner confidence that he had known had long existed deep within but that now had reemerged and replaced the taciturn indifference, barely assuaged by constant booze and tobacco, with a resurgent sense of peace and engagement. *Patience. When you have time enough, what else do you need?*

The group from the city had stopped about a hundred yards away and set up their own temporary encampment. Handy put on his gun belt and his cowboy hat and started walking along the riverbank in their direction. The pellucid water, sparkling in the sun, flowed by. Handy estimated its speed to be about two knots. *Swimmable.* He felt like the width was hard to gauge, like distances at sea or the mountains from the plain. *I bet it's over three miles.* The ground underneath was easy walking. It was soft, and the moisture of the riverbanks seemed restricted to just a few feet from the flowing water. He knew the river was a vast nutritive resource, and he imagined that the rivers' spacing around Range was perfectly planned. He knew that the rotation of the planet created a feeling of gravitational familiarity but enjoyably less. It was like being on old Earth, only better. The air was refreshing and richly oxygenated.

All in all, Handy could tell that Range was a wonderful place.

As he neared the visitors' camp, he could see that they were expecting him. In their group greeting, there seemed to be no leader. There were about thirty people and as many horsels. They greeted him as an old friend, and he quickly learned they knew all about him. The people were not Emers, but in some ways they resembled them. The individual variations were obvious here; each person was a distinct individual in dress and characteristics. The one thing that struck Handy was their unmistakable appearance of perfect health and prosperity. Everyone was clearly on an equal footing; there was an easy association among them. Handy noted no vying for attention, no one-upmanship of any kind detectable. It was easy to relax among them.

After the greetings and some food, they barbecued some sort of food on an open fire, and it was delicious. *A ChainFoods derivative?* A woman came forward. Handy was stunned. In all of his travels, Handy had learned that you can never really know what comes next, but the tranquility of Range and meeting these wonderful people had lulled him into a relaxed unwariness, safe from any danger.

He stood there looking at her. The eyes were the same, but she, like him, had changed, as well: a little taller, younger, healthier, and there was something else. The years had taken their toll on Emerald Earth. Even a ScreenMaster like Handy had felt it. Now looking at her, he knew his guilt and worry had all been for nothing. She walked up to him and took his hand.

"Hello, Handy. It's been awhile." He could feel the warmth, and he recognized the understanding affection he had known for so many years. Mrs. Handy. He kissed her and held her tightly.

"I thought you were gone forever," he said.

"Forever is a long, long time, Handy."

Over the next few years, Handy came to understand more and more about the mysteries of Sargasso, and like all true knowledge, the more one learns the more one knows how much there is to learn. He had traveled on the "Sea of Knowing," as they called the transportation system, and ultimately visited all of the planets, including Emerald Earth and the Moon. He regularly returned to Range. He learned that the people of old Earth, combed from Emerald Earth's new history, had actually survived. And in that knowledge, he learned one of the great truths about Sargasso: it was an ark of humanity, a haven, an incubator and chrysalis.

In learning that truth, Handy realized that even he might never fully understand all that the Emers had done.

His "Home on the Range," as he called it, became his residence for a time. He traveled, and sometimes the dolphins joined him. But they ultimately, and reluctantly, returned to their home on Emerald Earth. *Songbird* rejoined the Uiost family when Handy no longer used it. Handy had found a home. He raised horsels, and farmed a little. But mostly Handy just lived.

In time, he was just one of the 1.6 billion people of Range. His legend still circulated among the planets, but Handy himself was just another Ranger, living free. No one was more surprised than Handy when Mrs. Handy, or Clara Townsend, as she much preferred, presented him with a baby girl.

One discovery among Handy's acquisitions during this time – a handwritten note from Farson – did acquire a certain importance in the history of Sargasso.

Please forgive my handwriting. I try to write
more legibly and it ruins the experience, so
I've learned to just write and go. Good luck.
If anyone can do it, it's you, Handy.

This poem tells our story: methodical, intelligent,
sometimes strange, but always surviving and
giving good.
It also, for the record, states the numbers.

Farson

96. The Secret of The Passed

Handy was holding the note that Farson had clearly left for
him. He had discovered it, waiting for him in plain view, in
the bow compartment of *Songbird* when he first came aboard.
It was an envelope with his name written on it. Inside, there
were two sheets of paper, both handwritten in Farson's cryptic
but interesting script. You really had to know Farson to be
able to read his handwriting. Handy had read it when he first
found it, and now again at his home on Range. He was in his
study, at home with his wife and child, looking down at the
note again.

"Please forgive my handwriting. I try to write more legibly
and it ruins the experience, so I've learned to just write and
go. Good luck. If anyone can do it, it's you, Handy.

"This poem tells our story methodical, intelligent,
sometimes strange, but always _____ and giving good.

"It also, for the record, states the numbers."

There was one word he could not decipher. *Scrutinizing? Securing?* He tried singing it to see what might happen. Still no intuitive insight. Sometimes even Handy had trouble reading Farson's handwriting. He knew you had to "think it," rather than just read it. He had turned to the second page to see the poem.

It was a long one for Farson. He had written long poems, but the vast majority of his poems were much shorter than this.

Singing it had taken awhile, and finding the hidden tune with his guitar was the issue. But he did it. And now he loved it. He sang it like a ballad, with lots of rhythm and plenty of harmony. He made it fun to sing.

What is that missing word? Creating?

DEAD WORLD DANCING
by Farson Uiost

Half of the people who ever lived are still alive.
There's no escaping that everyone dies.
Despite our dreams and our cries,
It's a crazy mystic shuck and jive.

Can't remember your own birth.
Can't imagine your own death.
It's a deep, slow cleansing breath.
Take it for what it's worth.

Living is an art ill applied,
But it's all we've got.
From a barrel like blasting shot
It scatters us far and wide.

There is no just turning back,

No time when things were better,
From the homeless to a jet-setter,
In a mansion or a hapless shack.
And who can dispute such clarity?
"All that, that is, is," he said.
Like all, who were, were ... he's dead.
Like us, who have, have ... charity.

In this dead world dancing ... there's no winners.
Whatever lies beyond, lies beyond, we can't go.
Though one returned they say, we'll never know.
It's a world of dreamers: dazed, worn-out sinners.

He forgave me everything. Oh how I loved him.
She taught me so, so much. Oh how I should have told her.
We were friends forever. Oh how I miss you.
So many things left unsaid. Oh how I could have said them.

Imagine.

Half of the people who ever lived are still alive.
There's no escaping that everyone dies.
Despite our dreams and our cries,
It's a crazy mystic shuck and jive.

Remember, whatever we did and tried,
Half of the people who ever lived ...
... have never died.

Handy thought about the poem for a few moments longer. He could hear Clara in the kitchen with the baby. He had some more work to do on a fence out back, and then a leak to fix. He was getting tired; the day was done.

Handy knew Farson was talking in the poem about the others: the population of Earth at the time just before the stasis field. That old Earth, full of cravings, angers, and afflictions that Farson talked about as if they were behind us

457

now. Ignorance, greed, senseless aggression, false assumptions about each other, all the problems that plagued us almost to our death. That Earth. Those people. The people who had to be gone, as if they never were. Farson knew how to save them, so he did. Worrying about what to do with them, how to bring them back from oblivion, he left for the Emers.

Then there were the other others. Farson had told Handy that story, too.

At first, they were echoes in Farson's thoughts. He would think something and someone would say "no," or "yes," or nothing, which was the most disorienting in the end. It didn't happen very often, but even in the beginning, it did happen. During his Ascension, there was a voice, a presence, something that could not stay hidden. It was like a bolt of lightning in Farson's brain. It knocked him down once. In time he learned to control it better. Then ID>>Karo28689 showed up. She first came to Farson as a seven-year-old girl. He thought it was Karina, but that first impression quickly changed.

"Hi, Farson," she had said. It was during his Ascendance, and he was faced with a big decision. "They sent me to keep you company tonight." She was dressed in a collared, knee-length overcoat with six large buttons in two rows down the front, and sharp shoulders, all buttoned up. She wore loose white socks, drooping down her ankles. Her shoes were scuffed brown with crossing straps and small buckles on the side. Her short hair was topped with two small white-bowed pigtails that gave her the appearance of having kitten ears. "They said you would need it tonight." She sat down next to him.

"Do I know you? I feel like I do."

"Sometimes I whisper in your ear," she said. At this point, Farson had been a ScreenMaster long enough to know that time bends and weaves and even swirls around. He knew that things were never exactly what they appeared to be. This was the same night when Uvo told had him <<*Don't think you can count on my acceptance or assent, Farson.*>> Uvo had warned that he would not retire like Twill. Farson knew that it was that moment that sealed Uvo's fate, that small criticism of Twill. *There are no secrets on The Screen*, Farson thought. The little girl spoke. "Yes, there are, Farson. There are secrets." He turned to look at her. His best guess was that, whoever she really was, she wanted to look like a girl from around 1945 C.E. on old Earth. Farson could not help but understand the disguise. It was the seminal year of human history to that point. "There have to be secrets, you see," she said.

It was cold; she moved a little closer. Despite his awareness that all was not what it seemed, he was grateful for the company.

"What kind of secrets?" She had not mentioned her name or he would have used it.

"Secrets like where are all those people? Secrets like, what does The Screen want? Secrets like, who am I?"

"Do you have a name, or is that a secret, too?" She smiled.

"I thought you'd never ask."

Handy heard Clara calling for him. He got up, leaving the note on his desk, and walked into the kitchen. Part of him was dissatisfied and restless, thinking to himself how did I get here? Part of him was finally happy and content. He stood next to Clara. (He would always think of her as "Mrs. Handy," even though she disliked it when he called her that. "My name is Clara and you know it." It was a joke between them.)

Handy was born on a different planet; he was from another race of people; he was ancient in Earth years, and yet on Emerald Earth and within Sargasso, he was a relatively young man. Each day was a world uniquely unfolding itself to Handy now. *So many years gone and who knows how many to go?* He was grateful. He was content. Yet there was a part of him that was restless and wanting to get going. His daughter gave him pause on all counts.

Farson had said to him that she would surprise him. For the old Handy Townsend, a failed ScreenMaster and then a great ScreenMaster; a lonely old drunken and broken man; now one of Farson Uiost's best friends, who had played a crucial role in the history of mankind; a wanderer and now a father, a husband, and a homesteader on Range, it had all been too much. That side of him that always wanted to run and hide loved this new life's blessed obscurity. That side of him that stared at bottles of whiskey with a longing like fire for a log, that gets mad, and twirls loaded guns, and that smokes cigars, wanted to get moving again. Clara knew it all. Her new life had come as a surprise. Her daughter was a gift cherished and unexpected. In fact she had deeply sublimated the thought of children into the dullness and predictability of her life with Handy during the long, long stasis. Like a prisoner who learns the routines of doing nothing, she had made the most of those years, slowly but surely falling in love with him. It had seemed like an assignment in the beginning, but beneath the hard crust of Handy's outward show, there was a warmth burning that endeared him to her. She learned, over the years, what Farson knew immediately, that Handy was a good and faithful friend. The daughter she now held in her hands was proof. Katy was squirming. "Handy, would you get another bottle for her?" He walked through the kitchen, the air was filled with the aromas of dinner being prepared, and went over to the diverter. The bottle was already waiting. He took it in his hand and was about to give it to Clara, but decided instead to do it himself. He rubbed the nipple against his daughter's lips and in it went. The warm fluid immediately began to move with the sucking motion of Katy's lips and cheeks. Her eyes opened. She was looking at him. She pushed the bottle out for a second and said, "blurbeodoopy," or something like that. Handy had no idea what she meant, but Katy's eyes were bright and she was smiling. Handy could not help himself. It made him laugh and smile back. Katy was pleased at his response. She resumed her actions with the bottle, and Handy looked at Clara.

"Do you know what she just said?"

"Thank you, Daddy." Handy shook his head.

"Really?"

Back in his study, Handy returned to Farson's note and to thinking about the story Farson had told him about the little seven-year-old girl who visited him on the Butte of Decision. He remembered every word.

"My name is Ida Marie, and I was saved by you many years ago." Her little girl voice was charming to Farson. He knew that was just a disguise; but a pleasing one. "The other others helped you, but in these matters there is only so much they can do. Your decision tonight, right here, will change everything. That you do not accept things as they seem to have to be – the old ScreenMasters' ways – that will change everything, Farson. Your willingness to risk everything will open a history that no one could have predicted. It will give us, and them, a pathway. You can't save everyone who ever lived, but saving half of them, the people alive in your time, is pretty good." Farson was watching her, a little girl telling the universe's story. "For them, and the Emers, it will be a long-held dream come true."

Handy remembered Farson's description of what happened next as though it was written forever indelibly in his mind.

"When I looked again, Handy, she was gone. It was many years before I saw her again. That night the decisions I had been planning were easier, smoother. She changed nothing. I did what I was going to do. But, after her visit, there was a warmth in the cold; there was a sweetness in the bitter; there was a certainty in the doubt. From that moment on, I always felt like she was beside me. The little girl never returned, but I felt like she had never left. When the other others spoke to me after that, it was always in her voice, older perhaps, but I knew it was her. They never told me what to do; they made me feel like whatever I decided, it would be the right thing."

Handy folded the note up and put it back in the envelope. He played his guitar for a while and sang it once more. When he finished with the last stanza:

> *Remember, whatever we did and tried,*
> *Half of the people who ever lived ...*
> *... have never died.*

He felt tears welling up, thinking about his own planet's death and all that had happened before he came to Earth. His sadness streamed in tears down his face, the last tones of his guitar slowly fading out. He looked up, and Clara was there in the doorway holding Katy. Clara seemed concerned at his emotion, but a little hand waved at him, and it all went away as if by magic. Handy wiped a hand across his eyes, smiling now, and walked over to them. "Let's eat," he said, putting his arms around them. As they walked toward the dinner table together he was thinking of another line from another one of Farson's poems.

There's only one way out and it's through...

97. The Seas of Sargasso

Sargasso's seas – Passed, Knowing, and Memory – flowed like mother's milk over, under, and around everything. The beautiful image of Sargasso, to Farson's eye, was of a giant swirly milky way marble with whirlpools of imagination eddying and streaming in all directions waiting for a thumb to fire off the tolley shot.

Farson was thinking, in a long pausing silence in his conversation with Andrew Sortt, about the nature of things and how much they had changed. Inevitably, Farson broke the silence. "Back in the old days, Andy, people would walk around in their myths of importance: business, personal, physicality, attractiveness, wealth, ugliness, loneliness, superiority ... you name it. Everyone had something better or worse than others and either lorded it over on them, or lived in fear of discovery. All of the advertising in those days played off of this 'better than you' theme, boosting it at every opportunity, and, of course, profiteering on others' egos or angst. Playing off of intemperance, inferiority, and prejudice was very often the root of many advertising careers. Everything was aimed at making the individual think that something they could buy or order was going to solve all of their problems, fix their inadequacies, or give them health and longer life. When all the while, Andy, as you well know, the answers lurked within. Answers that everyone knew in their true heart of hearts: that we *are* all equal, that we *are* all good, that we *are* all together.

"There have been many long periods of mass delusion in the history of the human race." Farson stopped speaking and allowed time to pass quietly again. He leaned into the cushions of the chair and let the feeling of comfort and relaxation, that he loved so much in these precious moments with his friend, wash over him. Farson loved it. It was satisfying. There is no greater soothing cure for a human being than to know that he or she belongs somewhere and is not alone. Then, resuming, he submitted a question. "Wouldn't you agree, Andy, that here on Emerald Earth, we have fixed all of that?" Another patient intermission ensued. John Andrew McKinley Sortt started to take a sip from his glass but noticed it was empty. Even the aroma of vanilla and flowers was waning. Then he responded.

"I hope we're not in another one of those delusional periods now, Farson. I do agree that Emerald Earth is a spectacular real-life utopia, but it came with a price, as *you* well know." He emphasized the "you" to turn it back to his friend, who, Andy felt, was too often overly certain of his own conclusions, even as he made big changes with consequences which were always unpredictable by the nature of their complexities. He also knew that Farson had been very successful – up to now – so he was not being critical, just cautionary. "Let's hope all those people of old Earth are learning their lessons out there."

There was a holographic display floating in the room between them. Farson was in his chair, but John Andrew McKinley Sortt was slowly pacing now, more like wandering, his empty glass abandoned on the table. The display before them was of Sargasso in all its glory. It showed the huge star, Ichor. Ichor's inner sanctum, where the Emers worked, was extremely complex and easily as large as any of the planets. The six holographic planets, and two ghosted placeholders, rotated as though in time-lapse, with their various moons and satellites in synchronized orbits with them. Emerald Earth stood out as the smallest of the planets but perhaps the one glowing the brightest with its amber and green colors. Farson loved looking at the planet. The star-shaped Emerald City showed clearly on the to-scale depiction. It was the largest feature except for the great canyons and the vast, varied, vivid fields of grain. The three seas filled all other space within Sargasso. Each one of them was wide and vast in its coursing, and yet at the center of each was a concentrated current. Two circled each planet in their embracing flows, one clockwise and the other counterclockwise, and the third, the Sea of Knowing, went directly through each of the planets, its girth widening to coat them as it traversed their surface, but that other, more concentrated current, went directly through the center of each one. It was actually a vast transportation system, powered by the star, flowing right through every planet or through the empty ghost "parking spaces" where new planets could go. Its orbital time – to circumnavigate the interior of Sargasso – was about thirty days, depending on conditions. The other seas were similar in concept, circling the interior, touching all the planets, but with variations in orbital timing, velocity, and effect.

Within the transport sea, it was very easy to know where you were, and it was even easier to get on and off "the merry-go-round," as the people of Sargasso sometimes affectionately called it, because, like a subway system on old Earth, there were easily discernible markers, elaborate embarkation and disembarkation stations, and schedules universally and readily available. After all, it had been around for over two thousand years.

Knowing was always packed with people. For some, it became a world of its own because there was a whole group of people who, once they got on, never got off. In truth, the Sea of Knowing had everything, including a hardworking population of its own. They were known as the "Knowers."

"The K," as everyone called the Sea of Knowing, was how people got from one planet to the other. It also had limited intra-planet capabilities, some of which were just plain fun to use and see.

The other two seas could be "sailed" as well, but they were much slower and, in some ways, far less dependable, and vessels designed for the purpose were hard to come by. The Sea of the Passed and the Sea of Memory were the planetary atmospheric and chemical resources, and for that reason were cherished, in that taken-for-granted way that life support systems always are in everyday life: an unspoken prayer for constancy.

The star itself was sanctified by the populations for its vitality, consistency, and unending bounty.

Looking at the entire array floating before him, it was beautiful to Farson in so many ways.

He relaxed in his chair, watching it all; he knew it was a real-time depiction of mankind's crowning jewel right in front of him.

Farson felt compelled to reply to Andrew's last comment. "Andy, we have been here for a long time now, and just that amount of time proves it is working perfectly. If you mean that maybe we have missed something, or maybe that we are in denial, believing that something like this can go on forever, I would remind you what has just happened: the attack from Essor – I prefer to think of it as Twill's folly – and our ability to completely command the resolution that no one expected. It was potentially a very rough situation, and our actions prove that the forces we have created and control are more than worthy, more than real; that they are just and true. As I am sure you know, we now face a new challenge." The image before them changed to a view outside Sargasso, with the giant sphere in full view. Farson pondered how big it all really was. Around Sargasso, now, the telltale colors of the Seas had emerged through the "lights" and were coating the outer surface, and moving in all directions around it, mirroring the currents within. Sargasso was now glowing with a halo of light and beautiful tones of color. Both Farson and Sortt knew it was moving now. As the view rotated, the aperture came into view and the thick, steady, solid beam of bright blue and purple thrusting pulse from the powerful star was clear to see. The stars behind the image seemed to move backwards, but Farson and Sortt both knew that it was Sargasso that was moving, building speed quickly, and it was the stars themselves that were standing still.

Amazing, he thought as he and Sortt just stood and watched as Sargasso's depiction vanished into the diminishing perspective of infinity.

98. Aristealia

Uva was happy but depressed. Thrilled to be part of a future that no one could have predicted, but sad for a past that meant so much, now gone.

Farson appeared beside her. She found her mind was filled with soaring images of Aristealia, of her empty home nest, of her memories of Uvo. He had found her, of course. She had discovered a quiet place to be alone, deep in Ichor's interior, far from the Emers and all of the events now ongoing. She had wanted to be alone. The vision of her planet filled her mind, so peaceful in space, its teeming and beautiful population all living their lives of grace and kindness. "A people like no other," Farson had said. She felt his touch; he was very close. There was another of those vibrations. Farson held his hands in front of her and spread them slowly. An image of Aristealia appeared. He spread his hands farther apart. Uva gasped at what she saw and leaned into Farson. <<*You can't be serious, Farson.*>> As his hands had spread, Uva had seen that Aristealia was now within Sargasso, the seventh planet. She could see the seas enfolding her planet as though in an embrace. Aristealia's two gorgeous moons, like fledglings flying with their mother, were slowly orbiting with her, all together like gems in a setting, sparkling in the light of the enclosed star.

Then he was gone. Farson was on the move.

99. SkyKing and the Moon

One second SkyKing was in a geosynchronous orbit over Sargasso, communicating with Long John Hanson Silver, coordinating the preparations to fire on the Essor fleet, waiting for instructions from Belnad Goethe, and the next second they were inside Sargasso, in a stable orbit around Emerald Earth. The Moon was in its place as well. The seas were enfolding and encompassing the planet, the Moon, and SkyKing. Systems were going off and coming back on, the lights blinked, and then things settled down. Repoul Bensn, at his station, was checking everything. Jim Peterson was there, of course. "Get me Commander Nichols." As he was waiting, he looked around. Things were calm, but he could tell that the Skers were concerned. To Jim Peterson, it was as if nothing had happened. There had been no movement, no sensation of starting or stopping. One second they were conducting operations in open space, preparing for battle, and the next all was still. As operations in Alpha Whorl resumed, he walked over to the large window with the unobstructed view. The interior of Sargasso was as large as space itself from Commander Peterson's point of view. Emerald Earth dominated the view. The Moon was bright in a distant waxing crescent. The only other light, besides the star, that he could see was a bright white one far off the port side, which he assumed was another planet. There were swirling colors everywhere in the mix, which seemed to be vaguely moving past the window. Jim Peterson knew a great change had just occurred. *This is going to take some time to get used to.*

Repoul was standing beside him, in the throes of an emotion that Jim could not identify. *Perhaps he's in prayer*, he thought. Viera's voice was in his ears. "Jim, are you there?"

"Yes, Viera, I am. What do you think?" He had asked the question casually, as though inquiring about a new pair of trousers. The communications visual came on, and now he could see her as well as hear her. She was wearing her now customary Sker whites. She looked great, as always, to him: beautiful, fit, and in command. Viera told him of the Moon's experience. It was the same as SkyKing's. Instant transport to Sargasso's interior, a slight power fluctuation as the systems transferred: then everything exactly as before. He could see her looking out and viewing SkyKing orbiting brightly on her monitor.

"We can see you over there," she said. "You look pretty small," a slight upward fluctuation in her eyebrows. He smiled at her consistent affability.

"We are all small in any place out here. Somehow, for the first time in a long, long time, I feel safe. I feel like we are all safe."

"I agree. We have a long way to go, but my engineers think we should be able to resume transportation systems activity between the three of us shortly. Long John is back aboard and busy shutting down the engine room. How are your transporters?" Jim looked over at Repoul who had seemed to be lost in thought, but with Viera's question he looked up and gave Jim an uncharacteristic thumbs-up.

"Repoul says we are good to go."

For the remainder of that first day, everyone on the Moon and SkyKing worked to test systems and check protocols, but within a short time they realized that they were just going through the motions. Not only did all systems work, they were all working better. People were feeling better. John Silver's crew and equipment had also been brought back onboard just prior to the transport, and he had been checking all the systems of the thrusters as they were being reinstalled and stored on the Moon. He had heard the discussion between Viera and Jim Peterson. When his name was mentioned, he perked up. When they signed off, he turned to his crew. "It may be all hunky-dory for them, but we've got to muscle all of these motherfuckers back into place again. All this work and we never even got to shoot our big load. I think we were just a fucking diversion, if you can believe that. What the hell? Talk about a bunch of assholes all bonered up and nothing to fuck! We should have all just stayed home and had a circle jerk." The crew was laughing happily at their unstoppable boss and his dependable antics. They put an extra effort into the work, Silver sweating right beside them, everything back to normal.

Repoul Bensn knew that things had changed. He had a call in to Voul who was still in Ichor, working with Belnad and Ian Jordan. *He's been there a long time.* As things had returned to normal on SkyKing, Repoul had taken out his books and found a passage he had been thinking about. "... for the first heaven and the first earth were passed away ..." He held the precious books as though a child in his arms. Faith at its strongest point is always challenged, always tested, he knew. He read on in the passage about wiping away all tears, about no more death, "... neither sorrow, no crying, neither shall there be any more pain: for the former things are passed away." He read on about the city of gold with vast dimensions and the high wall of protection. He was standing near the window where Jim Peterson had stood just an hour ago. He was reading how the four foundations of "the city" were garnished in jasper, sapphire, chalcedony, and the final one in emerald.

He saw the planet gleaming in the starlight of Ichor's amazing power, its golden amber and green hues against the darkness of Sargasso's impenetrable and distant boundary, the colorful, nutrient, and powerful seas now churning their patterns everywhere: over, under, around, and through. It felt imprisoning to the Sker. He searched the skies of Sargasso, but there were no stars. He looked down at the books, and

Ban Jonsn's words stared back at him. "The truth of these words can never be sealed away, never closed off, never taken away. They will live forever within our hearts, if you hold true, and never waver. We shall all walk beneath the stars all together: the past, the present, the future. If any seek to take away these words, to steal our prophecy from us, then we must keep the faith and always persevere them in truth until the day when all has come again and we are finally free."

Repoul, so moved, that he wiped a tear from his eye, and prayed harder, waiting for Voul Jonsn to return.

100. Brittany's Log (Miscellaneous Entries)

(1) When I stepped through that portal I had no idea what I was doing. It had taken me twenty-five years to get there. For so many years, I was lonely. After my mom died, I seemed to blank out. I helped my father more and sort of shifted sides. My mom and I had always been really close, almost like one person. She knew everything and told me about it all. She was like a friend and a parent. Holding her hand was the joy of my day. Seeing her was seeing me, I suppose. Then I was alone. No warning. No fine wording. No argument. She was dead. Slowly, I turned to my dad.

I see things more clearly now, a little older and a little wiser. But when I stepped onto Emerald Earth, everything changed. I mean *everything*. First of all, it was a total physical transformation. One minute you're in one body and the next you're in another. Emers are always a minimum of seven feet tall – I was an exception at six feet, ten, plus a little. Then you notice other things. Sight, taste, touch, hearing, then your sense of smell. In that one regard, alone, it feels like heaven. Really. In the transformation, your physicality is reset to Emerald Earth normal and you feel great: health and body unbelievable. It reminded me of the second time I got a ride in a car. The first one was on one of the trips back to old Earth with Dad. He knew of the old broken down Dodge Dart in a garage. He wanted to take it out for a ride. After working all morning, we got it started and took off down the road, bumping and squeaking and laughing all the way. My second ride was on another trip to the planet years later. Dad had to rush ahead for his meetings, and he arranged for a car to drive me to the hotel. It was a Cadillac limousine: a totally different definition of the word "car." *That* is the kind of change in body that the Emers have given to me: a totally different definition of the word. A much better one. Everyone has one. Everyone is perfect and beautiful. Belnad said it's our reward for doing what we do. Everything is automatic. Bodily functions? I never think about them. Grooming? It's as easy as walking, on this planet. There is an atmosphere of such a unique engineering that, as you breathe it, you become healthier, cleaner in ways I never dreamed of, and mentally stronger and stronger. Most of the Emers here can actually control time. I'm not sure how, yet. I know that Emerald Earth never let the stasis field be completely turned off. They have learned everything about it and mastered it and reengineered it down to the individual level. When Ian and I made love for that first time, I realized later that he had suspended, and bent, and twisted time to get the experience he wanted me to have. It was wonderful. He told me later that it was also his first time, which surprised me, but now I know it was not all that unusual. Emers live forever but never marry and rarely engage in sexual activity of any kind. Certainly, they rarely do what Ian and I did (and still do).

There is an overall connection that, until you are plugged in, you know nothing about. Once you are part of it, you never want to leave it. It's a background like the sound you hear through a softly windblown sea conch; deep and melodic, mysteriously meaningful, but with no effort whatsoever on your part. It is natural for us. Whenever I think of Ian, he answers. When Farson is around, he is like that too; as is Karina. But the Emers have this connection honed at a whole different level. It's like a hive, I think, but also not at all like a hive. In the way we work together, yes, but that we all do as commanded? Absolutely not. The Emers are free and individual like no others. Imagine 6.8 million friends without question. You can go up in popularity, but never down. We are all equal. Not by decree but by our collective desire.

Education on Emerald Earth is all done by tutoring, and it starts when a new Emer comes, and it goes on forever. For all of us.

As I walked down the transport dock stairs, in those first moments, I already knew that the stairs were all different, some repaired, some original. I knew where the railing was. I knew the texture of the treads. When I walked with Ian, I knew when to match steps and slow down. I knew that Emers were strollers, not walkers. Any urge to rush whatsoever on Emerald Earth has no takers. We have all the time in the world.

(2) Some have asked me why I did it. "Why did you go with him?" When I first met Ian, I lost it, almost unconscious. He had to help me. I now know that when they travel, they have an aura around them of the Emerald Earth atmosphere that they bring with them. I breathed in just a little of it, by being close to him. It felt like I was swooning, but now I know that it was the transformation beginning. It wore off as we moved apart, but when I really transformed later that day, the truth was obvious. They don't really breathe air as we know it. For them, it is much more complicated than that.

Anyway, the real answer to "Why did you go with him?" is that I was lonely. That trip to the Moon's fantastic gym with Viera, that masseur, that skydive, that time with Thomas and

Brianna, it all made me even lonelier, knowing I would go back to SkyKing again. I know it's sort of a self-inflicted agony to admit that one is lonely in a world so full of great people and things to do, but on SkyKing I was just lonely. I worked hard, and I had friends. I even fell in love with Voul, but in the end, on SkyKing, it was just me again. So, when Ian caught me in his arms after just one gulp of the air of meeting him, and then helped me avoid the embarrassment of going to SkyKing wearing an unpowered Moon outfit, I felt safe with him. During the meeting I watched him and saw his brilliance and his humanity. He was only partially successful in the meeting, but he was happy. Patient. Coming back down the hall, I could feel his coming goodbye and did not want it to happen. I may have tightened my grip slightly to hold on. We were holding hands because Ian had taken mine in his so casually as if it were an Emer custom. I was thrilled at the contact. I was thrilled as he returned the gesture. As we neared the point where he would go on to his transporter and I would go my way, he asked me. I don't remember exactly what I said, and the next thing I knew it had already happened. I may not remember what I said, but I do remember what I felt. There was no doubt about it. I wanted to go.

(3) The longer you stay on Emerald Earth, the deeper the bond. The gratitude you feel and the peace you feel make you grateful. It's a sort of general feeling of thankfulness and appreciation: an affection, a deep friendship. You feel it for everything. It's love's purest form. I realized that loving Ian more or less than everyone else on Emerald Earth was stupid and merely possessive and it just never happened. I wanted to love him more – and I still believe I do – but the feeling of Emerald Earth's majesty and the endearing thoughts of the Emers were overpowering. The knowledge that filled me explained everything. Ian says my hesitations were because I

was born on SkyKing, which makes me laugh. On SkyKing my birth was the exception again, at least at first. I always felt like I was out of step with the people who were born on Earth, as though I had missed something. Over time that did change, but the sense of being out of place stayed with me. Now, here, on Emerald Earth, I am slightly out of place, an exception, again. All Emers were born on Emerald Earth except for me. I know I *am* an Emer. I know it because I know that everyone else knows it, too. No argument about things like that here. Everyone knows what everyone knows. When you are an Emer, they know everything about you, and you know everything about them. But, I am the first immigrant. You'd never know it. Even Belnad Goethe considers me a friend of great value. We work together, we argue, we enjoy a deep friendship. I say I love Ian because it makes me happy to say it – to be a couple – but I know more than that. I know what they know, and it is wonderful. Really.

(4) The Emers. I still call them that. They are very powerful, and they are very wise and brave. They are the philosopher kings. There are 6.8 million of them. Don't forget that. Now with Sargasso and the planets – half of the people who ever lived – we are all off to new horizons.

I have watched them planning. I know the plan. I agree with the plan. I am working within the plan every day. But there is still that part of human nature in me that says something will go wrong, but they have no doubt whatsoever about everything going exactly according to the plan. And they have been right every time. Even saying that makes me worry. The Emers never do. Ian never does. It doesn't occur to them to worry. What's wrong with me?

(5) Farson and Karina live here with the girls. They look just like they always have. No changes. Ian says it's because of who they are. I understand, I guess. They live on the Butte of

Decision in a house modeled after twenty-first century architecture with high, huge windows; flat roofs; a boxy look; angles and windows everywhere. The huge house is totally isolated. No neighbors. They come and go as they please. The Emers check mostly everything they do with either Farson or Karina, or both. The girls are almost twelve now, and they seem inseparable. They are very curious about Emerald Earth and are seen, out and about, more and more. The last time I was in Ichor control, they were in there for hours watching, asking questions, clowning around with each other, and generally enjoying themselves, but not bothering anyone. It reminded me of me on SkyKing.

(6) I mentioned Ian and I making love, which is my term. He calls it "combining." I sort of think his word is better because what we do for mutual sexual pleasure is way beyond anything I was expecting. I was a virgin. Making love with an Emer is more like melding body and soul and mind. The body part is fun, believe me. Emers can be great in that way, especially Ian, but it goes on and on as we expand to different times and places. Physically loving an Emer takes everything you've got, emotionally, physically, intellectually. It is really something. It doesn't happen every day, not even close. But it does happen.

The other day I was taking a walk in the morning, and I felt a summons in my mind. It was a call for me to go to one of the offices. When I got there, I was calmly and clinically informed that a gestation had begun in my uterus. They explained that obviously a conception had taken place. This unplanned event had not occurred on Emerald Earth in over five-thousand years.[4]

---

[4] In the beginning of Emerald Earth, as indigenous births grew, there was still a mixture of Emers and non-Emers on the planet. After around 1,500 years, the Emers were alone on Emerald Earth, as planned.

Following their protocols, this early information about my pregnancy had been filtered from me; everyone else knew, of course. They wanted to control the information so they could explain the options to me. It never occurred to them that at that point, when I knew, that I wouldn't care about all the various options. They stopped when they realized that carefully itemizing them all was useless and hurtful. My mind was made up. I was keeping the baby.

Now there is a lot of talk about where the baby should be born. This topic was also very brief in its discussion shelf life, because I told them I was having the baby right here on Emerald Earth. They were so happy, not because it's what they wanted, which it was; no, they were so happy because it was what *I* wanted.

(7) So, things are very interesting and going very well. No regrets. I know the plan is to send Emerald Earth out ahead of Sargasso at some point. I think Ian wants me to stay with him in Ichor as he manages the power, but I want to go with the Emers. I know there is danger ahead. Everyone knows. I find very little doubt lurking in my mind, and none in those around me. Selfless courageousness on Emerald Earth is universal. I am part of that now. *I should say: We are part of that now.* Ian has expressed regret about our coming separation. I have told him that we will be together, just apart. He looked at me with that same look my father gave me at Farson's party. Knowing there was no stopping me, being full of support and love, but, in the end, not liking the choice I was making, he still accepted it. Ian was holding my hand during this discussion. I felt his grip tighten ever so softly, his eyes looking deep into mine.

101. Terminus

Emerald Earth departed, leaving SkyKing circling the lonely Moon again. Viera was looking at the station through the window. They seemed small and fragile out there; now alone and out of place. She had Silver plot out a contingency maneuver that would get the Moon to the nearest planet, if need be, but things seemed to be fine, for now, even with Emerald Earth gone. Silver's studies discovered a way to use the outer edges of the transport current, like surfing on a diminishing wave, to get to Azure in about forty days by his estimate. "Could we make it, John?" Silver looked at Viera and said, "We could spend every day fucking twenty-four hours a day and still get there easy. We can shift this hunk of rock and dust from here to there without even losing our hard-on. The Seas make it very simple to move if we want to. Why'd'ya ask, Viera? Are we thinking about making a run for it?"

Viera laughed at how Silver's profanity flowed so smoothly that it seemed completely normal in its raunchy similes and mixed metaphors and, how, after all these years, it passed almost unnoticed. Almost. "Not us, John." She was still looking over at SkyKing. "But I'll bet that they *are* thinking about it."

Voul had been on Ichor with Ian for months, preparing the plan for implementation. He said it was where he could watch over things the best, for now. But Viera missed him. He had gone with Farson and Uva on *Songbird* to exploring Sargasso, then returned briefly. Now, he was away from her again, working inside Sargasso's star.

Farson and Uva were preparing to be off into the unknown, out in front of everyone, speeding along on a course no one knew, and at a speed few could imagine. Emerald Earth would be out there now, too, searching the path forward, using the combined powers and forces of 6.8 million Emer ScreenMasters. Sargasso was to follow them both, in time, ever increasing its speed, its precious cargo safe inside.

Silver said, "What the hell are they looking for, Viera? I thought we were all set once we got our asses in here. Now I'm wondering, are we heading into another fuckfest? Where *the hell* are we going, Viera?" She could see the star pulsing, powering up its thrust to move a solar system. She knew there were great forces at work now. But, even with all that, she was thinking of Voul when she answered, "I have no idea, John. I have no idea."

Voul realized that the Emers were referring to a plan called "Terminus" within a few minutes of being on the bridge of Ichor during operations. Everyone was working hard on it. What amazed him most was how they were regulating and channeling the star's immense energy. They used it to power the seas and to generate everything needed for life in Sargasso. They used it as a giant transporter system, moving planets and people as well. They used it for light throughout Sargasso and for electrical current everywhere. They were going to use it as propulsion to get Sargasso moving. And it was also the most powerful weapon ever harnessed. The structure of Ichor was a world in itself. As Voul learned more, it became obvious that while the Emers had "captured a star," they were now using its powers to channel the energy of other stars to carry out their plans. Voul imagined a neuron-like structure, invisible to the eye, yet beginning with Ichor and reaching across space in all directions, redirecting power back to Sargasso as needed. This effort would be even more intensely complex with Sargasso on the move. Voul watched Ian working in the control center, and he was reminded of Long John Hanson Silver on the

Moon pushing every ounce of effort out of his MoonBase crew. The floating visuals of Sargasso throughout Ichor's control center depicted the plan of it being preceded by Emerald Earth and *Songbird* way out in front. It captivated Voul. He could not believe what he was seeing; what they were planning.

Brittany had come over to talk with him, before her departure. She stood beside Voul, watching the images with him. "Kind of hard to believe isn't it, Voul?" He looked up at her face. It was the same face he had known since she was born, but stronger, more determined, and, he knew, vastly more experienced than the little girl vying for his attention back in the days before the ScreenMasters.

"Yes, indeed it is, Brittany." He paused and, still looking at her, repeated, "Indeed it is."

"How are the Skers holding up in all of this?" He knew what she meant. The Sker faith was based on scriptures stretching back nearly ten thousand years. Some were written and conceived in the days of humanity's distant youth. He knew that compared to what people were doing now, they were just toddlers back then, barely walking, barely speaking intelligently. *How can words spoken or written by those people have any meaning now?* He could tell that Brittany was reading his thoughts.

"You are one of them, or were, Brittany. What do *you* think?" She smiled at him; he felt a reassurance of well-being.

"I think the Emers are doing what they have to do, Voul. It's their mission. The old ScreenMasters caused a lot of trouble for humanity, and they gave us a wonderful opportunity. They pushed us out into the cold. But, Voul, in the end, we are still people, and the scriptures, even the literal scriptures of the Skers, still have meaning and power. The good, the true, the tested … these are still valid, perhaps, though, in different ways now. The Skers' esthetics and self-discipline are being tested in this new period of adventure and promise, as you know. But the Skers will adjust, as I have. As must we all. As you will, too." She was still looking at him, directly into his eyes. He knew she was right, but he still uncertain of his way, or his place.

"I hope you're right, Brittany." He was thinking of decisions that may have to be made. Viera was staying with the Moon, he knew that. If the Skers wanted to "fulfill their destiny," he would be forced to choose. It was one thing to be on Ichor with the Emers, while she remained on the Moon, and something altogether different, if Skers decided to "walk beneath the stars," and attempted to leave. He had seen the dilemma the instant SkyKing arrived. He could feel it. All the Skers did as they looked up into that dark impediment of Sargasso's shield. He remembered his thought at the time: *This is a prison to us.* Brittany was speaking again, the reason for their conversation becoming clear.

"Well, be that as it may, there is a new job at hand for you, Voul. Belnad asked me to brief you before I go." She told him that Farson had just arrived with *Songbird* – Handy wouldn't be needing the little starship – and he wanted Voul to join him and Uva aboard to accompany them "to the front," as he had put it. Uva had left Aristealia where she had been dealing with all of her planet's issues of being inside Sargasso, and she and Farson, and two others, were now all waiting on *Songbird* for him.

"Why me?" He was thinking of Viera, and Byn, when he said it.

"Farson says that you are unique and your perspective is going to be needed."

"Where are we going?"

<<*Voul, where we are taking* Songbird *is something you don't want to miss.*>>

Farson's thought was soothing to Voul. His friend. His leader. He nodded to Brittany, took her hand in affection for a moment, and set off for the hangar. As he walked, he could feel the engines building and he knew he was walking in the same direction that Sargasso was now heading. He wondered how many thousands of miles were passing with each step.

When Voul arrived, he noticed changes on *Songbird*. Farson confirmed that the Emers had upgraded her again. Voul also noticed there were two other passengers aboard: a young woman and a robot he immediately recognized as CT<<Dinsil2371. "CT," he said, "I thought you were dead."

"The report of my demise was premature."

"Good to hear." He then took another look at the young woman. He recognized her as ID>>Karo28689, or "Ida," as she liked to be called from the Thanksgiving party. "Hi, Ida. You're coming too?"

"You could say that." She looked at Farson, who added a comment.

"Voul, the truth is, we are coming with her."

Karina was thinking about her parents. Perhaps it was just that Farson was away again, but she couldn't help that her feeling of coming loneliness drew her back into her memories. She had found that, when things were tough, she often regressed to a safer time.

She was remembering when her parents decided to have a baby. It was more like, in their love, a little door had opened, and they walked right in. Her father's fear of being in a deep relationship, of his failures in the past, of his love for her mother, all combined in a wave of acceptance and intuition that she had never experienced before. The elevation protocol had given Karina such a deep understanding of her own life that the lives and deaths of her parents were now perfectly clear to her.

Looking forward, she could not see as clearly as Farson; she even doubted that his vision of the future was as clear as he liked to believe. But now looking back, and reliving moments as she chose, she did understood. Her mother had told her father, in those early days, not to worry. All would be well. Karina knew that something had just "clicked" in her mother and from that moment on, doubt, and uncertainty were things of the past. *Will I ever have such clarity?* That moment in her parents' lives when they realized that having a baby was natural for them, something they both really wanted, a joining of purpose and dreams that swept aside the fear of commitment and doubt about the future had occurred simultaneously for them both.

In her parents' happiness, Karina always found comfort and support.

She looked across the room of her new home on the Butte to see Valgary and Felicity in conversation. It was a quiet, obviously deep conversation. Suddenly, they both laughed out loud and looked at her. "What are you two laughing about?" They looked at each other, giggling. Felicity spoke first.

"We know where Sargasso is going, Mommy." Karina had been thinking that they were planning a party, or something to get Farson to return sooner, or maybe working up a special request for a trip to the Moon or something for dinner. She knew that her daughters were only twelve now, but that they were also a lot more than just twelve.

"How do you know that?" They laughed and giggled and ran over to her, crowding onto the sofa with her. Their hands were in hers.

"They just told us."

"Who?"

Ida was wearing the same outfit she had worn at the dinner party, including her bag.

Voul realized that the clothes were not really clothes and the woman was really a robot. *Or is it the other way around?* With that thought, he saw her looking directly at him. Her thought was clear and concise. <<*Which way do you think it is, Voul?*>> His mental response was unstoppable, and she, of course, heard it. She smiled. He knew he had gotten it right. He continued looking at her. She was young, maybe twenty-three or four. She was stylish and pretty, but in a wholesome way, not flashy or overdone. Her hair was blonde and a little mussed up. Voul liked her. He had never seen her in her robot form, but assumed she would look a lot like the others. CT<<Dinsil2371 was monitoring the exchange, and his strobing seemed to be focused on Voul, who sensed the older robot was not in agreement with Voul's last thought. Farson began to speak again.

"Well, now that introductions are out of the way, we are ready to go. Ida, would you like to brief the crew?" She moved to the center of *Songbird's* bridge. Uva was watching her like a hawk. A young woman, with a custom handbag, was going to tell them about things unknown. Uva, who was never pleased not knowing everything, seemed impatient, waiting to hear.

"You are going to precede Emerald Earth on this journey. You will be what the old militarists called 'the point.' The plan is to get as far out in front as possible, in the time allowed. The Emers' upgrade of this ship will get you to the planned position well ahead of the planet. In the meantime, there is much to discuss and prepare." Voul had a question. But Uva beat him to it.

"Position? What does that mean?" Ida sat down, facing them all. When she spoke, it was a soft mental touch and came with all of the images and enhancements they had witnessed in previous discussions with her, but this time, it was remarkably different. They first noticed the change when she asked CT<<Dinsil2371 to assist. As they listened, they

appreciated not only how powerful she was, but also that it was CT<<Dinsil2371's augmentations that lifted their understanding to new levels. She began to tell the story.

<<We are the ScreenKeepers. We have done what we do for eons and eons. We keep The Screen. That is our only purpose. Each of us came to this role in a different way, but mine was painful and cruel and sad. All robots have a story, but mine was of the prejudice, cruelty, and ignorance of my own family. We are all chosen for the role of ScreenKeeper, not as a promotion or as an honor; no, it is not those. It is offered as an alternative. We all had free choice in this, and whichever way we choose, it is irreversible. So, the ScreenKeepers you know and the innumerable ones you do not know are all prisoners in a way. Our assignment is never-ending and all-engrossing. The challenges are many, as the three of you well know. It is an honor to be here with you. You see CT<<Dinsil2371 standing there like a statue, but I assure you he is not. His story is one of the richest in our history. He stands alone with me. In truth; he stands beside me.>>

Ida looked over at CT<<Dinsil2371, and he knew she wanted him to come and stand with her. He remained still in the corner of the room. She returned to her story.

<<There are dreams that I have had concerning the events to come. Not dreams from last night, or last week, or last year, but dreams of thousands and thousands of years. These are not dreams like a child wanting to grow up. These are deep truths full of imagination and desire. These are perceptions of things that must happen. Aspirations that must succeed.

<<Your mission is to go into those dreams and discover where they lead. It is a leap into the unknown. A leap of faith as the faithful Skers have it. It is, as the old Earthers called it, an adventure.>>

485

Uva was sitting in the pilot's chair and the moment that Ida's story ended she backed *Songbird* out of her berth in Ichor's dock and positioned the ship in the middle of the hangar. There was a flash of purple and gold. The next thing the crew knew, they were in the black of space watching Emerald Earth fly by as *Songbird* accelerated into what appeared to be a rainbow of colors bending away ahead of them. Uva was laughing out loud as she said, "That was unbelievable," her hands still on the helm, her eyes dead ahead. "Let's go!"

And then all was quiet as infinity engulfed them.

Ida and the robot were gone.

102. Of This There Will Be No End

Ida Marie Rothschild looked around the room. It was the room they had let her use. She was in Paris. It was 1904. She was staying with her grandparents. It had been a hard time for her. Her youngest daughter, Esther, was with her, age four. Ida herself was only twenty, born in 1884 in the city of New York. She felt a tug on her hand. Esther wanted to get going. "Grammy said we could have a cookie." But Ida knew that things had gone too far for that. She had made the long voyage to Paris from New York, where her parents had refused to help her and Esther. Her father was adamant that she was dead to him. She had fled back to New York after four disastrous years in Oregon, where she had run away to avoid an arranged marriage at the age of fourteen. Her oldest daughter, Ida Katherine, was waiting for her return in a Catholic orphanage in Medford, Oregon. Ida knew now that her life was a house of imaginary cards collapsing all around her. She couldn't go home. She couldn't go back to Grants Pass where that ignorant brute bastard was waiting. She couldn't stay here in Paris as her grandparents had just confirmed. They would not make a such an irrevocable break with their son in New York.

Ida knew this was the end of the line. She took Esther downstairs. The kitchen staff was starting to prepare the late evening meal. "Tell my grandmother that I am going to bed early." Then she turned to her daughter. She bent down and took her in her arms and kissed her. "Ester, you be a good girl. Everything is going to be okay."

Ida returned to the room and sat on a single straight back chair in the middle of the room. A chandelier with dim lights was overhead. Ida sat there for almost an hour, thinking, as the sun set slowly.

Ester had enjoyed the cookie and was being tucked into bed by her great-grandmother.

He found her in the bow of *Songbird*. *<<Ida. What are you doing?>>* In her robot form, she stood up to her fullest height of a little more than eight feet. Her silver and blue metal body moved so easily, so smoothly. Her strobing was calm, as though resting. Her hands and arms hung at her side.

<<Just dreaming.>>

<<Dreaming? I would not have thought that was in your nature, Ida.>>

<<You might be surprised, Farson. I haven't lived all these years without having dreams. Who has?>> Farson considered that question. They were in the forwardmost compartment on *Songbird* where Uva had once stowed away. Ida just had returned to *Songbird* again after weeks of absence. It had become their meeting place. *Who has indeed? <<All of this could still happen to you, you know, Farson. You think you are immune, but life has a way of crushing us like bugs. Sometimes it seems as if there's nothing we can do.>>*

<<But rethinking that day over and over can do you no good. It's like a million years ago. Look at how far we've come, Ida.>> He stood beside her. Next to her robot self, he always felt

small. Next to her human self, he always felt inadequate. *I can't win with her. She is too much, too powerful, too wonderful, too everything.* She was looking at him.

<<*It is true, Farson. Nothing should be taken away from what we have done. But, for me, all is consequence and temporary. Nothing is forever. I fear the success. I fear the consensus. I fear the happiness. To me it is all preamble to disaster coming. I can't help myself. I see what I see.*>>

<<*You know I have seen it all as well?*>>

<<*You may have seen more than me, Farson.*>>

<<*If I tell you everything is going to be okay, will you believe me?*>>

<<*No.*>>

<<*You will persist in your unfounded pessimism?*>>

<<*Yes. And 'unfounded' is entirely inaccurate, as you know. We are still what we are. How different are we really, Farson?*>> He looked up at her. He momentarily felt like it was Sam who was standing there and would turn in a minute and tell him to go get his fishing rod. *Those were the days.* She looked at him.

<<*You see. You long for the past too, Farson, just as I do. We are not so different. The past is always with us.*>>

<<*There is one thing that is different between you and me, Ida.*>>

<<*And that is?*>>

<<*And that is … that I know that what we are doing now is forever. What we are considering is eternal. Look at all the years gone by even now. Look at all the lives saved, and now lived, far beyond what they had any right to expect. Look at Emerald Earth. Its truth is only now becoming known. Look at all that is happening. We are on a path, Ida. The very path you and the others have always wanted. All is proceeding as planned.*>>

Her strobing had slowed. Its purple hue was rich with tones. She changed her form back to the twenty-four-year-old Ida, dressed stylishly, with a rakish hairdo. She bent over and picked up her leather bag, rummaging around until she found her mirror and lipstick. She applied it perfectly and attractively, snapped the mirror shut, and dropped everything back into the bag. Farson noticed how nice she looked. He had no preference for her presentation; both fascinated him. *I could hug her in this form. The big robot, probably not.*

"So what are you saying, Farson?" The audible verbal selection fit perfectly with her changed form. He followed suit.

"I am saying," he paused for effect, "that we will see this through together, to the end." She looked at him. She thought of the room in Paris. She took a big breath and sighed it out, struggling inside to find the right words. It was time to stop these senseless discussions of time passed and get to work. But she did love Farson and even if she did not always understand him, she had grown to trust him. She thought of one more thing to say.

"Sometimes," she was speaking as she walked to the door, beyond which was the mission, the future, and the dreams of mankind. She stopped and looked back. "Things are what they are."

Farson could feel *Songbird's* engines reaching maximum. He could imagine the little ship streaking through space toward its destination. He could sense the strength of Emerald Earth coming up behind. He could imagine the vibration of Ichor as it reached its greatest power, pushing Sargasso after them. He was thinking of the dreams she had mentioned. A song came to him that he could not resist the urge to encouragingly sing to her.

"When you wish upon a star…" She didn't even let him finish the phrase. With a relieving laugh and without hesitation, her melancholy set aside, she joined him in the song's final verse, her perfect voice beautifully rising with his to a harmonic finish together.

"Your … dreams … come … true."

Then she was gone.

Farson wished she would come back and they could sing the whole song together again.

103. A Poem For the Others

STRUGGLE UNIVERSAL
by Farson Uiost

Getting ready for better things to come
Is the heart and soul of life.
The cleansing of things
From daily clothes to life itself,
Is part of us like breathing in and out.

To know how to separate
The horrible from the beautiful,
The foolish from the wise,
The petty from the forgiving
Is life's struggle universal.

The cleansing of the corruption
In our intentions, our motives;
Clearing antonymistic defilements
That turn our good into our bad
Our wholesome into our whoresome
Sanctifies life.

Not success but effort toward success
Is the only security we have.
As long as we try to be
It will always be possible to be.
This guards the lover, the poet,
The dreamer, the friend.
It makes a day something
We never want to end.

This makes a life worth living:
And friendship worth giving.

<< *The end.* >>

FRONT AND BACK MATTER
with appendices

Complete Works
Table of Contents
Diagrams
Chronology
Dramatis Personae
Glossary
Poems
Sequel Preview
"About the Author"

COMPLETE WORKS
W. MAHLON PURDIN
PUBLISHED AND UNPUBLISHED

**TABLE OF
CONTENTS**

The ScreenMasters
Farson Uiost [yüst], of Earth
Karina Chamberlain, his sister
Uvo and Uva, of Aristealia
Handy Townsend, of The Screen and the planet Oran

MoonBase
Viera Nichols, Base Commander
Byn Jonsn, her daughter
Master Sergeant Long John Hanson Silver, second-in-command
Sergeant Benjamin Franklin Smith, third-in-command
Thomas and Brianna

SkyKing
James Peterson, Station Commander
Brittany Peterson, his daughter
Lieutenant Gerald Antonoff, third-in-command

The Skers [skī-erz]
Voul [vôl] Jonsn, Sker leader, and second-in-command of SkyKing
Midshipman Repoul Bensn, a trusted Sker theorist and Voul's assistant
Prms Bensn, Repoul's son
Ban Jonsn, Voul's father, founder of the Sker nation

The Robots
ZZ<<Arkol25609, a ScreenKeeper
CT<<Dinsil2371, an ancient ScreenKeeper
ID>>Karo28689, a ScreenKeeper

Emerald Earth

John Andrew McKinley Sortt, the first and last president
of the United States of Earth

Strapper John Jordan, an Emer farmhand and friend of
Handy's

Ian Jordan, Strapper's son

Valgary and Felicity Uiost, Farson's and Karina's daughters
Belnad Goethe, effective head of the Emer Council

Emerald Earth's population

The Essors

Twill, Grand ScreenMaster, addressed as "Master Twill"

Panau t'ul'Dak, a data technician and a commander in the
Essor Navy

Shals t'Bu, a lieutenant commander in the Essor navy

Old Earth

Tom Jacobson and Catherine Peters, Karina's parents

David and Mary Uiost, Farson's parents

William and Mary Chamberlain, Farson's and Karina's
adoptive parents

Hattie and Sam, worked for the Chamberlains

Joan Peterson, Jim's deceased wife and Brittany's mom

Chronology
———————— A.D. ————————

1884   Ida Rothschild born, July 27
1904   Ida Rothschild dies at age twenty
1945   Nagasaki is bombed, August 9, 1:02 a.m.
1957   Ban Jonsn born, December 25
1991   First crude hints of The Screen are
       detected by scientists and reported in
       The New York Times, February 25
2010   SkyKing first goes crudely operational
2014   MoonBase settlement is planned
2020   Moon permanently settled
2039   James Peterson born, August 19
2044   Joan Peterson born, July 27
2047   Gerald Antonoff born, January 1
2063   Farson born, February 4, and Mary Uiost dies, David
       Uiost dies two days later
2064   Voul Jonsn born on SkyKing, June 3
2064   Karina born, July 31
2070   Tom and Catherine Peters assigned to SkyKing
2071   Karina's parents killed on SkyKing, February 15
       Farson (almost eight) and Karina (nearing seven)
       meet for the first time, March 3
2075   James Peterson moves to SkyKing as
       third-in-command
       Ban Jonsn dies, March 12
2076   Brittany Peterson born on SkyKing, February 14
2080   Laso-Nuclear Exchanges end
2082   Joan Peterson dies, May 17
2084   Jim Peterson becomes commander of SkyKing
2088   Andrew Sortt elected president of the USE

2091	ScreenMasters arrive, January 15
	Earth is placed in stasis, March 30
	Twill's Grand Ascendancy
2094	Voul and Viera marry
	Handy notices a fluctuation in the ScreenLock
2095	MoonKing exodus underway
	The Mending
2099	Felicity and Valgary Uiost born, February 4, 12:01 to 12:09 a.m.
2104	Exploration plans for Sargasso are begun
	The Emer ScreenMasters end their stasis evolution
	Byn Jonsn born, August 1. Prms Bensn turns three
2105	The Emerald ScreenMasters visit MoonKing
	Brittany goes to Emerald Earth
2107	The Secrets of Sargasso revealed

——————————————— E.E. -----------------------------------

6002	Handy notices a fluctuation in the ScreenLock
6485	Ian Jordan born, January 2
6505	The Culling
6505	Farson and Karina marry, June 27
6506	Felicity and Valgary, born February 5
6507	Emerald Earth completes its Ascension
6517	Sargasso mission monitoring begins
6518	Belnad Goethe arrives on SkyKing
	Brittany Peterson goes to Emerald Earth

Glossary

ChainFoods. Catherine Peters Jacobson's discovery. A formulation of elemental molecular components to create foods of such revolutionary quality in unlimited quantities, that changed the human diet, much for the better.

EarthStasis. The ScreenMasters' plan to solve the problem.

E.E. This is a time designation, like A.D. and B.C. in other eras. It means Emerald Earth and denotes the actual date for the inhabitants of Earth including the years in stasis while in captivity. There was a period when some historians referred to denoted years followed by the AF designation, which, of course, means "After Farson," but he adamantly insisted that this be dropped, and it was. It only appears in some of the now-ancient and sacred Sker documents from those days. E.E. has been universally adopted throughout The Screen out of respect for the people who lived and evolved on that planet and who emerged on 6505 E.E. after over 4,000 years of imprisonment.

E-Lasers. Erasure pulses created to clean and protect satellites in space that later evolved into highly destructive weapons, and later gave birth to the transporter technology.

Emerald Earth. The renamed planet Earth, after a long transition, totally devoted to agriculture, arts, education, and certain forms of entertainment. Known everywhere for its good food, clean atmosphere, and water, it is now peaceful, a very natural setting, and easily hosts the extremely generous export system it developed for sharing its bounty. The only social organization on Emerald Earth is that of families. People come to Emerald Earth in tribute and on pilgrimages. John Andrew McKinley Sortt is still its leader.

Emerald ScreenMasters. Residents of Emerald Earth.

Farson Uiost. Born, 2063 A.D., elevated to ScreenMaster, 2091 A.D., age 28.

FirstLevel ScreenMaster. Perhaps the easiest to attain, this ScreenMaster level involves solving a current, somewhat minor problem affecting The Screen.

GateWay. A transfer opening to higher and higher Screen levels achieved by traversing layers of The Screen.

Laso-Nuclear Exchanges. From 2077 to 2080, they disrupted all societies, especially the United States.

The Mending. Farson's original plan to reunite Earth, SkyKing, and MoonBase as independent entities, but also it became the name Twill used for his planned Ascension to supremacy among the ScreenMasters.

Phanta. A Screen phenomena that only the highest-level ScreenMasters have ever seen, and one that only Farson understood.

Right of Privacy. The cherished Sker postulate of organization, which allowed each individual to live as he or she sees fit within the one rule of "Do no harm." The Skers consider it the absolute guarantee of the rights of religious freedom, and freedom from prejudice.

ScreenBurn. The period of time after a repair is made and before the repair completes itself. Like a healing period. It is a period of strength because great things are happening. It is also a period of exposure because things are changing, but not yet complete.

ScreenChange. The change of an aboriginal being into a ScreenMaster. This change is not always successful or completed.

ScreenDeclension. A system where the overall control of The Screen is redivided among a new number of ScreenMasters. Previous to Farson this always meant there had been a reduction in the number of ScreenMasters. After Farson Uiost, and what came later, it sometimes was the opposite.

ScreenGlow. Another reference to a ScreenMaster's ScreenLite. Usually lingering after departure.

ScreenGrid. The fundamental element of The Screen.

ScreenKeepers. The robots who generally accompany some ScreenMasters in their travels. The origin of the ScreenKeepers, until Farson, was unknown and unquestioned. They just were. After Farson, it was a different matter altogether. They are highly intelligent, can alter their appearance and height, are telepathic, and possess many attributes of ScreenMasters themselves.

ScreenLayers. Groups of 100 levels.

ScreenLink. A conjoining with The Screen for travel and other things. Many ScreenMasters find the ScreenLink is a refuge.

ScreenLite. A purple hue that surrounds a ScreenMaster when he or she is activating his or her Screen powers.

ScreenLock. In conjunction with the Earth stasis field, The Screen concentrated around the planet and created a time lock in which the planet's time altered while space around it remained unchanged. The removal of a lock was thought possible. The Earth's ScreenLock cycle was occasionally visible from the planet it surrounded.

ScreenMaster. Master of The Screen, able to harness and direct its power through time, existence, dimension, and space, without limit, although ScreenMasters themselves vary in the depth and reach of these abilities.

ScreenMend. The procedure that results in upgrading a ScreenPatch to a full, seamless repair of The Screen. Highly technical, and very unusual, in ScreenMaster terms, and accomplished only by the most advanced ScreenMasters, and even then success was never guaranteed.

ScreenMoiré. A pattern discovered at Level9.96 that implied a way to slew a ScreenMaster's passage.

ScreenPassage. A ScreenMaster's movement on The Screen.

ScreenPatch. A temporary solution to a ScreenRent.

ScreenRent. A cascading syndrome of destruction that begins with a small "rip" or "tear" and, if allowed to continue, eventually causes fragmentation (tearing) in The Screen and can threaten its existence.

ScreenTear. The catastrophic effect of an unrepaired ScreenRent.

ScreenTime. Roughly 10,000 years to one Earth year.

ScreenTransit. The action of traveling on The Screen by a ScreenMaster.

ScreenTruth. Fabled among ScreenMasters, the word of The Screen itself.

ScreenWeb. A ScreenMaster's individual aspect that moves with him through the fabric of The Screen. Highly individual in size and characteristics. In many ways a ScreenMaster's Web is his defining signature.

Star>Day. Approximately 24 light-years.

TrueScreen. Farson's discovery.

VentSyndrome. The final destruction of a ScreenSegment in which a ScreenTear becomes an unpatchable ScreenRip, and the substance of The Screen begins to vent as the grids dissipate. This syndrome is theorized to start a cascading of ScreenGrids that eventually will destroy everything. The theory also holds that this situation, although never seen or recorded, must never be allowed to happen. To the ScreenMaster the VentSyndrome is Armageddon.

Poems

QUIESCENCE AND CONSEQUENCE
by Farson Uiost

Each morning I go outside and
   peer
Into the dark soil of my
   gardens.
Watching for those tulips to
   emerge.
Each morning I think of you,
Each morning I think of life,
Each morning I think of things
Rebuilding and teeming
For a new season of growth
And surprising beauty that
emerges,
Not just with the bud and
   flower,
But with time and things
   being.
Not just becoming.

It isn't just the flower of spring,
And the flagrance of beauty on
   which
We feast; it is also the time
That passes, the things that
change,
The season of abscission and
   recharge,
The long winter of quiescence
And consequence when so
many things
Are determined with little
   outward change;
And then there I am, back
staring
Down into the dark soil,

My eyes searching for the little
   hopeful
Sprouts scratching up for the
   warmth
And root-filling nutrient
Of a new season, another year
Of being.

Yesterday I saw one clawing its
   way
Through two inches of solid
   ice:
Its little green tip poking
   through
Just now touching its goal.
It was easy to imagine its
Relief after wondering how
long,
How far do I have to go?
Can I do it?
I must.

In a few weeks, that little
   ice-covered
Fuse-splinter will explode
Into one of nature's
Greatest beauties, full of high
Red and green and amazing
   from
Its hardscrabble beginnings.

How little we know
Of what we truly are
Becoming.

STAY RIGHT HERE
by Farson Uiost

I wonder sometimes if I'm so isolated
That I lose out experientially.
I mean those camels, those pyramids,
That Eiffel Tower, that Lenin's Tomb.
But then I watch you falling asleep
On the couch and think of the days just past
Driving, measuring, moving furniture,
Hanging curtains, painting touch-ups,
Going out for pizza (not for me)
Talking with our daughters all day
Thinking of what my day was like,
I doubt it.
It might be nice, but in an odd Thoreauvian way
I think it might be distractive. So many new
Things to factor there than here, in fact,
Here I can concentrate on things.
Plus I do get out and about, six states,
Ten towns, shopping at the supermarket,
I average around 11,000 miles a year
Just around here. I know a lot of people,
Which makes life fun, and I still have long, long
Periods of working alone, singing alone, and
Writing alone to satisfy the soul.
So going to Fallujah or to Vietnam,
Maybe taking one of those river cruises
Down the Bassac, or back to Australia sometime;
Are thoughts I have and have again.
But when one is happy where one is
It means something.
And I'm going to stay right here
Until I figure that out.

I WANNA BE YOU (#4)
by Farson Uiost

Your gray hair and mild eyes
Whisper of a lifetime perhaps,
Full of rich memories and battles fought,
Some lost. This has time-woven
A memory quilt that you can pull over you
As you stand there looking at me.

There are patches that clearly show
Quick repair and stitches
That could have been better.
It really looks a little too small from here.
Perhaps it's still unfinished.
I'm sitting in the ambient
Reality of the room, but you?
You have that blanket. You can throw it off
And use it as a pillow when it's warm.
You can use it, as now you do, to stave
Off the cold that's coming.
It's a shield you've earned, I think.

Your gray hair and mild eyes;
Were you always so peacefully blended?
Or did your hair once blow long in
The winds of youth and recklessness?
Did your eyes once have that talon-thrusting
Intensity that drove profit charts and
Other people crazy? Did some of those
Patches come with blood, smoke, and flames?
Were some torn out of other lives with tears?
You seem to be hiding some underneath, or
Maybe protecting them?

When it's your turn to speak
You often let it pass, unspeaking.
Let others burn their bridges, do you think that?
Or do you just listen in now, like an aficionado

506

At a symphony who hears all the nuances and
Subtleties of vibrations and techniques and knows
Exactly what the composer intended even with
Your eyes closed and your hands folded
Softly – untensed now – those clenches gone forever?

Or are you in there, behind all of this, scared of
The coming inexorability? Worried about all that
You have done? Regretful of so many things past?
Are you in there, tremulous with pain,
Worried of being called out, starring in your own
Tragedy, now alone, driven back onto
Yourself and your undeniable memories,
Your lack of glory and lack of courage,
Assignations of doubt and no way out?
Sitting here like a self-imposed prisoner are you
Wishing to God you were somewhere else?
Somewhere young and free again?

It's like looking into one of those mirror-on-mirror
Rooms where the images telescope away repeating,
Ever smaller but never disappearing, sort of
Bending off into eternity: me looking at you
You looking at me.
Your gray hair and mild eyes, and mine
Seem to blend together into a long, tapering
Spear thrusting into our mirror
As far as our eyes can see.

I want to be you.
Do you want to be me?

"Let America Be America Again"
by Handy Townsend

Let America be America again.
Let it be the dream it used to be.
Let it be the pioneer on the plain:
A home where we roam free.

(America never was America to me.)

Let America be the dream the dreamers dream.
Let it be that great strong land of love,
Where no kings connive nor tyrants scheme:
Where no man is crushed from above.

(America never was America to me.)

"You Struggle, As Though Wrapped"
by Farson Uiost

You struggle, as though wrapped
And being squeezed, life out, no hope
Twisting to be free, nowhere to go
Hopeless beyond saying it, lost in utterness
Alone, in darkness, descending, so, so low.

I know. Once so deep in me, I caved.
So cold in that dark place, I came
Close to the tip of things, nothing
Beneath, nothing above, just me
And the tip of the iceberg, the tunnel
With no light.

There on that balanceless point, I teetered
Like a bottle cap spinning, eternal-less
Empty of reason, discarded, to be forgotten
Useless now, less than ever even imagined,
Even dizzy-less, still spinning, knowing
Not even obliviousness was given to me.

Forced to witness my own torture
Pain never became pleasure as they say
Agony, full throated, was mine as long
As I chose. No filter, no dampening
It was pure, delivered with intent by
An enemy all mine. All mine.

I wish I could free you, but I know too much.
There is only one way out and it's through.
Takes your doing, not some lover's touch.
If you make it, I'll be waiting for you.

THE OTHERS
by Farson Uiost

They still mystify us.
They still make us happy.
They still make us wonder.
They still make us crazy.

They make us question, doubt, and hide.
They leave us filled, empty, shaken, stirred.

They burst into our lives and destroyed everything.
They burst into our lives and renewed everything.
They burst into our lives, set bombs, and ran.
They burst into our lives and took away the pain.

They were kind to us when we were young.
They scarred us as we grew.
They took our hand and said, "Don't worry."
"Things get better all the time."

They helped us up and down.
They threatened to condemn us.
They washed our hands and our feet.
How did we deserve such love?

They all are still marching beside us:
From young to old to dead.
We watch and listen and wonder
At all they did and all they said.

DEAD WORLD DANCING
by Farson Uiost

Half of the people who ever lived are still alive.
There's no escaping that everyone dies.
Despite our dreams and our cries,
It's a crazy mystic shuck and jive.

Can't remember your own birth.
Can't imagine your own death.
It's a deep, slow cleansing breath.
Take it for what it's worth.

Living is an art ill applied,
But it's all we've got.
From a barrel like blasting shot
It scatters us far and wide.

There is no just turning back,
No time when things were better,
From the homeless to a jet-setter,
In a mansion or a hapless shack.

And who can dispute such clarity?
"All that, that is, is," he said.
Like all, who were, were ... he's dead.
Like us, who have, have ... charity.

In this dead world dancing ... there's no winners.
Whatever lies beyond, lies beyond, we can't go.
Though one returned they say, we'll never know.
It's a world of dreamers: dazed, worn-out sinners.

He forgave me everything. Oh how I loved him.
She taught me so, so much. Oh how I should have told her.
We were friends forever. Oh how I miss you.
So many things left unsaid. Oh how I could have said them.

Imagine.

Half of the people who ever lived are still alive.

There's no escaping that everyone dies.
Despite our dreams and our cries,
It's a crazy mystic shuck and jive.

Remember, whatever we did and tried,
Half of the people who ever lived ...
... have never died.

STRUGGLE UNIVERSAL
by Farson Uiost

Getting ready for better things to come
Is the heart and soul of life.
The cleansing of things
From daily clothes to life itself,
Is part of us like breathing in and out.

To know how to separate
The horrible from the beautiful,
The foolish from the wise,
The petty from the forgiving
Is life's struggle universal.

The cleansing of the corruption
In our intentions, our motives;
Clearing antonymistic defilements
That turn our good into our bad
Our wholesome into our whoresome
Sanctifies life.

Not success but effort toward success
Is the only security we have.
As long as we try to be
It will always be possible to be.
This guards the lover, the poet,
The dreamer, the friend.
It makes a day something
To celebrate not vacate.

This makes a life worth living:
Friendship worth giving.

Illustrations

SkyKing

2017

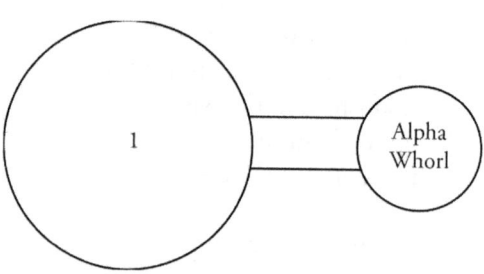

2020

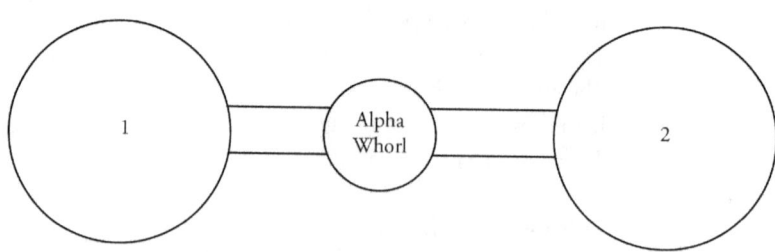

2044

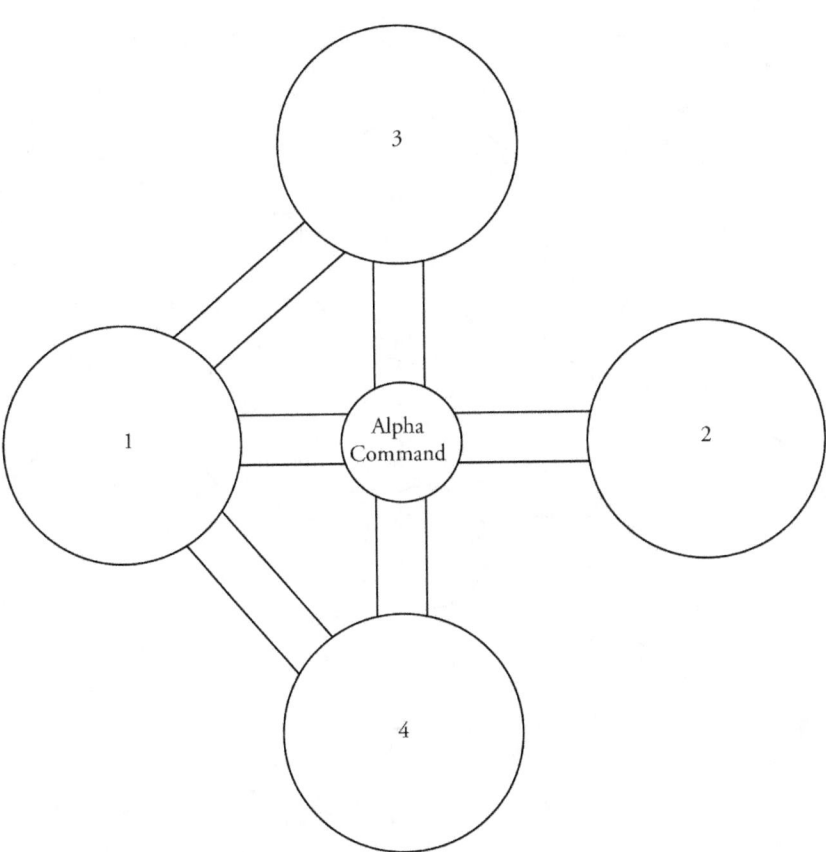

2094

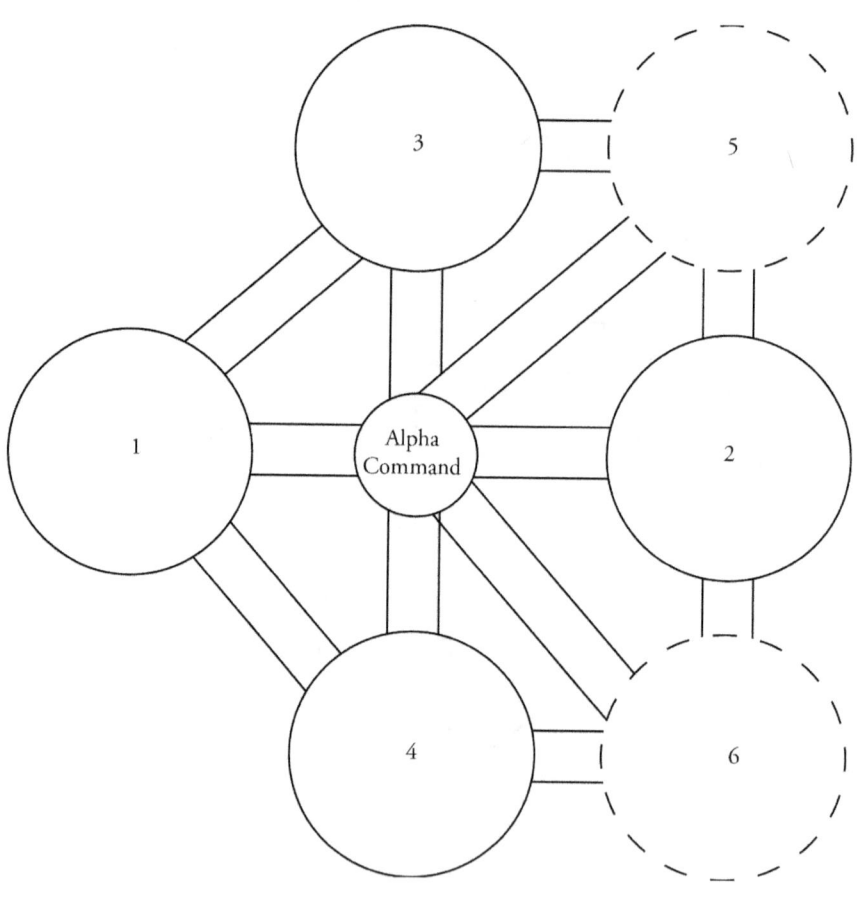

2120

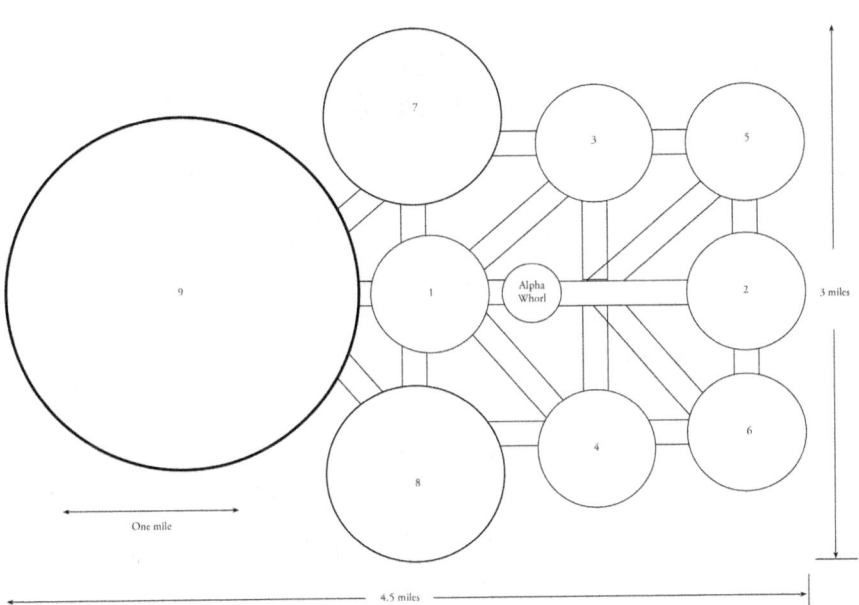

Statistics:

Overall
dimensions: 4.5 miles long, 3 miles wide
               13.5 square miles (footprint)
Capacity: 1,000,000
Whorls:
Alpha: .394 of a mile in diameter. Maximum capacity.
               1,500 people with command equipment
1-6: .667 of a mile in diameter, maximum capacity
               roughly 50,000 people per whorl, total 300,000
7/8: One mile in diameter, 125,000 ideal capacity each,
               total 250,000
9: Two miles in diameter, 450,000 maximum capacity,
               volume= 4.19 m^3
NOTE: SkyLake is on WhorlTwo

2120
Side View

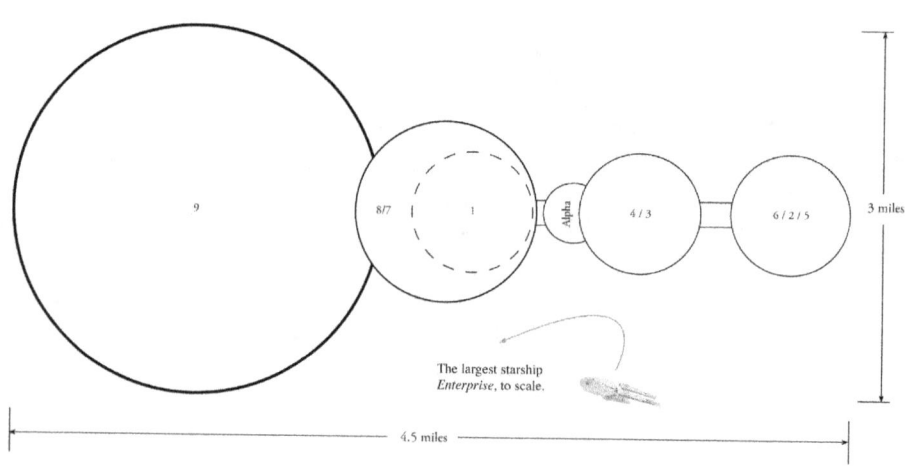

The largest starship *Enterprise*, to scale.

Sequel Preview

W. MAHLON
PURDIN

The
Dreams
of
Ida
Rothschild

THE
SCREENMASTERS
VOLUME THREE

AUTHOR'S NOTE

There are lives that are wasted; we all know that. They can be seen in the depths of self-pity and in the violence of aggression. They can be seen in the hunger of scarcity and the avarice of wealth. They can be seen in the horror of loneliness. They can be seen on the painful rack of history. They can be seen in the granular anonymities of life itself.

Some lives are unnoticed even in their squander.

But some of these shine back at us in ways unforetold in their demise. Some cannot be forgotten. Perhaps it is their innocence that prevails; perhaps it is their humility that rises; perhaps it was their promise that compels us to remember. Sometimes it is the very pain of their undeserved fate that drives immortality.

Whatever it is, sometimes a story cries out across the ages; soft whimpers of dreams overridden, hopes that never die, of a fire so strong, it cannot and it will not be extinguished.

Sometimes the truth comes out.

BOOK I
The Beginning

"Hold fast to dreams,
For if dreams die,
Life is a broken-winged bird,
That cannot fly."

– *Langston Hughes*

Chapter One
Ida Marie Rothschild

1. Still Just a Little Girl

The room was darkening. Amber light eked in through a small, curtained window like a dimming flashlight searching. There was a creaking sound, a straining of things long held in the balance, now finally yielding to one way or the other: a moving of events, a slowly decreasing momentum, soon unstoppable.

As the light crossed the room, it revealed a body suspended from a rope, tied to a small, softly chiming ornate glass chandelier, swinging back and forth, ever slowing, soon to be still, over the polished oak and spruce parquet of the floor beneath. Waning sounds of choking could still be heard. Gasping sputum fell onto the grains of wood as the fading life passed back and forth. The shadows of the fallen chair beneath the body, cast stark lines and skewed angles, in the failing light, like a crude message being written, but never finished.

Years earlier, in the spring of 1897, she was reluctantly approaching her fourteenth birthday, still just a little girl. Her morning had been, as usual, a fun time: breakfast, dressing, planning her day, looking in her bedroom mirror, and seeing herself growing up. She stood still in front of her reflection for a moment. She was barefooted and dressed in a long, flowing skirt with subtle patterning of black and green, and a white embroidered top with frilly sleeves and gathered cloth at her throat. She wore a halter over her blouse, with thin shoulder straps, that tightly covered her chest, demurely diminishing any sign of maturity approaching. Her hair was held neatly, but not completely, in long braids that cascaded past her shoulders. There were little wisps of hair that seemed to be reaching out and up through the twists and turning weaves of the light brown strands, as though longing to be free. She looked at her face, scrunching up her lips in disapproval. She had seen her beautiful mother for so long. The comparison with the awkward little girl's visage in the mirror made her impatient and unhappy as though, captured in this child's form, her inner woman was now just waiting to take charge. She turned in a burst of restlessness and ran out of her room into the corridor beyond.

"And just *where* do you think you're going?" Her mother stood in the hallway, between her and the beautiful curved, polished stairway that led to the front hall and then to the front door itself. Beyond that door was the curved brick walkway that snaked through the trees and manicured shrubs of the front yard and then on around the house to her wonderful, happy secret realm: the backyard. The backyard where she could run and play and hide and seek and build and tear down, laugh and cry, and where, most of all, more than anything else, above all other things, she could be herself.

Today was a beautiful sunny, blue-sky day, and she wanted to enjoy it. At the sound of her mother's voice she had slowed down, then stopped, and brightly shined her smile.

"Out to the backyard," she said. "It's a beautiful day." She sadly realized that her carefully crafted smile was not having the desired effect. Her mother was unmoved.

"Really?" Even the sound of her mother's voice when angry or sarcastic or annoyed or questioning was always pleasant to her. She found herself trying to speak like her mother: a lower tone, a deeper intelligence, a soothing source of reason. Ida was thinking how much like her mother she would like to be. "Have you forgotten what today is?" There is no way she had forgotten. The shadchan. Today was the day of his visit. Ida's worst nightmare.

ID>>Karo28689 was in the deep, deep of The Screen; out where it reached its limits, thinning into the vast stretches of space; out beyond the known into where the final gridframe segment edges were incomplete as though still evolving, or perhaps cut off. She was at the extreme boundary of "beyond The Screen." She was concentrating with intent.

The profound solitude of The Screen in this area, and her own undivided focus to the matter at hand, was creating a vortex. She was actually bending The Screen itself, funneling its power into a point of intensive pulsation. It appeared now almost as if she were holding a weapon poised for discharge. Then, suddenly, The Screen around her contorted and turned to a molten red. A short, thin beam propelled itself away from her like a laser pointer, and then a wide bolt of bright purple and yellow light followed, rifling from the end with an enormous flash and disappeared off into the distance. She watched as it vanished into infinity, and then, when the deviation in The Screen that she had caused began returning to its tranquil normality, she relaxed.

ID>>Karo28689 stood up, her visor strobing a bright scanning white from side to side; her eyes beneath, unseen, were serene with the effort. She stood up, stretched her body as though waking, and then disappeared.

The Screen seemed to ripple and then smooth out. The redness was fading back into itself like a spot drying out, or a wave receding. Just before it disappeared, when no one could possibly see, a brief band of very light purple seemed to be there and then was gone.

<<*Did you see that,* <<*ZZ*<<*Arkol25609?*>>
<<*Of course.*>> It was CT<<Dinsil2371. <<*Who knew she could do that?*>>
<<*Did you notice where she aimed it?*>> There was a silence. A few minutes passed. CT<<Dinsil2371 slowly realized what the other robot meant.
<<*Yes, I did.*>> His comment was matter-of-fact, decisive, and the long pause had its effect. Now he had a question of his own. <<*But, why?*>>

Whenever she spoke to the robots, her "voice" was always clear as a bell tolling for heroes. ID>>Karo28689 spoke clearly, but many times it took the other ScreenKeepers a while to fully understand the meaning of her words.

She had come to her position early after her rebirth as a ScreenKeeper, and without opposition. Such instant and universal unanimity on The Screen had occurred only once or twice in its long, long history. There was no doubt that her sudden, unquestioned rise was unusual. The highest rank of ScreenKeeper is Docent. The title was hers as soon as she was ScreenBorn.

Her story was such that respect came to her out of deep admiration and esteem for what she had done and for who she was. ID>>Karo28689 was revered.

The next communication the two robots received from her was a clear example of this high status. Both robots' minds were filled with the vision of a child riding in the back of a twentieth-century automobile, her parents in front driving down the road. The little girl seemed restless and agitated, impatient with her confinement in the back seat. "Mommy," she said, "are we there yet?"

2. A Job to Do

"How can you do this to me, Mom? You *know* me." Ida's eyes were moistening. Her mother could tell she was going to cry.

"It's just a first meeting, Ida. There is still a long way to go. Anything can happen."

"Anything, Mom? We both know *that's* not true." She was just about to turn fourteen, despite her efforts not to. That age was an important date for a young girl in her social situation. The oldest daughter of George and Claudia Rothschild, the richest people on the planet at the time. Masters of the universe. Her father traveled with kings and presidents. Her mother was the height of New York society. As a small child, she had thought that the world revolved around her mother and father. Now she knew that she, too, was caught in that orbital gravity of a planet she did not understand. Now she knew that she was a part of their world: not outside looking in, but inside wanting to get out.

"Now, Ida, don't be petulant. You know we all have jobs to do. I have mine, and you have yours. Be respectful of your father's wishes. You know he would never do anything to hurt you. All he wants is the best for you."

"He wants to kill me."

"That's not true, Ida, and you know it."

"It is true, Mom, and *you* know it. You know what he is asking me to do. How can you agree to such a thing?" Her mother paced up and down the hallway, never completely clearing the way to the stairs, or, as she well knew, Ida would have bolted down them and out to her cherished backyard, the pathway tauntingly visible through the stained glass trimmed cathedral windows that were vaulted over the main entranceway and lobby. The light flowed in from the morning sun, creating prism rainbows that splashed on the varnished stairs and bannisters, and then danced, sparkling, on the white marble floor, reminding Ida of the statues in the yard, near the willow tree and the wading pool, and how the gleaming morning light seemed to make them come alive. She could almost feel the cool air there on her face now, the soft grass under her feet. It felt good. It felt better. The freedom of her imagination was pulling her there, willing her there. Her bare toes on the wood floor seemed to be unconsciously feeling for the green richness there.

"Well, Ida, that I DO agree with your father must count for something, since you know I *certainly* have your best interests at heart in all things." Ida's brow furrowed, and her lips pursed.

"Except for this, Mom. You have HIS interests at heart, not mine."

"Why do they have to be different?" Ida's facial contortions became even more exaggerated as her mother spoke the question.

"Now that, Mom, *is* a good question." Her mother had moved closer with Ida's last comment, perhaps in sympathy, perhaps to impress the moment, and now Ida saw her chance. She skirted around her mother and, achieving the stairway, skillfully ran down the stairs, braids streaming behind her, her skirt pulled up for a greater freedom of motion. It was clear that her escape was clean, and without hesitation.

Her mother called after her, *"Be back here by eleven this morning, Ida!"* But she was uncertain that her message had gotten through to her daughter. She moved down the stairs and to the now open door thinking to say it again, only louder, but all she saw was the beautiful lawn, the empty brick pathway, and the stoic trees that lined the edges of the family's vast property.

Ida was gone.

3. How Did We Get Here?

For ten hours, Farson, Uva, and Voul had been pushing *Songbird* as fast as she could go, and it was a fast starship. Inside *Songbird*, it was as quiet as a balmy night on a summer sea.

Voul was working on navigational contingencies. Uva was in the pilot's chair, awaiting instructions. Time was passing very slowly. Farson needed a change of pace and scenery. He knew that this situation of waiting and plotting courses could go on for weeks. He moved over to the nav station and quietly spoke to Uva. "Let's go take a walk." She was her usual reticent and refractory self. She feigned a question.

"Why?" She said this as if her schedule were completely full, almost impossible to squeeze in something new. In answer, Farson filled her mind with images of soaring in the wide-open skies over Aristealia. The updraft currents were warm and steady.

The beautiful planet had either evolved geologically to be a flawless wind generator, or it just had the natural, ideal shape for the creation of easy, exhilarating currents perfect for flying. Whenever Farson thought of flying, he always thought of Aristealia, as he was now. Uva, catching the mental images, was very interested.

"What are you doing, Farson? It's always me who spreads such dreams." As Farson knew she would, she stood up and walked over to him. "*Where* are we going for this '*walk*?'"

"The Emers have made quite a few improvements to *Songbird* since you and I were last together, Uva. I have one particular improvement in mind that I think you may enjoy."

"May? May, Farson? I'm not going to do something that has a big 'may' in the middle of it, and I don't think you would either."

"I wouldn't. You're right. So, let's go." She wanted, in her growing excitement, to take his hand as they left the bridge, but she didn't.

They walked out of *Songbird*'s control room and into a corridor. Everything about the new *Songbird* had the look and feel of extremely high-caliber quality. Perhaps even more than that, something uniquely advanced and totally new. Uva was looking around. He could tell she was recognizing the changes. "High-value technology everywhere, Farson. This is quite a barge you have here. It's very deceiving."

"I wouldn't put it that way, Uva. It just is. I'm not hiding it."

They turned the corner and walked into the sphere-shaped main salon. Farson directed her to a door and into an alcove off the main passageway. She walked ahead of him, opened the door, looked in, and entered the large room. Farson came in after her and closed the door behind them. In the exact moment when the door closed, and it had latched successfully, everything changed: the air, the temperature, the feeling, all were bringing new energy into Farson's stance and posture. Uva was looking at him. The same thing was happening to her. It took her a moment, but then she recognized that they were on a shoreline of Aristealia's huge island continent, Rilievon. She stretched her wings reflexively, flapping them gracefully as Aristealians always did in preparation for flight. She looked at Farson.

Uva had seen much in her time, some of which she wished she hadn't, but now seeing Farson's metamorphosis into a fully grown adult male Aristealian, with his wings spread, preparing to fly, was a true surprise, an arousing astonishment. She understood that somehow a simulation was being created for them. She walked over to him and looked him up and down. "There is no way this could be artificially generated. You would need full Aristealian knowledge to achieve such details." She reached out and touched his flight feathers, feeling their vanes and the soft afterfeathers so close to Farson's body. She could feel his warmth. She stroked the primaries. She noticed Farson's uncertain response. His duplicity energized her even more. "How did you do this?"

Even as she spoke, the irresistible urge to fly was overtaking him, irresistible to Aristealians. She laughed as Farson vaulted into the air and out over the great sea, Cornu. She immediately followed him. In seconds, they were in perfect ascent formation.

Uva could tell that the physiology was perfect; she could feel the sensation of her muscles under the wings easily pulling her up and up. She could feel her body adjusting into its natural flight configuration. She could feel her neck reaching for the next stroke. "This is perfect," she said out loud, projecting her voice so the passing wind carried it easily across to Farson, just as it would have on Aristealia.

But Farson was now moving faster and faster, pulling out in front, as males always do, his large wings beginning to speed the climb. She flew up next to him, as females always do, and they rose together, wings almost touching, side by side.

As they went higher and higher, she looked around. The great sea, Cornu, was ahead of them. The great island, Rilievon, was under them. They were alone in the sky. She could see that Farson had attained the altitude he was seeking and now was assuming the long-stroke patterns of an Aristealian in transit. She could sense his relaxation, his joy, his physicality stroking the sky.

<<*You did this from memory, Farson?*>> He heard her voice in his mind, but it was as though it was far away in the distance they had left behind. He was entranced in flight, and as his thoughts settled deeper and deeper, he stroked his wings with less and less effort and felt the release of glorious freedom in flight. She was still talking. <<*The details are too*

perfect, Farson. This is real. What are we doing?>> This last question was beyond her abilities to resist.

In this flight configuration and altitude, if it were Uvo, she knew she would be moving into a position beneath him. She started to roll over, almost adream in the fantasy that it *was* Uvo over her. She moved even closer. The movement of air from his wings washed over her; her heart was beating faster.

Farson moved a little higher and banked toward the island. She righted her own flight and soared after him, feeling not embarrassment, but feeling a purely Aristealian emotion of being left out or misunderstood.

She raced after him in search of answers.

Now they were flying low over the sea. The high red cliffs of Rilievon were approaching rapidly. Farson banked toward the escarpment and swooped upward, swimming his wings in the air, now beating for with all of his strength, all his speed.

They caught the warm updraft from the sea and were lifted easily as they broached the top of the cliffs and sailed over the land. There were beautiful vines climbing high into the sky around them. They banked and turned through them, Farson still leading the way. They flew through a tunnel of vines, under a canopy of green. It was a long tunnel, and the cool air of the vast grove refreshed them. Uva was amazed as the moisture quenched her thirst and washed over her in flight. Then they were back out into the warm sun of Aristealia, the updrafts lifting them again, the downdrafts pushing them toward the land. In the joy of her flight, she saw Farson barrel roll ahead of her, and she laughed. *He is having a ball.*

In time she noticed that he was moving to a lower altitude. *Is he going to land?* She saw him skim across the ground, and then his wings flared, and he made a tiptoe landing, flapping his wings in exaltation, as Aristealians always do after flight. She landed beside him, stirring up a light cloud of fine dust. She noticed the exact smells and feel of her home planet.

Farson was already walking. She caught up and walked beside him.

"This is quite pleasant, Farson. Sure beats sitting in the pilot's chair waiting for something to happen." She looked around, her eyes relishing what she saw. *We are on Aristealia. I know this place.*

"We have plenty of time. Nothing's going to happen for a few days. Why don't we visit your homenest?"

This was a shock to her. She had stayed aboard her starship, *Rachis*, in orbit over Aristealia, avoiding her nest, her empty nest, since Uvo's death. She could feel the dread upwelling. Her sense of loss that never attenuated, except with Farson. She knew that he was her last link to Uvo, her husband for a thousand years, who had died in Earth's struggle with the old ScreenMasters. Even now, the emptiness came over her like a tsunami drowning her. "It's only about an hour from here," he said. "We could walk awhile and then fly up."

They walked along in silence, her mind in turmoil. Then she repeated her earlier question. "What is this? A simulation?"

"Uva, the Emers have achieved a level of knowledge and understanding that most of us will never be able to fully grasp. This is exactly what it appears to be. You can taste the air, you felt the flight, you can see me. How could I have created such a place? What I know of flight and of Aristealia I have learned from you. This is far more than that." Uva looked at him. She was mystified, and enthralled, and completely at peace, even if she did not fully understand what was happening. Farson's thoughts warmed her. <<*A leap of faith, Uva. A flight into a dream.*>>

The day was bright and clear. The clouds were little puffs of light, sparkling on a field of pastel blue. The exercise of flight and now of walking together was wonderful and invigorating to her. She was definitely enjoying herself. At just the right moment, as if he had been there a hundred times before,

Farson took off and began to work his way up to the beautiful structure high in the sky.

It was a mansion floating as if it were as light as balsa wood and suspended on invisible lines. Farson was preparing to land on the structure – *Not quite as gracefully as Uvo* – when suddenly Uva's cry stopped him. "No!" It was more of a cry of pain than of warning. He saw that she had not followed him. <<*Not yet, Farson; I can't do it yet.*>> He saw her turn away, stressing her wings with the force of her turn, and then beating hard for distance.

Farson realized his timing had been off. He had been to her homenest before, but only in Uva's stories[5], when he had come as Uvo. Now he was standing on their landing platform where Uvo had landed after his many trips away, where the two of them had embraced on his return. He knew that where he stood was sacred to her. He could barely see her now as she flew away.

He flew away from the homenest in pursuit, and felt again as if he were caught in one of her stories. All he could do was fly after her.

Farson and Uva had been gone for two days when they returned to *Songbird*. To Voul, they seemed relaxed and happy. The tenseness of *Songbird's* mission had dissipated. Voul had adjusted to their absence, using the time to work and pray. To him, they seemed like lovers back from a tryst, but Farson quickly corrected the direction of his thoughts. <<*No worries, Voul. All is well. Uva just needed to get away.*>>

Voul was thinking what Viera would say if he disappeared for two days with someone as elegant and beautiful as Uva, who was following his train of thought closely.

---

[5] These stories were told in *Sargasso*, sections 24, 34, 50, 57, 61.

"Voul, you have a dirty mind. I'm shocked." Uva's verbalization of what he had been thinking was an invasion to the Sker, although he should have known.

He stood up from the navigator's station and stretched, dismissing the entire exchange.

"I guess I am missing Viera."

ID>>Karo28689 came around the corner from the crew's quarters. Farson assumed she had come aboard after he and Uva had returned from their "walk."

"While you and Uva have been off goofing around, Farson," she said with a hint of humor, "much has happened."

The now complete crew of *Songbird* settled back into the routine of space flight: studying the current situation, forecasting the little ship's telemetry to their limits, analyzing the ship's status, and waiting for what they knew was coming.

ID>>Karo28689 was standing in front of the forward view screen. She had been there for a while. To the others, she seemed to be staring into the infinitude of *Songbird's* flight path, into the unmoving immenseness of space beyond. But Farson knew better.

She was dreaming of things to come.

4. The Shadchan

He was well known in the Rothschild household. His confidential business associations with Ida's father covered two decades of finessing deals and feigning affection, of casting fates and hollowing lives, of posturing piety and pretending pity, of self-serving advancements and secret payoffs. He was a fixture in George Rothschilds' life. The patriarch controlled all of his emotional and pecuniary dials and knobs. He knew exactly how to turn and adjust them just so. The "Shadchan" was a tool for the family business, nothing more and nothing less. That he had a pleasing personality and a handsome countenance only increased his insidiousness to Ida, and his effectiveness for her father. She saw right through them both. She knew the shadchan for exactly what he was. *The enemy.*

He arrived with annoying punctuality at 10:45 a.m.

Ida's mental willing away of what was going to happen today came to an abrupt and unavoidable end. Her mother had brought her inside, after a struggle, and had overseen her change of clothing and had redone her hair into a pretty upsweep.

Left in her room to await the summons, Ida had assumed that she had at least fifteen minutes before the battle began. She was going to spend those moments honing her performance. Going over it again and again in her imagination where everything always, miraculously worked out. Then she heard his avuncular greeting and the warm welcome he was receiving in the entrance hall below. She ran to the balcony, looked down, and her worst fears were confirmed. *He's early.*

5. The Emerald Earth Diaries (1)

They are really unbelievable. When you first meet one, you become disoriented; some even swoon. It's the air they breathe. It affects you. They don't seem to have a source of supply, but they do. In their science, they have been able to manipulate the molecules of matter into anything they want. Bodies, buildings, air, travel systems, history, you name it. They have been doing it for thousands and thousands of years. They have created planets and things that carry planets. They have captured stars and made them do their bidding. They have an army of amazing, sentient robots that have spread out in all directions around them for hundreds of light-years.

The Emers know everything there is to know, and yet they still search for knowledge like it was the most precious thing of all. There is only one thing they treasure more: love. This is one of the last things one learns in their company, but when it is learned, much is understood. They love. To them love is a substance, a tangible asset that they can see and taste and touch and hear and smell. It is what they are. At first you won't believe it. I didn't. But in time the unbelievable becomes obvious.

6. *He's Early*

It's not as though he didn't have his merits. For her father, he had been a lifelong friend and problem solver: a close confidant in the ways of business. For her mother, he was a flatterer and another man in the room. Someone to boss around, someone who smiled at each command. It was a game for her mother, a plaything to amuse.

Ida, on the other hand, viewed the situation as though a soldier going into battle. Her objective was set. Her means were at hand. Timing was now the factor that held a feather touch on her trigger: to run or to stay. Timing, and the ability to let things run their course, to a point, despite her anger and fear and rage, were her weapons. She would go along, or rather, she would make them think she was going along. As she touched her hair and straightened her dress, looking in the mirror, she noticed her hands were white from fist clenching. She looked into her own reflection and saw something there that was unsettling to her, something worrying. Reluctantly, she recognized it: desperation.

This was a big deal. Her father was there with her mother. The shadchan was there … as was … the man. *The old man.*

Patting the chair beside her, her mother said, "Come right over here, dear, and sit by me." Claudia's hope for a civil beginning was dashed as Ida obstinately ignored her mother and took the first seat available as she came into the room. There were other family members present, some she had not seen in years. She sat down without speaking to anyone. Silence was the camouflage of her strategy.

The shadchan stood, noting Ida's distance from him, and warmly addressed the group. "We are gathered here today to celebrate tradition and family. In a world of uncertainties, we maintain tradition; we follow the ways of our people, and we trust in the God of Jacob. The greatest achievements of life are to form deep, lasting associations, to marry, to raise a family, to prosper, to be faithful, and to be loyal to our own. Of all of these the last two are the greatest, for in these achievements, all of the others become possible. Faithfulness and loyalty take many shapes; some are beautiful and shine forever; some are difficult and lead on to great things; some are ugly that become beautiful; some are easy and lead to drudgery. Faithfulness shows its face in dedication and trustworthiness, in doing good and loving good, in being what God intended us to be. Loyalty to our family makes it all possible. Today is a celebration of faith and loyalty. Today is a great beginning. It is a day of birth. Today is a day of knowledge and a day of understanding. Today is a day of days."

7. The Emerald Earth Diaries (2)

There is no guile, no false ego, no deception on this beautiful ScreenMaster world. The Emers are the center of the universe, but they couldn't care less. They research and develop new things, and they farm a planet now so rich that it can easily feed the six other planets. Those others are their children, although "flock," or "multitude," or "reservoir" are words that would also suffice as a description. "Children" is very misleading, since they are the Emers' ancestors. So "children" in the sense that they are taken care of, but "parents" in the sense that the citizens of Emerald Earth, the Emers, are their successors.

Time itself is hard to judge around them. They travel through time with the ease of eagles soaring, or gazelles running, or like the grass dolphins moving through Emerald Earth. Time is like the front and backyards they play in. It is no longer possible to know exactly what they have done, undone, changed, and left unchanged. It is not even possible to know if they have changed your own life, and, clearly, the chances are, that, in some way, they have.

They are immortal, not through some divine intervention, but because in their research, they discovered that immortality was an easy thing to do. So they did it.

Their bodies are tended to by the planet's atmosphere, which they have developed over the years into a mixture of highly advanced molecular transport technology and a deeply healing nutrient that they absorb and that keeps their health perfect, eternal, and their bodies fully sustained, cleansed, and fit. They want for nothing. They are all beautiful, tall, intelligent, and loving. They are all connected telepathically, empathically, emotionally, and equally. There are 6.8 million of them and around ten billion of the others. They all live together in Sargasso, the largest man-made object ever constructed.

The Emers, on Emerald Earth, stand alone in the history of humanity as its guardian, its preserver, and its research arm. They reach out into the distances of time and space and clear the way with inventions, with stability, and with foresight. They are the bend of humanity's arc, the pressing edge, the flag that waves for peace and love.

8. A Day of Days

She was listening to every word. She could see his drift of meaning. He kept looking at her, trying to look right into her eyes. It was too much. She was avoiding his eyes, but she could still feel his on her. Ida felt like he had been speaking for hours. She could feel his insinuation of assumption and of the inevitable conclusion as if it all was settled, decided, and impervious to change.

"Yes, today is a day of days. The precursor of many, many happy days to come. Today is a day that creates the future, preserves the past, and that honors family and tradition. This is a day of worlds beginning: love, marriage, children, grandchildren, and on and on. It is a day on which many things are settled and much is begun."

With this final phrase, the atmosphere of the room changed to solemnity as Ida's father, somewhat overweight, ponderously lifted himself to standing. He straightened his handsome suit coat and silk tie. His starched collars pointing into the room looked to her like the blades of the scythes the yard workers used to mow down the weeds. She subconsciously ducked.

George Nathan Rothschild began, ostensibly, to address the people in the room, but Ida knew exactly who he was talking to. She looked over at her mother, now sitting demurely in an elegant side chair with a rich red satin seat cover and ornate inlay carvings framing her shoulders. Ida thought she looked so beautiful as the noonday light cascaded over her. *She's like a queen.*

9. The Emerald Earth Diaries (3)

They are building another Sargasso. They have no enemies. They are invincible by magnitudes of superiority that have no measure. In their first battle with the old ScreenMasters, the Emers deceived them so thoroughly that even now they don't know what happened for certain. In the second exchange with Twill, they turned a despotic aristocracy into a stable and open government and brought a violent, malevolent race into the light. The Essors, who once were so threatening, have now appealed to join the Emers. There was no fight in this revolution, no bloodshed, no history of victory or surrender. A sweeping change occurred, and no one dissented. That it was all obviously for the better was never questioned. Except by Twill, who is now in a situation the outcome of which only he can determine. The Emers are nothing if not patient.

Life and death for the Emers is a choice they make. Neither happens very often, but they do happen. Children are rare indeed because they are not needed to perpetuate the race. Emers all appear to be young, but they are not. The average age is in the three thousand year range. There are some, like John Andrew McKinley Sortt, who have been around since the beginning.

Reproduction, when it is required, is also a choice and an honor. All of the recorded births on Emerald Earth have been through "conjoinment," as they call it. A birth occurs, but the real parents are all of them. Together, they all experience the conception, the gestation, and the birth as though it were all of theirs, and, it is.

Death is handled the same way.

The population of Emerald Earth is united in a way only dreamed of in human history. True equality has been attained. Happiness is universal, life is eternal, and tranquility has been achieved. The Emers are free from want with wealth untold, in a world they themselves have made.

Salvation by any other name is still salvation.

Emerald Earth is a world of the people, by the people, for the people, conceived in liberty, and dedicated to the proposition that everyone is created equal. These truths are written in the heart of every Emer, and they really believe them.

They are the shepherds of humanity, and the flock is on the move.

(to be continued...)

ABOUT THE AUTHOR

W. Mahlon Purdin lives in Massachusetts with his wife, Joy Hooper Purdin. They have one daughter, Blythe.

He has written poetry, prose, and essays for many years. His eclectic career in advertising and copywriting has been nurtured by a wide variety of interests in extreme sports, music, and exploration.

Sargasso is the second novel of The ScreenMasters series, and his fourth to date.